Babycakes

Babycakes

DONNA KAUFFMAN

KENSINGTON PUBLISHING CORP.
www.kensingtonbooks.com

BRAVA BOOKS are published by

Kensington Publishing Corp.
119 West 40th Street
New York, NY 10018

All Kensington titles, imprints, and distributed lines are available at special quantity discounts for bulk purchases for sales promotions, premiums, fund-raising, educational, or institutional use.

Special book excerpts or customized printings can also be created to fit specific needs. For details, write or phone the office of the Kensington special sales manager: Kensington Publishing Corp., 119 West 40th Street, New York, NY 10018, attn: Special Sales Department; phone 1-800-221-2647.

ISBN-13: 978-0-7582-8050-3
ISBN-10: 0-7582-8050-5

First Kensington Trade Paperback Printing: November 2012

10 9 8 7 6 5 4 3 2

Printed in the United States of America

This one is for my youngest, Spencer,
who, in his dedication to all things wild and endangered,
has taught me so much.

Chapter 1

Her whole life had been about peanut pie.

Well . . . for the past twenty-nine years, five months, three weeks, five days, and—Kit Bellamy glanced at the digital clock on the dash of her car—about twelve hours, it had been about pie. Mamie Sue's Peanut Pie, to be specific.

As if there were any other kind.

She'd lived, breathed, walked, talked, dreamed, eaten, baked, boxed, shipped, and sweated over peanut pie, every single day of her life, for as long as she could remember.

So, she was having an understandably hard time embracing the idea that her future was going to be all about cupcakes.

Twenty-nine years. She might have been slightly off on the number of weeks and days, math not being her strong point—a painfully evident truth, given her recent life evolution—but she knew she had the hours part correct. Grandma Laureen hadn't told the story of Kit's mother going into labor right there in Mamie Sue's kitchen just once. No, that story had become part of the Bellamy legend, which was a rich and colorful one, even without the story of Kit coming into the world between the burlap peanut sacks and the six-burner Wedgewood stove. But then, as Grandma Reenie always said, "Bellamy women know how to make an entrance."

What Kit Bellamy was presently trying to figure out, was how Bellamy women—at least this particular Bellamy woman—made an exit.

There wasn't any historical lore on that point. As far as Kit knew, at least in the previous three generations, no Bellamy woman had ever walked away. From anything. Or anyone. Ever. Least of all family, and most of all, the family business.

Kit had done both.

Not that there was a business, per se, to walk away from—or much of a family, for that matter. She'd managed to destroy both of those first. She never should have trusted Teddy. "Having a few investors will allow us to expand Mamie Sue's into the kind of global empire she'd have been thrilled to see come to fruition," her brother-in-law had said, all earnest sincerity and gleaming dental perfection.

Never trust a man with puppy dog eyes and pearly whites.

Kit could hear her great-grandmother's words of wisdom as clearly as if she was sitting next to her. "Lesson learned, Grammy Sue," she murmured. "Lesson so learned."

The past thirteen months had been filled with lawyers, courtrooms, judges, shocking revelations, and the kind of utter betrayal Kit wasn't sure she'd ever recover from. Since Teddy's Big Reveal during what had turned out to be Mamie Sue's Peanut Pie Company's final board meeting she had stumbled from being frozen in shock, into utter devastation and guilt, on through blistering fury, and had only recently settled into merciful numbness.

The Bellamy women who had come before her were surely still rolling in their graves. Kit had fought back, and could only hope they'd have at least been proud of the grit and gumption she'd displayed in striving to save everything they'd all worked so hard for. But even that was a small consolation given that, in the end, Teddy and his fancy Westlake lawyers had won the day.

The company and the women who'd built it had each experienced their share of stumbling blocks and setbacks. "But none of them screwed up so badly they managed to let the damn thing be sold right out from under them," Kit muttered. "Much less to a vending machine snack company." She bit out those last four words as if she'd tasted one of their products. You couldn't call what they sold food.

Mamie Sue's deliciously decadent peanut pie—each and every one of them lovingly handmade with the very same ingredients Mamie Sue had used when she'd started the company in her own kitchen over seventy-eight years ago—should never, not ever, come in a cellophane wrapper. Or be shelved in the E5 slot of a Tas-T-Snaks vending machine, for a buck-twenty-five a slice.

"I should have shot him dead right there in the boardroom," Kit mumbled.

Would a jury have convicted her? She thought not. All she'd have had to do was submit footage of smarmy, self-important Teddy orating his way though any of the board meetings he'd wormed his way into over the last few years now that the older generations of Bellamy women no longer presided over such things.

It was probably just as well that Mamie Sue herself had passed on before Teddy had come on the scene. Kit had just graduated high school when, at ninety-four, Mamie Sue—who'd wielded a rolling pin pretty much every day of her long and bountiful life—had finally proven them all wrong and passed peacefully in her sleep. Up until that moment, they'd been pretty much convinced she'd live forever.

Mamie Sue's daughter-in-law, Laureen, and her granddaughter-in-law, Kit's mother Katie, had continued running the company they'd helped build just as confidently and assertively as Mamie Sue ever had. Unfortunately, soon afterward, Grandma Reenie had begun a rapid decline in health, with the devastating diagnosis of early onset Alzheimer's. Her merciful passing had been followed only a few short years later by the tragic death of Kit's mother and father in a car accident, leaving Kit, who had just turned twenty-four, and her twenty-two year-old sister Trixie, to head up the family company far, far sooner than anyone could have predicted.

Kit had, at least, been involved in the business since she'd been old enough to totter on top of a stool and smear flour on the rolling boards. Trixie's interests, however, had always been more focused on the lifestyle and prestige the family business brought her way—which was why Teddy, Trixie's husband of less than two years at the time of their parents' deaths, had stepped in and taken on what was Trixie's share of the company load.

Kit recalled how relieved the family had been when Trixie had settled on Teddy Carruthers. Trixie had barely turned twenty when she'd gotten engaged, but after spending most of her teenage years bringing home the most amazing array of users and losers—her way of "acting out" when her parents wouldn't enable the lifestyle Trixie was certain she deserved—they'd been so thrilled with her choice, they'd given the couple their heartfelt blessing.

Privately, Kit had always thought Teddy was a little too slick and a lot too full of himself, but all the family saw was that he was smart, ambitious, and came from an established Atlanta family, which meant he wasn't after Trixie for her money.

Even with his too-polished exterior, none of them could have predicted the true nature of Teddy's ambition or the depths of his greed. Least of all, as was now self-evident, Kit.

She allowed herself a moment to savor what the courtroom scene would have been like once the jury saw the heartless deviousness of Teddy's back-stabbing plan—one he'd concocted with the assistance of her "whatever you think is best, dear!" sister, who was far too busy with her new life as Trixie Carruthers, enjoying her country club groups and Junior League engagements, to pay any attention to what her husband was doing with her stake in the family company.

With the help of his slick, high priced, and oh-so-smug Westlake lawyers, Teddy had used his sneaky little investor plan to blindside Kit, the board of directors . . . and everyone else at Mamie Sue's, into giving him the leverage to sell the company to Tas-T-Snaks, which was interested only in owning rights to the name of the product itself. They'd be mass producing the product in another country and shipping it out in cartons, putting generations of employees who had invested heart, soul, and faith into the company out on the streets. Right next to Kit.

"Oh yeah. I'd have walked a free woman."

She was a free woman, all right. Free of the family business she'd loved with all her heart. Free of the family—if she could still consider Trixie or Teddy family—who had taken that beloved business and turned it into a colossal joke. All for greed. It begged the question, just how much money did two people actually need? Kit was even free of their equally beloved family home, with the very kitchen Mamie Sue had used to launch her fledgling little business over three-quarters of a century before. The same home Trixie and Teddy had summarily sold the moment the judge's verdict had been handed down on Kit's last and final appeal.

Yep, Kit was free to start her life completely over. From scratch.

Yippee.

She'd spent pretty much everything she'd had and all of what she'd gotten from the sale of the company to pay the lawyers she'd hired to fight Teddy and Tas-T-Snaks. Teddy had been astonished when she'd fought back, unable to comprehend why she hadn't been happy and just skipped into the sunset with the sudden windfall of income he'd procured for her from the sale. And Trixie had had the nerve to ask her why she was betraying her own sister like that, dragging family into court. Kit still almost had apoplexy just thinking about that conversation.

When Kit hadn't backed down, Trixie's righteous tears and Teddy's cajoling "there, there, it's just business" pats on the head had swiftly turned into downright fury when they'd had to spend their own money to fight back.

It wasn't much vindication—Teddy's family's pockets were deep—so Kit sincerely doubted he'd suffer from paying Westlake's steep legal tab, but it made her feel she'd at least done her best in the name of her family. That was what mattered to her, doing the right thing for all of those who'd worked so hard to make Mamie Sue's what it was. Or . . . had been, anyway.

Of course, now she was in the same boat they were—scrambling to find new work, trying to start over, figuring out what came next.

She frowned hard to keep fresh tears of anger and guilt from leaking out. She'd cried far too many already. It was just . . . how had she let it happen? Why hadn't she seen through his plan? Those two questions would plague her for the rest of her days. Through the shimmer of threatening tears, she spied the sign for the causeway over Ossabaw Sound to her final destination.

Sugarberry Island.

If a person was going to start her life over, Kit had to admit there was a storybook feel to the name alone, with a happily-ever-after implied, if not guaranteed. But she couldn't imagine what a happily-ever-after would even look like. She'd be happy to get through the days feeling as if she was contributing something important to something that mattered. Of course, if her business friend Charlotte was to be believed, Sugarberry offered her all that and more.

It had been two weeks since the courts had handed Teddy and Tas-T-Snaks their final victory. Fourteen days since Mamie Sue's officially no longer belonged to a single Bellamy. And almost the same number of months since she'd had regular employment. That she still had this particular job offer, one that was pretty sweet no matter how you defined it, was nothing short of miraculous. Charlotte had come to her with the possible offer right after the sale to Tas-T-Snaks hit the news the year before. But Kit had turned the job down when she'd decided to fight Teddy and Tas-T-Snaks.

A year later, that fight was over. After delays of her own, Leilani Dunne was still interested in finding someone to run Babycakes, the planned shipping and catering business that would adjoin her successful cupcakery, Cakes by the Cup.

Kit knew she should be jumping at the chance and thanking her lucky stars the offer was still on the table. The position was so important to her prospective employer though, Kit wouldn't have taken the position unless she'd stick with it. The last thing she could handle was disappointing someone else.

Hence the five-hour drive to the little barrier island off the Georgia coast—a big change from Atlanta, former home of Mamie Sue's pies, and, if all went well during the on-site job interview . . . former home of Kit Bellamy.

Charlotte had warned her Sugarberry wasn't anything like the city, or even like the ritzier islands down in the central and southern part of the barrier chain. Being one of the northernmost islands, it was still largely a wilderness area, only partly developed and inhabited. As she had defined it, it was a traditional small southern town, with a distinctly unique island flair. That part had sounded perfectly fine to Kit. Disappearing to a wilderness island after being front-page news in Atlanta for the past year sounded downright heavenly. It was the rest of it she was uncertain about.

Kit felt confident she had the skills for the job, but in every other possible way, it was about as different from the life she'd had at Mamie Sue's as it could be. She thought about all the stories her mom, Grandma Reenie, and Grammy Sue had told her growing up, about how her great-grandmother, as a young military bride, had started the company in the Bellamy House kitchen during World War I.

Kit loved those stories, had never tired of hearing them. They were inspirational and motivational, but she loved them mostly because of the reminiscing smiles they brought to the faces of the three women as they recalled the fond memories they shared. Kit had loved being a part of that bond, the passing down of so many traditions, feeling connected to something so important, the fruits of the hard labors and talents and dreams of those very same women.

Dreams she'd managed to shatter in the span of six short years.

Kit forcibly tamped down the guilt and anger living inside her. The day was about next steps and new possibilities. Her thirtieth birthday was on the near horizon. She'd sort of made that her mental deadline for getting her act together and having a new plan in place. If all went well, she'd be ahead of schedule on some of it, anyway.

"And we always like being ahead of schedule!" she said, a slight smile ghosting her mouth as she intoned the chipper phrase Reenie had been so fond of repeating.

If it wasn't for the grief and anger, Kit might have been truly excited about the idea of tackling a small, independent business and having her hands in on the initial growth and development. Being part of a new story with its own lore and legends was both an opportunity and a potential blessing. As she bumped over the grid at the far end of the causeway and turned onto Sugarberry, she imagined what words of wisdom, encouragement, or concern the Bellamy women might have offered.

"I know I let you all down," she said softly. "Horribly. Unforgivably. I trusted when I shouldn't have. I took my eye off the ball, because I thought it was safely tucked away. But if there's a way to make you proud of me again, you know I'll find it."

On that, the most optimistic note she'd managed since walking, stunned, out of that boardroom a year ago, she wound her way around the tiny, but charming town square and pulled into the little lot off the alley running behind the row of shops that included Cakes by the Cup. "Here goes nothing." *And everything.*

She tapped a quick knock on the frame of the screen door at the back entrance as instructed. She could hear music playing through the partially opened door behind the screen. The song was "Theme From a Summer Place," which made Kit smile. Mamie Sue had loved that song, mostly because she adored "that handsome Troy Donahue," who had starred, along with Sandra Dee, in the film of the same name in the late fifties. In addition, someone was talking quite animatedly over the music, making it impossible not to inadvertently eavesdrop.

"Well, I was as stunned as anybody, except maybe Birdie. Could have knocked me over with a feather when she told me that Asher's younger brother had claimed custody of her little grandbaby. But now that Morgan is actually here on Sugarberry, I just don't know what to think."

"Well, I think it's good," came a second voice, younger, steadier. "Great, even. I assume he's here because he wants Birdie to be part of Lilly's life."

"So he says," the older woman responded. "But can you really trust anything a Westlake says?"

Kit had lifted her hand to knock again, but froze at the sound of that name. *Westlake.* She shook her head. Coincidence. Surely the Westlakes who had helped dismantle four generations of hard work and dedication weren't the only Westlakes in Georgia. The older woman had said the names Morgan and Asher. Neither rang a bell with Kit, but that didn't mean much. She hadn't done any research on the firm Teddy had hired. She hadn't needed to.

The Westlakes were an Atlanta institution, as was their generations old law firm. Despite any successes her pie company might have achieved, the Westlakes ran in very different circles from the Bellamys. They were old money. Very old. Everyone knew of them, like everyone knew of the royal family.

Kit had never paid any attention to them or their frequent mentions in the political and social pages. They'd never been of any personal interest to her. Until they'd sat, with smug superiority, across the courtroom from her, she couldn't have named any one of them. All Kit knew was that Teddy had been a frat brother of one of the Westlakes, hence their prestigious name and power lent to Teddy's, and Tas-T-Snaks' cause. Trixie, on the other hand, probably knew their entire detailed history. Kit didn't think she'd be giving her sister a call on that anytime soon.

"I heard he bought a place on the north end of the loop," came the younger voice. "Which means he plans to stay. That has to count for something."

"We'll see," the older woman said. "We all just want what's best for the child, but given how Delilah let the Westlakes trample all over her and shove poor Birdie—her own mother—aside like they did . . . I don't trust this sudden change of heart."

"Didn't you mention something about Morgan being the black sheep of the family? By their standards, anyway. I've been so busy with all the craziness leading up to the cookbook release, I'll admit I haven't paid as much attention to the local gossip as I usually do. But what I have heard . . . well . . . I don't know. It sounds like he's trying to do the right thing. We can at least give him the benefit of the doubt, can't we?"

"Oh, he'll get a warm Sugarberry reception, all right."

The younger woman's tone was affectionate, but with a warning note. "Alva—"

"Don't Alva me, Miss Lani May. I don't have a single say in this."

"Other than being Birdie's closest friend for the past forty or so years."

"I just don't want to see her hurt again. Delilah was a late in life baby for Birdie, long after she'd given up hope of ever having a child. Everyone on this island knew she loved that girl with everything in her heart. What that same child handed her in return . . . and now she's gone as well . . ." The woman's voice trailed off.

Her voice was a bit more wavery when she continued. "I simply couldn't bear it if that family were to ruin things again. I've never met Olivia Westlake, and God help her if I ever do. I have more than a few words for that bitter old prune."

"She's not planning a visit so soon, is she?"

"Not that I've heard, but we need to be prepared. I wouldn't put anything past that—" The older woman broke off, and Kit found herself leaning closer to the screen door to hear the rest of what she was saying. "Birdie's been through enough. No mother should outlive her own child. She didn't attend the funeral, you know. Made the trip to Atlanta in her own time, paid her respects in private."

"Probably for the best, but a shame it had to be like that. I'm glad she has you looking out for her, Alva."

"She certainly does, and I've let everybody know about it, too."

"I'm sure you have," came the somewhat dry, but compassionate response. "And, of course, all of us will be rooting for her and little Lilly to hit it off. Have they reunited yet?"

"Not yet. Supposed to have a picnic or some such, but Mr. Morgan is taking his time."

"Well, given all they've been through, maybe that's not a bad idea. It's a lot of change in that little girl's life. And a picnic, whenever it happens, sounds lovely. It's been so warm this fall. I can't believe it's almost November and we're still having weather in the upper seventies every day. Not that I'm complaining." Lani laughed. "Neither Baxter nor I are missing those New York winters. Let me know if I can contribute anything to the picnic when the time comes. A few cupcakes could add some smiles."

"I'll mention it to Birdie. She loves your strawberry shortcake cupcakes. That might be just the thing."

"Done. Consider it my homecoming gift to Miss Lilly."

"Imagine not having seen your own grandchild since the day of her birth. Lilly just turned five, you know."

"I heard. Well, I still say we should give her uncle the benefit of the doubt going in. Sounds to me like he's trying to do what's best for the child, giving her family, a home, and roots. And, apparently going against that bitter old prune you mentioned, in order to do it. Pretty commendable if you ask me."

"I suppose you're right. He's unmarried, no kids of his own, you know," Alva added. "To turn your whole life upside down like that . . ." She gave an audible sigh. "If it were anyone other than a Westlake, I'd be heading the welcoming committee. As it is, I'm still doing some digging."

"On?"

"Him. For Birdie's sake, of course."

"Of course," came the dry response. "You're not thinking of putting him in one of your columns, I hope. I don't think anyone would benefit, least of all Birdie."

"Now, now, I wouldn't do that," the older woman said.

Even Kit, who hadn't met the woman yet, wasn't sure how sold she was on that score, and she didn't know what the "column" was they were talking about. With the comment about a funeral in Atlanta . . . there was no doubt which Westlakes they were talking about. Even during the trial, she knew the Westlakes had suffered a tragedy when one of the Westlake scions and his wife had died in a car accident. Kit had been too overwhelmed with what was happening to her and her employees—not to mention losing loved ones that way struck a little too close to home—to pay attention, especially when the name Westlake was involved. But . . . she was almost certain that was the situation Alva and Lani were talking about. And that situation had come to Sugarberry, too. Right along with her.

Crap.

"What I know is that he's thirty-two, wealthy, educated, and quite the looker as it happens. So," Alva said, sounding all conspiratorial, "what I wonder is, why isn't a man like that married? Must be something wrong with him."

The younger woman laughed. "Not everyone thinks marriage has to go hand-in-hand with the rest of that list."

"Well . . . we'll see. If he thinks he's bringing his playboy ways to Sugarberry—"

"He brought his five-year-old niece. I hardly think that would be his intent."

"Well, those rich folks usually pawn off child care to a nanny, so until we know what's what, we can't be certain of anything," Alva said, sounding quite put out. "And be assured, if it's there to be found, I'll find it."

"I'm sure you will," Lani said dryly, "but, if he is a playboy, I doubt he'd have come to Sugarberry. The island isn't exactly teeming with single women."

"Speak for yourself, missy," Alva said. "Besides, all the rest aside, nice scenery is never a bad thing."

The younger woman laughed outright. "Now that's the Alva I know and admire."

Kit knew she'd been standing at the screen door way too long, but her mind was spinning with all the Westlake talk. The doubts she'd had about moving to Sugarberry suddenly tripled. But she could hardly walk away without saying hello. She owed Charlotte that much for going to the trouble to set up the interview. At the brief break in conversation, she rapped on the door without further delay. "Hello?" she called out, over the conversation and the music. "It's Kit Bellamy."

The door suddenly opened and Kit had to lower her gaze almost a foot to meet that of a tiny, senior-aged woman as she popped into view.

"Well, hello there!"

"Hello." Kit smiled fully for what felt like the first time in ages. It was pretty much impossible not to. The woman—Alva, she presumed—barely topped five feet, with twinkling eyes and a welcoming smile, pearls clasped to her earlobes and strung around the starched Peter Pan collar of her lemon-colored blouse, which she'd paired with a moss green cardigan sweater. Pearl buttons, of course.

All of what you'd expect from a grandmotherly type, except, perhaps, for the hair, which had been teased into a spectacular beehive of curls and waves, and was a rather shocking, unnatural shade of red. Add to that, the entire ensemble had been topped with an apron that was essentially a movie poster for *Pirates of the Caribbean*—namely its star, Captain Jack Sparrow, as played by the very swashbuckling Johnny Depp. Kit couldn't help staring.

Alva followed her gaze, then looked back up, beaming. "I like pirates."

"I-I do, too," Kit stammered.

"Well then, I like you already." Alva stepped back and waved Kit inside. "Come on in. Welcome to Sugarberry."

Chapter 2

"Moggy, where's the mama turtle?"

Morgan Westlake knelt down in the damp sand near the nest of loggerhead eggs, his gaze level with the somber one of his niece, Lilly. "The mama turtle built this nest so her eggs would be safe. Then she had to go back to the water."

Lilly looked at the mound, under which an untold number of eggs were nestled. "Will she come back for them?"

Morgan ducked his chin. Without even trying, Lilly broke his heart every single day. He told himself often that wasn't a bad thing. She needed him to help mend her heart . . . and by doing that, maybe he'd mend his as well. He looked into her oh-so-serious blue eyes and smiled. "She doesn't need to come back. When the baby turtles hatch, they will know to head straight to the water."

"How do they know?"

"They just do," he said, then took her hand as he stood up and brushed the sand from the knees of his jeans. "Sort of like how babies know they're supposed to crawl."

"Won't the baby turtles be cold?"

"They have that nice shell keeping them warm."

Lilly seemed to think about that for a moment, then

nodded. "Can we come watch them when they get borned?"

He smiled. "That would be pretty cool. But from what I understand, they hatch at night."

Lilly immediately looked alarmed. "Then how will the find the water?"

Morgan crouched back down again, but kept hold of her hand. "Well, that's one of the things the researchers here are trying to figure out. They think it's because the moonlight reflects on the water and makes it sparkle." He knew the commonly held belief was that hatching at night enabled the babies to stay safe from as many predators as possible. But that was the last thing Lilly needed to be concerned about.

"It would be better in the sun. Then they can see the water by their selfs."

"That makes sense to me, but if they only hatch at night, then there must be a pretty good reason. That's why I'm going to help Dr. Langley get more grant money and donations. Then he can grow this research facility and find out more about why sea turtles do what they do."

Lilly thought about that as Morgan straightened again. Her hand tightened on his and he looked down at her upturned face. "Maybe they're scared—because they don't have a mama. So they come out at night when no one will see them." She tugged on his hand. "They aren't scared of the dark, are they?"

Morgan began to rethink his great idea about showing Lilly the egg mound. He'd thought it would be educational and interesting. He hadn't meant to give her something else to worry about. "I think maybe they're excited. After all, they get to go for their first swim."

Lilly's worried frown smoothed a little. "I like to swim. Miss Pam teached me."

"I like to swim, too." Morgan recalled his own swimming lessons, though he'd been younger than Lilly. His swimming instructor had been Mr. Hans. He and Asher had learned at the same time, even though he'd been a year-and-a-half younger. He'd been trying to catch up to his older brother pretty much from the moment he understood he had one.

"Who will teach the turtles to swim?"

"Well, I think they're all pretty good swimmers by nature. Remember how I showed you the pictures with their funny feet? Shaped like little paddles?"

"Paddle feet." She nodded, then smiled at that.

Just like that, his whole world smiled, too. "Yep."

"Why do they swim at night? You're not 'posed to swim in the dark."

He swung her around, and made her squeal. It wasn't often he heard that sound from her anymore. "Unless you have paddle feet. Then you can swim all the time."

"I want to be a paddle feet!" She let out a laugh, and he hugged her. He didn't know exactly what it was going to take to heal his heart, but hearing her laugh again was a pretty good start. He needed to figure out how to give more of them to her in return.

"Moggy, you're crushing me," she said with an exaggerated gasp only a five-year-old could pull off with any real credibility.

"Sorry." But he was still smiling as he kissed the top of her head. He carried her through the dunes on the sand-swept path, back to where he'd parked the car, then set her down next to his Range Rover.

He opened the rear passenger door and helped her climb in and get strapped into her seat. He kissed her on her forehead and tugged a lock of her dark hair, then ducked his tall frame back out of the SUV. He was about to close the door when he noticed Lilly was looking back at the dunes.

He glanced in the same direction, but didn't see anything. When he looked back at her, her serious face was back. She kept staring at the dunes.

"They're going to be okay, Lills."

She looked up at him almost defiantly. "Promise?"

Morgan's heart squeezed again. "We'll talk about it with Dr. Langley."

"He has the turtle fa . . . felicity?"

"Facility. Research center. He's in charge of taking care of the turtles here on the island."

"Will he help them swim like Miss Pam did . . . after they're borned?"

"That's why he's here."

"They won't be scared of him?"

"You weren't scared of Miss Pam, were you?" He thought again of Hans, and realized maybe he shouldn't have asked that. Hans had been pretty imposing.

Lilly shook her head. "I liked her. But I was scared of the water."

"Then Miss Pam helped you, and you liked the water, too, right?"

She nodded.

"The turtles won't be scared with Dr. Langley. You can usually tell when people want to help you."

"Like you helped me after mama and daddy went to heaven?"

Everything in Morgan went utterly still. It was the first time she'd mentioned them since . . . well, since shortly after she'd been told about the accident. That had been nine months ago.

"Yeah," he managed, though how he did it over the fist-sized lump in his throat he couldn't have said. "Exactly like that." He leaned in and kissed her on the cheek. "How about if you go see Dr. Langley with me? Maybe he can show you some of the turtles he's taking care of in the research center."

Her far-too-wise and wary gaze settled on his. "Real turtles?"

"Just like the ones that are inside those eggs on the beach."

"Yes, please," she replied, almost too politely.

It had Morgan glancing at her again as he straightened. He recognized that restrained note in her tone.

Her eyes were shining with delight, but she sat, ankles crossed, hands in her lap, and when she'd replied just then, she'd sounded like . . . his mother. Not that there was anything wrong with proper manners. He was all for folks being polite to one another. But a kid should, at heart, be able to relax and be a kid. Especially this one.

It was precisely why he'd left Atlanta at the first acceptable opportunity, though his mother and he had differed quite vociferously on what constituted acceptable.

"Okay." He climbed in the front seat and started the engine. Smiling at her in the rearview mirror, he gave her a wink and pushed thoughts of Olivia Westlake and that battle royal from his mind. "It's a date."

Lilly settled back in her seat, seemingly content. For the moment anyway.

He'd come back from Colorado for the funeral and to take on his legal role as Lilly's guardian. Asher and his wife Delilah had chosen him as Lilly's godfather right after her birth so he wasn't surprised they'd named him as her guardian in the unlikely event anything happened to them both.

He'd taken his godparent role happily and seriously and had made an extra effort to fulfill it, despite the geographical distance. But being the fun uncle was a world apart from being a full-time parent.

He'd stayed on at the family compound in Atlanta until after Lilly's birthday, but they'd been completely on their own, one-on-one, for the past month. He was still in the discovery phase of learning how many questions one little girl could ask. She'd had a staff of people to keep up with her, and he was swiftly realizing even they might have found it a daunting task.

Of course, being the insatiably curious sort himself, he rather liked and admired that trait in her. Though his rigidly formal family would have begged to differ, he'd always thought asking questions about any and everything was the best way for a person to figure things out. So much so, he'd made a career out of it.

He might know zip about child rearing, and a lot of what lay ahead was terrifying if he thought about it too much, but he knew there were certain things he wasn't going to do. He wasn't going to squelch a child's curiosity or stifle her unique voice, her desire to learn, to grow.

"Moggy?"

"Yeah, sweet pea?"

"How did the turtles get inside the eggs?"

He choked on a short laugh. *And you were saying, smart guy?*

Morgan ripped the tape off the bottom of another moving box, flattened it, and added it to the stack. His place on Sugarberry was smaller than the cabin-style A-frame he'd had in Steamboat Springs, but mostly what he missed was the big storage shed he'd had out west. Despite the fact that winter was almost upon them, he had a lot of winter-related gear he wasn't going to need on the far more temperate Georgia coast, and the small garage he had now barely held his truck. Maybe he'd rent a storage place over the causeway in Savannah. He'd originally planned on finding office space there, too. It was only a twenty-five minute hop from the island, not a bad commute. Lilly would be in school most of the time, once he got her enrolled, and by the time the following summer rolled around, he'd have something worked out for when she wasn't.

He was already in talks with another facility farther down the barrier island chain, on Jekyll Island, to help with some adjunct legal work they needed, when the research center thing had sort of landed in his lap. He and Lilly had only officially moved into the cottage a few weeks ago, but he was already finding a deeper connection to the island than he'd anticipated. He'd decided to relocate to Sugarberry because of Lilly's maternal grandmother—well, both grandmothers, just in different ways—and because it was as close to the way of life he'd sought out and found in Colorado as he could find and still keep Lilly surrounded and supported by what family she had left.

Sugarberry, it turned out, was as much wilderness retreat as it was small southern town, and the relaxed, slightly more eccentric island vibe surprisingly reminded him of the mountain town he'd called home for the past eight years.

Other than Dr. Gabriel Langley at the research center, he didn't know anyone on the island, as yet. But in the short time it had taken to find the cottage and move in, he'd found the same feeling of familiarity that he connected to, the same small town unity and sense of openhearted welcome he'd experienced when he'd set up his practice out west.

Knowing the rocky past Lilly's maternal grandmother had had with her daughter Delilah and with his own mother, Morgan had been a little uncertain of his initial welcome on Sugarberry. Ultimately, he'd felt confident that once the islanders met him and Lilly and realized how sincere he was in reuniting family and putting down solid roots, they'd be welcomed. He never would have moved there otherwise. While Sugarberry was already calling to him in ways he hadn't known it would, so was Lilly.

He loved her to death, had since he'd cradled her in shaky hands just after her birth. The first baby he'd ever held, she'd captured his whole heart with nothing more than a gurgle and a smile. Even though he hadn't seen her as often as he liked, that bond had only strengthened through the following years. With their lives turned upside down and wrenched inside out, she was surprising him and fascinating him at every corner, clutching at his very heart and soul in ways he couldn't have possibly imagined. He'd never felt anything like this before.

The idea of running his office from anywhere but Sugarberry, where he'd be right there when she needed him, anytime she needed him, seemed unthinkable.

"Moggy?"

He looked up from the next box he was slicing open to see Lilly in the doorway to what was going to be his future home office. "What's up, sweet pea? Did you get the rest of that page colored in?" He walked over to where he'd arranged his desk and filing cabinets in an L-shape and pointed to the side of the filing cabinets angled toward his chair. "I was thinking it would look great right there."

"I don't know what color the paddle feet are. I forgot."

Dr. Langley had pulled in just as they were pulling out of the research center lot earlier that morning. Morgan had turned the car around, they'd gone back into the facility, and Dr. Langley had given Lilly a tour. She'd been quiet bordering on painfully shy around the older man, but there had been no missing the avid curiosity and delight in her eyes when he'd taken her to see the turtles presently residing in the facility's rehab tanks. When she'd realized some of them were injured or sick, she'd whispered a dozen urgent and highly concerned questions in Morgan's ears for him to ask the good doctor. In turn, he had ever so graciously taken the time to gently explain why the turtles were there and what he was doing to help them get better.

Gabe had given her a loggerhead coloring book school kids received during their visits, and she'd been bouncing in her seat all the way back to the cottage. Then they'd had to go back out in search of crayons. What kid didn't have at least one giant, beat-up box of half broken and half worn-down crayons?

Well, him, for one. So, now they both had a fresh box.

"I'm not sure either," he told her. "You know, I have a bunch of stuff printed out about them right . . ." He turned in a slow circle, looking at the disorganized chaos surrounding him. "Somewhere."

She just stood there expectantly, so he began to dig.

"Aha!" He unearthed the folder Gabe had given him during their first meeting and started to hand her the fund-raising brochure right on top of the pile, which featured a big loggerhead photo on the front. Thankfully, he saw the sickly and diseased loggerheads on the back before she took it from his hand. Not exactly appropriate for five-year-olds, he tucked it back into the folder. "Uh, wait, let me find the perfect one," he said, flipping through the rest of the folder. He finally settled on carefully tearing the front cover off the first brochure and handing it to her. "Looks like they're kind of green, maybe a little brown."

She studied the photo with great intent, then looked up. "Thank you, Uncle Moggy."

He smiled. She might behave too excruciatingly proper at times, but other times her politeness was simply too sweet for words. "You're welcome, sweetheart. Let me know when I can come see it."

He watched her go back to the kitchen table, which he could see through the open archway of the den-turned-office. She was such an odd little mix. A lot of the quiet reserve was from the tumult that had so recently occurred in her life, turning her world and that of everyone around her upside down. But she had always been something of an observer, at least in the times they'd spent together. She'd always had a smile and a giggle for him, and early on in uncle-hood, he'd made it his mission to make her laugh as often as possible.

She'd always struck him as a pretty normal kid, naturally curious, smart as a whip—too smart for her own good sometimes—all wrapped up inside the perfectly poised and groomed little Westlake clone his mother was determinedly turning her into, much as she had with Asher, and again, with his young wife Delilah. Morgan had been her only great failure—at least, to her way of thinking.

It was precisely that way of thinking Morgan had been determined to get little Lilly away from as quickly as possible. When Delilah had been alive, she'd been able to run only a little interference, given Olivia had long since cowed her into submission. With Delilah and his brother gone, his mother would have been left with unfettered access to Lilly. No way was Morgan letting that happen.

He loved his mother in his own way, understood she was a product of her upbringing and a way of life that had worked well for the Westlakes for centuries. He understood her determination to stick with the program as set forth by their ancestors.

Morgan saw things differently—for himself and now for Lilly. His mother was, and would continue to be, an important part of Lilly's life. But she wasn't going to be Lilly's whole life. Exactly what that life would have been like under Olivia's control became immediately apparent, even as the funerals were being conducted. It was one of the main reasons he'd moved away from the family estate as quickly as feasibly possible.

With such a devastating loss, Lilly's life was in complete flux, so he'd thought it best to make the move sooner rather than later. Even so, it had taken the better part of a year to get them out the door.

Morgan might not know anything about raising a kid, but he had been a kid once himself. Specifically a Westlake kid, as was Lilly. He knew there was much more to do and see, to understand and learn, than the restrictive and suffocating boundaries their family environment would allow—not to mention how much more there was to feel. Morgan wanted to show Lilly all of that and provide her with access to the whole wide world, while hopefully keeping the bridges back to Atlanta intact.

A tall order, for sure, but having goals was a good thing.

He didn't want to take anything else away from her; he only wanted to add to her life. Worried about his decisions, his choices, where she was concerned, he had decided moving to Sugarberry was the best way he knew how to do that. Up until nine months ago, he'd only had himself to consider. But he knew for a fact, what life had been like for him, and would continue to be for her, in Atlanta. He wouldn't return to it, and he wasn't about to let her stay in it.

I Regarding that, he knew he'd made the right choice. Coming to Sugarberry? Bringing Delilah's mother into Lilly's life? Taking her out of such privileged surroundings and raising her in a cottage on the beach? Who the hell knew about those questions?

At the moment, he'd be happy to figure out how to make her laugh again.

"Moggy, I'm done," she called out, snapping him out of his reverie.

He tossed the folder onto the cluttered surface of the desk and went out to the kitchen. "Let's see."

She handed him the coloring book.

"You did great." It was clearly the work of a child, but he noted how painstakingly she'd made sure to stay inside all the lines. Was that her nature? Or a result of the How Young Ladies Behave indoctrination handed down from dear grandmama? He'd figure it out in time. "Can I do one?"

She nodded and flipped through the small booklet. "This one," she said, laying it on the table and pointing. "That's a boy turtle."

"It is, is it?" he said, charmed. He had a million things to accomplish if he was going to get moving on the project with Gabe, not to mention the consultant work he was still doing for his clients out west. But, for the moment, nothing seemed more important than doing a little coloring. He pulled out the chair and sat down. "So, was yours a girl turtle?"

Her eyes widened and she might have looked a little hurt. "Couldn't you tell?"

"Oh, sure, sure," he said, becoming a floundering guardian again. *Please don't ask me how I can tell,* he silently begged, needing all the parenting street cred he could build.

She slid the book away from him and turned back to her page. "See? Her tail is short." She turned back to his page. "Boy turtles have long tails." She looked up at Morgan. "Didn't you listen to Dr. Langley?"

Morgan didn't know whether to laugh or melt. Sometimes she sounded wise beyond her years, like a tiny little professor, yet she pronounced *turtles* with no /r/ sound, and added a good syllable or three to the esteemed doctor's last name. Feeling utterly defenseless in the face of her kind of nerdy adorableness, he could only hope he got a better grip on that before she grew any older or he'd be the worst kind of pushover. "I did. But I guess I missed that part."

"These are the colors I used." She slid the pile over to him.

"Are you sure these aren't girl turtle colors?" he teased.

"They're the same color," she responded. The look on her face told him she wasn't sure if he was as smart as she thought he was.

"Of course. I was just testing you." He'd been kidding, but she nodded, as if she expected no less than to be grilled on the accuracy of a simple coloring book picture. It made him feel like . . . well, like a Westlake. He generally tried to avoid that.

He started coloring, but his big boy hands and a little kid coloring book weren't always a good match. He didn't miss the slight intake of breath every time he went outside the lines. Smiling, he glanced up at her. "I'm not much of an inside-the-lines guy."

"That's why the lines are there," she said, in the way someone might gently help the totally clueless. "So you know where to stop coloring."

His smile grew. "I see them as more of a general guideline." When she kept looking at the page, frowning a little, he asked, "Does it bug you if it's a little messy? You know, you can color however you want. It's your picture. As long as you like it, that's all that matters."

She looked up at him, appearing truly curious. "Do you like it that way?"

He pretended to give his half-colored turtle a serious once-over. "I'm good with it."

"Okay." But clearly, she didn't agree.

Stifling a smile, he kept coloring and tried not to laugh every time she sighed when he went outside the lines. He might have done it a bit more than necessary, telling himself it was good for her to be exposed to new ideas. At least he'd learned it was her natural inclination and not something that had been drilled into her.

He signed his name at the bottom with a flourish when he was done, then spun the book around to face her. "There. What do you think?"

She studied it every bit as seriously as he'd pretended to earlier, then looked at him. "You did your best job, Uncle Moggy." She reached over and covered his big hand with her tiny one. "Can we go show our pictures to Dr. Langley? Maybe he will give you a book so you can practice and get better."

Morgan barked out a laugh, then lifted up her hand and kissed the back of it. "That sounds like a good idea." *Maybe it's just as important for me to be exposed to new ideas, too.*

Chapter 3

"As you know, I've been planning this for almost a year, but with everything going on, running the shop and finishing the cookbook with Baxter, making Babycakes happen was just one too many things to tackle. So, we're still in the beginning stages. Charlotte has said so many good things about you. I'm really glad it's working out for us to meet, though I'm so sorry about the reason for it."

Kit hadn't known what to expect from Leilani Dunne—Lani, as she'd asked Kit to call her—other than Charlotte's gushing about how amazingly talented she was and what a good friend she'd been. Kit was relatively close to her in age, and both had achieved a fair amount of responsibility and success already. Lani had made her own way, whereas Kit had been born into her career, but both paths resulted in the forging of two women who weren't afraid to tackle a big project and had the confidence to believe they could pull it off.

Lani had already proven that with Cakes by the Cup. For Kit, the question of whether she could build something entirely on her own, without the Bellamy women and Mamie Sue's team supporting her, was far more in question. For so many reasons, it was vital she find out what the answer would be. She needed to make amends for the loss she'd allowed to happen and to prove to herself that she wasn't a complete failure.

She was nervous bordering on slightly terrified, taking on such a big responsibility for someone to whom it clearly meant so much, but Kit couldn't deny she was a lot more intrigued and excited than she'd been when she'd rapped on the door almost an hour ago. Alva had made introductions, then gone out front to man the shop counter so Lani could conduct the interview. Kit had expected a thirty minute or so conversation . . . leading to a more serious, lengthy talk later if she took the job. Or a long drive back to Atlanta, if she didn't.

But an instant connection had occurred between the two, beginning with their mutual affection for Charlotte, extending into their shared love of pastry, and progressing into the more serious conversation about the trials and tribulations of running a business, though their individual endeavors had been on somewhat opposite ends of the spectrum.

They were finally settling in to the heart of the actual meeting.

"We've leased the space next door," Lani continued. "Used to be a tailoring shop, but when the owner became ill and had to move, Baxter and I snapped it up, thinking it might be our only chance, if we want to expand." She grinned. "Folks here don't run businesses for only a few years. It's a life commitment, sometimes for generations. We weren't sure when we'd ever get another chance."

"I understand all about generations of commitment," Kit said, her smile somewhat bittersweet.

Lani surprised her by reaching across the desk and taking Kit's hand. "I know, and . . . honestly, I hate what happened to you. It's because you have that kind of commitment and dedication that you're so appealing and special to me."

"Thanks." Kit meant it. The compliment didn't exactly mitigate the guilt she still carried around, but it was good to know her entire life hadn't been a complete waste, that what she'd learned and earned was worth something to someone else. "You understand, and that means a lot to me, too."

Lani grinned and settled back in her seat, her expression lighting up with excitement again as she talked about her new endeavor. "The building has the space for conversion, but it will take a lot of renovation. It might seem premature to be hiring someone to manage the place, but I thought it would be a good idea to have that person get involved, literally, from the ground up."

"I think it's a solid idea. Speaking for myself, I'd like to be involved as early in the process as possible. I know it's ultimately your show," Kit said, "but working as a team always seems the best way to go."

"Well, that's exactly the thing. We each bring something different to this project. With my work here, and even back in New York running Baxter's place, Gateau, we did everything but mail order. Gateau did catering, and we do a fair share of small scale parties and orders for events here on Sugarberry. But we don't have the capacity to do anything bigger, not on a regular basis. Charlotte's catering business in Savannah is really taking off and though they do both sides—"

"I really like how she and Carlo set up their business," Kit offered. "That's how we met, working together on some events in Atlanta. I think Sweet & Savory is a great idea, a great business name."

"Right?" Lani agreed enthusiastically. "And her connection to us is getting out there, too, so requests are coming to her to work with us and bring Baxter's whole Chef Hot Cakes cache to some of the bigger functions."

"How does that go over with Charlotte?"

"Fine, fine. We both know word of mouth is how to grow a business. While it's important to me to keep Cakes by the Cup small and intimate and focused on life here on Sugarberry, Charlotte has bigger dreams and hopes for her company. She knows I send every request we can't handle her way, and her business has really profited from that. But she's almost got more than she can handle now, and she and Carlo don't really want to expand quite yet."

"So, what is your ultimate goal in opening Babycakes? And where did the name come from? It's so cute. Is it because it's the offspring of the cupcakery?"

"Well, that, and it's also something personal to me. A nickname my dad calls me."

"Aw." Kit smiled. "I love that."

Lani's eyes shone with love and emotion. "Me, too. And I can't talk about it or I get weepy, which is ridiculous."

"I bet your dad is really honored."

"He'd rather I was naming a child after him. His hints are of the brick to the side of the head variety. But then, the sheriff isn't known for his subtlety. I think he started approximately two seconds after Baxter and I said our vows. But yes, he was very touched."

"I think it's really sweet. And the perfect name."

"We did, too. I can't believe we're really doing it, but we are. With the publication of Baxter's first cookbook last year, followed by the feature about us done on his cooking show filmed here on Sugarberry, and his show going to network TV filming in Savannah, things are taking off more swiftly than I ever imagined. Certainly a lot faster than I envisioned when I left New York and came down here. A lot of the added interest is for mail order to folks who can't get here but are curious or interested in us, and more catering offers are coming in. I thought by opening an adjunct business to strictly handle those things, I could keep my initial shop the same, which is what I truly want."

"And this next cookbook features you and your husband's joint story, right? How you met and worked together. So that's probably going to increase demand."

"Given how things have gone so far since Baxter's arrival here . . . " She trailed off, smiled, and that thing, that twinkle, that . . . special knowledge in her eyes as she talked about her new husband reminded Kit of a look she'd witnessed in her own mother's eyes and in Grandma Reenie's as well. They'd become Bellamy women by marrying Bellamy men, and those bonds had been just as strong, just as loving.

Kit had always wanted to have her own "special one" some day. Though she thought she'd been there a few times, she'd never felt . . . that thing she saw shining from Lani's eyes. She always figured that was how she'd know for sure. "I've seen his cooking show about the two of you, and yeah . . . I'm pretty sure you can expect another upswing in business after your joint cookbook hits the shelves."

Lani laughed even as she blushed a little. "It's doubtful we could get the place open by the time the book is released, but I'd like to be close. We started work on the cookbook just a little over a year ago, and with everything else going so well and momentum building, the publisher pushed us to get it done in record time. Now they're pushing hard to get it ready for release. Lead time is usually ten to twelve months. We turned it in early in August and they're releasing in March."

Kit's eyes widened. "That's just five months from now."

Lani smiled, but that twinkle was still there. "I know." She lifted a hand to stall whatever else Kit might say. "Like

I said, we don't think we'll be ready by then, but I'd like us to have a solid opening date to promote, if nothing else. We were hoping by the first of June."

Kit leaned back. "That's a lot to think about."

"I know. It's a tall order. But that's the other reason you intrigued me and Baxter. You've had experience running a massive commercial operation. Your input and expertise would make this entire effort a great deal easier."

"Well, I don't know about easier. It's going to take time and a lot of hard work, no matter who is on board."

"It might help us make fewer missteps, though," Lani said. "And talking with you today . . . I'm feeling more certain you're the right person for the job. But I need you to be certain, too. This might ultimately be my show, as you called it, but I want someone who feels as strongly about the whole thing as I do. Someone who knows where things may go in the future and what opportunity there might be. I want to run and nurture my bakery. I don't want to run Babycakes, too. Not now and not in the future."

Kit tried to take it all in. "It's a lot to think about."

Lani smiled. "I'm sure you have more than a few questions. Why don't you take some time, look around the island? Baxter's at the studio in Savannah. He'll be done right about the time I close up here. I thought maybe we'd head over the causeway and grab some dinner in Savannah, just the three of us. Talk more. We could book you a room, if you'd like."

Kit hadn't even thought about accommodations. She hadn't been sure she wouldn't already be making the long trip back to Atlanta. "Oh, that's gracious of you, but I— you don't need to do that. As for dinner, I'd like that very much, but—"

Lani's expression fell.

"No," Kit laughed, "not that kind of but. I just—I agree

about getting to know the island a little better. If Baxter will be heading back to Sugarberry later, is there somewhere here we can grab a bite? I'm not fussy."

"Yes, but there wouldn't be much privacy."

"I guess having a famous husband—"

"Oh no, not that." Lani laughed. "We're family here now, the whole celebrity aura with Baxter has long since worn off. I mean, everyone is proud to call him one of their own." She grinned. "And take credit, of course, for the success of the cupcakery, the cookbook, and anything else that happens. In this case, you'd be the person of interest. Being family here means everyone thinks your business is their business. So we'd have some nosy stoppers-by, being neighborly." She framed the last word in air quotes. "Checking out the new girl in town."

Kit laughed. "Actually, I know a little bit about that. Mamie Sue's was it's own small world. A village unto itself. We had families, generations of them, in fact, who'd worked for the company from the early days onward." Her smile faltered, turned poignant. "I miss that part the most."

Lani's smile shifted, too, then faded. "I'm so sorry. I can't imagine how hard that has been on you."

"That's okay."

"No, it's not. I saw, of course, in the papers and in the news, but—"

"They made it sound like I was some kind of ungrateful, spoiled heiress. I can assure you—"

"No, Charlotte told me the real story. The whole story. It's"—she paused—"just me and my dad now, family-wise. I never had siblings, but I was close to my mom and my grandmother. I even remember my great-grandmother. And I can't—I just can't imagine that kind of betrayal."

"Thank you," Kit said, surprised by the sincere heat she heard in Lani's voice.

"I left New York, came here to take care of my father after he had a heart attack. I'd lost my mom—"

"A few years before that." Kit smiled briefly. "You forget, because of Baxter's show, your whole life is part of the fairy-tale legend. The hunky British television chef and the prodigy pastry chef-turned-cupcake baker."

Lani blushed, laughing at the same time. "Yeah, I keep forgetting people outside Sugarberry Island know all that. I want to let you know I realize this isn't where you'd choose to be, that if you could, you'd be running the pie empire built by the Bellamy women, equally legendary in their own way. I know it's all still fresh, the loss. The timing might not be exactly what you wanted. All I can tell you is that you feel like the perfect fit to me. You just need to figure out if we're the perfect fit for you."

Kit smiled. "Well, then we're definitely eating on the island tonight. If it turns out I'm going to be part of the island family, I want to get to know them and they me, sooner rather than later."

Lani grinned as she pushed back her chair and leaned across the table, hand extended. "You are *so* hired."

Kit took her hand and squeezed it. "Thanks. And, you're right. I also want—need—this to be the right thing for me. I know that much."

"Well, fair warning. I'm not above using my incredibly hot husband to woo you with his even hotter British accent and worldly, charming ways."

Kit laughed as she reached for her sweater and purse. "I should be so lucky."

Lani came around the desk. "Speaking of that . . . the papers never mentioned much about your personal life, other than the Bellamy family history in general."

Kit gave her a wry grin. "That's because I don't have one."

"Oh. Well, I'm not prying . . . or even asking. I'm

just—the only reason I mention it is, if you did, I wanted you to know . . . we're happy to work with you on that, help with transition—"

"It will just be me. And I'm sure I'll figure something out"—she flashed Lani another smile as she walked back through the kitchen to the back door—"if, you know, I take the job."

"I'm also not above using my cupcakes as leverage," Lani warned. "They're no Mamie Sue's Peanut Pie, but they're pretty addictive"—she looked at Kit with a twinkle in her eye—"she said humbly."

Kit drew in the sweet scents of vanilla and chocolate and sighed. "Yeah, well, that might be more persuasive than the already taken hot British guy."

Lani laughed. "You're going to take this job, you know. You fit here."

Kit looked around the kitchen. She hadn't even seen the retail space of the cupcakery, much less the space they were planning to use for Babycakes. But this place felt like something between Grammy's old kitchen with its lovingly restored antique appliances . . . and the far more cavernous warehouse kitchens that housed all the appliances and equipment used to produce Mamie Sue's pies on a far broader scale. As the company expanded and grew under Laureen, and later, her own mother's watch, they had worked hard to keep the ambience of those industrial size kitchens as homey and warm as possible. Mamie Sue had demanded only one thing, that there would always be "real hands, making real pie." And that's how it had always been.

Lani's bakery kitchen was like a tiny slice of that, and Kit felt naturally at ease. It was a place where she felt she could fit in. She glanced back at Lani, who was quietly allowing her to size up the place. Kit could see the pride she took in her shop and the worry that it wouldn't measure up to Kit's expectations.

"I do have one very important question."

"Shoot," Lani said, worry more evident on her face.

Kit motioned to the Beatrix Potter themed apron Lani had on. "Will I get to wear awesome aprons at Babycakes?"

Lani blew out an audible sigh of relief. "Absolutely."

Kit left the shop smiling, feeling lighter of heart than she thought she might ever feel again. "You'd like her," she murmured under her breath, feeling the presence of Mamie Sue, Grandma Reenie, and her mother, as surely as if they were walking beside her. *She's not a Southern girl, but she understands family.*

Kit got in her car and pulled out of the lot with the idea of taking a slow, wandering tour of the island, then coming back to the town square to stroll around the shops, maybe peek through the windows at the space next to Cakes by the Cup that was going to house Babycakes.

In all honesty, the interview had far outshone any expectations she might have had. Partly because she'd worked really hard at not having any. Why set herself up for more disappointment? What was important was to put aside the burgeoning little flicker of excitement and the natural urge she felt to tackle this new challenge and think the whole thing through as rationally and objectively as she could.

But it was hard to ignore the little thrill of anticipation, and the relief that came with it. After the past year, it was a gift she hadn't expected to receive.

So, given that, it made no sense she was, once again, fighting tears as she took the loop road around the back, ocean-facing side of the island. It was what Lani had said about family. Kit missed hers so much. Even her sister, who, despite everything, she loved. She didn't know what twist of genetics had made Trixie so different from the rest of the Bellamy women, but Kit understood, on a level far deeper than the superficial irritation and frustration Trixie had elicited from all of them, that her younger sister really couldn't help herself. Trixie simply wasn't hardwired like the rest of them. She wasn't connected to the family, its history, the bond they all shared, the way Kit was. And nothing was ever going to change that.

Which left Kit . . . where?

"Here." Kit stated it out loud, trying it on for size. Like a confirmation. Or an affirmation. "It leaves me here. On Sugarberry Island."

She smiled a tentative smile as she imagined herself there. Sugarberry was a surprising blend. The island was small, intimate, with fishing docks on the south end and the lively little town square located just north of that. The cluster of shops and central park area were surrounded by a small grid of narrow lanes dotted with houses. The narrow lanes turned to a lazy sprawl of development ending along the north end of the island, which was largely swamp and wilderness. Cottages periodically dotted the road looping around the exterior of the island. A few faced the sound, but most of them were on the ocean side, ranging in size, spaced somewhat sparsely, and nestled among the dunes, with the ocean lying just beyond.

Kit cruised past the last one, then drove a stretch of road bordered only by dunes and sea grass to her right and untamed, swampy wilderness to her left. A contrast to the developed end, it was what made the place feel like an island, rather than an extension of the mainland that just happened to be across a short bridge. The beach, the dunes, the salt spray. Even with her windows up, she could hear the sounds of the surf.

At the northernmost tip of the loop, she saw a large sign

announcing a wildlife sanctuary and research area. Her attention was caught by the image of a sea turtle beautifully carved into the wood. She slowed, curious, but the dunes blocked anything beyond them from view. Well, almost everything. She noted a bright green kite dancing in the sky, far above the skyline. She smiled at the whimsy of it, as it also happened to be a sea turtle. She assumed it was meant to mark the research center, perhaps attract tourists and visitors, but wondered, briefly, how they kept it flying.

Just past the sign she noticed the narrow crushed shell and packed dirt road leading, presumably, to the research center. Glancing at the clock on the dash, she saw she still had plenty of time before her dinner meeting with Lani and Baxter, and she'd already found Laura Jo's diner, their designated meeting spot, so she knew right where to go when the time came. So . . . why not explore?

Only two vehicles were parked in the tiny lot fronting a rambling, weathered, one-story building. She thought about poking her head in, but found herself drawn down the path through the dunes instead, toward the ocean . . . and the turtle kite. She'd have thought it would be attached somehow to the main building, but maybe there was more to the research facility than that.

She drew her sweater closer around her. It had been a very warm autumn in the South, but it was late afternoon, and the steady winds on the beach were making the temperatures feel a bit brisk. "Good day for kites."

She emerged from the end of the dune path to find a series of narrow, open air, pavilion-style buildings with what looked like rows of worktables bolted down to cement slabs. Beyond that was a wide stretch of empty beach.

"Look, Lills! Paddle feet are good for flying, too!"

Kit spun around at the sound of a man's voice. About twenty yards down the beach she spied him holding the kite. A few yards farther down the beach a little girl was crouched down, looking at something in the sand.

Kit watched as he coaxed the kite into staying up in the air while closing the distance between himself and the child. The little girl looked up at him and he bent down, looking at something she was showing him. Then he held out the stick the kite string was wound around.

The surf and breeze snatched their conversation away, so Kit couldn't hear anything they were saying, but the little girl was clearly skeptical. Finally, the man took her hand and helped her to her feet, then positioned her in front of him, with her body backed up against his. Using his body as a brace and a shield against the wind, he lowered the kite string in front of her. After looking up for reassurance, she took the string. He held on for good measure, then slowly let his fingers lift away.

Kit could clearly see her face when she lifted it to the sky, wonder and amazement clear in her expression. She looked up to the man, then back to the kite. Kit smiled, watching them. Simple things, like flying a kite, could bring so much joy. Her gaze shifted back to the man's face. She'd expected to see him grinning or laughing, but he was watching the girl with . . . well, she couldn't exactly say. He was a bit too far away. But she could tell he wasn't smiling . . .

Until the little girl looked up at him again. Then he immediately beamed back at her. When she looked back to their dancing turtle kite, Kit noted he wiped at his eyes. The wind, maybe?

A moment later his gaze shifted as if he felt the presence of someone else on the beach . . . and fell directly on Kit. His smile turned polite and he nodded a short acknowledgment of her.

Not knowing what to do and suddenly feeling as if she was intruding on a private moment between father and daughter, she automatically lifted her hand in a short wave, giving a brief smile.

Good-looking father, too, she thought.

He was tall and lean, with dark hair a bit on the shaggy side. Or maybe that was just the effect of the wind. But he had a lot of it to blow around. Nice smile. She couldn't tell from that distance, but she'd bet on warm eyes. The little girl looked a lot like him. She had a small frame, but matched the dark, thick hair, at least if the ponytail sticking out from the back of her little baseball cap was any indication.

Kit's smile returned. Both had on hoodies—his navy blue, hers pink—and sported sandy, damp knees on their jeans. *Like father, like daughter.*

Pretty charming pair, she thought, then decided maybe it was best to turn back to the path and leave them to their private moment. Her smile remained as she headed back through the dunes, even as her thoughts turned a bit more poignant. She hadn't gotten any kind of time like that with her own dad. He hadn't been the outdoor type. Or much of the dad type, truth be told. He'd followed the male tradition in the Bellamy family started by Mamie Sue's brother, who'd been too frail for the war and had gone into banking. That was where the men of the family had made their contribution to the family business. Her father had been a shining example, working long hours and showing the same kind of dedication as the women of Mamie Sue's.

Kit had loved him very much and had known, absolutely, she was loved in return, but their time together had mostly been spent at the dinner table. Despite being used to not having him around much, she still missed him every day now that he was forever gone.

She thought about the man on the beach and sighed a little as she pulled open the door to the research center. Life brought with it so many unexpected changes. She hoped that little girl realized how lucky she was.

Chapter 4

Morgan reeled in the kite, with help from his little assistant. "Sun's starting to set. Getting a little chilly. What do you say we go get some dinner in town?"

He was gaining ground on the whole unpacking thing, but hadn't quite gotten ahead of the curve on the buying food and feeding the child part. He was used to grabbing whatever was handy whenever he came up for air from working and realized he hadn't eaten in hours. Little people required something a bit more regulated than that, not to mention nourishing.

"Where?" she asked.

"Well, there's a little diner on the town square. Laura Jo's." The other options were the pub or the tiny pizza place, neither of which seemed suitable for their first joint venture into public. He'd wanted to get unpacked, let her settle in a bit, before springing more new people on her—including the grandmother she'd never met. Well, the grandmother she wouldn't remember, since she'd been a newborn at the time they first met.

Actually, the more he thought about it, maybe the diner wasn't such a good idea. There was no telling whom they'd run in to, or how people would react when they realized who he was . . . and who Lilly was. He should probably test the waters first. "Do you like pizza? We can order one to take home."

"I don't know."

"You don't know if you want pizza?" he asked. *Since when did kids turn down pizza?*

She shook her head and explained. "I don't know if I like it."

Right. She was a Westlake. They didn't "do" pedestrian food, much less eat anything that could be carried out in a box.

He bundled up the kite, then took her hand as they headed down the path back to the research facility. "Well, what do you say we go find out? If it's a bust, we can always go to the little grocery store and find something we like." He'd been working from the stash of cereal, sandwich fixings, soup, and frozen casseroles the head housekeeper Coraline had surreptitiously asked the cook to load into his truck before he'd left Atlanta. Plus there was the always-dependable peanut butter and jelly he'd picked up on their trek in from Atlanta, but, after a few weeks on the island, supplies were running low.

"Okay," she said.

"Great. Let's go give the kite back to Gabe—Dr. Langley—then we'll head to the pizza place." He'd get the number from Gabe and call ahead, so he could just buzz in, grab the pie, and they could head back out to the cottage.

"Can we see Paddlefoot again first?"

Morgan smiled, thankful she was too young to understand the wry curve to it. He'd thought the turtles would be interesting to her, provide a little distraction from . . . well, everything else, but again he'd found himself back in careful-what-you-wish-for territory. In a single day, she was quickly becoming fixated on them. "Just for a minute. And only if Dr. Langley says it's okay."

Her grip on his hand tightened as they sped up the path. He was definitely going to have to work a lot harder on that whole not-being-a-pushover thing. Today it was turtles, tomorrow it would be . . . God, he didn't even want to think about it.

They opened the door and pushed through the screen of thick, dangling plastic strips designed to keep birds and other creatures from flying into the building and walked on into the welcome area. Morgan heard voices coming from the lab, which was through the door on the opposite side of the small foyer, so he headed that way. It was also the direction of the rehab facility.

He spied the doctor talking to the woman who'd come out to the beach a little bit ago. She was listening while Gabe was explaining . . . something to do with his work, no doubt. Morgan smiled, thinking he couldn't recall seeing Gabe quite so . . . animated. In fact, when the woman laughed at something he said, Morgan could have sworn the older man's deeply tanned, sun-grooved cheeks flushed a little. Not that his reaction was entirely surprising.

The young woman was a little taller than most, with an average build. She had on khaki trousers and a light blue sweater, so he couldn't see distinct curves, but that wasn't the reason for Gabe's blush or Morgan's more thorough perusal. Her hair was a show-stopping—and quite natural, he believed—auburn shade of red, cropped short around the ears and neck, but left longer on the top. Thick tufts tossed about by the wind sprang up, giving her a just-woke-up look that . . . well, on her was pretty damn sexy.

He was about to turn Lilly around and tell her they'd have to come back another time, when Gabe spied them and motioned them forward. "Hello, Miss Lilly," he called out. "How was the kite?"

Lilly's grip tightened on Morgan's hand, and he felt her

press against his hip. He glanced down. "It's okay. You know Dr. Gabe now."

She glanced up at him, then straightened a little and looked at Gabe. "It was very good," she said, giving it her best Westlake. "Thank you for letting us borrow it."

Gabe beamed. "You're quite welcome. You can borrow it anytime."

Morgan smiled, glad Lilly had spoken up for herself, but well aware it was a command performance. Her grip hadn't let up one bit. He hated inadvertently playing the Olivia role. He had faith that, in time, as she healed and moved on in life, Lilly would eventually let her guard down a little and feel more comfortable around new people.

"Thank you." She tugged on Morgan's hand, and when he looked down, she whispered, "Can you ask him about Paddlefoot?"

It was another in the rapidly multiplying series of moments when Morgan questioned his options. Part of him wanted to gently encourage her to speak for herself, if for no other reason than to allow others into her world who could help make it better, more interesting, give her comfort and attention, or even just be friendly. The other part of him wanted to wrap her up in something soft and warm and keep the world at bay until she was good and ready to deal with it.

"You can ask him," he said gently, quietly, just between the two of them.

She didn't say anything to that, but let her eyes do the pleading for her.

"Okay, we can take turns. I'll ask this time, and you can next time. Deal?"

She nodded, and he rubbed his thumb over the slender fingers still in his grasp.

He glanced back at Gabe. "Any chance we can go say

hello to Paddlefoot one more time today? Lilly drew him a picture."

She glanced up sharply at him and he wasn't sure what he'd done wrong. Then her gaze went to the woman, then down to the floor. Ah. Apparently he was revealing too much to strangers.

"That's wonderful," Gabe was saying. "I'm sure he will love it. Maybe you can show the other turtles, too—if you don't mind sharing. They don't have anyone drawing them pictures."

Lilly looked a little distraught about that, then blurted out, "Moggy drew one, too."

Gabe chuckled, his gentle demeanor soothing and completely nonthreatening, despite his rather tall, somewhat knobby appearance and the gray beard he sported. "Fantastic."

Walking a short distance from her, he crouched down so he was on eye level with her. "You know, maybe we could make a bulletin board back there and encourage people to bring their drawings or anything else they want to share with the turtles during their stay here. What do you say? Would you be willing to help me with that?"

Lilly looked up at Morgan, squeezing the life out of his fingers again, but maybe for different reasons. "Can I, Uncle Moggy?" she whispered with such honest yearning in those sad eyes of hers. he was pretty sure any piece of his heart she hadn't already shattered, had fissures shooting through it.

"Of course. I think that's about the best idea ever."

She looked back at Dr. Langley. "Yes, sir. Thank you. Very much." She spoke politely, with emotion vibrating in every word.

Gabe grinned and pushed to a stand. "Well then, consider it a plan. Go on back and say hi, maybe look around and see where you think the board should go, okay?"

"Yes, sir. Okay," she said directly, without needing an intermediary this time.

Morgan smiled. Little steps—but big, too, in their own way. A part of him relaxed a bit. The interaction helped confirm Lilly was ultimately going to be okay. She was too interested, too curious, and too determined to let the hardships of life keep her down for long.

She tugged on his hand and nodded toward the rehab room.

Morgan chuckled. "Lead on." He turned to follow the all but vibrating child, then looked over his shoulder and made direct eye contact with the woman still standing just behind the doctor. "I'm sorry we interrupted."

"Oh, don't apologize," she said with an easy smile. "I'm just wandering through."

She had the pale, creamy skin that often went along with being a natural redhead, but what caught his full and undivided attention were the green eyes that completed the package. They sparkled when she smiled. That and a flash of white teeth and he found himself somewhat rivet—

"Uncle Moggy," Lilly whispered almost fiercely, tugging at his hand with all she was worth. "Please?"

Morgan chuckled again and lifted his shoulders in an apologetic shrug. "I must go." He nodded toward Gabe. "Be careful around this one or he'll have you volunteering your time and your checkbook."

At Gabe's raised eyebrows, Morgan's smile turned self-deprecating. "On second thought, since I'm supposed to be helping him with that, forget I mentioned it."

"I can think of worse things to do with both," the woman said with a fast grin. "And, who knows, if I end up sticking around, maybe I'll do exactly that."

"Great," Morgan said, with Gabe echoing the sentiment. "You thinking of moving to Sugarberry, then?"

"Moggy," Lilly said, drawing out the syllables into a classic kid whine.

Nice to know she can beg, he thought. "Nice to meet you," he called as he stumbled along behind Lilly. "I'm Morgan, by the way. And the tiny terror is my niece, Lilly."

Her smile faltered at that. "Ah. Uh, I'm Kit," she answered after a moment, more polite afterthought than sincere offering.

Morgan smiled through the surprised little gut punch her reaction had given him. She was just passing through. God only knew the reaction he was going to get when he mingled with the folks who actually lived here. "Enjoy your stay, Kit." With that, he disappeared into the rehab center.

She didn't disappear from his thoughts quite as easily.

So, Kit thought, *that was Morgan Westlake. Figures. Hot, handsome, and adorable with his niece.*

And single, she recalled as the conversation she'd overheard between Alva and Lani floated through her mind again. It competed with the far stronger memories of her months spent in court, going up against those unbearably snotty lawyers from his family's firm. The last thing she needed or wanted was to tangle any part of her new life with anyone remotely connected to ending her old one.

"Sorry," Dr. Langley was saying, "didn't mean to leave you standing there."

"No, no, not to worry," she assured the older gentleman. He was pretty much the textbook description of what she'd imagine if she was asked to picture a doctor of ecology and wildlife conservation. She pegged him somewhere in his mid-to-late sixties.

He was tall and lanky bordering on bony, with longish gray hair a bit on the wispy side, as was the accompanying beard. He sported wire-rim glasses, a lab coat over faded khakis, and exceedingly well-worn hiking boots. The few pens in the upper pocket and a folding knife sheathed to his belt completed the outdoorsy-nerdy combination. He had a calm quiet voice, but his hazel eyes sparked to life when he talked about the plight of the endangered species he clearly loved and was dedicated to helping.

Kit had liked him on sight. "Actually, I'm truly curious about the work you're doing here." Surprisingly, it was the truth.

The court case and complete dismantling of Mamie Sue's, not to mention the family turmoil caused by sitting across a courtroom from a vengeful Trixie and smug Teddy, had overwhelmed Kit for what felt like forever. Add to that the emotional toll of trying to figure out what was next for herself . . . and it felt like it had been ages since she'd thought of anything outside the takeover.

She certainly wouldn't have guessed sea turtles would capture her attention, and she wasn't sure anything more than a pleasant and interesting conversation with the good doctor would come of it . . . but she couldn't deny it was blissfully restorative to step outside her problems and think about something—anything—else, even if for only a short time.

Kit continued the conversation. "What got you started here? Why the turtles?"

"I've always been interested in working with animals. Grew up in the Smokey Mountains. My dad was a park ranger and taught me a lot about them, how they manage themselves and how the environment can affect them. As for the turtles, I moved to Savannah to take on a teaching position at a college there, got involved with a few professors who were already studying turtles." He smiled and his eyes brightened. "One in particular really . . . engaged my attention."

Kit smiled. "Ah, so it was true love, was it?"

"At first sight . . . the lovely professor and the turtles. She—Anne—actually started the work here almost twenty years ago."

Kit wanted to ask the obvious question, but didn't want to thoughtlessly probe something that might not be a happy memory.

But her curiosity showed on her face. He lifted his hand and flashed a simple gold band on his ring finger. "She's working in Savannah at the college, but is helping me here when she can. We live on Sugarberry."

Kit's smile broadened and she might have sighed just a little. "I think that's wonderful. Both love stories. How great that you can share something you're both passionate about."

"You are absolutely right about that." Not a trace of smugness appeared in his tone, just sincere joy and happiness.

"Do you have children involved in the family passion as well?"

"No children for us, unfortunately," he said easily. "The turtles get our undivided attention."

"Then they're the luckiest turtles around." She stepped forward and stuck out her hand. "I don't know what my immediate future holds, but if I end up staying, I'd like to talk some more, maybe find a way to help out. I need a, well—"

"A hobby?" he asked not unkindly, but perhaps a bit . . . probingly.

Kit didn't blame him. She was sure people thought volunteering was cool and interesting and fun—and no doubt it was all those things—but first and foremost it was a research center, and the work they were doing was serious and important. "I was going to say I need something other than my immediate world to focus on for a change. I'm starting over, I guess you could say, and this time around,

I want more of a balance between work life and personal life." She grinned. "Any personal life would be a major step in the right direction."

"Sounds like a healthy plan and I admire your optimism and fortitude." He shook her hand, then squeezed it before letting it go. "Let's talk more when that time comes. I can always use the help and enthusiasm of someone who truly wants to contribute. As for Sugarberry, it's a good place for starting over or just plain starting. And an even better place for staying. And building. And growing. We'd be happy to have you, Miss Kit."

She grinned. "Well, if the rest of the residents are like you, you might as well get a lab coat ready for me."

He smiled and gave her a wink. "Guess I should go and see how my newest little volunteer is doing."

Kit's smile didn't falter. She was feeling too good and . . . relaxed, and wanted to hold on to the feeling for as long as possible. "Mr. Westlake's niece?"

Dr. Langley's gaze sharpened a little. "Yes, the delightful Miss Lilly. We've only just met ourselves, but she's going to be a wonderful addition to our growing family here. I hope we can be the same for her."

"I do, too." At the doctor's questioning look, she added, "I'm familiar with . . . his family. And I overheard in town earlier about his moving here. None of my business, really. I just—it sounded like they've been through a tough time and I think it's cool she's found something that interests her."

Dr. Langley studied her for a moment, then said, "Yes, I agree. Perhaps that's something you know a little bit about yourself?"

She smiled briefly. The good doctor was a very perceptive observer, but she guessed that's what made him good at his work. "Perhaps."

"Well then . . . I hope it works out for you both."

Kit wasn't entirely sure what he meant by that, but nodded and smiled. "Me, too." She took a step back and turned to leave. "Thank you again. For your time . . . and for . . . the encouragement. I hope to see you again."

"As do I. Safe travels, Miss Kit."

"Oh, I'm not travel—" She broke off when his wise eyes warmed with knowing. She laughed shortly. "Very clever."

"Sometimes you just have to know the right questions to ask yourself."

She was smiling as she walked back toward the welcome area. She glanced over her shoulder to find him still standing in the same place. "Very lucky turtles, indeed," she called back to him.

He smiled, lifted a hand, and waved.

She waved back and headed outside. "So," she said, walking toward her car. "So."

The sun was low on the horizon and the warm air had cooled significantly. She took in a deep, cleansing breath as she made a slow turn, looking toward the dunes. She remembered the dancing turtle kite, and thought about the little girl who'd lost her parents and found, perhaps, some unlikely new companions in a few stranded turtles. She tried not to think about the hunky, kite-flying uncle, but he was hard to block out. Unfortunately, so was his last name.

Still . . . she was smiling as she finally climbed into her car. Sure, she would have much preferred a Westlake-free environment, but, given the rest of the items on the plus side of the list, it was a compromise she was willing to make. It wasn't like they had to spend time together.

Kit turned her thoughts to Lani's job offer, to the excited and passionate pastry chef and her sexy, British husband, and to the lively little senior, Alva, and her love of pirates. Making her decision, Kit gave a pound to the steering wheel. "Ready or not, Sugarberry. Here I am."

Morgan was leaning in the doorway behind Gabe as Kit left the building.

The older man didn't seem all that surprised when he turned and found him there. "Nice young woman. Good spirit. Good heart."

"You got all that from a ten minute chat?"

The good doctor smiled. "It's easier to read some than others. No pretenses with that one. She'll let you know how she feels." He slid the clipboard out from where he'd tucked it under his arm and studied something on the top page. "She certainly did with you," he added casually.

Morgan already knew that despite his somewhat absent-minded professor demeanor, Gabriel Langley was anything but.

"Never saw her before," Morgan said. Though, admittedly, he was intrigued enough—despite her reaction to his name or maybe because of it—to hope their paths might cross again. "Can't say why she reacted the way she did."

"I believe it was your last name that gave her pause."

"Oh, I got that part. I just don't know why. I know the islanders might be concerned, given my family's history, especially with Birdie Wiggins. I think they'll come to see I only mean to make things better—for Lilly and for Birdie. I have their best interests at heart. I do."

"Oh, I think you're right about that. Just give it time."

"But she—Kit—isn't from here, so I don't know how she even knows anything about me."

"I believe she mentioned something about overhearing a conversation in town."

"So, folks aren't saying kind things then, huh?"

"I didn't say that. Just that she heard something about you being here and about the situation with Miss Lilly. Might be she understands a little something of that. Personally, I mean."

"Why do you say that?"

Gabe looked up, pushed his glasses up the bridge of his nose. "A look in her eyes. Sometimes a person can just tell. Maybe that was why she reacted to you the way she did. Hard to say. Seemed right friendly, otherwise."

When Morgan didn't have anything to add to that, Gabe flipped a page on the clipboard and went back to reading. "Sounds like she plans to stay on Sugarberry, though," he said, at length. "Maybe she'll see your good intentions, too. Change her mind."

Morgan grinned, surprised, but kind of touched at the same time. "You playing matchmaker, doctor?"

"Oh, I don't play at that." A smile ghosted around his mouth as he flipped another page. But he didn't bother to elaborate.

Still grinning, Morgan said, "Lilly and I are going to head out, get out of your hair. It's dinnertime. Do you, by chance, have the number for the pizza place?"

"Take-out menu is in the folder on top of the cabinet over there."

"Great." Morgan crossed the room. "I really appreciate your patience and understanding. With Lilly, I mean. I had no idea she was going to become so fixated on the turtles, but—"

Gabe looked up, his smile soft and clearly filled with affection. "The turtles can use all the attention they can get. She's welcome here."

"I—thanks. That means a lot. I don't always know what to do with . . . well, everything, when it comes to taking care of her. But this is the first thing I've seen her take a real shine to, since . . ."

"I'm happy and touched the turtles mean something to her," Gabe filled in when Morgan trailed off.

"I know this is a lot to ask, but I don't want her to worry about them. About losing them, I mean. I'll keep her away from the ones that are in need of more . . . intensive care. I just—she doesn't need more loss."

"I understand. There are plenty here who will be just fine, if not perfect, when we release them. If you would like to be involved with that, we can get her following the few who are closest to that stage."

"They don't need to be perfect, just preferably not dying. In fact, she's taken a shine to the big guy back there. She calls him—"

"Paddlefoot." Gabe smiled. "So, I heard. He'll be with us a good while longer, but he's doing well."

"Sounds like a good fit then."

"He'll be released eventually," Gabe warned.

"Hopefully, by then, she'll understand that's a good thing for him. Do you do the releases here?"

Gabe nodded. "Right off the beach."

"Well, maybe we can be involved in some other releases before he goes, so she understands how it works, what's in store for the turtles, and why it's good they get to go home again."

"I think that's a wonderful idea."

"I also showed her the egg nest. I thought it might intrigue her, or at the very least, be a distraction. She's very concerned about them."

"So are we, to be honest," Gabe said. "It's late in the season for a nest to hatch. Not unheard of, but it's not as usual this far north. There's only the one nest left."

"It's been pretty warm this fall."

Gabe nodded. "But it still cools off quite a bit at night, and temperatures could become less moderate at any moment. If it gets too cold, the eggs stop incubating. We've been testing the temps in the sand, and keeping an eye on them. The mother picked a good location high up on the beach, not at risk for flooding, and we haven't had any big storms or heavy rains, so we staked it out, fenced it from predators, and we'll let it go as it goes."

"Do you know how many are in there?"

"We inspected the nest early on. One hundred sixteen eggs by our count."

"Wow. What percentage do you think will make it?"

"It's anyone's guess, but the sooner they hatch, the better chance we have of getting as high a percentage as possible."

"Could you dig them up, hatch them inside?"

"Not here. They should hatch in the next two weeks, so we think it will go as well as can be expected."

"Will you be out there? Or monitoring it in some way?"

"We have a camera mounted under the pavilion awning closest to the nest. It's still a bit of a distance, but we'd see the surface disturbance enough to know they're coming out."

Morgan entered the pizza place's number into his phone and put the folder back. "How well will they do once they come out? I mean, do you think they'll mostly make it?"

"Their chances of making it to adulthood are rough, but if we're lucky enough to be there when they hatch, we can do our best to keep the other creatures away, and at least help them to the water. The crabs and birds won't be a threat at night. We mostly work to keep the manmade barriers, trash, netting, that sort of thing, to a minimum to help keep their path clear to the water. And keep the lights off, so they don't get confused." He flipped the papers back on his clipboard and put it under his arm. "If any of the film comes out well, we can show Lilly an edited piece of the babies digging through the surface and trekking to the water. It really is a sight to see."

Morgan smiled. "That would be great. I'd be happy to help with that, if you need me to. I've put a lot of film together for clients . . . for in court and for fund-raising, so I've gotten pretty handy with that sort of thing."

Gabe smiled. "Good to know. Careful what you offer."

Morgan's smile spread to a grin. "It would be my pleasure. Something to balance out the work life."

Gabe's expression turned knowing. "Funny. Kit said something along the same lines."

Morgan shook his head and chuckled. "Glad to know you're not matchmaking." He headed back toward the door to the lab where Lilly was keeping Paddlefoot company.

"I didn't say that." He smiled, a sage look on his face. "Just that I don't play at it."

As Morgan neared the doorway, he could hear Lilly singing quietly, and that lump came back to his throat. He looked back at Gabe, barely registering what the man had said. "Thank you. Again."

Gabe merely lifted a hand in an easy wave and headed toward the front of the building.

Morgan paused at the door to the rehab area, not wanting to intrude just yet. Lilly was singing so softly he couldn't make out the words, but it sounded soothing and comforting, rather than sad, which, he discovered as he listened, soothed something inside him as well.

The song ended, and he stepped into the room so she could see him. "Hey, sweet pea," he called out, just loudly enough that she could hear him. "Pizza time."

She slid off the stool he'd parked her on and said goodbye to Paddlefoot, then said her good-byes to each and every other turtle.

Morgan had long since lost track of the number of tears he'd shed in the past nine months, but at least the moisture gathering in his eyes this time was from happiness. Heal and be healed. He'd seen enough of life, knew enough about himself, to know that would happen for him, eventually. Already, he'd learned Lilly would be a big part of the healing process. Maybe it was going to happen for her, too.

He scooped her up and swung her lightly around. "What do you think about pepperoni?"

"I don't know," she said, wrapping her arms around his neck.

"What say we go find out?"

She leaned her head on his shoulder. "Okay."

Her body was relaxed and more than a little heavy, but he relished every ounce of the weight. They'd had a very big day, and she was understandably tired. For once, it was from a day well spent, doing new and interesting things. There would be more days like this to come, too. It bolstered his confidence that he'd done the right thing, taking her to the turtle hospital.

She was already half dozing as Morgan ducked through the door to cross the lab. He nodded at Gabe, who smiled at him and his sleepy cargo, and nodded in return. He turned his back to duck through the long plastic flaps across the reception door and saw that Gabe had followed them to the front door.

"You know"—Gabe spoke quietly, so as not to disturb Lilly—"you should think about finding out why."

Morgan paused. "Why what?" he asked, keeping his tone soft.

"Why your last name gave Miss Kit pause."

"Why does it matter?"

Gabe smiled, his alert focus sharpening his gaze. "Well, since you're helping with the funding, and possible video editing, and Miss Lilly there might be of some help this winter break when I lose my student interns from the college . . . it's my guess you're going to be seeing a lot more of each other."

"We will?"

"She'll be back. And often, I'm thinking. Best to clear the air now. It's important things remain calm around here."

"I doubt she'd be combative about it. I know it doesn't matter to me, one way or the other."

Gabe smiled again. "Maybe it should. Find her and figure things out."

"How do you propose I do that?"

"It's a small island. Can't be too hard."

"But—"

Gabe folded his arms, and Morgan was reminded that he used to be a college professor. *Heaven help the student who underestimates the kindly old guy.*

"You're a lawyer," Gabe said. "I hear they're supposed to be pretty good with words. I'm sure you'll find some."

Morgan smiled and shook his head. Cradling his sleeping niece, he crossed the lot to his truck. Intrigued by Gabe's persistence and his own attraction to Kit, he thought, *Yeah, but will the words I come up with be the right ones?*

Chapter 5

Five whirlwind days later, Kit found herself knocking once again on the back door to the cupcakery. It was time to meet up with more than just Lani and Baxter, who had indeed, turned out to be swoon-worthy. Big and blond, with charm to spare and a killer accent, he and his wife had been ridiculously adorable together the night Kit had had dinner with them. She only hoped the evening went half as well as that dinner had.

Alva opened the door and motioned Kit in. "Chilly out there. Hurry on inside where it's warm."

With the winter season almost upon them, the Indian summer temperatures had dipped unseasonably low the night before and had barely reached fifty that afternoon. For the Georgia coast in November, it was downright frigid.

Kit ducked into the kitchen area and Alva quickly closed the door behind her.

"You changed your hair"—Kit smiled at the older woman—"And here I thought we'd be Team Redhead."

Alva patted her bonnet of artfully teased and lacquered curls, which weren't red any longer, but retained quite a pink hue. "It was just a rinse I was trying out. Laura Jo's been bugging me about it ever since she went red last year. I told her it wasn't me, but you know she won't keep quiet until she gets her way. She claims it's what got the attention of Felipe, her man friend who runs the bait shop. Well, I tried to tell her I didn't need any such help, but Lord knows she has her own mind about things. Before I knew it, I was in the chair at Cynthia's place."

"Well, what matters most is that you feel comfortable with it. People give me a hard time for keeping mine so short, but when you work in a hot kitchen all day, every day—"

"By people, I'm guessing you mean men," Alva interrupted. "I'll never understand their unending fascination with long hair. Why, just the other evening, we were watching television and Hank was making a comment about that actress—oh, what's her name—who went and chopped her hair short for some role she was playing."

"Is Hank your husband?"

Alva surprised her by blushing six shades of pink—none of them matching her hair—and fluttering her hands over the ever-present pearls at her throat. "Why no, that would be my dear, departed Harold. Love of my life, that man. Hank Shearin runs the grocery at the corner. He's forever blocking our alley out back with his delivery trucks. A more frustrating man you'd never meet. Annoying you with his bullheaded opinions one minute, charming you right into having dinner the next."

"Ah," Kit said, unsure if she should squelch the smile she was feeling. "Well, whatever the fascination they have with long hair, they'll have to get over it when it comes to me." She skimmed her palm over the unwieldy tufts of hair poking up on the top of her head and flicked back the ones that constantly fell across her forehead. "I'd shave it, given half the chance."

"You know, some women do. You might have the head for it. Our Miss Dre does. Have you met her yet?"

"Not yet, but now I'm even more interested in doing so. Completely shaved?"

"Not completely. She still has some in the middle. So, do you have a gentleman friend? A husband?"

"No to both." Kit smiled in surprise at the question.

Alva smiled right back and patted her arm. "Well, we'll just have to see about that, won't we, dear?"

Before Kit could get past the sudden choking sensation in her throat to consider formulating a response, Alva was sliding her arm through Kit's and steering her into the kitchen. She patted Kit's hand and leaned in to add, "If you do it right, you only need one to fill both positions."

With no clue how to respond, Kit smiled, feeling a little more nervous about the evening ahead.

Lani walked over to her wearing a chef's coat with GATEAU stitched over the breast, left over from when she had managed Baxter's bakery in New York City. Her hair was pulled up in a simple ponytail. "I'd hug you, but I've got pastry dough hands." She wiggled flour-covered fingers. "Come on, let me introduce you to everyone."

For Kit, the days had been a blur of business talk, contract negotiations, celebrating, and jumping straight into helping assemble a small army of local tradesmen and subcontractors responsible for transforming the tailoring shop into a mail-order catering site. It was overwhelming in many ways, but such a welcome relief from what she'd dealt with for the past year, and had a far more positive end in sight.

However, the evening was social, not business. Usually quite confident in that area, she was coming to realize how decimating the trickle-down effect of utter betrayal could be. Intellectually, she knew only Trixie and Teddy were responsible for what had happened, but she couldn't help feeling less than confident about her own judgment after being so grossly taken advantage of by the ones she'd trusted the most.

So far, everyone she'd crossed paths with had been quite welcoming, but she had no idea how she'd be received in a social setting or if she was up to reading the subtle nuances that came into play when meeting a group of people who'd already established a tight bond with one another. She knew Lani was hopeful they'd all become fast friends. Kit was just as hopeful. But it was a lot to take in, a lot to tackle—all at once.

"Everyone? Meet Kit Bellamy, new friend, fellow baker, and"—she paused for dramatic effect, much to the detriment of the knot already forming in Kit's stomach—"our new manager of Babycakes!"

A cheer went up from the small group—which thankfully included Charlotte—and Kit saw nothing but sincere goodwill and joy at the announcement. The knot loosened up . . . and so did she.

She gave a little wave. "Hello, everyone. Thanks for inviting me."

"Welcome to Cupcake Club," Charlotte said, beaming with a certain amount of pride.

Whether it was for the club itself or for being the one to bring her into the fold, Kit had no idea, but it was all positive, so she ran with it. "Thanks. I'm happy to be here."

"Rule number one," Alva said, stepping forward. "What happens in Cupcake Club—"

"Stays in Cupcake Club!" everyone finished in unison, with the occasional brandished spatula or pastry bag.

Kit grinned. When you had an eighty-four-year-old, five-foot-nothing senior standing in front of you sporting pink hair, pearls, and another pirate apron—Errol Flynn this time—it was pretty much impossible not to. "Got it."

She made a zipping motion across her lips. "Thanks for the warm welcome. It smells incredible in here."

"It's my new recipe," Alva offered, ushering her farther into the room. "With Thanksgiving here in just a few short weeks, I wanted to celebrate the season." She picked up a cupcake from an industrial-sized cooling rack positioned on one of the rows of worktables. "My very own Sweet Potato Tater Cakes. Have a taste."

Kit took the proffered cake. "That sounds . . . amazing."

"Cardamom Cream Cheese frosting. Lani's recipe," Alva added.

"Can I?" Kit began peeling off the wrapper.

"Of course!" everyone said, again in unison.

She peeled off half the wrapper and used it as a cup to catch the crumbs as she sank her teeth into the cupcake. "Oh," she said with her mouth still half full. "Wow."

Alva beamed with pride. "I'm serving them at my holiday poker party next week."

Kit took another bite, then thought *did she say* poker *party?*

Before she could ask, a tall, muscular, and very swarthy young man approached, took her free hand, and bent over it in a deep, Gallic bow. *"Bonjour."* His voice was a pleasant, deep rumble. "Pleasure to meet you, Mademoiselle Kit." He straightened and smiled. "I am Franco."

Wow, again, Kit thought. *Handsome, at home in the kitchen—and French.* The evening was getting better by the second.

"Wait . . . Franco? As in Charlotte's—" She realized she was speaking out loud and broke off mercifully, before adding "gay best friend." *God.* Five minutes in the door, and she'd already put her foot in it.

"Partner in crime?" he finished, but with a twinkle in his eye that said he knew what she'd been about to say.

"*Oui, monsieur.*" Kit laughed, recovering more quickly given his good grace. "I've heard great things."

"Of course you have, *mon amie,*" he said, still grinning, "for I am a great chef."

Kit laughed again, charmed. "I'm not usually so clumsy, sorry. I'm excited and happy to finally meet you."

"Forget about it," he said, in his native Bronx accent, which made Kit laugh yet again.

She knew he was a close friend of Charlotte and Lani, going back to their days in New York, and had made the move south the same time as Charlotte. He worked with her and Carlo in their catering business and as an assistant chef on Baxter's television show. The times Kit and Charlotte had crossed paths at the same catering functions or foodie events, she'd talked a lot about Franco, but Kit had never had the opportunity to meet him.

She wasn't quite sure she recalled what Charlotte had said about why he'd adopted the whole French persona thing, but, he worked it so well, and was so damn over-the-top charismatic with it, she really didn't much care.

She turned to Charlotte, who'd woven through the tables to meet up with them. "You didn't mention how good looking he is."

"Please stop now or we shall never hear the end of it," Charlotte instructed, her lovely Indian accent accentuating each word. She glanced at Franco . . . who was preening. Even sporting a Pink Panther apron with Chef Clouseau stitched on the front, he managed to look hot as hell. "Although there really is no stopping him."

"I'm a force of nature, *ma charmante amie.*"

"*Oui,*" Charlotte said. "Of the Category Five variety."

They all laughed.

"I love the aprons, by the way," Kit said.

"Oh, I almost forgot!" Lani picked up a flat, folded bag

and carried it over to Kit. "Dre made one for you. She'll be here later. It's a little different from our usual silliness here, so if it's not 'you,' don't worry. We just wanted something to celebrate the new business and your arrival."

"How is our Miss Dre liking her new job?" Alva asked. She'd gone back to her table and was presently swirling cream cheese frosting on the remaining Tater Cakes.

"We haven't really talked much." Lani nodded at Kit to open the bag. "She's only putting in time here on weekends now, and I'm thinking that's not for much longer—which, totally selfishly stating, is killing me—but I'm thrilled for her. After all those years in school, I'm so happy she found something in her field so soon after graduation." Lani turned to Kit. "Dre is a graphic artist. She designed all the signage and business cards and what-have-you for Cakes by the Cup. That's how we initially met. She's just landed a job with a small marketing firm in Savannah that works mainly with gaming companies, graphic publications, and things like that. Go ahead"—she waved her hands at Kit—"I'm dying to see it."

"You haven't seen it?" Kit asked, dusting the flour from Lani's hands off the bag.

"She said she wanted to do something for Babycakes and to welcome you."

"That's so sweet." Kit was truly touched. "I look forward to meeting her."

"*Open it!*" the other four shouted in unison, all but bouncing on the balls of their feet.

"Okay, okay," Kit said, laughing, already feeling at home.

She opened the paper and carefully slid out the folded apron wrapped in tissue. She laid it on the nearest clean work surface and folded back the tissue. Her gasp of surprise and delight was echoed by the rest as they crowded around the table. "Wow. Just . . . wow."

Kit looked up at Lani, stunned. "She designed this?"

Lani was beaming like a proud parent. "Sure did. She's brilliant and amazing."

"And then some." The apron was a mural, top to bottom, side to side, of a rich, vibrantly colored fairy world, rendered in such elaborate detail it was truly breathtaking. A banner at the top, held up by tiny fairies, read BABYCAKES in beautifully stylized Old English script.

"Oh, look!" Lani said, pointing. "It's the shop. Wait, it's all of Sugarberry!"

Lani was right. The apron featured the whole island, transformed into a fantastical fairy world, with cupcakes perched in trees.

"Ha! There we are!" Charlotte pointed at the seven fairies flitting about over the town square with tiny cupcakes in their outstretched hands.

Kit smiled as she figured out some of them. The Alva fairy had perfectly coiffed silver hair and pearls around her neck. Lani's fairy wings had an elaborate pastry with a heart in the center as part of the diaphanous detail. Charlotte's fairy also had creative wings, a wedding cake etched on one side. Kit pointed to the red dash on the wings. "Is that a . . . chili pepper?"

Charlotte smiled and her cheeks bloomed with a little color. "Yes. Carlo's family is Cuban." She reached out and traced the tiny wings and the heart that was on the tip of one of them.

"Where's Franco?"

He pointed to the fairy with the French beret tilted at a jaunty angle. His was bigger than the others, and sported black peg-leg pants rather than a dress.

"Who knew guy fairies could be so sexy?" Kit said, sending him a fast smile.

"Oh, honey," Franco drawled, "I've known that for years."

Everyone laughed.

Alva pointed out the Dre fairy, who was the most . . . well . . . macabre of the bunch. Something of a punk fairy hairstyle, with a tiny eyebrow ring and detail of whimsical dragons in the wings made Kit even more curious to meet her.

"Who's that?" She pointed to a fairy with blond curls and a big smile. "Is that a Band-Aid on her wing?"

"That's Riley. She did all the photography for Lani and Baxter's cookbook." Alva traced the tiny bandage on the wing. "And she's fine. She's just what you might call a little . . . ungraceful, at times."

"She did the food styling," Lani said, "not the photography."

Alva's neatly penciled brows furrowed. "I still don't understand why you need to pose the food. You put it on a nice plate, maybe add a pretty candle."

Lani looked at Kit over Alva's head and they smiled. "She's amazing. Wait till you see her work in the cookbook. We should be getting advance copies in soon."

"I can't wait. Where is she? Does she come to these bake sessions, too?"

"She's one of us," Charlotte said. "You'll love her. Everyone does."

"She's on book tour with her significant other right now." Alva wiggled her eyebrows. "Really big deal."

"Oh?" Kit asked, surprised. "She's a cookbook author, too? Or . . . he is?"

"Oh, no. He's Quinn Brannigan."

"Quinn Branni—wait. *The* Quinn Brannigan?" Kit had seen his handsome face smiling at her from the back covers of his books for years. "I didn't know he lived there."

"Moved in just this past summer," Lani said.

"Whirlwind romance," Alva added, hands clasped under

her chin. "Real fairy tale." She smiled up at Kit, eyes twinkling. "He's a real hunk."

"First, Baxter Dunne and now Quinn Brannigan? What, is this like the Island of Hot Authors or something? And, if that's the case, what was I doing in Atlanta all these years? Where do I line up?"

Alva patted her hand again. "I told you, dear, just give us a little time."

Grinning and shaking her head—but not entirely sure Alva was kidding—Kit looked back at the apron. Riley's fairy had a little heart on her wing, too. She noted that Dre's didn't . . . and neither did Franco's. Maybe that signified who had a love in their life and who didn't. She noticed Alva's had a heart on hers. And the heart itself had little angel wings. She felt a tug in her own heart at that. The late Harold, she was guessing.

She looked up at the group gathered around the table. "You all are amazing."

Lani put an arm around Kit's shoulders, leaned in, and pointed with her other hand. "There's you."

That tug tightened a little more when Kit spied her own fairy likeness—short red hair . . . and a slice of pie in her hand—and gave a soft gasp. "Oh."

Lani's arm around her shoulders tightened. "I'm sure she meant it as a tribute, not to hurt—"

"No," Kit said quickly, which was hard to do over the sudden lump in her throat. "I love it. It's just right." She blinked back the threatening tears and smiled. "I can't wait to meet Dre and thank her. This is just . . . tremendous. I don't know how she did this so quickly. I haven't even been here a week—"

"I think she had a lot of the apron done and was just waiting to see who the newest addition would be."

"I'll cherish it. I almost hate to think about actually wearing it. I wouldn't want to mess it up."

"It was meant to be worn," Lani said.

"I know, it's just, I'd feel awful if anything hap—"

"Put it on!" everyone shouted, once again in unison, making them all laugh, Kit included.

She wanted to look at it longer, but did as commanded and slipped the apron loop over her head. Franco brushed her hands away and took the side straps, making quick work of the bow, then snugging it tight and flipping the ends with a flourish. God, he was so cute.

"Give us a show, *mademoiselle,*" he said, twirling his finger over her head.

Kit held her arms out and spun in a circle.

Alva did a fierce wolf whistle, surprising a laugh out of Kit and loosening her up a little more. She shook her hips and turned again, much to the delight of Franco, who swept her into his arms and twirled her effortlessly around the table. She squealed in surprise, but did her best to keep up with him.

"Just go with it," Lani said.

Someone punched on some music, and a moment later they were all shaking their groove thing. Yeah yeah. Alva and Charlotte were doing The Bump and Lani was doing some kind of backup singer line dance.

Kit thought they were all a little nuts . . . and kept right on dancing with Franco . . . and laughing like she hadn't in far, far too long.

She might not have a heart on her fairy wings, but her own heart was much fuller. Welcome to Cupcake Club, indeed.

Chapter 6

"Can I wear my green skirt?"

Morgan looked up from the papers he was sorting through on his recently uncovered desk. "Let me see."

Lilly held up the bright green skirt. It was made mostly of long netting with what looked like sparkles attached all over it. "Where on earth did you get that?" He smiled, unable to imagine Olivia ever allowing something so . . . frivolous.

Her expression smoothed. "I wore it to Mallory Worth's birthday party. We all dressed as fairies."

"It's quite . . . amazing," he said, not meaning to dampen her spirits. He propped his elbows on his desk. "Does it come with proper wings?"

Lilly's mouth tilted tentatively at the corners and she nodded. "It's my very favorite dress in the whole world."

"Then of course you should wear it. This is a very special day. Wings, too."

"Yes," she whispered, then turned to run out, but stopped short and turned back around. "Thank you, Uncle Moggy."

So polite. He sighed, but it was accompanied by a sincere smile. "You're very welcome. Hurry and get dressed. We don't want to be late."

He expected her to dash off, but she hung in the doorway a moment longer.

"Do you need me to help you with it?" He was still a bit awkward with the whole dressing the little girl part. Mostly he let her choose what she wore, just making sure she was warm when she needed to be and cool enough when it got hot. He supposed that would change when it came time to put her in school, but he had the holidays yet to sort that all out.

"No, I can do it. But"—she looked at the dress—"do you think Grandmother Wiggins will like it?"

Morgan laid the newly found folder down and pushed back from his desk. "She'll love it."

He walked over to Lilly and crouched in front of her. "She'll probably wish she had one of her very own."

Lilly cracked a smile at that. "Grandmothers don't dress like fairies."

Morgan had an immediate image of his mother in such a getup and choked a little. "Maybe. But I bet some grandmas would think it's pretty cool."

Lilly thought about that. "Will Grandmother Wiggins think that?"

"I have a pretty good hunch she might. And I bet she'd really like it if you just called her Grandma Birdie. But let's go find out for ourselves. Hurry, we're picking up cupcakes on the way."

Lilly's eyes widened. "Cupcakes?"

Morgan nodded. "Birdie—Grandma Birdie—asked if we'd bring dessert to the picnic. And there's a bakery on the square that makes very special cupcakes. Good idea?"

"Best idea." She turned and raced down the hall toward her room.

Morgan stood and stared down the hall, even after she'd closed her door. Some days with Lilly were good days, some were more challenging. It was starting out to be a good day. A really good day. He prayed he still felt that way when it was over. His own stomach was in knots over the pending picnic. He couldn't imagine how Lilly was feeling.

"Watch the wings," Morgan cautioned Lilly as he pulled open the door to Cakes by the Cup.

"I am." She stopped as soon as she stepped inside, blocking Morgan in the open doorway. "Whoa," she marveled.

Morgan shuffled her inside and closed the door behind him. The cold snap had gone, but it was still cooler than usual. "Whoa, indeed."

The shop was outfitted like a retro ice cream shop—except it was for baked goods. At least that's what he equated it to. Antique glass display cases topped with old-fashioned glass domed cake stands were filled with amazingly decadent-looking cupcakes.

"Awesome fairy dress."

Lilly and Morgan turned toward the voice and saw a twenty-something girl manning the register, which was also a gorgeously restored antique. Behind her was a set of floor-to-ceiling inset shelves filled with kitschy retro baking items and a display of cookbooks written by the shop owner's husband. Morgan recognized him as Baxter Dunne, television's famous Chef Hot Cakes.

However, his attention was focused exclusively on the counter help. In his defense, given her stubby, purple Mohawk and the multiple silver rings piercing one eyebrow, it was kind of hard to look anywhere else.

"Thank you," Lilly said, responding to the compliment, her private-tutor voice back on display as she edged closer to Morgan's leg.

"I've got fairy wings, too," the girl said. "Wanna see?"

Morgan felt Lilly press her body more firmly against his leg, but she nodded, her eyes wide.

The girl came out from behind the counter, revealing an apron with Gandalf from *Lord of the Rings* on the front. It was rather stunning, actually, with a gorgeously designed backdrop that almost looked hand painted. Lilly crowded against Morgan as the girl came closer.

Morgan noted the stitched word *Dre* on the top border of her apron and extended his hand. "Hello, Dree, I'm—"

"Morgan Westlake," the girl said, with no hint of derision. With no hint of anything, really. "Small island. And it's pronounced Dray."

"Ah. Well, hello, Dre. We're here to pick up a few cupcakes."

"For the picnic—with Birdie Wiggins."

"How could you know that?"

A hint of a smile played around her surprisingly makeup-free mouth. Maybe she'd used it all up around her eyes. "Really small island," she repeated, then crouched down to Lilly's level and spun so her back was to them. She reached back and lifted up the Mohawk spikes that covered her neck.

Lilly drew her breath in. "Does your hair hurt?" She sounded concerned. "It's very pointy."

The question surprised Morgan, and Dre, too, if the smile she shot Lilly was any indication. "My hair? No. Feel it. It's spiky, but it's soft."

Looking alarmed and curious, Lilly shook her head, then added, "No, thank you."

Dre's smile widened. "No problem. But ask me again if you change your mind. I just wanted to show you these." She dipped her chin down and tugged the open collar of her top a bit wider, revealing a tattoo of a very elaborate, beautifully detailed and intricately colored pair of fairy wings, which wrapped partly around either side of her neck and disappeared under the neckline of her shirt and presumably down her back.

Lilly's eyes grew as big as saucers. "Are they real?" she asked, her voice a hushed whisper.

"They're as real as yours are," Dre said. "You can touch it if you'd like."

Morgan wasn't sure how smart it was for Lilly to check out a tattoo. He could already imagine the ensuing conversation they'd have when his five-year-old niece begged him for one. But, it was too late.

Dre turned back around, but remained in a squat, resting on her heels. Morgan almost spoke up, unsure of what the young girl might tell his impressionable niece, but, in her fascination, Lilly had forgotten to be shy and spoke first. "How did you get them?"

"They're like a drawing."

Lilly's eyes widened further. "You colored on your own skin? Didn't you get in trouble?"

To her credit, Dre glanced up at Morgan, who merely smiled and lifted one shoulder in a half shrug. She'd gotten herself into it after all.

"No," she told Lilly. "When you get to be my age, you can make those kinds of choices for yourself."

"How old are you?"

"Lilly—"

Dre waved off Morgan's concern. "Just turned twenty-two."

"I just turned five."

"So I heard."

Lilly frowned. "Who told you?" She glanced up at Morgan, then back to Dre.

"Little bird." Dre smiled again when Lilly's frown turned wary and whispered, "Your Grandma Birdie told me."

Back to wide eyes again, Lilly said, "You know her?"

Dre nodded. "I do. She's very good friends with Miss Alva, one of the other ladies who helps out here in the shop." Dre spared a short glance at Morgan again, but went on without waiting for approval. "She's very happy you're here."

Lilly pressed against Morgan again, and he laid his palm on her head, careful not to dislodge the fairy antennae headband. He was ready to move the conversation along to cupcake purchases, when Lilly spoke again.

"I am, too," she whispered.

Morgan's hand, which had shifted to her thin shoulder, tightened reflexively as his heart knotted up all over again—in a good way.

Dre smiled. "Good. So let's pick out some cupcakes for you to take to her. I know which one is her favorite. But why don't you tell me which one is yours?"

She started to straighten, but Lilly impulsively reached out and touched her shoulder, then yanked her hand back as if surprised by her own impulsivity.

Dre just winked at her and turned around one more time, tugging a little at the neck band of her shirt and giving Lilly one last look at the fairy wings.

"They're very pretty," she said almost reverently. And Morgan started to formulate his speech against the tattooing of minors.

Dre stood up and turned to face them. "I thought so, too. Come on. Let's go look at cupcakes."

Shocking him speechless, Lilly put her hand in Dre's and off they went to examine the display cases.

Morgan stood there, wondering exactly when he'd completely lost control of the situation. Of all the people in the world he'd thought Lilly would feel comfortable with, the Mohawked, tattooed, multi-pierced Dre would not have made even the long list.

"Moggy!" Lilly exclaimed a moment later. "Come here. They have turtles!"

Oh boy. He walked over to them. "Turtles, really?"

"They don't look like turtles, but Miss Dre says they're called turtles anyway."

Other than the time Lilly spent with Paddlefoot and his fellow rehabbers, which had been for part of every day since Morgan had shown her the egg mound a week-and-a-half ago, it was the most animated he'd seen her since the accident. Certainly the most chatty—in public, anyway. He smiled to himself, thinking Lilly might have interesting taste in whom she chose to place her trust, but he admired her for being her own person and making the choice without worrying what someone else might think.

He leaned over her and read the little sign. "Mmm. Turtle cupcakes, with chocolate, caramel, and pecans. Those might be my favorite, too."

Clearly thrilled with that pronouncement, Lilly reached for his hand and held it tight. "Can we get some?"

"Sounds good. Do you think we should find out what Grandma Birdie's favorite is?"

Lilly nodded and turned to Dre, who said, "That's easy. Strawberry shortcake."

Lilly looked at Morgan. "Have I had that?"

"If you have to ask, probably not," he said with a laugh. He looked at Dre, who had moved behind the display case. "We'll take three of each, please."

She nodded and went about boxing up their order as the bells jingled on the door, announcing another customer. Lilly's hand tightened in his, as did his on hers. It was their first real foray in public together on the island, and though he knew they'd have to be prepared to start meeting people, he'd hoped, since it was a weekday, that it would be more of a trickle than a steady stream.

"Hey, Dre, is Lani in the back? I have a question about the—oh, sorry. I didn't know you had customers."

Morgan turned to find the redhead he'd met at the research center standing just inside the door. She looked . . . different, though he couldn't quite put his finger on it. "Hello, again. Kit, right?"

"Right," she said, stepping all the way inside and closing the door behind her. "Mr. Westlake."

"Morgan, please. You remember Lilly."

She gave a little wave to Lilly, who apparently had become empowered by the fairy costume, or by meeting the intriguing fairy-winged Miss Dre, or maybe it was a sugar rush from the smell of cupcakes, because she gave Kit a short wave back.

"Here's your order," Dre said, pulling his attention away.

He turned back to the counter.

Lilly let her hand slip from his and moved to the door. Near Kit. "We're having a picnic. Did you know, too?"

Who was this kid, Morgan wanted to know, and what had she done with his quiet, shy, little niece?

"I might have heard something about it," Kit said, and Morgan appreciated her honesty.

"Do you know my gramma, too?"

"I just moved here, so I haven't met her yet. But I hear she's a very nice lady. My friend, Miss Alva, is her best friend. I think if Miss Alva likes her so much, I will, too."

Lilly seemed to think that over. "We're getting her cupcakes. She likes shortberry cake. I got the turtles."

"I like turtles, too. Cupcake ones and real ones. You know Dr. Langley, don't you?"

Lilly nodded and looked a little wary.

"He introduced me to your friend Paddlefoot."

Lilly's eyes all but goggled. "He did?"

Kit nodded. "He told me the turtles really like you. And your pictures. They're really good."

"Uncle Moggy did some of them." She looked at Morgan as if debating whether to say something, but remained silent.

Kit looked up at Morgan. "You colored turtle pictures?"

"Sure did. I'm not as good at staying in the lines as Lilly."

He thought he heard her say, "I'll bet" under her breath.

"He's practicing to get better," Lilly assured her, and Morgan noticed Kit fought to keep from laughing outright.

"Do you want to draw some?" Lilly asked. "Dr. Langley can give you a coloring book. I have a box of colors if you don't have any."

"That sounds like fun. I'll ask him the next time I see him."

"We'd better go." Morgan handed the money to Dre, who had gone back to her dispassionate, young-punk demeanor. Apparently she was only animated with folks under four feet tall.

"Cool kid," she offered as he took the string-tied box.

He smiled at that. "She is that. Thank you."

"Anytime."

He wasn't sure if there was a bit of warmth in Dre's response, but chose to think maybe Lilly had bought him a little headway. Taking Lilly's hand, he remembered what Gabe had admonished him to do, but it was hardly the time or place. He nodded to Kit. "Good to see you again."

"Have a good picnic." Kit's smile shifted to something a little less warm as she lifted her gaze from Lilly to him.

Perversely, it made his smile spread fully across his face. Dre might have a bit of a wall up, and he could understand the reserve. He was still a stranger to them, his motives concerning Birdie unproven. But this woman had an entire fortress erected . . . and she didn't know Birdie or him. He was suddenly just as curious to find out why as Gabe had been. On impulse, he said, "We're going to the research center again tomorrow afternoon. We'll bring the crayons."

Lilly looked up with an animated face and hopeful smile. "You can come color with us." She looked at Dre. "You can come, too."

"I'll be at my other job," Dre said, warm smile instantly back in place. "But maybe next time."

Lilly nodded, then looked expectantly back at Kit. "Can you come?"

"I'm pretty busy getting the new shop ready," she began, but when Lilly's little shoulders sagged, Morgan could see her relenting. Good to know he wasn't the only softie where Lilly was concerned.

"Around three?" he prompted.

She flashed him a look that, though she was smiling, told him she wasn't keen on his using Lilly to manipulate her into going. His smile grew, and he was completely unrepentant about it. He didn't mind folks having something against him, but thought he should know what it was he was being condemned for, at least.

"I'll try." She smiled at Lilly, leaving him out of it.

Lilly smiled up at Kit, then waved to Dre as Morgan moved around her to open the door. Dre lifted a hand, nodded, and gave Morgan an unreadable look.

"Tough crowd," Morgan murmured dryly as they exited to the sidewalk.

Lilly all but skipped beside him, and it was such a flashback to the child who'd charmed him all the years leading up to the accident, whatever frustration he felt immediately dissipated. He realized more each day that he'd done the right thing by coming to Sugarberry and his confidence had grown with the realization—which was good, considering his main reason for doing so was presently waiting for them at the local community center.

Although only a short block and a half off the main

square, the closer they got to the building, the slower Lilly's steps became. Her grip on his hand tightened and she drew closer to him, all the bravado she'd achieved at the cupcake bakery having fled as swiftly as it had come. When they got to the walkway that led to the front doors, she stopped altogether.

"What's wrong?" he asked gently.

She kept her gaze on the doors. "Do we have to go in?"

"I think we should. You remember how Kit and Dre said your grandma was excited about the picnic."

Lilly nodded, but she looked as if she was facing the gallows rather than a fun picnic outing.

The mild irritation Morgan had felt back at the bakeshop, presumably for being judged by the actions of his family, paled in comparison to the flash of real anger he felt toward his own mother in that moment. He hadn't had a say in what Olivia had done to ostracize Delilah from her own family, and later, Delilah's daughter from the same family, but he wished he'd at least tried. All the adults who mattered most in Lilly's life had failed her in varying degrees, himself included.

Because of that, the picnic mattered more to him than he'd realized. It would be a first step toward doing right by her.

Morgan crouched down and gently tugged Lilly's hand so she turned to face him. "Why don't we go in, say hello, and take her our cupcakes? We can see how it goes from there."

"Could we leave then?"

"If we really want to. I hope we won't, though."

Lilly turned and buried her face on his shoulder. Surprised by such a complete turnaround from just minutes ago, Morgan instinctively gathered her close and hugged her. Her fingers dug into his shoulders for all they were worth. He was on the verge of telling her maybe they'd try another day, when she whispered, "What if she doesn't like me?"

"Oh, baby." Instant tears sprang to Morgan's eyes, which he blinked back as he kissed the top of her head. He gently pried her loose and looked at her face. "She loves you. She always has. It's just . . . sometimes families make decisions for reasons that don't make sense to anyone else. But Grandma Birdie has always wanted to know you."

Lilly seemed to take that in, but Morgan hadn't any idea if she believed it, much less understood it. How could he explain someone like Olivia to a five-year-old? "Let's go in and say hello like we talked about, and then we can decide how to go from there. Okay?"

Lilly nodded, but her heart clearly wasn't in it.

"I wouldn't ask you to do something if I didn't think it was okay, or might be bad for you. You know that, right?"

She nodded again, with a little more conviction.

"You liked Miss Dre, didn't you?"

"Yes. She has funny hair. And earrings in her face." Lilly said it solemnly, as if everyone knew those things constituted automatic friendship.

Morgan grinned and simultaneously decided he was locking her in her room until she was eighteen. Maybe twenty-one. "And you liked Miss Kit."

"She likes turtles. Her hair is a color book color, too."

"I like her hair," Morgan said. It suited her. A lot of other things about her would have suited him, too. Like those flashy green eyes and that luminous skin—if, of course, she didn't loathe him on sight. "So, you already met some nice people today. I think most people on Sugarberry are nice."

"Why?"

"Well, because it's a nice place to live. They're happy here."

"Do you like it here?"

Morgan nodded. "More and more every day." He was hesitant to ask, but knew he couldn't pass up the chance to find out how Lilly was really feeling. "Do you like it here?"

She had such a contemplative look on her face, Morgan wanted to hug her again. She was such an amalgamation, one part reserved, polite child and the other an inquisitive, social little girl.

"I like the turtles. I like the beach. I like my room. It's blue."

Having seen her studious and conservative bedroom at home, Morgan had known, going in, he wanted her to be a big part of choosing how her new room was decorated. He'd offered to paint it any color she wanted—within reason—thinking she'd go for something girly and pink. They'd picked out the paint swatches together, and all of hers had been some shade of blue. They'd settled on a pretty sky blue, with a pale chiffon yellow ceiling and window trim. No curtains yet, or bedspread, just window blinds and a regular blanket, but she liked it. It was . . . cheerful.

He wished he knew how to make its occupant feel the same way at the moment. "Pretty good start, right?"

She nodded.

He straightened and took her hand. "So, let's go inside and see if this is something we can add straight to the like list."

"The like list?" she asked, scrunching up her face as she looked up at him.

"Yep. The official What We Like About Sugarberry List. It's growing pretty quickly already."

She thought about that. "Okay."

Just like that, they were heading inside.

Morgan breathed a quiet sigh of relief . . . and decided

right then and there if Birdie Wiggins wasn't pretty much Glinda the Good Witch of Grandmas, they were heading straight back out. The emotional roller coaster was wearing him out.

Chapter 7

"Pretty hot. For an uncle."

Kit shot a look at Dre as she ducked behind the counter with her, then headed toward the kitchen to see Lani. "He's a Westlake."

"Doesn't mean he can't be hot. For an uncle."

Kit let out a little sigh. Her hormones were still jumping all over the place from their surprise meeting, which made it next to impossible to pretend he hadn't affected her. "I know. Dammit."

Dre might have cracked a small smile; it was hard to tell. She was an ambiguous mix of I'm-so-over-it cynic and creative genius, but sometimes Kit had to remind herself this was the same person who had designed and made her that incredible, whimsical apron.

"Tell Lani we need more turtles," Dre said. "They've been popular today."

"Will do." Kit bumped her hip against the swinging door and entered the kitchen. "Lani, I—" She paused while Lani picked up the remote control for the stereo and cut Elvis off right between a little more action and a little less conversation. Lani didn't play the music as loud during business hours as Kit had come to discover she played it when baking solo in the early morning, pre-opening hours, or late night after hours, but music was usually on if she was baking. When Kit had asked her about it, Lani had explained she'd gotten used to baking to music since opening the shop, claimed it helped her creativity.

Having grown up in a family of strong-willed, slightly eccentric women, Kit understood that explanation completely. "Dre says we're low on turtles."

"I know. I peeked out when I heard that deep voice. He's pretty—"

"Hot," Kit finished. "I know. For an uncle."

"For an anything." Lani wiggled her eyebrows. "I also might have been peeking out there when the two of you were making googly eyes at one another."

"We were not. There was no googling of eyes, I can assure you."

"Say what you like," Lani said dismissively, then shot Kit a wicked grin, "but I know googly when I see it."

"I say run a background check." This from Alva, who was standing at a worktable on the far side of the kitchen, taking cupcakes from their pans and lining them up on the cooling rack.

"On who?" Lani and Kit asked simultaneously.

"Whoever it is you're Googling."

"What?" Lani asked. "Oh. Not that kind of google."

Alva merely shrugged and went back to what she was doing. "Last week I Googled Hugh Jackman. Dee Dee Banneker said he takes his shirt off a lot. Turns out, Dee Dee is right." She continued lining up the cooling cupcakes. "I like that about him."

Lani laughed and Kit just stared, slightly openmouthed. She was still getting used to the various sides of Alva Liles. Kindly, sweet older woman in many ways . . . and an octogenarian who held a monthly poker night and wrote a gossip-slash-advice column for the local newspaper that was like a mash up of Dear Abby . . . and TMZ. Kit never knew what to expect. Admittedly, that was part of the fun.

Smiling, Kit turned back to Lani. "I was just on the phone with George, the electrician's brother? He was recommended for the demolition we need on that one wall, but he's not available for another two weeks."

"Can't you just take a hammer to it? When my Harold and I moved into our first house, he tore out three walls with nothing more than a big mallet and some serious determination to make our dining room and kitchen one big area." Alva paused and smiled. "He took his shirt off a lot, too." After a brief sigh, she went back to work. "I still miss that."

Kit heard Lani sigh beside her and glanced her way.

"What?" Lani said, smiling. "I hope I still feel that way about Baxter when I'm eighty-four."

"I've seen you two together. I'm pretty sure that won't be a problem." Kit leaned closer so only Lani could hear, and, in a hushed whisper, added, "Alva mentioned something about Hank, the guy who runs the grocery store? Are they an item?"

"Well," Lani replied, also sotto voce, "she plays it like the two of them are at odds over his always blocking our back alley with his delivery trucks—which he does—and her always getting into trouble with the local council, on which he's a leading member—which she does—but we're pretty sure they're not always at odds. Every Thursday they both kind of disappear around lunch time."

Kit smiled. "It's sweet that they have a weekly lunch together."

"You can all it 'lunch' if you want to," Lani said, making air quotes around the word.

Kit laughed, then stopped when Lani just nodded.

"Seriously?" Kit looked over at Alva, who was humming Elvis and swiveling her hips as she frosted. "I so want to be her when I grow up." Kit's voice held a fair amount of reverence. "Well, maybe without the pink hair."

"It goes well with the raspberry velour track suit, though," Lani said.

"True." They glanced at each other and smiled. "So, what should I do about the wall demo?"

"Call the electrician back and see if he has any other heavy-handed brothers?"

Kit smiled. She had only been on Sugarberry for ten days, but it already felt comfortable. Lani was open and easy to know, as were the rest of the Cupcake Club crew. As was everyone she'd met on the island, truth be told.

Her thoughts immediately went to the one person on the island who made her uncomfortable. And not just in the ways he should. Morgan Westlake bothered her all right. At a time when she should be completely focused on this new path and getting Babycakes up and launched, the very last thing she needed was a six-foot-one distraction with thick dark hair, broad shoulders, and the most beautiful blue eyes she'd ever—

"She tell you she has a hot crayon date with Uncle Hunk?"

Kit blinked and visions of a smiling Morgan vanished as Dre came bumping through the swinging door with an empty display tray in her hand. It took a moment longer for her to realize what Dre had just said. It was a moment too long, as it turned out. Nothing got by the Cupcake Club ladies.

Lani's eyes widened in surprised delight as Kit scrambled to backpedal. "We don't have any sort of date."

"Do too," Dre said, sliding the empty rack into one of the large industrial sinks and sliding a rack of freshly frosted turtle cupcakes from the tall, rolling cart.

"I knew it!" Lani said. "Googly eyes tell the truth every time."

"We were not—"

"What's a crayon date?" Alva wanted to know. "Is that some new sort of sex thing? Because back in my day—"

"No," Kit said in a hurry, not sure she was ready to hear anything about what Alva might or might not have done with crayons, or finger paints, or God knew what, on any day. "His niece—"

"Who is completely adorable, by the way," Lani said, then added, "I told you, I was peeking. Cute little costume she had on. Isn't today the big day she meets—"

"Birdie," Alva finished. "It sure is. And I can tell you, Birdie is as nervous and excited as a new mother. I don't think I've ever seen her like this. Told her she better get a grip on it before she had a stroke. Had to talk her out of buying out the kid section over at Tolliver's."

"Well, it's understandable she's anxious to finally get to be a grandmother," Lani said. "Lilly is her only grandchild. I still can't imagine what she must have been feeling, all these years, being cut off from any kind of communication."

"I still say give me five minutes with that old battle-ax, Olivia Westlake and I'd give her a solid piece of my mind," Alva exclaimed. "I'll never understand that kind of poisonous behavior."

"Me, either," Lani said. "I'm glad Morgan had the—"

"Balls," Dre supplied. "Me, too. Special kid. I like her." With that she took the tray out front . . . and Lani and Alva turned their attention back to Kit.

"So," Lani said, with the kind of speculative gleam in her eye that, even in Kit's short tenure, she'd learned meant she hadn't a prayer of diverting the topic of conversation. "Tell us about this date."

Finished with emptying the cupcake pans, Alva wiped her hands on a towel and crossed the kitchen as well. "Why crayons? Sounds kinky. He didn't look like the type to me. Though I suppose you can never tell. Why, I remember when Harvey Rickenbottom was found out in the back shed with two of Louise Granger's—"

"He didn't invite me, really. Lilly did," Kit blurted almost desperately.

Lani caught her eye and mouthed a silent thank you.

Kit smiled and went on. "Lilly was telling me about the turtles and I shared that I liked them, too." She shrugged. "So, she asked me to color some with her. That's really all there is to it."

"You've been over to the research center a few times since you got here, right?" Lani asked.

Kit nodded. "I went in that first day, the day we interviewed, on a whim, and well . . . I like Gabe and I really respect what he's doing down there. And"—she took a steadying breath, smiled—"with this new change in my life, I decided it would be smart of me to develop outside interests, something other than work. I loved Mamie Sue's, but it was my whole life, it was work and home—because I wanted it to be. I think maybe that was why I didn't have any real perspective."

"Family businesses can be like that even in the best of circumstances," Lani said. "You got handed a really big responsibility when you were pretty young. Then you had to deal with your sister's husband, too. It must have been challenging."

"It had its own special brand of challenges, yes. But, even with the loss of my grandma, and my mom and dad, mostly it was wonderful. It saved me, really. It was the one constant thing I had, the one thing I could count on to always be there. I loved the business. Truly. Every part of it. And I think that really blinded me. I was so deeply entrenched, I sort of took for granted that everyone was as devoted to it as I was."

"Well, from what I understand, they were. Except for Teddy—"

"And the members of the board he bribed." Kit waved a hand when Lani started to say something. "It's—okay. You don't have to defend me. I know I made some big mistakes. It wasn't until it all ended, and so abruptly, that I realized I hadn't just lost my job, or my vocation. I had lost everything. My whole life was suddenly empty, because I hadn't ever built anything else. Sure, I had friends, family. But my friends were all Mamie Sue employees, and my family . . . "

Lani laid her hand on Kit's arm. "Family shouldn't turn on family. No one sees that coming. We're all so sorry about that."

Kit covered her hand. "I know, and I really appreciate your support." She looked at Lani and Alva. "I've learned that if I think about my life in terms of things lost, I'll never move on. In just as many ways, I could never have expected to be blessed with such a wonderful new path. And I'm really grateful for it. For you. All of you."

Alva laid her tiny hand on top of theirs and squeezed. "We're happy to have you here, Miss Kit. You're family with us now."

Kit felt her eyes well up, and it was only then she realized she'd gone a whole ten days without crying. That alone was cause for celebration. "It means more to me than you know. You all, and . . . well, everyone here. That's why I've gone back to see Gabe—Dr. Langley. I really admire him, but I also really enjoy his company. I met his wife Anne the other day. They're both wonderful, and together . . . well, it's a special thing they have."

"It is," Lani agreed. "I like them both, too."

"He's . . . well, he's nothing at all like my dad." Kit laughed, trying—and failing—to imagine her father even chatting with someone like the doctor. "But I guess I have that same comforting feeling around him. I know it makes no sense—"

"It makes perfect sense." Lani spontaneously put her arm around Kit's shoulders and squeezed. "You know I came down here to be closer to my dad and . . . well . . . we had our share of hard times, especially after my mom passed. I'll be honest, for a while I didn't know if moving here was the right thing. I mean, I knew it was, but he didn't. And that wasn't going to be good for either of us."

"But it's good now," Kit said. "I saw Sheriff Trusdale just the other day and he all but bursts at the seams talking about you."

Lani smiled and her own eyes sparkled with a glimmer of joyful tears. "He's a hard man in so many ways, but such a special guy in the ways that matter most. And, yes, I'm so glad we've figured things out." She one-arm hugged Kit again. "Finding a feeling of family with Gabe, or Anne, or any of us, is a really good thing. That's all I was trying to say."

"Thank you." Once again, Kit was stunned by the honest and sincere compassion and empathy she'd received from friends so newly made. "I really am fascinated by his work, so it's something I'm happily pursuing. When I can, anyway."

"What about the Westlake connection?" Lani asked. "I mean, I think Morgan seems like a really good guy, trying to do the right thing. His niece is totally cute, and you can't help falling a little in love with her. I know his family's law firm was involved in the sale of Mamie Sue's—"

"How did you know that?" Kit hadn't told anyone about meeting Morgan that first day, or her misgivings about there being a Westlake living on Sugarberry. It was her problem, not theirs.

Alva smiled. "I Googled him, too. And I might have read a few things about the sale of your family business." She laid her hand on Kit's arm again. "Don't worry, dear, he seems to be nothing like his family."

"And she'd know," Lani added. "If there were any skeletons to be found, then—"

"Now, Miss Lani May, don't make it sound like that. I wasn't snooping. I was merely looking out for a dear friend." Alva turned to Kit. "Turns out he got himself into something called environmental law. Moved all the way to Colorado over a half dozen years ago. Hasn't had a thing to do with his family during that whole time. Normally, I'd say that's a shame, but given what I know about his mama, I'm thinking he had the right idea. In fact, I'm surprised he stayed on the same continent with that nasty bi—"

"I think what she means," Lani jumped in, "what we both mean—is it looks like you don't have to worry about him being anything like the parts of the Westlake clan that helped your brother-in-law."

"Well, that's good to know," Kit said with mixed emotions. "I know the word is he's here to do the right thing by his niece, which is really admirable. I just don't want to start my new path by tangling it up with any part of my past one—especially the bad parts. He might not be involved in what happened, but he's directly related to the ones who were. And that's an extended family I don't want any part of."

"Hear tell, neither does he," Alva said. "That's why he came out to Sugarberry."

"Wonder why he didn't just take Lilly back to Colorado?" Kit asked, curious even though she knew she shouldn't be. The world was filled with other guys she could meet and be interested in, whose last names weren't Westlake. She should save her curiosity for them. If she could just get those gorgeous baby blues and that wicked fast grin out of her head, she could get right on top of doing that.

"He stayed here so he could give Miss Lilly a chance to know the rest of her family," Alva said.

"And keep her close to her Westlake relatives, too, I'm guessing," Lani added.

"And that's a move I applaud," Kit went on. "I know he just lost his brother and sister-in-law, and now he's raising a small child, and he's helping Gabe fight for the lives of endangered turtles, so he's almost a local hero already, but—"

"And he's a hunk," Alva offered. "Never hurts. I wonder what he looks like with his shirt off." She seemed to ponder that while Lani grinned.

Kit just sighed. "Yes, he's completely, one hundred percent white knight material. I get it. But I have no intention of getting close to him. There are a million other men out there who aren't related to anything about Mamie Sue's or the sale, or . . . any of it. I don't want to get involved with the Westlakes on any level. I just . . . don't need that." She looked at the two women who were quickly becoming good friends. "I hope you can understand that."

Lani smiled and squeezed her shoulder. "I do, honestly, I do. I just think that—" She broke off. "Never mind. It doesn't matter what I think, just what you do. I don't know and can't know what it was like to go through what you did. And steering clear of all things Westlake probably does feel like exactly the right thing to do."

"It does." Kit slid her arm around Lani's waist and squeezed back. "Thanks. For supporting me even if you don't agree with me."

"Oh, I get it. I just . . . " She grinned. "Well, I'd want to see him with his shirt off, too. Just sayin'."

"So . . . does this mean no one is going to tell me what you young people do with crayons that constitutes a date these days?" Alva straightened her apron and smoothed her netted hair. "I have a column to write and this sounds like something juicy I could use."

Lani and Kit laughed. "I'm sure you already have plenty of other juicy tidbits to share," Lani said. "You always do."

And I hope I'm not one of them, Kit silently prayed. She'd heard so much about Alva's column, she'd taken the time to read a few of her pieces. And, well, let's just say she was hoping it would be a good long time before Alva offered her any advice in print. She had a way of illustrating her points by using stories about other island denizens. Generally not the most flattering ones. Kit had had enough of being devoured and spit out by the press. She'd take a bye this go around. For life, if she could get it.

"So, are you at least going to go color with Lilly?" Lani asked. "I mean, I know she's a Westlake, too, but—"

"I'm not going to turn down the poor little orphan girl, so stop looking at me like that."

"I'd have used that exact line on you if you had made even the slightest noise about backing out. Just so you know," Lani said, smiling.

"I had a feeling," Kit said, smiling back. "But whether or not her uncle is there is secondary to doing right by the child, okay? We all understand that?"

"We do," Lani said, but Kit didn't miss her and Alva exchanging a knowing wink.

She sighed in defeat. For now. "You know, I don't think I'll need to call the electrician back after all. I think I'll go smash down that wall all by myself." She left the kitchen, realizing the other side of all this compassion, friendship, and empathy was that they'd be sticking their noses into every part of her business from now on . . . and she'd better get used to it.

She heard Lani's laughter and Alva saying, "So, are they dating then? They'd make such a nice pair."

Dear Lord help her, what had she gotten herself into? Seriously.

She was walking to the front door of the shop when Dre said, “If you need a big mallet or an ax, I have one of each in the trunk of my car.”

Of course you do, Kit thought, waving, shaking her head, and laughing all at the same time as she let herself out.

Chapter 8

"Is Miss Kit here yet, Uncle Moggy?"

"Not yet, sweet pea," Morgan answered, just as he had the last dozen times she'd asked. "We don't know for sure she can make it. She's pretty busy getting the new bakery shop ready."

"But they already have a bakery." Lilly looked up from her latest Crayola masterpiece. "With the fairy lady."

"Her name is Miss Dre."

"I like her."

"I know you do."

"Maybe she can come color with us sometime."

"Maybe."

"Why is Miss Kit having a bakery?"

Morgan paused with a hammer in one hand and the bulletin board he was hanging in the other. At the rate Lilly's questions were coming, he'd never get it put up. He supposed he should be grateful she was chatty today. Yesterday had been a completely different story.

The picnic with Birdie hadn't gone well. Between Lilly's last-second ambivalence about meeting her estranged grandmother and Birdie's nervous excitement, it had been somewhat strained and awkward, which was a first for him since arriving in Sugarberry. Unfortunately, it had happened with the one person he'd hoped Lilly would instantly befriend, as she had Kit and Dre. Maybe Birdie needed green hair or some interesting tattoos.

Or course, Birdie wasn't at all what her name might imply. She'd been quite friendly and outgoing when they'd spoken on the phone, so that hadn't been a surprise, but, given the nickname, Morgan had pictured a tiny, more fragile type. In truth, she was quite tall, thin to the point of gangly, and significantly older than he'd expected. He knew Delilah had been a later-in-life baby, but had assumed her mother would be somewhere in her sixties, not much older than his own mother. Birdie, however, was in her mid-seventies, at least, which meant she'd been in her forties when she'd had Delilah.

Still quite energetic and sharp, Birdie was a little flamboyant with her short blond bob and brightly colored caftan. And she was chatty. Very chatty. Her exuberance over the reunion—understandable as it was—along with her towering height and boldly patterned clothes, had been more than a little intimidating to Lilly, who had hid behind Morgan almost immediately. He'd made gentle efforts to get her to at least come out and be polite, if not social, but he could feel her physically trembling. Unlike his mother, he didn't put social niceties over compassion and empathy.

To Birdie's credit, she immediately realized her faux pas and tempered her enthusiasm, but by then, the initial damage had been done. Morgan had eventually coaxed Lilly to take a seat at the table inside the rec center that Birdie had so beautifully set with their indoor picnic. But Lilly had eaten little and said even less. Morgan made his own small talk with Birdie, hoping Lilly would see that she was a nice woman, and otherwise harmless, but his efforts hadn't made any obvious difference. Finally, Birdie had stepped in and suggested perhaps they could meet again another time, in a place of Lilly's choosing.

Birdie had pulled over a bench seat from the table behind them and sat down near Lilly without getting too close—her aging knees and hips made it impossible for her to crouch down. Gently and kindly, she told Lilly how happy she was they'd met and she hoped they would eventually come to be fast friends. She reminded Lilly it was a blessing to have people in life who loved and cared about her.

Lilly had nodded, though she hadn't made eye contact. Morgan had instead, with an apologetic expression. Birdie had merely winked at him, making it clear that while she was surely disappointed, she wasn't offended in the least.

Birdie had packed up enough lunch goodies to keep them fed for a week, insisting they take all but two of the cupcakes they'd brought with them. She kept one of her favorites, and one of Lilly's, and mentioned that next time they got together, they could talk about which one they each had liked best.

Morgan suspected she'd had more than a few little gifts for Lilly, if the bags stuffed under a neighboring table had been any indication, but she'd chosen to give her just one thing before they'd left. Morgan had mentioned in their conversation that Lilly and he were helping at the research center, in hopes it might encourage Lilly to join in the discussion. She hadn't, but Birdie had clearly been paying attention.

She'd given Lilly a special coloring book and paint brush set, explaining that if she brushed water over the pictures, they would magically turn colors. Morgan had yet to see Lilly pick it up since they'd gotten back home, but she had managed a whispered thank you to Birdie when the older woman had given it to her.

Only Morgan had noticed Birdie's eyes swim with joyful tears, and that had made his own eyes burn a little, too. Birdie didn't want much, or even expect much, and he knew that even though the day had not gone as hoped, seeing her only grandchild, for any amount of time, had been a gift she'd likely never thought to have. Morgan had intentionally put the meeting off until Lilly had settled somewhat on Sugarberry, and perhaps he should have pushed it even further back, but he'd wanted Lilly to start getting to know the folks on the island and for them to be out and about more together. The initial meeting with her grandmother was important . . . not something he wanted to have by accident if they happened to bump into each other.

He might still question the timing, but the look in Birdie's eyes in that one single moment had answered any remaining questions he might have had about relocating to Sugarberry.

He took solace in the fact that everyone on Sugarberry that had any involvement with the two of them, clearly wanted what was best for Lilly so he remained sincerely hopeful that with time and the development of trust, it would all work out.

"Is Miss Kit's bakery gonna have cupcakes, too?"

Morgan pulled himself from his thoughts and positioned the corner of the bulletin board where he'd marked the wall. "Actually, Miss Kit's shop is part of the cupcake bakery."

"How?"

"Well, the bakery where Miss Dre works will sell cupcakes to people like us who live here and walk in to buy them. Miss Kit will run the part next door that makes cupcakes for big parties and to send to people who don't live on Sugarberry, but want cupcakes." Of course, he hadn't known any of that, but Birdie had filled him in when they'd given her the cupcakes.

"Don't other people have cupcakes where they live?"

"Maybe. But you tried Miss Lani's turtle cupcake for lunch today and you thought it was pretty good."

"Ah-mazing."

Morgan missed the nail and hit the frame of the cork bulletin board instead. He turned to grin at Lilly. "Ah-mazing, were they?"

She nodded enthusiastically at that. "The bestest."

"Well, see? If someone wanted the bestest, most ah-mazing cupcakes, now they'll be able to get one no matter where they live."

Lilly went back to drawing and Morgan made good use of the brief moment he had before the next barrage of questions began, sinking the nail in the wall with three short raps.

The sound of the hammer was still echoing from pegging the other end when Lilly said, "Can we call Miss Kit?"

Morgan sighed, but he smiled when he glanced at her. "Not today. Maybe we'll stop by and see Miss Dre later. We can leave a message there for Miss Kit and ask if she can come next time."

Lilly paused in her drawing and looked up. "Is she mad at us? We didn't buy her cupcakes."

"No, sweet pea, she's not mad. And she sells the same cupcakes as Miss Dre. But she's very busy getting the shop set up and probably couldn't make it."

"Can we go see her bakery being made?"

Morgan didn't know where the fixation with Kit was coming from, any more than he had with the turtles. He supposed he should be grateful Lilly wasn't grilling him about fairy tattoos—though he knew better than to drop his guard in that respect. "Maybe we can take a peek. I don't think there's much to see yet. I'll check later, okay?"

He turned and made a grand sweeping motion with one arm toward the bulletin board. "What do you think?"

Lilly looked up and studied it for a moment. "It's crookded."

Morgan looked over his shoulder. "Crookded, huh?"

Lilly nodded and pointed. "That side isn't the same."

Morgan turned fully and studied his handiwork. "Huh. You're right."

"Can you fix it?"

"I can try, but I'll need to go borrow a few more nails from Dr. Gabe." He put the hammer on the cabinet. "You keep drawing and I'll be right back, okay?"

"Okay."

She went back to her picture in progress and Morgan swung out of the room—smack into Kit. He reached for her arms as she stumbled back and both staggered a step or two before coming to rights. "I'm so sorry. I didn't see you."

She let out a short laugh. "That's okay. No harm done. I don't think, anyway."

He got caught up in her eyes and didn't respond. Green and sparkling, lit by her open smile, it was such a contrast to the wary expression she'd sported when they'd spoken at the bakery the day before, he found himself staring.

"Morgan?" Her smile faltered. "Are you okay?"

"Fine," he murmured. "Just fine."

The dark centers of her eyes expanded and a different kind of awareness crept in. Morgan's body responded swiftly to the message and his gaze shifted to her lips.

Her gaze did the same; then they looked again into each other's eyes. Morgan might have started to dip his head, the tiniest fraction toward hers, and her lips may have parted, just slightly, on the softest of sighs.

Flustered, she straightened, eyes blinking and wide.

"Okay, well, that's good. I'm good, too. Fine. Really . . . fine."

Morgan let go of her arms as she stepped back. Well . . . he certainly hadn't anticipated that little . . . moment. And he definitely hadn't anticipated her instinctive response to it—to him. There was no denying it had happened. Intrigue added to intrigue, and he couldn't stop thinking about her mouth . . . and what it would have tasted like.

"Is, uh, Lilly here?"

He lifted his gaze to take in her entire face, his mind—and body—still hung up on their almost . . . something. Her cheeks had pinked with a light flush. He bet she probably hated that about her pale, Irish skin. He found it rather charming. "She's in the lab, coloring. I'm putting up a bulletin board so we can post pictures the kids draw of the turtles."

"What a nice idea," Kit said, sounding casual . . . except she was looking at her hands, her feet, the room—anywhere but at him.

More and more intriguing. Morgan's grin widened. "I've been informed I hung it a bit *crookded,* so I'm off to hunt up more nails."

"Crookded, huh?" She smiled naturally at that and their eyes met again.

He held her gaze and was rewarded when she didn't look away. "I could use some help getting it straightened out. If you're game."

She searched his face, as if trying to figure out if she should read something into his words. Her smile stayed, though it turned a shade wry. "As long as you don't plan on my wielding a hammer."

He cocked an eyebrow. "Am I in some kind of danger?"

Her smile spread briefly with a flash of white teeth. "From me? No. I'm just more adept at hitting my thumb than I am the head of a nail. I try not to repeat my mistakes."

Morgan wondered whether there were lines there he should read between, but he didn't push. "You hold the board in place, I'll hammer."

"I think I can manage that."

"So, are you planning to contribute to the art board?" He nodded at the coloring book in her hand.

"From Dr. Gabe," she explained. "But I'm afraid I'm all out of crayons."

"Well, I happen to be the proud owner of a brand-new sixty-four pack."

"Lilly mentioned she had crayons."

"She does. But these would be my crayons, thank-you-very-much."

Her eyes danced. "Ooh. Your very own. The kind of set that comes with a sharpener?"

"The very same."

"I always wanted that set when I was a kid. Had to settle for the twenty-four pack. I tried to explain that I needed more colors, but my mom thought twenty-four was more than enough."

"Well, I don't think there's such a thing as too many colors. And I play well with others, so I'll share."

She nodded, the whimsy still in her smile. Morgan found himself more than charmed, more than simply intrigued. With her thatch of red cropped hair, fair skin still glowing pink, and green eyes dancing, she was like a fairy sprite. A fairy sprite with a knowing smile. Hell of a combination, as it turned out. Damn sexy, too.

"Fair warning," she said. "I have been known to be a little hard on my crayons. I especially liked cerulean."

"You like blue, then? So does Lilly."

"Blue's okay. I just thought it was a really cool name.

Cerulean." She drew out the syllables. "Sounded exotic, even to a five-year-old."

"So, you're a coloring veteran then."

She cocked a brow. "When did you start coloring?"

He grinned. "About ten days ago."

"What, your kindergarten teacher didn't believe in crayons?"

"My private tutors were more interested in teaching me about the aesthetics of oils versus watercolors."

"When you were five?"

Morgan merely smiled, mentally kicking himself for inserting anything about his Westlake upbringing into the conversation. He wasn't entirely sure what it was about his family name that had turned her off the day they'd met, but things were progressing well at the moment. He'd very much like that progression to continue.

She didn't make any comment about the privileged upbringing implied by private tutors. Instead, that knowing smile deepened slightly. "And?" she queried.

"And . . . what?"

"Watercolors . . . or oils? Which did your five-year-old self prefer?"

He flashed a grin then, surprised—quite pleasantly—by her dry humor. "Oils. I guess I've always been a bright colors kinda guy."

Her eyes sparkled again. "Well, given we're coloring water pictures today, you might want to keep an eye on your cerulean. I'd say it's definitely in jeopardy."

He took a step closer, not because he'd intended to, rather simply because he felt a natural pull to do so. She didn't step back, and—to her credit and his further delight—she didn't look away, either.

"So noted." He took in her soft lips . . . pink cheeks, and something of a considering look still in her bright eyes. While he was loathe to do anything to dampen the rapport they'd easily found, he couldn't ignore the fact some other underlying . . . something was still going on inside her head, and it wasn't likely a good something.

"Can I ask you a question?"

"Sure." She didn't pull away or put her guard up, but that considering look was a lot less subtle.

"Did I say or do something to cause you to have an issue with me?" He watched her eyes. "Not today, but . . . before?"

Her smile faltered at that and she looked honestly surprised, possibly a little abashed, at the question. "Why do you ask?"

His grin returned. "I thought it was only lawyers who answered a question with a question. Or . . . are you one?"

Her eyebrows lifted slightly. "Me, a lawyer? God, no."

He chuckled. "So, is that it, then? I'm condemned by profession?"

"Oh." She realized her faux pas. "Sorry. No. I know from Dr. Gabe that you're helping him with some research funding. That's really great of you. I wasn't meaning . . . never mind."

Gabe had been telling her about him. The good doctor had been telling the truth. He didn't play at matchmaking; he was quite serious about it.

Morgan found he wasn't at all put off by that. "So . . . not a lawyer. And yes, I am one and, yes, I am helping Gabe. I work mostly on environmental causes."

"I know."

"Ah."

"Small island." Kit seemed to debate saying more. Coming to a decision, she added, "And yet, you don't seem to know who I am."

For some reason he didn't think her comment had been the one at the root of the mental tug of war. "I know you're going to work for Lani Dunne, running the side business to her bake shop."

"Did you know my last name is Bellamy?"

"Yes." He couldn't recall if she'd told him or if that had come from Birdie or Gabe. "Should . . . that matter to me in some way?"

"Doesn't ring a bell then?"

"I'm sorry," he said sincerely, suddenly feeling lost. "Should it?"

He wasn't sure what he'd expected when he'd asked what issue she had with him. He'd supposed it was about him being a Westlake, which could elicit any one of a number of responses—many less than positive—from various people. On Sugarberry, he'd assumed it likely had to do with his mother ostracizing Lilly's maternal grandmother. But with Kit, it sounded rather a lot more . . . personal. And he had no idea what to think.

She paused and seemed to take stock. "No. No, it shouldn't." After a second brief pause, she tried on another smile. It wasn't at all wary, but didn't quite reach her eyes any longer. "Well, now that we have introductions out of the way, where's this crookded bulletin board of yours?" She turned toward the lab door, conversation apparently over, but he stopped her.

"If I had known your last name was Bellamy, what would I also know about you?"

She glanced back. "Nothing important. Forget I asked."

"I wish I could."

She turned back to him. "Meaning?"

He smiled. "I'm a curious sort. Gets me into all kinds of trouble. Of course, it also got me into my chosen profession, and probably makes me better at it, so I can't be too annoyed."

"I'm sure any one of the locals would be happy to fill you in."

"True, but hearsay and secondhand information can be colored by the teller's perspective. It's always better to hear it direct from the source."

She fought a smile, but he could see it teasing the corners of her mouth. A mouth he found himself watching . . . and still wanting—quite badly, actually.

"Apparently you can add tenacious to curious," she said, a wry note in her voice.

"Guilty as charged."

"I'm sure that's another trait responsible for your success in your chosen profession."

"It's come in handy, from time to time."

"Yes. It would seem to be a family trait."

His smile faded. "Meaning?"

"Meaning I've been witness, firsthand, to how tenacious Westlake lawyers can be. Can't say the same about the curiosity factor, though. They didn't really seem to want to know much of anything about me or what was going to happen to me. Their only interest was winning—at any cost—which, I understand, was a very pretty penny. Since my brother-in-law is a Carruthers, he certainly had the means to take care of their tab."

Morgan's smile was completely gone, but he kept his tone steady and pleasant, despite being totally lost as to what she was referring. "I'm not part of the family law firm. Never have been."

"I know."

"Yet, I'm to be tarred with the same brush, apparently."

"No, not at all. I don't believe in the whole sins-of-the-father bit."

"So, you have something against me personally? What would that be?" His thoughts went to Lilly again, but he couldn't imagine Kit had an opinion on his guardianship one way or the other. Her beef seemed to be with the family law firm. Neither he, nor Lilly, had ever played any role there.

"Actually, I don't. Not really." A little of the starch went out of her shoulders. "In fact, you seem like a pretty decent guy. Or I wouldn't have been laughing with you a moment ago."

"But . . . we're not laughing now. And I get the distinct impression we may not be laughing again, anytime soon. For that, I'm truly sorry. I enjoyed it. Very much, in fact. Maybe I shouldn't have brought it up, but I knew when we were first introduced that there was a problem and I just . . . wanted to clear the air."

"No, that's okay. I'm glad you did. I'm just still a little . . . raw. Maybe a lot raw. From my experience dealing with your family, I mean. When I heard you were a Westlake, it was natural, I think, to be wary."

"Understandable, yes. Until you realize that I have nothing to do with them, their cases, or how they conduct their business." He smiled, but was certain it didn't reach his eyes, either. "I'm what they'd call the black sheep of the family."

"To hear it told here, you're the white knight, and the rest are the black sheep."

He smiled more naturally at that. "It's nice to know the islanders think of me kindly. It's important to me that Lilly and I fit in here. I want to put down roots, build a life here for us. How anyone feels about my extended family or the firm is their prerogative, certainly, but I can't do anything to change that, nor am I particularly interested in trying. My relatives have earned that reputation and whatever comes with it. That doesn't involve me, one way or the other."

"Understood," she said. "And appreciated."

"So . . . still wary? Or are we okay?"

"Mmm, maybe a little wary still. Just being honest. Not so much with you, specifically, but more with our . . . um . . . " She trailed off and suddenly was back to looking at her hands, her feet, the walls. But not before her gaze had gotten caught up in his again, with a little side trip to his mouth.

His smile spread to a grin. "So, it's the our . . . um . . . part. Is that because you don't want to be attracted to anyone associated with the Westlakes, and, I'm guessing, most certainly not a blood relative?"

Her chin flew up at his question, and her eyes widened when she realized he'd moved another step closer. She lifted her gaze to his, and he watched that delicious punch of awareness enter her eyes again . . . and knew his own reaction mirrored it, perhaps even surpassed it.

"I'm not attracted—"

"Kit"—he interrupted her attempt to duck what they both knew was true—"I could say I'm as surprised as you, about our . . . um . . . but I'm not."

"You make a habit of almost kissing someone you don't know?"

"See, I thought it was an almost kiss, too. And no, not once, have I ever." His gaze drifted, lingering on her mouth, and he saw her throat work. His was a little dry, too, come to think of it. "I still want to. What I meant was that I wasn't surprised I wanted to. I was attracted to you the first time we met."

"You're drawn to women who are clearly wary of you?"

"I was confused by the wariness, but still interested enough to at least find out why."

"And now you have." Her tone might have smoothed . . . but her gaze was still soaking him up.

Made a man want to take a little swim. "Indeed." He didn't bother attempting to mask whatever she might be seeing in his eyes.

"Well, then," she said, though there was a slight tremor in the words, "at least we've cleared that up." She tried to clear her throat, but had to pull her gaze away from his mouth again, to look into his eyes. "As I said, I have no personal beef with you. I even think you're a nice guy. You obviously love your niece, and you're doing good things for Gabe. So, to that end, we're okay. I just don't want to become . . ."

"Chummy?" he helpfully supplied, a grin kicking at the corners of his mouth.

Her lips curved as well, but she held on to the smooth tone. "Anything other than friendly acquaintances."

"I respect that. Disappointed, but respectful."

She allowed a small smile, and the warmth was back in her eyes. "Thank you. I appreciate that."

"Although, if you'd like to just remain . . . friendly acquaintances, you might want to stop doing that," he advised.

"Doing what?"

"Staring at my mouth like you missed a few recent meals."

Her gaze flashed, flying up to his . . . but the most delightful flush to her cheeks told the real story.

Caught in the act, she still gave denial her best shot. "We can add arrogant and egotistical to the list."

"Not at all. Observant," he offered, then let a slow smile cross his face. "Confident in what I know to be true. Curious about what I don't know. And . . . always hopeful."

"Well, please observe then, this is me telling you I'm not interested. I can't be clearer than that. So . . . don't get your hopes up."

"Too late, I'm afraid. But, message received." He lifted his hands, palms out. "Friends only."

"Thank you."

"You're welcome." He shoved his hands in his pockets.

"Just so we're clear though, on the our . . . um . . . thing." He shifted his stance slightly when her gaze went straight to his mouth, and her own opened, just slightly, on an in-drawn breath. She really had to stop doing that. His jeans were getting more uncomfortable by the second. "If I weren't a Westlake, would you be interested?" He waited for her gaze to lift to his. And what he saw there prompted him to finish the question with a smile. "In finding out more about our . . . um?"

"It . . . it makes no difference. The answer is no." The flush in her cheeks deepened, but her eyes had their flash back, only it wasn't a spark of desire.

He wished he could say that was a turn off, but it wasn't. At all.

"And, with me, no means no. It's not a veiled invitation to try harder."

He grinned, laughed. "Yeah, that tenacious thing has also gotten me into trouble from time to time."

"Not surprised to hear that."

Considering her dismissal of all things Westlake, he replied, "No, I imagine you're not."

He took several steps back, keeping his hands in his pockets. So far her gaze had only drifted as far south as his mouth, but he didn't need to risk it drifting any lower. "I won't apologize for my family, as I'm certain they're not very apologetic regarding the matter, so that would be disingenuous of me at best."

The heat faded somewhat from her cheeks and her eyes.

"However, I will apologize for my own behavior. I've long since distanced myself from their actions, but I do take full responsibility for my own. I didn't mean to make you feel personally uncomfortable just now. I was just . . ." He trailed off, surprised to find himself far more disappointed than the situation seemed to merit. They hardly knew each other, had barely crossed paths, so getting shot down shouldn't be more than a cursory blip—a welcome one, even—considering everything on his plate.

But it wasn't. And he couldn't help that it felt more . . . monumental than it should.

"Hopeful," she supplied for him, collected once again and at ease enough to inject a dry note into her reply.

"Yes," he said, smiling in response. "Always and in all ways."

She smiled briefly then, too. "So . . . an optimistic lawyer."

He shrugged. "I'm trying to save the planet here. I kind of have to be."

She laughed, and seemed surprised by it. But it did lessen the tension. The bad kind, anyway. "It's good to have small goals."

He matched her smile. "Sometimes the smallest goals are the most challenging to achieve. And the most vital."

"Yes. True," she said, then broke eye contact altogether as she stepped away from the worktable. "So . . . Captain Environment, where is this bulletin board that needs uncrookded-ing? We have masterpieces to create that the world needs to see. Or, at least, some very large turtles."

She turned and strode toward the door leading to the rehab area and he grinned at her very straight spine. She wanted him to see the starch, but he'd already seen the heat. And it would be some time before he forgot it. "Let me grab a few nails, then it's right this way, Madame Cupcake."

Chapter 9

"And you just told him no? Straight up?" Lani shook her head and poised her pastry tip over another rack of hollowed-out cupcakes. Death by Chocolate cupcakes, to be exact.

It was a good thing Kit was so distracted by the fact that her personal business was being bandied about at the current evening's Cupcake Club soiree—otherwise known as the Bitch 'n' Bake, according to Alva, who had delighted in explaining that to her—or she might have lunged across the table and planted her face in all that deliciously warm and ridiculously rich truffle filling. If chocolate cured all ills, Lani had just solved the world's problems with a single decadent recipe.

While Kit couldn't speak for the whole world, she'd vouch it would definitely go a long way to improving her little corner of it. She was beginning to think the whole "get a personal life" thing was highly overrated.

"I just made it clear to him I wasn't interested in anything other than casual friendship. And I only mentioned it so you all would stop with the nudging. He's nice, but I don't want to get involved with anyone right now," she explained. "It's not the right time."

"That's what everyone says," Alva offered. "And they end up alone. The right time is whenever you meet the right man." She went back to sifting powdered sugar on the tops of her gingerbread cupcakes. "Don't look a gift hunk in the mouth." She paused, sighed, then went back to sifting. "I certainly wouldn't."

Lani laughed at Franco as he grinned and sent Alva a smooching air kiss. Charlotte smiled as she continued intricately decorating a row of cupcakes, turning them into turkey tops, and Dre . . . well, after three weeks on Sugarberry, Kit still couldn't read Dre.

"How long has it been, dear?" Alva went on.

"Been?" Kit repeated, swiveling her gaze back to the tiny octogenarian. "Since . . . I was in a relationship?"

Alva sent her a sweet smile. "That, too, but I meant how long has the dry spell been? Since you had sex?" she clarified, as the stunned look on Kit's face led her to assume she hadn't understood.

Oh . . . she'd understood.

"Well, good sex," Alva quantified. "Bad sex never helped anyone."

"Don't answer that, *mes amie,*" Franco warned.

"The column," everyone in the room mouthed silently in Kit's direction. Behind Alva's back, Lani made a slicing motion across her neck.

"That's not the point," Kit hurried to say.

"Dear, if it's been so long you can't answer the question, then it most definitely should be the point."

Lani and Charlotte snickered, though they quickly hid it behind their respective pastry bags when Kit shot them both an incredulous look. Sensing the total loss of any control she might ever have over her private life, she blurted out, "Even if it was the right time, and I wanted to . . . to break the dry spell, as it were . . . it wouldn't be with him."

Everyone paused in his or her respective task. Even Dre.

"Really?" Lani said, peeking over her pastry bag with raised eyebrows, drawling the word in a way that made it sound . . . lascivious and . . . promising.

Dammit.

"Is it because he's a Westlake?" Alva asked.

Sighing in defeat, Kit's defiant posture deflated. "Not in the way you think. I know he's quickly become, like, the island hero, rescuing his niece, reuniting her with her other grandmother, but the fact is—"

"The fact is he distanced himself from his family a long time ago," Lani said, albeit somewhat more gently. "You can't hold him responsible—"

"I know that. We talked about it, and I don't."

As one, they gave her a look clearly indicating they didn't believe her for a second.

"No, really. I know he had nothing to do with what happened to my family's business. He didn't even know anything about it. It's just . . ."

"It feels like he's tainted by association," Alva said. "Is that it?"

"Not tainted, exactly."

"Why, then?" Charlotte asked.

Kit shot her a surprised look. As the one person she had history with, she'd counted on Charlotte to have her back. Of course, Char's longer and deeper history with everyone else in the room clearly trumped that.

Kit really didn't want to get into the whole Westlake defense, mostly because she didn't want to hear how lame it would sound to her own ears. It mattered more how she felt. "I'm not ready to get involved with anyone at this point." She shot a look at Alva. "On any level."

Part of her brain was still boggling that she was discussing her sex life with a group of women who—other than Charlotte—she'd only laid eyes on for the first time less than a month ago. And Charlotte had been more business contact than personal friend. They'd certainly never discussed their intimate relationships before.

"So, don't get involved," Lani said. "Just . . . enjoy his company."

"*Oui, oui,*" Franco said. "Do not be so quick to dismiss those other levels."

"Exactly. No one is saying you have to marry Uncle Hunk, dear," Alva said.

"Uncle—Hunk?" Kit choked on the bite of Death by Chocolate she'd just given into tasting. Sheer desperation had lowered all her usual chocolate defenses.

Alva's eyes twinkled. "That's what we call him. Lani May started it. But I kinda like it." She added another scoop of powdered sugar to her sifter. "Suits him. I'll say that much."

"I will second that." Franco sighed. "Hunka, hunka burnin' uncle. Speaking of which, we haven't had an Elvis night in a while."

"That's because last time . . . well, we still haven't gotten over last time." Lani paused and the other's gazes swiveled toward one person, with Kit following after.

Alva looked up to find them all staring at her. "What? I thought I was pretty good." Her expression shifted to one of fond memory. "I remember the first time I saw him in concert." She clamped a sugar-dusted hand to her apron-covered heart. "Oh my, it was simply *scandalous*. The way he moved his hips." Her eyes twinkled and her cheeks flushed. "I loved every minute of it."

"Wait," Charlotte said. "He was popular in the late fifties. You would have been—"

"I had just turned thirty. Harold took me to the concert. Now you see why I loved that man." She smiled and turned back to her cupcakes. "With some men, you're always a teenage girl at heart." She didn't clarify whether she meant Harold or Elvis . . . but she bumped her hips to one side, then the other, and hummed the chorus to "Hound Dog."

Kit laughed along with the rest as they picked up at the chorus and sang it, and soon they were all dancing. Only then did she know she'd end up telling them anything they wanted to know. Who could resist cupcakes, impromptu dancing, and group Elvis impersonations?

Franco finished up a particularly rousing rendition of "Jailhouse Rock"—figured he had a killer singing voice—and ended up sliding with a flourish, right onto the stool next to Kit. He pressed his head against her arm, looked up into her eyes, and in a deep baritone, said, "Thank you, thank you very much."

Kit was laughing too hard to respond. It felt good. Really good. She needed more laughter, more silliness, and more spontaneous acts of craziness. It felt good. And . . . safe.

That was exactly it. She felt safe. She trusted these people. It was a huge thing, given the events of the past year. They weren't nosing into her business for their own prurient interests, but because they cared and wanted things to go well for her.

Morgan Westlake, on the other hand, made her feel very . . . well, not safe. He felt dangerous and made her want things unrelated to good judgment.

With his head still pressed dramatically against her arm, Franco said in a weird, hybrid French Elvis voice, "It has been a rough year for you, *cherie.* No one would blame you for having a little fun." He wiggled his perfectly arched eyebrows. "In fact, we here in the Elvis Impersonators Cupcake Club applaud this idea of having *ze* fun."

"Speaking of *ze* fun," Lani said to Franco, "what's the latest with your special someone?"

Charlotte made a low hissing noise, trying to make a slashing motion from behind where Franco was perched, much as Lani had before, but it was too late. Franco had already straightened on the stool, his smile remaining, but it didn't warm his beautiful brown eyes any longer.

Lani immediately looked contrite. "Sorry, forget I asked." She winced and sent Charlotte a *why didn't you tell me?* look.

"When have you had time?" Charlotte said, as if the question had been actually asked.

"I know, I know. With the cookbook promotion starting and finally getting Babycakes off the ground, I'm behind on my nosiness." Lani sent a soft smile Franco's way. "I love you, you know. And I'm sure he's a rat bastard who will die a sad, lonely death."

"I do know," Franco said, his responding smile sweet with just a little sadness. "And thank you." Then, swinging directly around to Kit, broad smile right back on his handsome face and his Bronx roots fully back in his voice, he asked, "What will it take for us to persuade you to jump the hunka hunka hunky uncle's bones, sweetheart?"

"Persuade me to have a . . . a fling with someone I don't want? Why would you even do that?"

"Oh, you want." Dre, who didn't so much as glance up from her own project, spoke for the first time. "I was there. I saw."

"Googly eyes," Lani provided. "I saw them, too."

"Oh, for the love of—" Kit lifted her hands in utter defeat.

"Googly eyes never lie," Alva added, smiling with apparent remembered pleasure, then started humming "Teddy Bear."

Cornered, Kit's gaze circled the room . . . and landed on Charlotte.

Recognizing what she saw in Kit as desperation, Charlotte said, "There is the child to consider."

Kit pounced on her comment like the shamelessly desperate woman she was. "Exactly. Thank you." To the room, she added, "Little Lilly has been through the worst kind of hell a child could imagine. I was in my early twenties when I lost my parents and it leveled me. Still does, from time to time." *Like pretty much every day for the past year.*

She would have given anything to have had her mother with her during the trial, even for a day. "I can only imagine how it must be affecting her. She doesn't need her uncle complicating her life by introducing new people into it."

"Well, she's meeting a lot of new people here on Sugarberry," Lani offered. "It's her new home, so that will only continue. Besides, I thought she was adorable."

"Awesome kid," Dre said, remaining focused on her project, which was creating a series of sketches, rather than baking. Everyone who'd seen the apron she had made for Kit in honor of the upcoming Babycakes launch had so completely swooned over it Lani had asked Dre to find a way to work the elements into something that could be used for a store logo and other marketing for the mail-order shop, much as she had for the cupcakery.

"She is a great kid," Kit agreed. "I had fun with her, turtle coloring. She's bright and sweet, smart, and clearly adores her uncle. But she's still—"

"She invited you to the rehab center to color with her," Lani said. "Sounds like she's the one reaching out to you."

"Yes, she did, and it's great to see she's doing that. For all that she looks like this tiny wisp of a thing, she's strong, and the more people she has supporting her, the more it will help her adjust—"

"Seems to me Morgan is also responsible for that," Lani said. "I mean, bringing her here to Sugarberry and getting her away from Olivia Westlake showed he's not afraid to take a stand, do what he thinks is right." Lani expertly shot warm truffle filling into another row of dark chocolate cupcakes as she talked. "From what I understand, his mother is a pretty formidable force."

"To put it mildly," Alva added. "Morgan is doing right by Miss Lilly, bringing her here, letting her get to know her maternal grandmother."

"How did that go, by the way?" Lani asked Alva.

"It could have gone better. Birdie was moved to tears just getting to spend some time with that darling girl. Imagine, being kept from your only grandbaby. It was a might overwhelming for the little one and Birdie felt just awful for being too excited. Though you can hardly blame her."

"Well, they are here to stay, so there will be plenty of time," Lani said. "I think it will work out eventually. It has to. Everyone who meets Lilly loves her."

"I agree," Alva said. "Of course, all that said"—she cast a sly glance in Kit's direction—"adults need adult time, too."

Kit merely sighed and gave up any hope of keeping the conversation off her pathetic social life. "It's a good thing I already love you guys, you know."

"We nudge because we care, *mi amor,*" Franco said.

Kit laughed. "If this is nudging, I'd hate to see outright pushing."

"You're right about that." Lani grinned. "I still have their collective boot marks on my backside."

"And look where that got you," Franco said. "Blissfully married to a hot, handsome Brit."

Lani sighed dreamily. "He is that."

"We got Riley hooked up with Quinn, too," Alva said. "And Charlotte—"

"I took care of that one all by myself," Charlotte corrected.

"True," Franco said.

"Overachiever," Lani added.

Charlotte smiled. "I just waited until no one was looking."

"Making notes . . ." Kit murmured and everyone chuckled, then looked at her expectantly. She gave them all a level look. "It's not going to happen. Not with Morgan, or anyone. Not right now. It's good for Lilly to have supportive people in her life, but that's not the same thing as having someone intimately involved with her uncle."

"Kids are more resilient than you think. Besides, love and support is never a bad thing, no matter how it's packaged, or with whom." Alva lifted a hand to stall Kit's response. "But, if it's not to be with Morgan, you might want to keep in mind the pickings get pretty slim. Sugarberry doesn't have too many bachelors. Under the age of seventy, anyway."

"There's Dylan," Dre offered.

"The mechanic?" Lani thought about it. "I guess. If you like brooding James Dean types."

"And the problem with that is . . ." Dre left her comment to trail off.

"You interested in him, *ma petite amie*?" Franco wanted to know.

"I don't go for guys born more than a decade earlier than me," Dre said dryly. Then paused in her drawing. "But, you know, if I did . . ." She surprised them all by smiling and wiggling her pierced eyebrows.

"Well, sometimes age is just a number," Kit offered.

"Sometimes," Dre said. "Not this time."

Kit waited for the inevitable prodding and nudging. But everyone went back to work. Apparently there would be no boot prints on Dre's backside. Just on Kit's. How fortunate for her.

"Well, dear," Alva said, a few moments later, "if you're planning on rejecting Mr. Westlake's advances, then I hope you don't likewise reject any future overtures from Miss Lilly."

"Of course not," Kit said. "I wasn't that harsh about it. I just think, given everything that's happened recently in both our lives, we'd be asking for trouble to even consider—"

"So . . . you have considered it then," Lani prodded, grinning unrepentantly.

"I didn't say that. But while we may not be rebounding from broken relationships, we are rebounding from some pretty major broken life events."

"I can think of worse ways to drown your sorrows than by having really hot sex," Lani said.

"And she would know," Char offered.

Kit let her chin drop and just shook her head.

"That's the best kind of trouble to get in," Franco added.

"I'm taking a pass on any kind of trouble for the time being. I'm sure Morgan and I will form a nice friendship. We already have. It's a small island, after all. Plus, I still want to help out Dr. Gabe with the turtles, and I know Morgan is doing work for him, and Lilly is involved with them, too. If she asks to see me, I'll say yes. I want to reinforce her reaching out like that." Kit lifted a hand to stall their collective replies. "But that's it. I mean it. So you can stop with the boots on the butt. I'll jump when I'm ready, with whomever I'm ready for. Just not right now. And not with him."

"Him, I'd jump," Dre offered casually, head still bent intently over her sketch pad. Everyone's head turned as one toward her. Feeling the scrutiny, she looked up and her lips curved just a little. "Sometimes age *is* just a number." When everyone continued to stare, she scowled. "What? I'm twenty-two for God's sake. Haven't we had the sex talk already, moms and dad?"

"Speaking of *ze* sexy talk, *mon amie,* whatever happened with that divine grad student you were seeing?" Franco slid closer and Dre got a lot more interested in her work.

"Seeing, but not dating. He's a friend."

"You always say that," Lani said. "And yet, you go on about this active sex life—"

Dre looked up. "Friend. And not the kind with benefits."

Franco pulled up a work stool and sat catty-corner to Dre, propped his elbows on the table and his chin in his hands. With a knowing smile, he leaned closer. "So . . . if he didn't make the 'with benefits' list, I'm dying to know who did."

Dre sighed. "There is no list. At the moment."

Kit knew then she was a small, small person, because she didn't feel a bit of remorse for being taken out of the hot white glare of the sex life chat.

Lani executed another perfect row of cupcake filling shots. "Everyone has a list."

"You mean you used to have a list," Charlotte said. "You're married. The icky, gooey, googly-eyed-in-love-with-your-husband-forever kind of married. Give your sadly neglected list to someone else. It's the charitable thing to do."

"Takes one to know one," Lani shot back. "Just get Carlo to an altar somewhere already."

"Carlo and I are not icky, gooey. We actually show restraint."

Everyone in the room snorted at that, including Kit, who had worked with the lovebirds in the past and knew them to be quite capable of being exceedingly over the icky, gooey line.

"Even when my Harold was alive, I had a list." A wistful smile curved Alva's bright red, lipsticked lips.

Once again, as one, everyone turned to Alva with a mixed look of anticipation and possible dread at whatever she might say.

"Really?" Lani bravely ventured.

Alva placed a sugarcoated palm directly over her heart, half covering the head of the purple-maned My Little Pony on her apron. "Oh my, yes, dear. Harold and I had a deal. If Tab Hunter, Paul Newman, or that handsome, young Jimmy Stewart ever crossed my path and gave me so much as a wink and a smile . . . well, my Harold, bless his soul, would have understood. Some things a girl just doesn't say no to."

Charlotte frowned. "You wouldn't really have—"

"Well, dear, now that they've all gone to their great reward, I suppose we'll never know." Alva smiled and the twinkle even Kit had come to recognize for the mischievous glint it was, made her faded blue eyes sparkle. "Now I have a new list. And no Harold." She smiled as if reviewing the list and went back to work. "It could happen."

"I'm not asking." Franco sent a look of warning around the room. "Some things are better not left to the imagination."

"Did Harold get a list?" Kit wanted to know.

"Audrey Hepburn, Grace Kelly, and Mitzi Gaynor."

"And?" Lani asked with an eyebrow wiggle.

"Skunked, both of us," Alva said with a light laugh.

Everyone chuckled; then Lani said to Kit, "Oh, before I forget, I took those extra pillows and linens I told you about upstairs to the apartment earlier."

"Great, thanks. I appreciate that." Since agreeing to take the job, Kit had been staying in the small, one-room apartment over the main bakery, which also doubled as a storage room for overflow store supplies. She'd thought she'd have more time to look around for a place to rent, but once she'd signed on, Lani had jumped straight into the new project like a kid with a new toy. Not that Kit could blame her. To have an idea and see it come to life was pretty exciting. She was well caught up in Babycakes, and just as dedicated to making it happen by their self-imposed deadline of the cookbook publication as Lani and Baxter were.

What felt like all the time in the world would disappear sooner than they thought. The past few weeks had already gone by in a blur. Kit was thankful for the all-consuming focus a project of that scope demanded. It felt like a life preserver, one she was clinging to for all she was worth.

She had to stay equally focused on the whole balance thing. She'd already talked to Dr. Gabe about volunteering through the holidays when a lot of his interns had family obligations. She'd figure out how to handle things when she bumped into Morgan again. She'd thoroughly enjoyed the coloring session with Lilly, despite the lingering sexual tension that had continued to sizzle in the air between her and Morgan Surely that would die down in time if she ignored it long enough.

Surely.

Fortunately, Lilly had been blissfully unaware of the adult undercurrents in the room, focused totally on her newfound love of turtles. Kit's heart had melted when Lilly had introduced her to the rehab turtle she'd named Paddlefoot. Honestly, only someone with a heart of stone could spend time with Lilly and not be captivated by her. Oh-so-serious one moment, too quiet the next, shy at times, and quite direct at others, she'd smile like the little girl she was at something silly Morgan would say to her. Something he did often, Kit had noted. Perversely, it made the whole tension thing even thicker. Hunky uncle, indeed.

But respecting his efforts and commitment to raising his niece was not going to sway her decision to remain uninvolved. She could adore Lilly, respect and like Morgan, and be turned on like crazy whenever she so much as thought of him, and still manage not to jump into bed with him. She really needed to stop thinking about that, and would, as soon as everyone stopped trying to nudge her there.

"Whom will you be spending Thanksgiving with?" Alva asked.

The question sent a direct ping to Kit's heart, catching her off guard. The last one had been strained, as the court case had been just getting under way. They'd all still lived in the family home, then. This Thanksgiving would be the first holiday in her whole life spent anywhere but the family home.

It was only when Charlotte answered that Kit realized she'd been lost in thought and missed part of the conversation.

"We're going back to New York to spend time with Carlo's family."

"With the engagement ring *on* this time?" Lani asked, somewhat pointedly.

"Yes," Charlotte said, wiggling her hand, where a small but beautifully set antique diamond resided on her ring finger.

"Good," Lani stated. "It's about time."

Kit had already heard the saga of Carlo's extensive Cuban family having met Charlotte the previous fall and liking her a great deal . . . as long as she was only their beloved son's business partner. Their enthusiasm had waned considerably when they'd found out this past summer that he'd actually proposed to her before meeting them. With a family heirloom ring, no less. One they hadn't actually seen her wear yet.

Charlotte sighed. "Yes, well, Carlo's grandmother still

has a curse on me, but his mother no longer refers to me as *that woman*."

Lani smiled dryly. "Progress, then."

"At this rate, I'll be cleaved to their bosom . . . oh, sometime around my seventy-fifth birthday."

"What about your folks?" Alva asked. "Are they coming back this year?"

"Of course not. Why would they when there is no wedding date? That's fine. Once in nine years is all I can handle."

Kit also knew Charlotte had left Dubai at eighteen to come to the States to attend culinary school . . . and escape her parents' control over every aspect of her life. To hear Alva tell it, Charlotte's parents had planned out her entire future, including whom she would marry, the number of grandchildren she would bear them, how far apart they were to be born, and would have specified gender, and in what order, if they could have arranged that, too.

The one thing Kit had learned from her short time with the Cupcake Club was that having family issues was apparently a lot more the norm than she would have guessed. Even Morgan could be included in the group.

"Why not elope?" Kit asked.

"We'd be universally disowned by both families."

Privately Kit thought that didn't sound like such a bad trade-off, but she of all people understood the complexities families represented.

"I try not to think about it, but to be honest, it's been over a year since the engagement and . . ." Charlotte, who was possibly the calmest person Kit had ever met, looked somewhat flustered and dropped her gaze to her engagement ring, prompting Franco to slide his stool almost the full length of the worktable from Dre, stopping it a fraction of an inch away from Char.

He lifted her left hand and pressed a kiss to the back of it, then looked up with those heartbreaking eyes of his. "*Ma cherie,* just give me the word, and I will have them all killed." He dropped the French accent and went straight back to the Bronx. "I have connections."

Charlotte laughed, even though her eyes were suspiciously glassy. And, yet again, Kit wondered why all the good ones were gay.

"Thank you." Char hugged Franco's shoulders. "You guys are all the family I need."

"Maybe you should stay here for the holidays," Alva suggested. "Start new traditions." She clapped her hands together. "We should have our own holiday dinner together. I'll host!"

Lani opened her mouth, then closed it again, and appeared thoughtful.

Charlotte shook her head, but there was a distinctly wistful look in her eyes. "Carlo's family would definitely never forgive me if I kept him away."

"Sounds like he needs to grow a pair if you ask me," Alva commented, sending them into snorts of laughter, Charlotte included.

"You're not necessarily alone in that opinion," Charlotte said, "but their culture is very different, very matriarchal, especially in his family."

"Well, you'll be the matriarch of the family you and Carlo begin . . . why not start your reign of rightful terror now?" Lani asked, a conspiratorial smile on her face. "Besides, I heard from Riley last night that she and Quinn will be back on the island the day before Thanksgiving."

Charlotte's eyes lit up, and she appeared to waver.

"At least think about it," Lani asked.

Alva was already grabbing a pad of paper and pen. "My goodness, it's less than a week from now. We hardly have any time to plan."

Franco stood and walked over to Alva and put his arm around her diminutive shoulders, which, given the disparity in their height, was somewhat comical. The fact that he had on his Pink Panther apron again, while Alva was sporting her purple-maned My Little Pony apron made the duo even more amusing. "You're talking to a room full of trained chefs, *ma petite belle amie*. I think we can pull this off." He took Alva's hand and bowed low over it, then pressed a kiss to the back of it. "Just tell me what you need done."

Alva, who had surely been on the receiving end of Franco's charms for as long as they'd been on the island together, still blushed a pretty pink behind her carefully applied layers of foundation, rouge, and powder. "You're a scamp."

"You have no idea," he replied, and everyone laughed.

"You know, I think I love this idea," Lani said, excitement building in her own voice. "We should do it. A Cupcake Club family dinner. My dad will want to come, of course. You know, Charlotte, you could always invite Carlo's family down here. Since Quinn and Riley will be back, we could see about having the meal at their house." She looked at Alva. "Not to take away from your lovely offer, but they have the most room."

"And the kitchen of the gods," Franco added reverently.

Quinn and Riley's whirlwind romance had happened during the fall of the year before, when he'd come to the island to write his newest book and Riley had been hired to stage the house he'd ended up leasing.

"What do you say, Kit?" Lani asked. "Dare to join us?"

Kit had been looking forward to meeting Quinn and Riley, but hadn't thought much about what she was going to do over the holidays. She'd tried to avoid thinking about it, actually. She supposed she'd figured on working. There was plenty to be done. But now . . . she had an offer. She couldn't deny it made her feel warm and welcomed and . . . happy. She smiled. "Well, it depends."

"On?"

"How gauche would it be to ask Quinn to sign one or ten of his books over turkey and canned beets?"

Everyone laughed.

"Don't think just because he's part of the family now that we haven't gotten him to do the same thing. Every one of us."

"Good to know," Kit said. "I might have to slide a cookbook in front of your husband, too. I know I asked this before, but how is it again that two members of the club have snagged famous husbands?"

Lani just smiled. "We blame it on the cupcakes."

Kit looked at the half eaten Death by Chocolate cupcake still in her hand and carefully—very carefully—placed it back on the table.

Lani laughed, Charlotte smiled, Alva winked, and Dre shook her head. Franco, in the meantime, took Kit's hand and spun her expertly into his arms, then into a deep dip. "It's too late now, *mon amie,*" he told her as a slow smile spread across his handsome face. "You have bitten *ze* cupcake, Cupcake. There is no going back."

Kit didn't know whether to laugh or be afraid. Very afraid.

Chapter 10

"Coraline, I know you miss her, that you all do." Morgan shifted the phone to his other ear and, after peeking to make sure Lilly was okay with her lunch at the kitchen table, he stepped farther into his office. "But we're going to stay here on Sugarberry for Thanksgiving."

"Mr. Morgan, Miss Lilly should be with family, as should you."

"She is with family," he told the Westlake's head housekeeper calmly, gently. He'd been expecting this call. He was only surprised they'd waited until the Sunday before the holiday to make it. "We've just settled in here and, for now, we need to keep doing that."

"You'll be home for Christmas, then."

"Cora—"

"The missus is suffering, too," she said, her voice shaking with emotion. "She lost too much. Too much. She shouldn't lose you and that child, too."

Morgan sighed then. He didn't discount the pain that was clear in her every word, but he knew it was Coraline who was feeling it. For all of them. "Cora, she hasn't lost us. We're just not going to live in the same house. I appreciate how much you and the staff all personally miss Lilly. I promised we'd come back for a visit when the time is right, and and I meant that. Still do. But, it's not time yet."

"But, Missus Olivia—"

"Cora, you know as well as I do that my mother hasn't a sentimental bone in her body about this time of year." *Or any time of year,* he could have added. "To her, the holidays merely represent business opportunities for the firm. All those holiday functions are like a press junket to her."

"Now, Mr. Morgan, this is a time for family—and you and Miss Lilly are all the family she has left."

"I know. We miss you, Coraline. All of you. I have a great deal of respect for your loyalty to my mother, but"—he sighed again—"let's not pretend here, okay? We're all suffering because Asher and Delilah are gone, especially now, facing the holidays without them for the first time. I know losing Asher was devastating for my mother, even if she has a hard time showing it."

"She has to be strong," Cora said.

"Yes," Morgan said, resigned. "She's always that. She made sure we all knew she never missed a single day of work, even if she had to work from home, for propriety's sake, right after the accident. She took whatever she was feeling, bottled it all up, and just kept on going. Have you seen her shed a single tear? Or appear to be incapacitated by what happened in any way?"

The silence on the other end of the line grew lengthy.

"I know that was harsh, and I'm not trying to be, truly." He softened his tone. "But we need to be honest about the reality of the situation. I need to be, for Lilly's sake." *And my own,* he thought. Coming back to Georgia, even after years of being gone, even after finding his own way, happy with his life, had been much harder than he'd anticipated. And not just because of the tragic circumstances.

"People all grieve differently," Coraline said, somewhat stiffly. "And someone has to stay on top of things at the firm." What went unsaid was tnow that Asher was gone, it should have been Morgan stepping in to help, at home and at the company.

Morgan didn't bother to mention Asher had never been anything more than a puppet figure, that his mother had always held the reins to the firm in a tight, unyielding fist, never giving up an ounce of control she didn't have to. That most certainly wasn't going to change now. Asher had thrived on the glad-handing and social whirl required in their circles, but it had never been Morgan's path. As tragic and painful as the loss of Asher and Delilah had been, he would never be stepping in to take his brother's place. He couldn't play the role Asher had, and there was no way his mother would relinquish her hold on the firm. Not even if he wanted her to—which he most decidedly did not.

"Yes, people do grieve in their own way," Morgan agreed. "But you need to understand my mother's dedication to the family firm has and always will be her first and foremost priority. I think Lilly would be better served by being around people who are more . . . openly supportive of her specific needs right now." He'd been about to say more openly loving, but that would have been a direct slap at the household staff, who did love Lilly very much. To their credit, they had always done their best to show her . . . as they had shown him.

However, Morgan knew their first loyalty would always be to his mother, whose demands would be met regardless of their personal opinion on what might be best. Even when it came to her children . . . or her grandchild. Without Asher or Delilah to serve as a buffer, there was no way he'd have left Lilly there to fend for herself. Hell, he wouldn't leave himself there. Taking Lilly back into that environment, when they'd just begun settling into their new life, would not be good.

"I will tell her not to expect you, then," Cora said, coolly professional.

He knew he'd hurt her, and regretted he'd had no other choice. "Thank you, Coraline. And thank you for calling to check up on us. We're doing well here. Lilly is okay." It was why she'd really called. He doubted his mother knew she was calling or had thought one way or the other about the holiday itself, other than how it would look to others that her surviving son and her only granddaughter weren't present at this holiday function or that one.

Growing up, Thanksgiving dinner had always been a stuffy, rigid affair, complete with formal dress, full staff, and a table full of people Morgan had never met and who seemed disinclined to talk to children. He missed—greatly—being in Colorado with the close friends he'd made there . . . but he didn't miss being in Atlanta. He hoped Sugarberry would become to him and Miss Lilly what he'd found out west. The Thanksgivings he'd known there were full of the true holiday spirit he wanted her to experience.

He had no doubt Olivia would make the rounds, handling things efficiently, with polish and poise sharpened to a bright luster, with ruthless determination, and an attention to detail that made her the envy of everyone around her—just as she always did. Not that any of those around her were close to her personally—Olivia was more the type for allies, rather than actual friends—but they did covet her position, her fortune, and how expertly she wielded it.

He imagined she'd be lauded for putting on such a brave face, for soldiering forward in such difficult times. But he wasn't going to let her trot Lilly out as some kind of little Westlake show pony, not this year or any other. At least while he was her guardian.

Morgan used to feel bad for having such thoughts, and

had struggled with guilt for a very long time. But as he'd gotten older and made his own way, he'd eventually come to understand the truth was . . . simply the truth. Far more difficult had been accepting that nothing he did would ever change it.

"Please tell everyone that Lilly says hello. And that I do, as well. And wish them a good holiday. I'll tell her you called." He heard Cora's shaky sigh, and wished things were different for her and the others, if nothing else.

"You have a good Thanksgiving, Mr. Morgan," she said, her tone softening once again, emotion seeping back in.

Likely that honest emotion caused Morgan to add, "If any of you would like to come to Sugarberry, you know you're welcome." He was pretty sure the silence on the other end was from shock.

"I—why, thank you," Coraline said at length. "We'll be tied up through the holidays, but perhaps afterward . . . " She trailed off, as if unsure whether he'd really meant it or was just being polite in the spirit of the holidays.

"We'd like that," he said, smiling, absolutely sincere in his invitation. "Please, just give me a few days advance notice and we'll get everything set up."

"Okay," she said, an edge of excitement and awe in her tone. "We'll do that." For the first time in as long as Morgan could recall, she sounded like a normal person.

"Have a good Thanksgiving, Cora."

"We'll do our best. And please, hug Miss Lilly extra tight for us, will you?"

"I will." He hung up, unsure of what lunacy had prompted him to cross that invisible line, but he was happy for whatever confluence of emotions had caused him to do it. If anything, Cora and the rest of the staff had been Lilly's true family. He was tempted to go tell Lilly, but decided against it for the time being. Until there were concrete plans in place, he didn't want to get her hopes up.

He wasn't sure whom Cora would get to travel with her, but even if only she came, it would make him and Lilly happy.

He wondered if Cora would tell his mother about the invite. And what Olivia would think of her paid staff heading out to Sugarberry to visit her granddaughter when she hadn't received a similar invitation. He smiled, then chuckled. He had absolutely no idea. But it was fun to think about.

He tucked his phone away, then snagged an envelope off his desk and went out to the kitchen. "You about done there, sweet pea? Dr. Gabe is waiting for us."

"I'm done." Lilly slipped down from her chair and took her plate and glass to the sink. "Can I wear my fairy skirt?"

Just when he thought they'd get out the door without The Negotiation. "Sweetie, what you have on looks great. Besides, you've worn that the last few times we went out there."

"Paddlefoot likes it. It's his favorite."

"I'm sure he does like it, because it's really pretty. But remember how we got a little messy with the finger paints Dr. Gabe got you?" Morgan might not ever entirely forgive him. Clearly Gabe had no idea how hard it was to get that stuff off clothes, skin, hair . . . and fairy skirts. "I haven't figured out how to clean it yet and I don't want to ruin it."

Lilly paused, and Morgan took shameless advantage of the rare breach in her normally rock solid negotiation tactics. "Why don't you wear that pink sweatshirt with the sea turtles on it?" He'd ordered it online back when she'd first shown a real love for the turtles, thinking it would be a good stocking stuffer . . . then had caved the moment it arrived and let her open the package immediately. He definitely had to work on that before Christmas rolled around. Or they'd need a bigger cottage. "Paddlefoot would be happy because you're wearing something that looks just like him."

She thought about it, and Morgan sent up every prayer he had. This was why he wasn't a trial lawyer.

"Okay." She skipped off to her bedroom to get it.

Morgan let out a sigh of relief on par with having just negotiated someone down off a ledge. "Why can't it always be so simple?" he murmured.

Lilly came out a minute later with two ribbons, three coated elastic bands, and a plastic headband. "Can I have braids?" She held out the beauty parlor assortment.

Morgan's chin dipped straight to his chest. "You're going to make a great defense attorney someday."

"I wanna be a turtle doctor. Like Dr. Langley."

Gabe had asked her to call him Dr. Gabe, but Lilly stuck with his formal name. Morgan liked how she still straggled out the last name, so he didn't buck her on it. "Well, you'll be very good at that, too."

He took her hand, wondering if he could Google how to braid hair. It had gotten him off the hook when she'd asked for a manicure the week before. So, it could work. Maybe. He'd need fully illustrated, step-by-step drawings, though. "Why don't we wait until we get back for the braids?"

"Maybe we can ask Miss Kit to help," she suggested easily. Too easily.

Morgan paused as he reached for the front doorknob and glanced down at her with a narrowed, speculative gaze. "Definitely defense attorney."

They went out the door and he helped her into the backseat of the SUV. "I don't know if she'll be there today, but if not—"

"She's coming today," Lilly said confidently.

"Okay, well, we'll still have to ask her."

They hadn't crossed paths with Kit since their meeting

with the coloring books the previous week. Gabe had said one of his new volunteers would be happy to keep watch on— *Ah.* Morgan smiled at Lilly in the rearview mirror. She'd answered the phone when Gabe had called the day before to set up the meeting. Apparently they'd had quite the chat before he got out of the shower.

Yep, he was so locking her up the minute she hit thirteen. Maybe ten. Or perhaps starting next week. She was too clever for her own good, that one.

He turned down the short, crushed shell road to the center. A handful of cars were in the lot, which wasn't entirely surprising for a weekend, even in the off-season. Although, with it being the Sunday before Thanksgiving, he'd figured the place would be deserted. Assuming everyone was traveling to see loved ones, he didn't think there'd be much, if any, tourist trade.

Lilly was already unbuckled by the time he got out and opened the rear door. They'd been to see the turtles pretty much every day since he'd first shown her the egg mound, even if just for a quick hello to Paddlefoot. Morgan worried she was getting way too attached, worried what would happen if one of the turtles didn't make it through rehab, or when they were released or shipped out to a long-term facility. But then he'd look at the excitement on her face and think . . . that had to be a good thing, right?

Since their first visit, none of the turtles had been released nor had the eggs hatched, but he'd been thinking maybe they should start talking to Lilly about how the process worked.

"Come on," she urged, taking his hand.

He had stuffed the hair paraphernalia in his jacket pocket, so he grabbed the manila envelope from where he'd set it on the roof of the truck. "Okay, okay." He had to admit, her enthusiasm was always contagious.

As soon as they entered the doors and pushed through the hanging plastic strips, Lilly immediately pulled back and tucked herself close to his legs. At least a dozen folks were milling about in the front visitor area, all adults.

Morgan instinctively rested his hand on her shoulder. Usually Gabe and occasionally, his wife Anne, along with the small crew of college interns and volunteers, were the only ones in the facility. There had never been more than a couple visitors, dropping in to check out the facility.

Morgan spied Gabe on the far side of the room, talking with two of the members of the group. He lifted a hand in a short wave, but the good doctor was so intent on whatever conversation he was having he didn't notice.

Suddenly Lilly was tugging on Morgan's hand again. He glanced down and noticed she was looking through the sea of bodies to the doorway leading to the labs and the rehab area. He followed her gaze . . . straight to Kit, who was standing in the doorway.

She lifted a hand in a wave. They waved back, Lilly's a little more enthusiastic. Morgan was just hoping for the best, and wished he knew what that was.

Kit was wearing a turquoise blue lab coat with the center's sea turtle insignia stitched over one pocket. The rich color offset the vibrancy of her red hair and made her creamy skin look luminous. He wasn't close enough to see her eyes, but he bet that turquoise added a little flash to the green. His thoughts went to how that green had flashed when they'd almost kissed and how much he wouldn't mind seeing them flash like that again. He wasn't sure any amount of time was going to change his reaction to her.

"Come on, Moggy," Lilly whispered, and somehow managed to stay all but glued to his leg while simultaneously winding them through the throng with laserlike precision.

"Hey," he said to Kit as they arrived at the doorway. "What's with the crowd?" Yep, up close, everything about her was luminous.

She smiled easily at them, and he relaxed a little, telling himself he'd be happy to find a comfortable middle road. For Lilly's sake. Speaking for himself . . . he still wanted more. But it was what it was.

"One of the professors from the college in Savannah where Gabe occasionally teaches has family in for the holidays and they're doing some sightseeing. Apparently several of them are in the same field and wanted to see firsthand the work Gabe was doing."

She leaned a little closer, which surprised him, until he realized she was peering past him through the doorway. "I think I heard something about a donation." She straightened and smiled. "A sizable one. Apparently Gabe's professor friend is from a family with some pretty deep pockets." Almost immediately her smile faltered. "Uh—yeah." Her smile turned self-conscious, but her green eyes sparkled with humor. "Awkward."

"Nah. You don't get to pick your family." His smile froze for a moment. "Now I'm sorry." He smiled. "Awkward."

Her smile spread. "Well, you're right, you don't get to pick your family. Or, more to the point, who certain members of your family choose to marry. So . . . I guess you did your research on me. All that curiosity and tenacity, huh?"

He lifted a shoulder in a half shrug, but his smile was unrepentant. "I did. Nothing invasive, just wanted to know what happened. Seems like neither of us is a stranger to family issues."

"Mine are a more recent acquirement. My family is—was—the best."

"I'm sorry."

"For? I thought you didn't apologize for your family."

"I don't. Can't. My apology was for the loss of your family business. From what I read, it seemed you and the Bellamy women who came before you were a dedicated, passionate bunch. I think that's pretty great."

"I thought so, too."

She didn't add anything more, and the silence grew beyond a few seconds.

He didn't want to offer what would surely sound like empty platitudes to her, no matter how sincerely he meant them. Regardless of the fact that he'd played no personal role in the matter, he doubted she cared much what any Westlake thought of her recent misfortunes. Instead, he asked, "What was it like, growing up in a happy family business?"

She took a moment to consider the question, or more likely his possible reasons for asking it. "It was unique, different, to be sure. But it was my whole world, so I didn't know anything else. I absolutely loved it."

She smiled, and the sincere affection and love he saw reflected in her eyes caught at something inside him.

"My mom, my grandmother, and my great-grandmother were wonderful women, great role models. It was impossible not to get caught up in their passion and enthusiasm for what they were doing. Well, impossible for me. My younger sister was clearly immune."

She tried to pass that last bit off with dry humor, but he hadn't missed the flicker of pain, of hurt, and the even greater flash of guilt. It had been so recent, he understood why she was still feeling raw.

"Well, not everyone falls easily into the family way of life," he said wryly. When her chin came up, he added, "Of course, I just walked away from mine."

"Right." She considered him for a moment. "Growing up in your family business was probably a great deal different from mine."

"You have no idea," he said, maintaining the humor.

"I'm sure I don't." She said it simply and honestly.

Her expression shifted again, and the walls lowered once more. "I'm . . . I never got the chance to say it, but I'm very sorry for your loss, too. I—" She broke off, glanced down at Miss Lilly, then quickly back to him, looking a little stricken that she might have spoken out of turn, with the child present who'd also suffered the same tragic loss. "I'm . . . I didn't—"

"It's . . . don't worry," he said. "And . . . thank you. I know you've experienced loss of loved ones, too. It came up when I read some articles on you," he explained. "I wasn't prying—well, I was, but . . ."

"I understand. A lot was written about the court proceedings over the Tas-T-Snaks sale, so you could hardly miss the details about every aspect of the Bellamy family. I guess we've both been through . . ."

"A lot," he finished for her, when she seemed unsure just what to say.

"Yeah." She offered up a brief smile.

"It was a great story, your family business. Your great-grandmother starting up a pie business in her own kitchen during the war, then taking off with it as she did. Very unusual for a woman at that time."

"She had the support of her brother. He was infirm and couldn't go to war, but he had this mathematical genius brain and put it to work to help grow the business."

"He was in banking, right?"

Kit nodded. "All the Bellamy men were. It was as much their tradition as it was for the women to run the pie business. They invested the money Mamie Sue made, and Mamie Sue, her daughter-in-law, and hers after that—my mother—all relished the challenge." Kit smiled briefly, and he saw the love and the loss . . . and the guilt starkly in her eyes. "I did, too."

He wanted to cup the curve of her cheek with his palm, ease the sadness, the self-recrimination. From what he'd read, she never saw it coming. Her faith in Mamie Sue's had been as blind as it had been absolute. He didn't fault her for that, but he was certain, from the look on her face and the emotion that colored her words, that she did. Unfortunately, he doubted she'd be receptive to any kind of solace from him.

"I am sorry, Kit," he said, realizing he was speaking of the loss of her business, but also for the loss of the opportunity to ever find out what could become of this . . . thing they had between them. It was still there, just as palpable as before. More so, perhaps, given their determination to ignore it. She captivated him, and that feeling was deepening with each subsequent meeting.

"I'm just glad they didn't live to see how horribly I screwed it up."

"From what I read, you didn't. You trusted your sister and your brother-in-law to have the company's best interests at heart, just as you did. Given Carruthers's own personal fortune, there was really no reason to think otherwise."

"Did you know Teddy? I think he was a frat brother to one of the Westlakes. That's how he came to hire the firm."

"Maybe my brother, Asher, or one of my many cousins, but no, not me. I know the family name, though."

"Your . . . family business," she said, after a moment. "How did that begin?"

The question surprised him. "I'm not entirely sure."

That wasn't true. He'd been educated in the Westlake ancestry by his tutors as if it had been another schoolroom subject, right along with geography and science. But he doubted she really wanted to hear the murky details.

"Westlakes have been working in various positions within the court system so far back, those courts were originally run by royals rather than judges."

"Quite a history, then."

"Yes . . . it is that." The corners of his mouth curved up. "I managed to crush not only my mother's hopes, but those of veritable legions of my ancestors, by not taking my rightful place in the family empire."

"You did follow their footsteps into law, however."

"It was the wrong kind, so that didn't count."

"Wrong kind?"

He smiled. "Helping those in need. The kind who generally don't have deep pockets to pay for big hourly billing."

"Ah."

"Indeed."

"How did you manage it? That's a lot of pressure."

"It took some doing, plotting the big escape."

"My guess is that's an understatement." Kit's attention became more focused then, more personal. "So . . . when, exactly, did you know you wanted out? My sister never had the slightest interest in peanut pie or the business of making and selling it. No interest in any aspect of it, even as a little girl."

"Maybe not as early on as that. It took me a while longer to figure out what I wanted . . . and what I didn't. I think maybe in your sister's case, it wasn't the family, just their chosen profession, she wasn't interested in."

"True. So . . . it was the other way around for you?"

"I actually like my profession, very much, in fact. I just had to find a branch of it that called to me personally."

"And that wasn't good enough for your family? I mean, you did follow your ancestors at least to some degree."

His tone was quite wry, as he said, "In my family, there are no degrees, no shades of gray."

She surprised him by smiling back with the same bit of a dry twist to her lips. "Well . . . yeah. I got that."

Both were smiling as they shook their heads. Still, the differences between them, their pasts, the roles they played in their own family dynamics, and how those dynamics had impacted them . . . and in the case of his family, impacted her directly . . . couldn't have been more clearly stated.

He was going to have to accept that his interest in her, his attraction to her, had no future. It meant he was going to have to stop thinking about her like that.

Their gazes caught just then and their smiles widened easily, naturally. The amused kind of smile that spoke of personal jokes and shared, insider knowledge. They "got" each other, as the saying went.

It was the kind of connection he'd never shared with anyone. *Good luck with the getting over it part,* he thought.

Lilly chose that moment to squeeze in between them and slither through the gap in the doorway. "Can I go see Paddlefoot?"

"Sure," he said, reluctant to end the conversation, but grateful for the intrusion. No point in furthering things. "Let's go on back and—"

"Morgan?"

Morgan turned at the sound of Gabe calling him. Lilly was still tugging on his hand.

"I'll take her back," Kit offered.

Morgan's head swiveled from Gabe back to Kit, but before he could say anything, Lilly let go of his hand . . . and took Kit's extended one.

"I wore my sweatshirt for him," Lilly was telling her. "Moggy got it for me. It's got a turtle on the front."

He traded smiles with Kit over Lilly's head as the two

headed back to the rehab area. *Thank you,* he mouthed, then shook his head as he turned back to Gabe. Lilly was such a mystery to him. On the one hand, she was shy and withdrawn around new people, new things. On the other, she'd take the hand of someone she'd only recently met and walk off with her, chatting up a storm. He should probably have a talk with her about that, but . . . in this case, he couldn't say he faulted her instincts.

"Hey," Gabe said as he met Morgan in the doorway. "I need a favor. A big one."

Morgan turned to face him. "Sure. Big how?"

"Can you spare me a few hours?" Gabe seemed flustered.

Morgan's eyes widened briefly. "What's up?"

"As you can see, I have a contingent here, and—"

"Kit said it was the family of one of the professors you work with in Savannah."

Gabe nodded, glancing back at the milling group. "Yes. Several of them are professors with the same interest. I'd like to show them the facility, give them the grand tour."

Morgan leaned closer, smiling. "I hear there might be some donation money at stake here."

That seemed to fluster the good doctor even more. "Yes, quite possibly." He glanced over his shoulder again. "Quite."

"Gabe?"

The doctor turned back. "Right. Actually, I'm as interested in getting the other professors more personally invested in my project here as anything. They carry considerable clout and could get some favorable attention paid to us, in the form of grant monies and the like, over the long haul."

Morgan began to see why he was so nervous. "A lot of opportunities, then. That's good."

"Great, in fact. I just—I wasn't prepared."

Morgan had only planned to be at the center for an hour or so. Enough time to let Lilly visit with her turtles and for him and Gabe to finalize some paperwork. Morgan was still doing consulting work on a number of cases back in Colorado, as well as Utah and Arizona, and his preliminary work with Gabe's center had already attracted attention from two other facilities; one on the Gulf coast, the other in the Florida Keys. All of which he was planning to devote some time and energy to that day.

But one look at the stark expression on Gabe's face when he finally shifted his full attention to Morgan, and he was already mentally juggling everything. "What can I do to help?"

"The facility on Jekyll called. They need to make room for an emergency rescue that was brought in this morning. A big one. We need to go and get some of their turtles."

Chapter 11

"Their facility is easily four times the size of yours," Morgan said, surprised at the news. "How big is big?"

"Three mature loggerheads. Two are over three hundred pounds. And a nine-hundred-pound leatherback. All of them are in pretty bad shape. The leatherback was a boat hit and the others were longlines," he explained.

Standard practice for some fisheries was to set long trawling lines, with hooks that often snagged sea turtles. Being reptiles, the turtles needed to surface periodically to breathe, and, when hooked under water, they would either drown or tear themselves up trying to get free before the lines were checked. Getting caught in longlines, trawling nets, and other commercial fishing gear was the biggest threat to their ongoing survival and a big reason they were on the endangered list.

"That's a lot of turtle," Morgan said.

"Right."

"So, what are we bringing up here?"

"Five young turtles; three are loggerheads, two are very young hawksbills, so they're pretty small, and one mature loggerhead, running about two-hundred-seventy-five. All of them are out of danger, health-wise. They are either waiting for release or for adoption into a zoo or long-term facility. We'll keep them here until that happens or until Jekyll can take them back." Gabe's expression was bleak. "There didn't seem to be a great deal of optimism on the new arrivals, but just in case . . ."

"I'm sorry. And sure, I can go. Just tell me what to do."

"I need to send two people—one to drive, one to monitor the turtles during transport back. I have two new interns coming in shortly, but was thinking maybe, since you know Kit, the two of you—"

"Wouldn't the interns be more experienced? I mean, than either Kit or myself?"

Gabe shook his head. "When I said new, I didn't mean just new to me. They're coming here to help out for the holiday break. Today is their first day. Ever."

"Ah. Wow."

"One is nineteen, the other eighteen, both freshmen, so, I'd feel better with someone a little more . . . seasoned. The folks down at Jekyll will know what to do to get the turtles loaded up and will explain what you need to do during transport. They're healthy, so it's more just keeping them safe during the drive. It's not that far, it's off-season, and a Sunday, so it shouldn't be too bad a trip. Once you get back here, I can help oversee the off-loading and getting them situated. I'll put the interns to work prepping for their arrival."

"Okay, okay, no problem. Wait—what about—can Lilly come with us?"

"I don't think that would be a good idea. I can't guarantee what she'd see down there. Things are a little . . . frantic, at the moment."

"Right, okay." Morgan glanced behind him to the rehab area. "Maybe leave Kit with her and send an intern with me? She trusts Kit, and if Kit's willing . . ."

Gabe smiled for the first time. "I'm sure she'd be happy to. She's a very sharp girl and seems genuinely interested in the work here. And in Miss Lilly."

Gabe's expression implied Kit's genuine interest might extend beyond just Miss Lilly, but Morgan hardly thought Gabe was in the frame of mind at the moment to continue his matchmaking efforts.

Just then, both interns arrived and wound their way through the group still clustered in the greeting area, heading toward Gabe and Morgan.

"Dr. Langley?" The shorter one was maybe five foot tall, at best.

If she weighed more than a hundred pounds soaking wet, Morgan would have been surprised. *Probably not a good candidate for big turtle transport.*

"We're the interns, from the university?" Intern number two was male and more closely resembled a college fullback than a scientist.

Morgan's hopes went up.

"I'm Flip and this is Greta," he went on to say.

"Hi," Greta chimed in. Perky, blond, and energetic, she was the cheerleader to Flip's football player. "I'm here for as long as you need me today, but Flip is just—"

"I had a call from my family," Flip broke in to explain. "My grandmother—she's eighty-two—just went to the emergency room. I'm really sorry to duck in and run, but it's the holidays and everyone is at my house and my mother is—I really need to—"

"He was my ride out here," Greta said, talking over him. "He made sure to get me here and wanted to at least meet you. He's really dedicated to this, Dr. Langley. And we're super excited to get to work with you and the loggerheads. I hope this doesn't mean—"

"Once I get to the hospital and find out what the deal

is, I will call," Flip promised. "I really want to be here, Dr. Langley."

"Oh, he does," Greta assured them. "We both do. Really."

Gabe and Morgan had been watching the two young students as if they were observing a high-speed Ping-Pong match.

Gabe reached out and shook Greta's proffered hand, then shook Flip's hand as well, probably more to stem the word flow than anything else. "I'm happy to have two such dedicated individuals. Your enthusiasm is duly noted. Flip, please, head on out and my good wishes and Godspeed to your family. I'll keep your grandmother in my thoughts. Don't worry about things here; we'll figure out a schedule for you later."

"Thanks, Dr. Langley." He glanced at Morgan, seemed unsure what to say to him, then lifted a hand. "Okay, so, I'm outta here." He looked at Greta and paused. "Will you be able to get back okay?"

"We'll work something out," Gabe assured them.

Flip nodded. "Okay. Cool." He wove his large frame back through the crowd.

"He's really great," Greta said, looking after Flip, with—if Morgan wasn't mistaken—a bit more in her eyes than simple admiration for his scientific dedication.

That made him smile. And hope like hell he didn't look at Kit like that.

"I'm sure he is," Gabe said. "Listen, we've had a few things drop in our laps today, so it's not a normal routine at the moment. Far from it. I need to . . . take care of a few things, and then I'll be with you to get you settled in. In the meantime, go ahead and take a good look at the facility, the labs, the rehab area."

Greta's face shone with excitement. "Excellent. I'm on

it, Dr. Langley!" And with that, she ducked past him and began her exploration.

"Wow," Morgan said. "I think, right at this moment, this is the oldest I've ever felt."

Gabe chuckled at that. "It only gets worse, my friend. It only gets worse. But I'm happy for the enthusiasm. Keeps me young."

Morgan turned back to Gabe. "I'm not sure what to do about Lilly. She doesn't know anyone here yet that she's really comfortable with, other than you, and, I guess, Kit." He wished things had progressed better with Birdie, but that was going to take time.

"I can keep her with me on the facility tour, then let her color while Greta watches her."

"You don't need to be dealing with that. This is important for you. And Greta seems to be a nice girl, but Lilly isn't always good right off with—"

"Hey, Doc."

Gabe and Morgan looked up. The body of the person belonging to the voice was kind of lost, weaving through the crowd, but he'd recognize that purple Mohawk anywhere.

"I have samples," Dre said as she made it through the throng. "Big crowd today."

Cupcake samples? Morgan thought that was kind of odd, but maybe the bakery offered samples to local businesses. Then she pulled a manila envelope out of her black messenger bag.

"Let me know if this works. I think I captured what you wanted with the graphics and got the information organized in a way that would encourage a person to actually read it."

Gabe opened the envelope and slid out a couple brochures for the center. His face instantly brightened. "These look great. I'd like to go over them more thoroughly." He looked up at her. "Things are a bit crazy at the moment—"

"No problem. I figured as much. Actually, I was going to ask if it would be okay to look around, maybe hang out a bit. I was working off your other material and our conversation, but . . . it kind of got me interested in finding out more. I have some ideas I'd like to talk over with you." She lifted a hand. "Don't worry, doesn't have to be today. And it isn't going to cost you anything. It's . . . just something I want to do."

"Sure, of course." Gabe's cell started buzzing in his lab coat pocket. He checked the screen. "It's Jekyll. Let me take this."

"Okay," Dre said. When Gabe stepped away she turned to Morgan. "I'm glad you're here."

His eyebrows lifted. "You are?"

"Well, glad, meaning if you're here, your niece is probably here, too."

Sounds more like the Dre I'd met, Morgan thought, amused. "She is. What's up?"

"Cool kid."

He smiled. "I think so. She liked you, too."

Dre smiled, and it struck him how dramatically that altered her otherwise . . . interesting visage. Between the Mohawk, the multiple piercings, kohl-heavy makeup, and fairly gender non-specific clothing she wore, he didn't know quite what to make of her. But, when she smiled, she was actually quite a beautiful young woman, in an uncommon kind of way.

He thought about the elaborate, delicate, and quite feminine fairy tattoo on her neck, and, when she smiled, it all seemed to make a little more sense.

"Cool. So, while I was doing this work for the doc, I went ahead and put together a little book for Lilly. Kit said she's really taken with the turtles, and I know she likes to color." She reached in her messenger bag and pulled out a spiral bound notebook about half the size of a standard coloring book, but about three times as thick. "It's nothing fancy, but"—she shrugged and handed it to Morgan—"I thought she might get a kick out of it."

The cover was sturdy black mat board and featured a beautiful print of a wide blue ocean with a single sea turtle swimming in the midst of its rich vastness. Below that, in a whimsical print evoking images of mermaids and other nautical fantasies, it said *The Adventures of Paddlefoot & Friends.*

Morgan flipped it open and discovered the contents were separated by a half dozen tabbed dividers. Between them were a mix of pages with outlined images of turtles and seascapes, some very simplistic, some far more detailed, along with lined journal paper, and other pages that were entirely blank.

"I thought it was something she might keep. Color in the easier stuff now, maybe the more detailed stuff later. If she wants to write stories, or just her thoughts, the lined paper is for that. And the blank paper is for whatever she wants to do. Draw her own pictures, write more. The paper I used is for multimedia, so she can color, paint, marker, anything."

Morgan continued to flip through the book. "This is . . ." He looked up to find Dre watching him closely, her normally unreadable expression replaced by one of . . . nervous anticipation. She was trying to sound casual, but clearly it meant something to her.

"It's stunning," he finished. "Thoughtful and . . . really wonderful. Thank you. Very much. She's going to love this."

Dre beamed, and he wanted to tell her she should do that more often. She really was a beautiful young woman, inside and out. "Good. I'm glad."

"Where did you get these drawings? These prints? They're amazing."

"Oh, I did those."

His mouth actually dropped open and he flipped through the book again. "Wow. This is . . . a lot of work."

"Not really. I mean, I drew up a ton of things for Gabe, and, well, for myself. Turns out these guys kind of grab at you, the more you get to know about them. And . . . well, it's my thing. It's fun."

"It's definitely that. You're . . . amazingly talented."

Her lips twisted in a wry half smile. "You sound surprised."

He looked up, instantly contrite. "No, not at all."

"Don't sweat it. A lot of people underestimate me. I'm used to it."

"I'd like to think I'm not that person. But . . . maybe I was, a little. My apologies." He smiled. "Never hurts to take a good look in the mirror once in a while. I appreciate the opportunity."

Her expression turned to one of studied observation. "I was prepared not to like you before we even met."

His eyes widened, not because the comment surprised him, but because she'd admitted it. "I gathered as much, that day in the bakery."

"I guess we both need to look in the mirror every so often."

He grinned. "Apparently." He lifted the journal. "Would you like to give this to her? She's going to absolutely be head over heels about it. And coming from you . . . well, she was really taken with you, and she doesn't warm up so quickly to many people."

"Ditto," Dre said. "I'm not much for blending in."

"I got that," Morgan said, and they both exchanged wry smiles. "But I think you enjoy standing out."

"It's . . . amusing. At times. I'm just being who I am, though."

"That's all we should be."

She gave him a more pointed once-over. "You'll do, Westlake."

He chuckled, then cradled the book against his chest and stuck out his hand. "Ditto."

She shook it; her fingers were long, slender, her hand far more delicate and soft than he might otherwise have anticipated. An odd amalgam, Miss Dre.

"I probably shouldn't tell you this," she said, "and don't let it go to your pretty head, but we're rooting for you."

Morgan frowned. "Rooting?" he said, confused. "For me? How?"

"You've got it all over the mechanic dude. He's a good guy, but totally not right for her."

"What mechanic dude?" For a moment, Morgan thought maybe she'd been referring to him and Lilly, making their home on Sugarberry and being accepted by the locals. But . . . *what*?

Dre sighed the sigh of young people everywhere, when their elders didn't get the drift. "You have more of a shot than you think you do, that's all I'm sayin'." She shook her head, when his brow furrowed more deeply. "Okay," she muttered under her breath, "so maybe age always matters."

"I'm sorry, I really don't get—"

"Just tryin' to help."

"Dre, Morgan." Gabe walked over just then, looking truly concerned. "That was Jekyll. They really need us down there, pronto."

"What's up?" Dre asked.

"We need to lend an assist with temporary housing," Gabe told her. "I'll just have to send Greta with you, Morgan, and see if Kit will watch over Miss Lilly."

"I can watch Lilly," Dre offered. "How long?"

Morgan turned to her. He wouldn't have thought of her as babysitter material, but opinions change, and his had. Plus, Lilly liked Dre. "It would be at least a few hours. Maybe even four or five?" He glanced at Gabe, who nodded in agreement. "Gabe's got this tour, and new interns, and—"

"Say no more. I'm on it." Dre held out her hand. "I'll take the book back and send Kit up."

"You sure?" Morgan asked. "I mean, Lilly will love it, but that's a lot to ask."

"You're saying more and time's wasting. When I'm on it, I'm on it." She wiggled the fingers of her extended hand. "Gimme."

Morgan's wry smile returned as he handed her the spiral bound journal. "Appreciated."

"No worries." She smiled and brushed past him. "Besides, now you'll owe me."

"I'll be happy to help you whenever there's something you need."

She paused, looked back. "I think you mean that."

He grinned. "Just being myself."

"Huh. You know, we may be more alike than you think."

"Scary, right?"

Dre's lips twisted in that half smile and she started toward the back again.

"Just don't shave her head or tattoo her, and we'll be fine," Morgan called behind her.

"Not to worry," she called back, turning and continuing to walk backwards. "I only shave and tattoo on Wednesdays."

"Very funny."

"Besides, she's not the type for tats."

"Good to know you feel that way."

Dre paused just before pushing the swinging door that led to the rehab area. "Oh, she'll be the type for something. But probably not that." She grinned. "Probably." Pushing through the door, she let it swing shut behind her.

"I'm sure they'll be fine," Gabe said, looking worriedly at Morgan.

"Oh, I know they will." Morgan glanced toward the back, then heard a loud girlish squeal of delight coming from the other side of the door. "That's what worries me." But though Dre was a complex young woman, , anyone who would put that much thought, care, and personal time into making such a gift, simply because she wanted to, was all right in his book.

Lilly burst through the swinging door a moment later, carrying the journal clutched to her chest. Kit came through the door just behind her.

"Moggy, Moggy, look!"

Morgan crouched down and caught Lilly as she all but ran over him. "I know, awesome, right?"

She showed him the book, her eyes shining more brightly than he could recall seeing in a very, very long time. "Amazing." She drew out the word, then giggled when he laughed. "Miss Dre is going to stay with me. Miss Kit said you and her are going to get more turtles."

"We are. Will you be okay with Miss Dre?"

Lilly nodded without hesitation, but asked, "Can't we come, too?"

"I'm afraid there's no room. But you can see them when we get back and watch us unload them."

Gabe bent down and propped his hands on his knees. "Maybe you and Miss Dre can help us get their tanks set up."

Lilly looked at him, her expression one of absolute awe. "Can we?" she asked in a hushed tone.

"I'll talk to Miss Greta, and she'll come get you in a little bit, okay?"

"Okay," Lilly said, her expression the kind normally worn by kids on Christmas morning. "Thank you, Dr. Langley."

Gabe beamed. "You're very welcome, my dear. I appreciate the help."

"Okay," Morgan said, "you go on back with Miss Dre. We need to get going."

Lilly hugged Morgan tightly, then skipped back through the door to the rehab area, journal still clutched to her chest. Morgan could hear her excitedly telling Dre about their new job.

He straightened and caught Kit's expression as she was watching Lilly's exit. Her face was filled with the amusement of someone utterly charmed, but there was also a look of true affection. Something about the unguarded honesty of her expression caught at him and caused a funny little flutter in his chest.

"That was a pretty awesome journal Dre made," she said, turning back to him.

"She's very talented."

"I know. You should see the apron she designed for me for Babycakes."

"I'd like to." He quickly added, "Lilly wants to come by and see how your shop is coming along. I've been trying to explain how it works, but seeing it would probably make it clearer to her." He smiled. "She's afraid your feelings will be hurt if we don't buy your cupcakes, too."

"Aw. Sure, that would be fine. We're done with demo now, so it's a mess, but not dangerous."

"Great. Thanks. And thank you for being so good with her. It means a lot."

"Oh, of course. She's delightful. I enjoy spending time with her."

"Um, can I show you the transport truck?" Gabe interrupted.

"Oh." Kit's cheeks turned pink. "Right! Sorry. We were just—"

"That we were," Morgan said, shooting a fast wink at Kit, then saluted Gabe. "Lead on, MacLangley. Your turtle transport team is on the job."

Chapter 12

On the way down to Jekyll, Kit sat up front with Morgan. "This is my first time seeing this side of the operation. I didn't even know he had his own transport truck. Pretty cool, actually."

"Used to be an emergency vehicle. Gabe got it at auction a few years ago. Had to overhaul the engine, then had it refurbished to handle a different kind of patient."

"Makes sense, really."

"Actually, from what he told me, the idea came from a guy here on Sugarberry. Dylan Ross. He runs an auto shop down by the docks on the other end of the island. Gabe said he did most of the work gratis . . . as a contribution to the center. Gabe just paid for parts."

"Good idea from a good guy, then."

"From what I hear." Morgan seemed to get lost in his train of thought for a moment, and she thought he murmured something like "that mechanic dude?" under his breath, but she didn't question him on it. "You, ah, you know him?" he asked a moment later.

"Who? The auto mechanic? No, haven't had the pleasure. Why?"

"No reason."

She cast him a sideways glance, but his attention was on the road, and a smile hovered around his mouth. They fell into an extended silence as Morgan continued to make his way south. It wasn't uncomfortable, but it wasn't easy, either. Much as Kit had been staying focused on getting Babycakes up and running and on her new volunteer work at the center, Morgan had still managed to factor into her thoughts far more often than she'd like to admit. The tension simmering between them was exactly why. It led to restless nights and vivid dreams about things her conscious mind knew better than to explore . . . but with which her subconscious mind was having a veritable field day.

If she thought about it too much, she'd be squirming in her seat.

Though it appeared he was going to honor her "casual acquaintances" request, there was still a particular . . . look in his eyes when their gazes connected. It was not quite amused, not quite knowing, or maybe a little of both. Apparently, no matter what social barriers she put up, there was going to be no stopping that heightened sense of awareness they shared.

Of course, he'd come right out and said he was attracted to her. After she shut that down, she figured a man who looked like he did wouldn't waste more time on a dead end like her, but would move on to a more willing recipient. Given his looks and his family name . . . finding someone couldn't be all that challenging. Even on an island as small as Sugarberry.

She hadn't heard any whispers to that effect, though. Not that her fellow Cupcake Club bakers would have bothered to whisper. She wished they'd taken the hint as well as Morgan had.

She hadn't been certain how she'd feel when she saw him again. He'd been the subject of much chatter in the kitchen, and even more in her own, private deliberations, but none of it had changed her mind. She'd hoped, upon seeing him again, she could be pragmatic.

She sent another sideways glance in his direction, only to find his gaze connecting with hers. He shot her a fast grin, and there was that look again . . . like he knew exactly what she'd been thinking. Had she been fidgeting in her seat, after all?

She shifted her gaze out the front window as casually as possible, but no amount of casual kept the heat from warming her cheeks. Not to mention other, more sensitive parts of her body. *Honestly, Katherine Mary Margaret Bellamy. Get a damn grip.*

All that made her think about his hands. She'd noticed them straight off, when he'd handled the kite. Big hands, but gentle when they protected Lilly during her shy phases and skilled when they hammered nails and hung bulletin boards. She knew what they'd felt like on her, too—on her arms anyway. And . . . she really needed to stop thinking about them or she would be doing more than shifting in her seat.

"Do you have plans for the holiday?"

His deep, smooth voice didn't so much jerk her from her guilty thoughts as feed straight into them. "Thanksgiving?" she managed, though she had to discreetly clear her throat to get the sex kitten out of it. What was wrong with her? Alva's preoccupation with her "dry spell" filtered through Kit's mind. *It has been a long time. A really long time. Dammit.*

Morgan sent a sideways smile her way. "That would be the one."

She smiled, too, feeling beyond ridiculous. What was she, sixteen? "We're ah, we're all having a group dinner."

"All?"

"Oh, sorry. I mean the Cupcake Club."

He grinned outright at that, and it was infectious. "You have a club for cupcakes? Sounds like my kind of organization."

More relaxed and more stimulated, all at the same time, she laughed. "It's a group of Lani's friends and associates who get together every week and do some after-hours baking. Kind of like a quilting club or book club . . . only we—"

"Commune over cupcakes."

"More or less. It's a rather . . . eclectic group, but I like them a lot." She grinned. "Okay, so maybe I fit right in. It's nothing like Mamie Sue's, but it fills a certain void, not working with the crews every day anymore."

"I think I've met a few of them. They seem like a nice bunch." He laughed. "Though I admit, I had my reservations about Dre. Or she had them about me, or maybe both. She changed all that today, though."

"She's like that, very unexpected, but you'd want her having your back."

"Definitely would rather that than the alternative."

Kit laughed. "Well, that, too. They're very loyal. We haven't known each other long, but with the shop and everyone in and out all the time, I feel like we've already become friends. It's been nice. More than nice. Definitely unexpected."

"Sounds like a good entrée to island life."

"It has been. I'm thankful . . . and grateful for them."

"Sounds like a good reason to give thanks together, then."

She settled back more in her seat. "You know, you're right, it certainly does. I didn't know how I was going to deal with . . . well, everything, moving forward. Actually, the holidays coming made me a little sad—maybe a lot sad—but that was really the least of my worries, all things considered. Still, I can't say I was looking forward to them. But now . . . well, I am. Very much."

"They're always saying life moves in mysterious ways."

She laughed. "Exactly. So what about you? Are you and Miss Lilly heading home for the holidays?"

Being part of a fractured family herself, she felt a connection to him she hadn't anticipated. For family reasons—she missed hers and he was intentionally escaping his—they'd come to be in the same place at the same time, as part of a new life cycle. She wasn't sure how she felt about having personal understanding of him. It was a lot like the road trip they were on . . . not exactly uncomfortable, but not simple, either.

"We're staying on Sugarberry," he said. "We haven't been here all that long yet, and I want to keep Lilly's life and routine as steady and stable as possible before we bring family back into it. Well, my side of the family anyway."

"I hope this isn't too personal, but—"

"I'm pretty sure, given everything we know about one another already, that's one thing we don't have to worry about."

She smiled. "Yeah . . . maybe not. I was going to say that Alva mentioned the picnic with Birdie wasn't as great as you'd hoped. I haven't met Birdie, but I've heard Alva talk about her at length, and I know she's so grateful that you're trying."

"We are. We'll get there. It will just take a little time."

"Understandable," Kit said. "Poor thing has been through so much. You, too. I'm guessing this first round of holidays since . . . everything happened can't be easy. I'm sorry. We don't have to talk about it. I probably shouldn't have asked."

"No, that's okay. Actually, I haven't talked about it with anyone and . . . it's almost a relief."

Kit wasn't sure what to say to that, or how she felt about him opening up to her, but she'd asked. Given how grateful she was to the cupcake crew for their friendship and support, she wouldn't turn away from him if he needed the same. "How are you two coping? Is she doing okay? Do you think she'll handle Christmas all right?"

"I honestly don't know. I haven't spent the holidays at home in a very long time, but I miss Asher and Delilah, and I worry all the time whether I'm doing right by Lilly.

"I've always made time for her throughout the year, ever since she was born. The holiday season is a very intense one at the Westlake household, and not in a good way, so I would come and visit her and the family at other times of the year. This is really our first Christmas together, and . . . I can't make it not hurt and I can't make it not hard, but I do want it to be as relaxed and as easy on both of us as I can. I want her to have sentimental traditions and goofy traditions and believe in Santa and all that . . . so, maybe not too much this year, but enough so it's something she looks forward to next year."

"Didn't you have those things? Growing up, I mean? I'd think a family as old and established as yours would have some really deeply rooted traditions."

"Oh, they do." His tone was wry . . . and weary.

"Sorry," she said. "I don't want to stir up—"

"No, that's okay. My family." He let out a humorless laugh. "God, where to begin? We had traditions, but I can't say they were the kind that made you feel all warm and fuzzy. My mother isn't really the warm and fuzzy type, but it goes much farther back than that. Let's just say the Westlakes aren't so much a sentimental bunch as a family that never fails to find a way to turn any occasion into a potential boon for the family business. The holidays are seen more for their usefulness in networking and making sure to impress all the right people with just the right social engagements than they are about family or . . . well, any of the things I always wished Christmas and Thanksgiving could be about."

"I'm sorry," she said, not in a pitying way, but simply meaning it. "Sounds . . . removed. And lonely, actually."

"Yes, it was. Fortunately, Lilly is young, so there's still time to give her the kind of Christmas I always wished I'd had. Growing up, my friends would talk about their holidays, and since I've been in Colorado, I've experienced them firsthand like that." He shrugged. "Let's just say I know which way I prefer. And I want that for Lilly, too."

"Do you miss your friends out west?"

"I do, yeah. A great deal. We've been keeping in touch, though, and I still do consultant work that keeps me connected out there, so it's been okay. Better than I thought it would be, anyway."

"Did you consider taking Lilly back there? I mean, it was your home."

"When everything happened . . . it was so sudden. I'm Lilly's godfather, and I knew Asher had wanted to name me guardian in full, should anything happen. None of us thought it would ever be needed, but . . . now it has. And I love her so much, I'd do anything for her."

He slowed the truck as they bumped over the grids to another bridge and briefly glanced at Kit. "Our lives got turned inside out on that single night. So, nothing was going to be the same, anyway. I knew I wasn't going to stay in Atlanta, at least not at the family estate. But I was never interested in taking Lilly away from my mother entirely, for either of their sakes. I don't want her to ever forget her mother, her father, or her time in Atlanta. I want her to have *all* the family she has, around her."

"You mean Birdie."

He nodded. "I decided it was best to stay here—enough distance for me to take care of Lilly the way I want to take care of her, but pretty close to everyone."

"You want to give her a real home, and not a family compound."

He glanced at her again. "Exactly. Is that what you had?"

"No." She smiled. "We're new money, and most of that went back into the company. We kept the house Mamie had during the war, which went way back in the family. As things grew, so did the house, with additions stuck on here and there, every which way, but . . . even as things changed, they stayed very much the same." She sighed. "I loved that house. I used to spend hours looking through all the old photo albums Mamie kept. So much of what we had was pretty much what I saw in those photos, just updated and expanded. We had traditions, tons of them, but they were . . ." She paused, then let the sentence trail off.

"Exactly what I'd want Lilly to have," he finished quietly, but also with an easy smile.

"Thank you. That's really nice of you to say. They were everything to me. Let's just say we're both missing things from yesteryear this time around."

"I'm sorry," he said, and she understood what he meant.

"I am, too. You know, it's funny, but for all that losing the company was devastating to me, because it was my life and my extended family all rolled into one, and because I felt like I'd ruined everything my family worked so hard to build—"

"You didn't ruin it, you—"

"I let someone else ruin it, which is just as bad, maybe worse. It'd be one thing if I just couldn't make a go of it, tough economy, whatever. I'd have gone down fighting, anyway."

"From what I read, you did fight. Hard."

"I did. I put everything I had into it, literally. But, as I said before, Teddy had deeper pockets than I did. And pricier lawyers."

Morgan shot her a glance, but she was smiling, albeit tightly. "If it hadn't been your family firm, it would have been one equally cutthroat." She winced. "Sorry."

"Don't be. They are."

"The thing is, it should never have come to lawyers and lawsuits. I should have known, should have seen it coming, but I just—"

"You trusted your brother-in-law, your family. It didn't all rest on your shoulders; you didn't have complete control. Your sister had half of it, didn't she? I mean, she's responsible for how she handled her part, and you're—"

"Trixie never had a clue about the business and didn't want one. I think the reason I never saw it coming is that Teddy is from a family almost as old as yours, with easily as much money. I think that's why my family welcomed him into the fold. Not because we liked him personally, all that much. He can be a bit . . . overbearing. But he honestly seemed to love my sister, and we knew he wasn't after her money, because he had more than enough for several lifetimes. That's what blinded me. Even though we became a successful family, we poured a lot of our earnings back into the business, and family always came first. The money was security. We lived very comfortably, but not ostentatiously." She smiled. "We're strong Irish stock and being frugal was also a big Bellamy tradition."

"Hence the twenty-four crayon pack."

She laughed outright. "Exactly."

"Nothing wrong with that."

"No, although my sister would beg to differ. But, see, even there, we thought, hey, this solves everything. Teddy could—and did—give her the life she'd always thought she deserved, and we didn't have to worry about someone taking advantage of her, and by extension, us.

"I just never saw it. Teddy was very aggressive in business. He wasn't just a name on the letterhead; he had a part in continuing the growth of his family fortune. When Trixie turned over her share of our pie company to him to handle, rather than me, I was okay with it. He demonstrated very quickly that he understood what he was doing, and seemed truly and sincerely interested. In that regard, I actually respected him. He seemed devoted to his part in the company, to the family, and though we differed in some ways, especially where it came to tradition and not everything having to be bigger, better, faster, I honestly thought he understood what Mamie Sue's was all about."

"If you respected his ideas, his decisions, it stands to reason you'd trust him."

"We had different goals, but I trusted his business acumen. He was all about Mamie Sue's making more money and I was about keeping it grounded in what we believed in, why we were in business in the first place. We had our struggles, our boardroom debates, but there was always balance, and I always felt, when push came to shove, he deferred to my ideas and decisions. Ultimately, he worked for his family full-time, and his work for us was just a sideline, something he did for his wife, and because, frankly, he was good at it. I knew he equated success with the bottom line, but I never thought he'd actually undermine us."

"That's because it was never about the money to you, so you don't understand the mind-set," Morgan said, not unkindly. "It's hard for someone who is living well, doing well, who feels happy and successful to understand that not everyone is motivated by living well and being happy. Someone like Teddy—I don't know the man, but I know many like him—sees growing a company as a contest, even if it's just with himself."

"But we were a big, successful company already. He

certainly didn't need more money. We didn't need more money. I mean, we wanted to keep growing, but we weren't failing. We were doing well."

"It's not about greed or saying you have *x* amount more money in your bank account than before," Morgan said. "It's about winning. Conquering. Owning, controlling. Not because you need to, but because you can. Because you're good at it. It's like a climber can't look at a mountain and not want to climb it. Teddy looked at Mamie Sue's and . . . couldn't help himself. That's how his mind works. Money and growing the bottom line is how the contest is measured. It's not because he needed more or even wanted more."

You're right. I don't get that. I didn't then and I don't now. How can a well-educated, smart man destroy something that meant so much to so many people? It was his own family. Well, his wife's family. Would he have done that to his own family business? I understand that he's good at making companies make as much money as they possibly can, but he could and did do that in his own world. Why do it to ours? Why do it to ours if it meant dismantling what we'd worked so hard for? Tearing it apart meant nothing to him."

"You said your sister never wanted the business, maybe . . . well, I don't want to say something out of line here, but—"

"No. I know what you're going to say, and I've asked myself the same thing. Did he sell off the family business because Trixie couldn't be bothered with it? It wasn't like Trixie actively wanted out, not that I knew about anyway. She was never in. She never had to lift a finger for the company. Teddy could have managed her shares hardly lifting a finger, if he'd chosen to. It's not that I never felt overwhelmed by the responsibility that had been so suddenly thrust on us—well, on me. I did, all the time. But I was handling it, and would have continued to do so, single-handedly and gladly. He could have left all of that to me and kept his focus on his own damn job. But it was like—"

"Crack to an addict," Morgan interjected.

"Exactly!"

"I know you don't get it, Kit, and that's a good thing. You're not supposed to get it. I never got it. People like Teddy and my own mother are all about the game. That is life to them. That's what makes it exciting and what feeds them. It's not about people—never something as emotional and human as that. People are too challenging and emotions are messy. Better to rise above all that and stay in that place where you can control everything in your environment. Then it all becomes like an elaborate, wily chess game. For those people, the stakes of day-to-day life just aren't high enough. They're born into money and know they're never going to lose everything. They're always going to live a comfortable life. So, they have to get their thrills somewhere."

"You make it all sound so—"

"Clinical? Cold? Unfeeling? It is. Or it certainly can be, if that's your mind-set. If Teddy is as much like my mother as it sounds, I'm sure what he did wasn't personal to him. He probably is as clueless about why this hurts you as you are to how he could do such a thing in the first place."

"Yes, he is completely clueless! You're exactly right. He was utterly blown away that I was going to fight the sale to Tas-T-Snaks. He couldn't fathom why I'd do that. My share of the buyout was quite healthy. I don't know what the heck he thought I'd do with a pile of money and no family business, but—"

"That's just it. He never would have thought of it that way. He'd figure you'd either do like your sister and enjoy your new life of leisure, or turn around and jump into some new game."

She slumped back in her seat and sighed ruefully. "Well, I guess he was right on that score. I had to jump somewhere."

Morgan shot her a wide grin. "Yeah. You don't strike me as a rest-on-her-big-buyout-payoff type."

She could have told him she wasn't the rest-on-her-broke-ass type either, but that really wasn't any of his business. After racking up legal bills that eclipsed her share of the buyout, she'd put her share of the family house up for collateral. In the end, she'd lost, and the lawyers had taken her buyout payoff and everything she had left, including her share of the house after Teddy and Trixie sold it.

The lawyers had told her if she'd been fighting anyone else, they'd have had a good chance. The legal fees alone were daunting, but since Teddy had deep pockets, he could go in for the long haul and not get hurt. Beating her in court was just the cost of doing business, no matter the fees involved.

Her financial adviser, in his last act before she had to let him go, too—no need for one when there was nothing left to advise on—had told her she should be grateful she wasn't in debt to her lawyers, the IRS, or anyone else. She was starting over from scratch, sure, but, hey, she wasn't in the hole. She was still having a hard time being all rosy about that. "That's the part that kills me the most."

"What part is that?"

She hadn't realized she'd spoken out loud. "Oh. Sorry. I was just—"

She really didn't want to talk about it. She was afraid she'd cry again. But she'd worked up a fair head of steam and as he'd said, talking about it, especially with someone who wasn't connected to it . . . She chuckled at the irony.

"What?" he asked.

"I was thinking I didn't want to explain, because it would likely make me cry. That's so becoming and all, plus, just what the designated driver in any road trip wants, a crying navigator."

"I don't want to make anyone cry, but if you want to talk it out—"

"That's what made me laugh. I was also thinking that you were right, talking about it was kind of a relief. Specifically, talking to someone who wasn't involved. And then I thought . . . how odd, that I'm unloading on a Westlake, of all people, about this particular tragedy."

"Maybe that's your karmic payoff," he said, laughing himself.

"More of those 'mysterious ways,' huh?"

He shrugged. "Might be. But I'm not connected, really, so . . . fire away."

"Well, it may be my karmic payoff, but it's certainly not yours to have to listen to it."

He looked at her, his expression open, easy and simply asked, "So, what was the part that killed you the most?"

She held his gaze for a moment; then he had to look back to the road. She kept looking at him, though. He really was a decent, good guy. And a Westlake. If that was karma, she didn't want to know how they'd gotten to this point.

After an extended silence, she answered his question. "Losing the house. If I had to choose between pie business or house, I'd have chosen the pie business. Which I did, and that's why I put my share of the house up during the court battle."

"What happened to it?"

"I couldn't buy my share back, so . . . it's gone."

"Gone, gone?"

"Trixie owned the other half and she's always hated it. She considered it an embarrassment to what she perceived as her social standing. It was a ramshackle, crazy house. It sat on a fair amount of property, though, and I guess I thought, if anything, maybe she'd just give it a giant makeover once it was all hers."

"But half went to your lawyers. Did they force a sale to get their share? Surely Teddy could have just bought them—"

"Oh, trust me, it never came to that. Trixie had it on the market almost before the judge's final rap of the gavel had finished echoing in the courtroom." Kit folded her arms loosely around her waist, looked out the window, but didn't really see anything. "I miss the business like crazy. But I'm getting back some of the personal fulfillment I got from it, here with the new bakery. Entirely different, but it's filling that void, as much as anything ever could, anyway."

"It's a much smaller endeavor."

"Yeah, but, I don't know . . . it suits me. Suits my life as it is now, or maybe it would have always suited me. After all I've been through, it's about as much responsibility as I want. I can work with Lani and Baxter; make sure to do whatever I need to, to make her vision a success. But I'm not responsible for hundreds of employees' livelihoods, and I'm okay with that." She snorted. "I'm sure the employees of the world are sleeping more soundly because of that, too. I'm hardly a good risk as an employer these days."

"I can't imagine what it's like to go through what you went through, but I know you're being too hard on yourself. And if Mamie Sue's employees knew you, and knew what was really going on . . . well, I can't imagine they blame you, either."

"Well, they're certainly not cheering the fact that I lost the company to a corporation that had no intention of retaining any of them."

"Still—" He decided not to push it, turning to sympathy instead. "I'm sorry you lost the house, too."

"In the scope of karmic fairness, a lot of my former employees ended up losing theirs when they couldn't find work after the layoff, so . . . it is what it is. I shouldn't complain."

"You're not complaining. You're mourning—as are they. No matter how it all came down, you're human and you lost everything that mattered to you. You're allowed to grieve without feeling guilty about that, too."

She looked at him. "Do you ever miss what you've let go? Do you ever feel like it's unfair that you had to give up everything to take on this new role?"

He slowed the truck and stopped at a red light, then looked directly at her. "For a long time, I felt guilty for wanting out of my family and the family business. I don't, anymore. I took a lot of flak from the extended clan for taking Lilly away from my mother . . . but you'd have to know my mother to understand it's not as cruel a thing as it appears to be. My family was only upset because of how it might look to others. If anything, it's been a blessing to my mother, not having to deal with raising a small child and what a painful reminder Lilly is to her. You have to realize, she doesn't view people as . . . well, people."

"I'm so sorry," Kit said softly. "I shouldn't have—your loss is so much more personal than—"

"No, we're both putting it out there and we've both lost. We've both suffered, are suffering. You understand what that is. You've suffered personal loss, too. We both know life can be hard, sometimes a whole hell of a lot. But I can honestly say, nothing about having Lilly in my life, except the reason for it happening in the first place, is bad.

I am terrified, pretty much daily, that I'll screw it up, but I feel . . . honored and grateful, to have a hand in raising her."

"You love her. So much. You won't screw up."

Morgan smiled and pressed the gas pedal as the traffic flowed forward again. "Yeah, well, I'll believe that as soon as you believe you shouldn't feel guilty for being pissed off."

She laughed and so did he.

"God, this is all so . . . odd. You're nothing like your family, or those I've met anyway. I think I see what you're saying about them. I've never met your mother—the court proceedings were well underway when the accident happened. It was all over the news, of course, but I was so swamped with the court battle, I really didn't pay attention to it, except I knew it was the son of the woman who owned the firm currently fighting me in court. I wondered if . . . it would stall anything, or change anything, or . . . I don't know . . . cause the lawyers to be less—"

"Vicious?"

She shrugged. "Maybe. That's a horrible thing to say, but they were relentless. The accident was so tragic and I couldn't help wondering—because I lost both my parents the very same, very sudden way—how they could attack at the same time they were suffering such a loss. But there was never even a blip, not in court. Not so much as a time extension for them to handle things. Nothing. I realize it's a big firm, but there were lawyers at that table with the same last name as yours, so I assumed . . ." She shook her head. "Never mind. I shouldn't have said anything. I understand now, at least a little. That's all I was trying to say."

"Just as I understand why hearing my name made you take such a big mental step backward."

She slid a glance his way, but his attention was on the road. "Teddy is a lot like your family. So, I guess, is my sister. Do you know she was furious with me, utterly furious, when she heard I was going to fight the sale? She said I was betraying family, taking Teddy and the snack company to court." Kit laughed, albeit with no humor. "I felt like I'd stepped into an alternate universe where everyone else was suddenly speaking an entirely different language."

Morgan surprised her by chuckling. "You just described pretty much every day of my childhood."

Smiling with him, she glanced his way. "Maybe it's just us, and we're the weirdos."

"If we're the weirdos, I'll take that over normal every day and twice on Sundays." He looked over at her just then, and though he held her gaze for only a moment, the connection between them was as palpable as if he'd reached out and caressed her. "Thanks for keeping me company in Weirdo World."

She laughed, but her body was having a far more . . . involved reaction. He was just so . . . wonderful, really. She wanted him. Wanted the real touch to go with that palpable, imagined one.

"And to think, I'm still single, with lines like that," he said dryly. "Shocker, really."

"And to think I took it as a compliment," she replied, laughing. "We really are in Weirdo World."

"Well, I'm off to rescue mutant-sized turtles, and I've left my only niece in the care of a Mohawked, multiple-pierced young woman who has a fairy wing tattoo that my five-year-old niece seriously covets, so, I suppose Weirdo World really is somewhat applicable." He laughed. "It's a good thing my family can't see what's going on or they'd sue to get her back."

Kit raised her eyebrows as her libido took an instant dive. "You've seen Dre's tattoos?"

"Tattoo," he replied. "As in one. Singular. She showed it to Lilly the day we stopped by the shop when Lilly had on her fairy costume." He glanced over at Kit and his eyes widened. He chuckled as he turned his attention back to the road. "You didn't seriously think that I'd—I mean, she's at least ten years younger than—" He shook his head. "Now who's the weirdo?"

Kit shrugged, but she was fighting a laugh. "She's an amazing young woman, and, as she says, age is just a number."

"You know, she said something like that earlier, back at the center, only I don't think it was supposed to be a compliment." He slowed the truck and made the turn toward Jekyll. He was silent for a moment; then, as if he'd been debating saying it, he kind of blurted, "She also said they're rooting for me, whoever 'they' are. I wasn't sure what that meant. It was when she made the age crack."

Kit had to smile or be mortified. She couldn't believe Dre had told him the Cupcake Club was trying to play matchmaker. Well, she could believe it, but never considered they'd actually take a hands-on approach. Okay, Alva maybe. And Franco. She sighed, then laughed. Or all of them. "What does it say about us when we're the weird ones and Dre is the one who gets it?"

Morgan chuckled. "I don't think I want an answer to that."

Kit glanced over at him and smiled. "She calls you Uncle Hunk." Fair was fair, after all.

Kit thought Morgan might have choked.

"What?"

"Oh, come on. Surely it's not a surprise that women find you appealing." She grinned. "Alva calls you that, too."

"Birdie's friend, Alva? She's like, what—"

"Eighty-four. See, your appeal knows no age boundaries." Kit laughed again when she saw a bit of color bloom in his cheeks. God, he was sexy, charming, and ridiculously adorable. She was in so much trouble. "She and Dre are both Cupcake Club members."

She realized her mistake when he turned his very knowing grin on her. "Ah. So that would be who is rooting for me, I'm guessing. Hmm. Rooting for me in what manner, I wonder?" He slowed at another red light. "I don't suppose you'd care to . . . illuminate?"

"I don't suppose I would." She strove to sound prim and proper, which was totally ruined when he snickered and she joined in, helpless against it.

They were still laughing when the light turned green. "Weirdo World, indeed," she said, when she could find air.

He grinned at her. "We're quite the pair."

"So you keep telling me," she said dryly. Their gazes caught, held for a moment, as he slowed to take a turn.

They bumped into the parking lot of the research center. "Maybe if I tell you often enough, you'll believe me."

Chapter 13

"Oh, my goodness. Morgan, look how small they are." Kit walked around the holding tank for two of the little Hawksbills they were taking back to Sugarberry, a look of delight and wonder on her face. She crouched down to watch them through the glass. "Oh, no, look. That one has only three flippers."

Morgan came around her side and bent down to watch with her. "Seems to be doing pretty well with them, though."

"Yeah, he does. Still . . ." She turned her gaze to his. "Lilly is going to totally fall in love with him, you know."

That was the moment it hit him. Truly, for sure, it hit him. Right next to a turtle holding tank on Jekyll Island.

He'd lost count of the number of times he'd heard the "when the right person comes along, you'll just know" advice. He'd never really believed it. He'd dated, often, in fact, during his years in Colorado, and could recall, quite fondly, the women he'd spent time with. They'd had lively, deep, stimulating conversations about politics, the environment, world peace, and philosophy. Wasn't that what connecting and chemistry was all about? He'd always thought something would slowly evolve from there. But . . . it never had.

Not until that moment by the turtle tanks. Staring into green eyes and an open, honest smile, it finally had evolved.

In the short time they'd known each other, he'd opened up to Kit, talked about himself, his family, his goals . . . something he'd never done before. She had, too, and he doubted that was the norm for her, either. Maybe it was the unusual connection they'd had to one another that had allowed it to happen so swiftly; he didn't know.

He used to think it was about time spent together, that a relationship eventually would grow if given the right amount of attention . . . but this road trip was the longest they'd spent in the company of one another. Over the past two hours—hell, every time they'd had even a brief conversation—it had been meaningful in ways that had nothing to do with deep thoughts about current world events, and everything to do with connecting to each other on an intimate, personal level.

The karmic joke was on him. He finally understood, finally *knew* . . . and he was the last man on earth she wanted to get involved with.

But that sense of rightness, of connection was there. It wasn't just him, and it wasn't going to go away just because she wished it would.

Just be there, involve yourself . . . and see where that takes you, he thought. Worst case . . . she stuck to her friends-only edict and he ended up with someone in his life who was important to him, special, and who cared about Lilly.

Best case? Well, he didn't want to think that far ahead. One step at a time.

"Morgan?"

He snapped from his reverie . . . and curled his fingers into his palms to keep from cupping her face in his hands and lowering his mouth to hers. The urge to . . . what, claim? Yes. Claim. That was the only way to describe the primal feeling coursing through him. It was crazy. He'd never been the stake-his-claim kind of guy. And yet . . . with her . . .

"I was just imagining Lilly's face when she sees this little guy."

That wasn't entirely true. At that moment, he'd been wondering what she'd do if he leaned in and kissed her. If he started by claiming her mouth . . . and went from there.

Her eyes softened. "I know. Can't say as I'll blame her, either. Do you think . . . have you thought about her getting attached to these guys?"

He fought to get his thoughts—and needs—back on track. "Yeah, it worries me, a little. She doesn't need more loss in her life right now. I've talked to Gabe, and he's suggested that we let her be part of the releases, when the time comes. So she can see the turtles going back to their homes. I figure—as unfortunate as it is—there are always going to be new temporary residents for her to get involved with. If she sticks with it, stays interested, then she'll just have to learn that her role in their lives is to help them get back home, and see that as a good thing."

"That's a great idea." Kit's smile spread, warmed, as she continued to hold his gaze.

Such a change from where they were the last time they'd spent time in each other's company. He couldn't squelch the leap of hope, didn't want to. He wanted to slide his hand in hers, tuck her next to his side, and share the moment with her. Such a simple desire, and yet nothing about it was simple. It was complex and richly layered, and felt oh-so-good. *Our . . . um . . . .indeed.*

"I know you're worried," she said, mistaking his silence for concern. "About taking care of her, raising her. God knows, I'd be terrified half the time, too, maybe all the time. It's a huge responsibility. You clearly love her, but what will get you through is that you are looking out for her."

"Thank you. I'm just doing the best I can."

She laid her hand on his arm. "That's all anyone can do." She squeezed, then let go, turning her attention back to the tank.

As swiftly as his grand ideas of slowly romancing Kit had come to mind, the reality of where that would inevitably lead crashed his fanciful dreams right back down to earth. Even if she could get past the fact that he was a Westlake and decide she was ready to take on the emotional challenges of a relationship, the fact was, he didn't come solo. He was part of a package deal. With everything she'd been through, the new challenges she'd taken on, and starting her life over, he sincerely doubted she was looking for a ready-made family to top things off. No matter how much she cared about Lilly. And he couldn't blame her.

It made his desire to turn her face back to his, then lean in and take her mouth in a slow, deep, claiming kiss all the more difficult to deal with.

"Morgan? Kit? We're ready for you in the back."

They rose and turned as the research center tech guided them to the rear of the facility to help load the mature turtle onto the truck. As they started to go through the swinging doors, the tech turned back to them. "Fair warning. Our newest residents are back here and they're not in the best shape."

"Okay," Morgan said. "Thanks."

Kit was in front of him and he could feel her hesitation. He leaned down and quietly said, "I can take care of this part if you want me to. You can use the regular exit, meet us back there by the truck."

He wasn't sure how the offer would be received; she was a pretty independent sort.

She glanced up at him with sadness and concern in her

gaze. "If I want to deal with these turtles and be a volunteer, then I need to see this, too."

"Are you sure? Because—"

She nodded. "Yeah, I am. But . . . thank you."

It has hard not to comfort her, the inclination was so natural, so normal. He tucked his hands in the lab coat they'd given him to protect his clothes while they moved the turtles. It was that or tuck her next to his side.

Evidently, the Westlake training had stuck with him, since he'd never thought of himself as a nurturing type. He'd never had the chance to show it or a reason to feel it. Then Lilly had come into his life and brought out his nurturing side. Reflecting on that, he realized his whole career was indicative of that quality. So . . . maybe that's what this desire to reach out for Kit was all about. She needed. And he needed. Maybe that's all it was.

And yet . . . he felt that he *knew* her. And she knew him—possibly better than anyone ever had.

The tech pushed through the heavy swinging doors and Kit followed, with Morgan just behind her.

He'd seen plenty of photos of turtles in all stages of distress. None of them had prepared him for the reality of what the folks at the research center were dealing with, firsthand.

Kit gasped when she saw the condition of the huge leatherback. The side of his powerful jaw was mangled, his shell had been badly damaged, and one flipper had been torn completely off. Her hand flew up to her mouth and her step faltered.

As naturally as he did with Lilly, Morgan took her by the shoulders and turned her around, into the shelter of his body. She didn't fight him. He could feel her trembling, and bent his head, pressing his lips against her hair.

"Morgan," she said shakily, and he could hear the tears threatening.

"I know, I know." he said quietly.

"My God." She shuddered, and he drew her fully into his arms and held her.

He caught the eye of the tech, who'd turned back to see where they were. The young man nodded and mouthed *sorry*.

Morgan nodded back. "Just give us a minute, okay?"

"Sure. Meet you out back."

"I-I should be able to handle it." Kit's voice was barely above a whisper. "They need us. I mean, I knew that, but now . . ."

"Now you'll just work harder," he murmured. "They need help through all the stages of recovery. Anything you do, any step you involve yourself in, helps them." He felt her nod against his chest and gently eased her head back, tipping her face up to his. "We don't have to do it all. We just have to do what we can, what we're able to do. Lilly, me, you."

Her eyes were full of unshed tears. "Right. You're right." She took a steadying breath and started to turn her head toward the techs who were working, but Morgan shifted her face back to his.

"Let's go out back, help the ones we can, and get back on the road to Sugarberry." When he thought she might resist, might force herself to look again, he cupped her cheek with his palm. "We're helping them, Kit. And by getting these other guys out of here, we're helping that guy, too. Okay?"

She nodded, and he shifted next to her, providing a screen between the work going on and the path to the door. He kept a soothing hand on her back, guiding her toward the tech motioning them through another door.

"Thank you," she told the young man, as they followed him to the holding area. "For what you're doing."

He smiled with understanding. "Thank you for what you're doing."

Kit sniffled one last time before wiping her eyes, then shook it off as best she could and forced a smile. "Okay. So . . . what do we do?"

The tech smiled at her. "Right this way."

She glanced up at Morgan, who hadn't taken his eyes off her. "Thank you, too."

"Anytime," he replied, feeling his heart begin that long, steep slide.

He was in serious trouble.

Chapter 14

"Why doesn't he swim crookded?" Lilly pressed her face against the tank, watching the young turtle.

"He's figured out how to swim with just three paddles," Morgan told her. "Turtles are pretty smart like that."

Lilly looked up at him. "Will it grow back? The other one?"

Morgan shook his head. "That's why he's here. To learn how to get around okay with three. We'll make sure he can swim really, really well, then we can let him go home again."

"To the ocean?"

Morgan nodded. "Maybe, when the time comes, you can help us get him back to his home."

Her eyes went huge. "Can I?"

Morgan smiled. "If Dr. Gabe says it's okay. But I think he'll be happy you want to help."

Lilly looked back at the turtle tank. "What's his name?" She looked up. "Can I name him?"

Kit had been watching the entire byplay between the two, her heart tugging the whole time. When Morgan shot her a fast grin and a wink, she felt an entirely different kind of clutch in her chest. She grinned right back, wishing she was able to just go with the flow. He made it such an easy flow.

"His name is Donatello," Morgan told Lilly.

Kit knew the turtle had been named after one of the Teenage Mutant Ninja Turtles, which she'd somehow missed seeing in her formative years. Maybe if she'd had brothers, but alas, no. Morgan, however, knew all about them and had regaled her with stories of their feats of amazing ninja turtle prowess during the trek back to Sugarberry with precious turtle cargo.

She'd stayed in the back of the truck, monitoring their passengers, but it had been an easy drive, so she'd been able to chat with Morgan as they drove. Since the turtles were strapped to gurneys and boards, she'd been more a glorified babysitter than anything else. She was thankful that had been all there was to it.

She wished she'd been able to cope better with seeing the torn-up turtle. Knowing those images would be vividly imprinted on her mind for a very long time, she was thankful for peaceful turtles and Morgan's funny ninja turtle stories to help keep her focused on the matter at hand.

"Do-na-tello," Lilly said, sounding it out. "That's a funny name."

"It's a ninja turtle name," Morgan told her.

He'd already told Kit that Lilly was probably still a little too young for the cartoons and movies but his stories had been so cute and funny, she'd urged him to tell Lilly about them, edited as he saw fit.

"What's a ginja turtle?" Lilly wanted to know.

Morgan launched into a tale about Donatello and his brother turtles, Michelangelo, Raphael, and Leonardo. "Donatello was the smart, scientific one."

"Like Dr. Langley?"

Morgan chuckled. "Exactly like Dr. Langley, in fact."

Kit's phone beeped in her pocket and after checking the text message, she slid off the worktable she'd been sitting on. "Hey, guys, I have to get back to the shop. The inspector is finally there." She took off her lab coat and hung it up on the row of hooks along the back wall.

"Are you coming back tomorrow?" Lilly's attention temporarily swayed from tank.

"I don't know yet." Kit scrunched up her nose. "But I'll let Dr. Gabe know when I'm available this week, so he can tell you. Okay?"

"Okay." Lilly looked again at the swimming turtle, then back at Kit. "Thank you for bringing Donatello here. He's happy."

Kit smiled. "Yes, I think he is. You should draw a picture for him in your new journal."

Lilly's face lit up. "Okay!" She headed back to the research area, presumably to get the journal and her crayons.

Kit turned to Morgan. "Sorry, hope that was okay."

"More than." He straightened from where he'd been crouched down next to the low tank. "Come on, I'll walk you out."

There went that little flip inside her chest again. "You don't need to do that."

He smiled. "I know."

Lilly came bouncing back in, and Morgan said, "I'm going to walk up front with Miss Kit. You start on your picture, okay? No hands in the water. Just because he's small—"

"Doesn't mean he can't bite me," she finished. "I know. Dr. Langley told me and Miss Dre that if we put our hands in the water, it scares the turtles and we can't ever be here again if the turtles get scared."

"Way to go, Dr. Gabe," Kit murmured to Morgan under her breath, giving him a sideways smile.

"I owe him," Morgan murmured back. "That's exactly

right," he told Lilly. "I'm glad you understand. Draw Donatello a good picture, okay? I'll be right back."

She had her head bent over the spiral bound journal, which looked huge across her tiny lap. "Okay," she answered absently, already immersed in her creative masterpiece.

Morgan followed Kit up front where she retrieved her purse and sweater. "You really don't have to—"

"I know," he said again, then held the door to the parking lot open for her. "I just wanted to thank you for going today, for helping out. I know you're swamped with stuff."

"As, I imagine, are you. The glamorous life of us turtle volunteers, right?"

He chuckled as they walked to her car.

"Well, it got a lot more interesting today, anyway. I was glad I could manage the time. Lani was happy to fill in for me."

"I'm glad we had the time to talk. Clear the air a bit more. It was . . . really good. You're easy to talk to, and I appreciate your listening."

"I am, too," she said, realizing how much she meant it. "And I can ditto the rest, too."

She turned to him. It must have been that warm, fuzzy feeling that had her opening her mouth and adding, "I know you said you wanted to stay here on Sugarberry for Thanksgiving. Would you . . . would you and Lilly consider joining me—us—for dinner? They're a good group, a lot of laughter. I don't think there will be other kids there, but Lilly knows Dre and Lani and me. She'll love Alva and Franco. If you think it wouldn't be too overwhelming for her, it might be a good way to jump in and start becoming part of the island community. Well, more than just out here at the center. Maybe Alva can invite

Birdie. Maybe in a group like that, it would be easier. I don't know. I'm just—" She stopped the sudden gush, and her lips twisted in a self-deprecating smile. "I'm just sticking my nose in, I guess. Tell me to stick it right back out again, and I'll understand."

Morgan had his hands shoved in his pockets and was just standing there, smiling at her.

"I just thought . . . well, the invitation stands," she stammered, realizing her heart was beating way too fast in anticipation of his answer.

"How would folks feel about me being there? I wouldn't want to make anyone's holiday—"

"Trust me, it would be the highlight of the season for them." She paused as she realized the true implications of what she'd just offered. If she'd thought the cupcake crew had been pushing her and Morgan together before—oh, dear Lord, what had she been thinking? Well, she'd been thinking she didn't want Morgan and Lilly sitting home alone on Thanksgiving. That was all.

Probably, that was all.

Surely, she could make the Cupcake Club understand it had just been an offer from one island newcomer to another.

"Does that mean you'll consider it?" she asked.

"You realize what you're offering. As a single guy, I've never had to cook the traditional feast. I have no idea what I'm doing. It's beyond tempting to take any excuse to duck that."

"Did you already buy a turkey?"

He shook his head. "I was wondering if maybe one of our new traditions might be Chinese carry-out on Thanksgiving." He grinned. "We just got unpacked. Seems like a bad idea to risk burning the place down so soon."

She laughed. "Yes, well, when you put it like that, a

chopstick Thanksgiving starts to sound like the wiser approach." She gave him a considering look. "How are you with canned cranberry sauce?"

"That, I think I can manage."

"Okay, that can be your contribution. Well, if Lilly's game, anyway. Let me know? And, about Birdie, I won't say anything—"

"Actually, that might be a nice idea. But only if the rest of the group thinks so."

"We'll figure it out. I'm glad you'd like to come. Everyone has been so good to me here and well, I'd like for you and Lilly to experience that, too."

His smile deepened, as did the way he was looking at her.

When the silence lingered for a few seconds, then a few seconds more, during which they just seemed to get more tangled up in each other's gazes, she finally found her voice. "But don't feel you have to—"

"I don't." He stepped closer. "You're a special person, Kit Bellamy."

"I—thank you." She felt all flustered with him standing so close . . . and not in a bad way. She was having the devil of a time recalling why it was she didn't want him in her personal space . . . because it felt pretty damn good.

She remembered being wrapped up against that broad chest of his, how sturdy and solid he'd felt, and how gently he'd comforted her. She couldn't look at his hands without remembering how his wide palm felt, cupping her cheek. Or how good it felt to hear his deep voice, soothing her, encouraging her.

He'd made her feel stronger, rather than weak and wimpy. It should have been awkward, if not in the moment itself, surely afterward, but . . . it hadn't been. At all. Quite the opposite.

"You're welcome." His gaze drifted lazily down to her mouth.

Her body responded as if he'd drifted those wide palms right over the tips of her nipples. No amount of restraint in the world could keep her gaze from drifting to his mouth, too . . . and wondering how his tongue would feel sliding over those same now-tightly budded tips. She had to swallow a small moan, but didn't do a damn thing to stop him when he stepped forward again and closed the distance between them.

And then that palm was easing along her cheek again as he tipped her face up to his. "Just a taste, Kit," he murmured.

"Just . . . a taste."

His lips brushed hers, taking her mouth slowly, exploring as if he had all the time in the world and intended to make good use of every second.

She sighed against his lips and let her eyes drift shut as a shiver of pure pleasure coursed through her.

He took full advantage, sliding his hands into her hair and easing her head back. Tasting and teasing, he took the kiss deeper.

She slid her hands to his shoulders, then scraped her nails along the nape of his neck as she wove her fingers into his thick hair. He groaned deep in his throat, and the slow, sweet exploration took on a starker, greedier hunger. His arm slid around her waist, pulling her tight up against him. Her fingers knotted his hair as she urged his mouth more firmly onto hers.

The embers they'd been stoking since that first day they'd met, sparked and caught fire. He molded her body to his, leaning her back against the side of the car, and kissed her like it might be the last time he ever had the chance. She forgot where she was and who he was, and sank into it right along with him.

The sudden shrill chirp of her phone, vibrating between them where it was trapped inside her sweater pocket, startled them both. She jumped, and he lifted his mouth from hers, but kept her wrapped up against him as they caught their breath.

"I don't know about you," he said, with a gravelly edge to his deep voice, "but that—" He shook his head, in wonder or denial, she wasn't sure. Looking as stunned as she felt, he took in all of her—her eyes, her mouth, her hair—his gaze as intimate as his kiss had been. Then he looked into her eyes again. "Kit, I—"

"We probably shouldn't—"

"I know." His gaze moved to her mouth again, and he briefly closed his eyes. "I know. You've made it clear what you want and what you don't. Starting anything with me would complicate your life in so many ways . . ."

She'd been about to say they probably shouldn't stand in the parking lot where anyone could come out and see them, but he was apparently already past any immediate issues of possible impropriety and thinking well beyond that moment. She was still trying to gather her thoughts over the sound of her pounding pulse.

"Morgan—"

He was searching her gaze again, and she could see he didn't want to do what he knew was best. What he thought he knew, anyway. "I just wanted to know if I was right. I-I didn't expect that." She felt his fingertips flex on her scalp. "But then, I didn't expect you."

Kit was such a jumble of emotions and needs at that moment, she couldn't begin to sort through them. Her brain was still scrambled by a single kiss that had felt more intimate, more . . . carnal, than if she'd stripped down and had sex with him on the hood of her car. Come to think of it, that sounded like a damn fine idea.

Oh boy.

"I-I didn't, either," she managed, struggling to rein in her—well, everything. She knew that much was true.

"So . . . I won't. We won't. I'll, uh, let you go. You go take care of your inspection. I'll go . . . take care of Lilly. And we'll just . . . be friends."

Everything in her rejected that idea. Except, rationally speaking, objectively speaking, he was probably right. They were at a crossroads in their lives. His was especially complicated. He had more than himself to consider when making decisions about who to spend time with and how serious he wanted to be about it.

Even if she could get past the idea of tangling herself up with the extended Westlake clan, she had no idea how she felt about dating a single parent. She'd been so busy rejecting the idea of a relationship, she hadn't seriously considered how his guardianship of his niece would affect anyone but Lilly—namely herself.

"I guess that means I need to stop holding you like this." A bit of the humor that usually colored his words had edged in, but didn't make it anywhere close to his eyes—which were still drinking her in.

But he didn't straighten, didn't slide his arm out from around her waist, didn't step away. Instead, he brushed at the strands of hair on her forehead, traced a fingertip along her bottom lip, and made her tremble with a want so deep she didn't know how to contain it . . . much less decide on whether she should act on it.

She didn't want him to step away, didn't want to lose the warmth of him, the strength of him. Didn't want him to never look at her again the way he was looking at her.

"I could get lost in you, Kit Bellamy. Hell, maybe I already am."

It was only when he let his hand fall to his side, and she felt him begin to loosen his hold on her, that she made a move. If she'd thought about it at all, she'd have lost her nerve and played it safe. And there was nothing safe about how Morgan made her feel. "Maybe I need to know, too."

She pulled his head back down to hers and kissed him.

"Oh, thank God." He was grinning as he kissed her back.

The kiss was different this time. Every bit as ardent, and the intensity was crazy . . . but that edge of do-or-die-trying had been replaced with the joy of discovery. And she was doing some of the discovering herself.

They broke apart when her phone chirped again . . . and then again, and they laughed, albeit a bit breathlessly.

"I think someone is trying to send me a message."

"Hopefully it's just about your inspection." The light in his eyes was infectious, as was the devilish glint to his smile.

She smiled at that. "I do have to get over there. We've been waiting a week for him to get out here and approve the permits we need."

"I know. I need to get back inside, too." He loosened his arm around her waist, but slid his hands down her arms and took her hands in his. "I know this was just a kiss . . . but it wasn't just a kiss. Was it?"

She shook her head. "No, but—"

"It's not something to take lightly. I don't."

"I don't know what I want," she said, then laughed. "Well, there are a lot of things I want." Her laughter faded, but her smile stayed as she looked up into his handsome face. "I just have to figure out if it's something I should want right now." He started to reply, but she stopped him. "I know I invited you and Lilly to Thanksgiving dinner, and my reasons for wanting you both there haven't changed, but—"

"But, this complicates things," he said. "Possibly a lot. I do understand, Kit. I do. I know—"

"I need to think, to really . . . consider . . . everything."

He brushed the backs of his fingers across her cheek. "I know. And I want you to think about . . . everything. If you'd still like us to attend, I can talk it over with Lilly, and if I think she's ready for it, we can be there . . . as your friends."

She gave him a dry look. "Given the events of the past ten minutes, do you honestly think we could pull that off?"

He laughed outright. "See? That's why I kissed you. Why I've been thinking about kissing you, pretty much since the day we met."

"Why? Because I don't pretend? Wait, you have?"

"God, yes." He grinned.

She couldn't help it, she grinned right back. Honestly, it was like they were two mischievous school kids, playing hooky and trying not to get caught.

"Well," she said on a laugh. "Now that we've gotten that out of the way—"

He scooped her right back up against him again and bent his head down over hers. "Oh, it's not even close to being out of the way."

He made her pulse pound in the most delicious way. "I—you may have a point."

He straightened again and let her go, but kept his hands on her arms. He was the tactile sort, she realized, but rather than feeling pushy or invasive, it felt . . . comforting, solid. He was that way with Lilly, too.

"Listen," he said. "The holiday is just a few days away. Lilly and I will be fine on our own."

"With kung pao turkey? And fried rice stuffing? I don't know, Morgan—"

"I do. It's a small island, and our paths are going to keep

crossing. Better to figure out now what's best, before involving anyone else."

"It is a small island." She sighed, because she knew he was right. "And though I already love them dearly, my new friends are not the types to sit back and just let nature take its course . . . or not. They'll poke and prod. They already are. I wish it was less complicated. I just . . . want to be fair. To you. To me. To Lilly. I can't jump first, and figure it out later."

"Neither can I." He slid his palms down her arms again, took her hands in his, and squeezed them. "Much as I want to. Thank you."

"For?"

"Being honest. I probably shouldn't have kissed you at all. Maybe neither of us is in a place where we can act like two unattached adults and let the chips fall where they may." He gave a gentle tug on her hands, so she moved back up against him. "I'm just having a really hard time regretting a single second of it."

He smiled, leaned down, and pressed a single, simple, sweet kiss on her mouth. "One for the road."

It was the one that branded her. Not the deep, crazy primal kisses, but the sweet, honest one. Go figure. How was she supposed to think rationally when he kissed her like that?

"Yeah," she said with a half smile.

He finally let her go for good and stepped back.

She couldn't remember ever feeling so bereft. It was silly, but there was nothing funny about it. It took considerable willpower to remain standing by her car when he turned to walk back into the research center. "Morgan?"

With one hand on the center's front door, he turned back.

"No regrets, either," she said.

Her phone chirped again, making them smile. She lifted

her hand in a short wave, and climbed into her car. She watched him go inside, then pulled out of the lot. "Except maybe letting you walk away," she murmured under her breath.

Chapter 15

"Hi, Gabe, just checking—"

"She's fine. She and Dre are coloring up a storm and writing a story about Donatello and Paddlefoot. Dre will bring her back by dinner. Don't waste your alone time talking to me."

"Right, right. I know. I just haven't—" Morgan stopped himself. "I'm hanging up now."

Gabe chuckled. "It gets easier."

"You and Anne don't have children."

"We've had hundreds of them—in our classrooms. Speaking of which, I have some four-footed ones who need me. Now stop bugging me already."

Morgan smiled, albeit somewhat sheepishly. "Yes, sir. And thanks. For letting Lilly and Dre hang out. And for the boot to the butt." He hung up and steered his hybrid SUV into Sugarberry's town square. Birdie had called him and asked to see him. Hence the babysitting setup.

Her home was a few blocks on the other side of the square, near the fishing docks. He pulled into the drive of the tidy little cottage, and spotted her in the open doorway, waving to him before he had the engine turned off.

"Thank you for coming, Morgan," she said, welcoming him inside. "Care for some tea?"

Seeing that she already had the tea set up on the coffee table in her living room, he nodded. "Sure."

He sat in one of the two chairs facing the davenport and the large picture window with a view of the front yard.

"I appreciate your coming by. I hope it wasn't too much of a bother."

"No, not at all."

She fussed over tea and he took a moment to scan her place. The interior was as neat and tidy as the exterior, and decorated about the way he'd assume someone her age would have her home set up. Antique furniture, well kept, but showing its age. Hurricane lamps, throw rugs on the hardwood floors, and doilies. Lots of doilies.

What stood out were the framed prints on the walls. Interspersed among the traditional family photos in heavy old frames and a few oil paintings that had seen better days were a number of watercolor paintings, seascapes and beach scenes . . . of Sugarberry or the other islands, he presumed. Varying in size and style, they were clearly by the same artist. They begged a closer look, lending a certain serenity to the place that was a good balance to the contained energy Birdie seemed to carry with her at all times.

"Oh, please don't mind my art," she said, noticing where his attention was focused. "An old woman's vanity." She handed him his tea on a dainty saucer.

He took it, praying he didn't break anything. The cup alone was rather lost in the palm of his hand, and the empty saucer felt like a fragile wafer. "They're really beautiful. I was just thinking they add a nice, soothing ambience to your home." He looked back at her. "Are you saying you painted them?"

She nodded and a blush stole into her cheeks, despite the deeply tanned, grooved skin she sported from a life spent on an island. "It's a hobby I took up about five or six years ago." She looked away then, busying herself with her tea.

It didn't take Morgan any time to figure out that she'd taken up painting right about the time her only grandchild had been born—and removed from her life. "Did it help?" he asked gently.

She looked startled for a moment, then sighed. "Some." She let out a short laugh. "Well, you can see how many there are, so maybe it was more the doing of it, than the result, that helped." She sent him a smile topped by a sharp but kind gaze. "I figured it beat taking to the bottle."

Morgan nodded, smiling in similar fashion. "Good point. Well, I think they're lovely. Is that why you gave Lilly the paint book?"

"It was something I thought we might share in time. But not to worry if it's not something she finds an interest in."

Morgan didn't want to tell her that Lilly hadn't touched the paint book. He didn't want to hurt her feelings, but felt it wasn't right to lie, either. So he told her the truth as he saw it. "Do you know Dre, that young girl who works over at the cupcake shop part-time?"

"I do, indeed. Quite the artist, herself."

"Yes, she is. She put together a journal for Lilly, filled with all kinds of turtle pictures and such, and they've been working on writing a story about a new resident we have out at the research center, so—"

Birdie laid her hand on Morgan's arm. "Dear, there's no need to explain if she hasn't taken an interest in the painting book." She smiled kindly. "It will be there for her if and when. I was just glad to get to meet her."

Morgan's heart squeezed, and he tamped down the anger over his mother's high-handed machinations that had cost this lovely woman—and Lilly—so dearly. "Well, I hope that was just the first of many meetings to come."

"That's actually why I invited you here. I wanted to talk with you about possibly seeing my darling granddaughter again. I had been thinking about the upcoming holiday, but when our picnic didn't turn out as well as hoped, I thought, perhaps, that wasn't a good idea. I wasn't certain of your plans, but my friend, Alva Liles, tells me you'll be staying here on Sugarberry."

"We will." Morgan didn't bother to wonder how a woman he'd yet to meet knew of his holiday plans. Small island. Then the name struck a chord. "She—Miss Alva—is one of the ladies who bakes over at the cupcake shop, right?" *She must be a friend of Kit's.*

"Yes, dear. And that's part of this, too. You see, I thought it might be too much to have a big meal here with just you and sweet little Miss Lilly, but Alva tells me they are having quite the feast over at Quinn and Riley's place and have extended an invitation for me to join them."

"That sounds nice." Morgan had no idea how Birdie traditionally spent her holidays or if she had other relatives. He knew Delilah had been her only child, and though they hadn't been in touch for a number of years, this holiday season would have to be hard for her, mourning the loss of her only child and any future chance at reconciliation.

"Alva tells me that darling Lilly has become friendly with several of the girls at the shop and she thought . . . well, there's room for more, and . . ." Birdie's quick chatter drifted off suddenly and her tea cup rattled on her knee.

Morgan steadied her by placing his hand on her arm. He set his cup and saucer aside, then took hers and set them on the table as well, before taking her hand in both of his. "Birdie, I know we haven't spoken much, about . . . things. We're both in mourning. Lilly, too."

Her voice was rough with unshed tears. "Please don't feel I'm pressuring—"

Morgan gently squeezed her hand, feeling his eyes burn a little. "No, I'm not saying that. At all. I'm saying that I want us to be a family. I know the timing is hard, with the holidays upon us, but make no mistake—I want you in Lilly's life, in my life. Don't apologize, ever, for wanting the same. I know your heart is in the right place and you want what's best."

She trembled a little and reached for a hankie she'd tucked into the edge of her sleeve. "You have no idea what that means to me," she said, dabbing at her eyes.

"It means just as much to me. That's why we came here, are making a home here."

She nodded and seemed to get some of her lively spirit back. Another dab at her eyes, then she smiled. "I just thought . . . it might be a way for Lilly to enjoy the company of her new friends, a nice thing for you to have good company on the holiday, and a way to have me about without a forced one-on-one situation. That's all. I know it's just days away, but . . . would you think about it?"

Morgan could see how much it meant to her, and, were it not for the extenuating circumstances with Kit, he'd have been truly pleased with the invitation. He had thought a lot about it since she had asked him the day before and knew it would be a much better alternative to spending the day alone, just him and Lilly. He'd figured they'd spend it with the turtles, to distract Lilly, and maybe himself. But he'd much rather spend it with new neighbors and friends.

"I will," he promised her. "I'll talk with Lilly, feel her out a bit, and let you know as soon as I can."

Birdie's face lit up and she squeezed his hand with a great deal more force than he'd have assumed her capable of. "Oh, that's just about the best thing I've heard in . . .

well, in a very long time. And please, don't concern yourself if you feel you need to say no. I'll understand, I will. We'll just figure something else out. But that you're willing—"

"Birdie, of course I'm willing."

She sighed, taking a moment to catch her breath and collect herself. "Of course, of course. It's just taking some getting used to. I-I couldn't be happier, Morgan, that you've come. You've given me such a gift. I don't know that I can ever thank you enough."

He stood and drew her up as well, then gave her a gentle hug. "We're family, Birdie. We're family."

She nodded several times, then dabbed at her eyes again, too overcome with emotion to speak.

"I'll talk with Lilly and give you a call. By tomorrow morning, at the latest."

They said their good-byes, and Morgan was back in his SUV, heading toward the town square, trying to sort things out. He pulled up and parked in front of the bakery, thinking he needed to talk it over with Kit. Despite the Birdie connection, he and Lilly were the interlopers. He didn't want to make Birdie happy, only to make Kit uncomfortable, and have Lilly in the middle of it all.

As for what he wanted . . . well, he wanted it all. That's what he wanted.

What had happened with Kit the day before had dominated pretty much his every waking moment and had played a starring role in all of his sleeping ones. He had no idea where she stood on any of it, now that she'd had time to think things through. He'd planned to wait for her to contact him, allowing her to move at her own pace, and had assumed she'd let him know in some way regarding the holiday dinner invite, but he'd honestly figured it would be just him and Lilly.

Whatever had begun between him and Kit might be

better pursued after the strain and external pressures of the holiday season were over. At least, that was the conclusion he'd drawn and what he'd been prepared to tell her when they spoke.

But with the invite from Birdie to the same dinner, he didn't have the luxury of waiting any longer for an answer.

He went directly to the smaller building next to the bakery rather than ask after her at the bakery and alert anyone else to his presence. Not that he was sneaking about—no point in even trying that, plus he'd parked right out front—but no need to announce it, either.

The front door was propped open by a five-gallon paint bucket, and he could hear the sound of saws, hammering, and a radio blaring, so he didn't bother knocking, but stepped over the paint bucket and ducked inside. Since no one was in the front space, he followed the sound of the radio. Winding around the ladders and draped tarps, he emerged into the back room, surprised to see only Kit. She was hammering away at a set of shelves, bopping her hips to the music on the radio. The buzzing of the saw was coming through the back screen door. Whoever else was working was out in the back parking lot.

He didn't want to startle her while she was swinging a hammer, so he took unabashed advantage of the moment and simply watched her. She was wearing jeans that were old, worn, and fit her in a way that made him want to peel them right off her. The pale green Henley was soft and clung to her slight curves in all the right places. Her pretty red hair, a few ends tipped with cream-colored paint, stuck up in thatches around her head as if she'd raked her hands through it more than once. Splotches of the same cream color decorated her hands and her shirtsleeves, as well.

He wanted her so badly it made his teeth ache.

The song ended as she laid the hammer down. He was

just about to speak when she turned and spied him from the corner of her eye. Startled, she banged her elbow against the shelves and backed into the can of paint behind her.

He sprang forward and grabbed her arms before she could trip over the can and paint tray beside it, pulling her toward him. They stumbled, and he banged up against a framed-out counter, still holding her.

"Sorry, I didn't mean to—"

"You scared the life out of—"

They started to speak at the same time . . . and stopped at the same time, as their gazes got all caught up in each other.

"Hi." He smiled into her dazzling green eyes.

"Hey." She smiled self-consciously. "How, um, how long were you standing there?"

"Long enough to say with some authority that you've got much better rhythm than I do."

Pink stole into her cheeks, and warmed every part of him.

He reached up and gently peeled off a splatter of paint from her chin. "You look good in"—he glanced down at the can of paint, but it was too splattered to read—"whatever color this is."

"Sunlight cream," she supplied.

"That, too," he said, looking back at her, liking that neither of them had made any move to disentangle themselves from one another. "I didn't mean to interrupt, but—"

"I was going to call you. At some point today."

"Well, before you say anything, I need to tell you that I just got done visiting with Birdie."

"You spoke to Birdie, about—"

"She invited me for tea and a chat."

"Oh. Wait, where is Lilly?" Kit started to pull away, as

if suddenly realizing Lilly might be standing somewhere right behind him.

He held on to her, just firmly enough to keep her right where she was. "She's with Dre and Gabe at the center, writing an ode to her newest, bestest friend."

Kit smiled. "Donatello."

"The Adventures of Donatello and Paddlefoot, I believe."

Kit's expression softened. "That's really incredibly sweet."

"Yeah." *As are you,* he wanted to say. It would be so easy to dip his head, kiss her hello. Kiss her a whole lot of things.

Her gaze followed his thoughts and drifted to his mouth.

He was already tilting down to take a taste, when the buzz saw stopped abruptly, and they were jerked back to the moment at hand.

Kit gripped his arm to lever herself away without upsetting the paint tray and can, and Morgan straightened and moved off a respectable distance in case whoever was working out back happened to come through the screen door.

"So, what has you stopping by?" she asked a bit too brightly, her gaze darting to the screen door.

Morgan didn't take her sudden shift personally. He understood, but wished it didn't have to be that way. "Alva invited Birdie to your Thanksgiving feast, and she's extended the invite to me and Lilly."

"Ah. Oh." Kit focused her attention back on him.

"Yeah. So, I came straight here, because . . . well, to talk to you about it."

"If Birdie has asked and you think Lilly would like to—" She stopped and started over. "I mean, please, don't not go because of . . . you know."

"This past week has been a real change for Lilly. She's

settling in, feeling more comfortable now that she knows people. I'm hoping to figure out a way for her to meet some other kids, though I guess that will happen once I get her in school. I think she'd really enjoy spending the day with everyone. But I don't want to make things uncomfortable. They're your friends, it's your holiday, too, and—"

"And we're adults," she finished. "We can make it work. I've thought about yesterday—a lot—and, you know, it was a pretty big day, quite emotional, seeing those poor turtles, and . . . I think we just got caught up in that and let our attraction balloon a little out of control."

Morgan hadn't been sure what her choice was going to be, but he hadn't expected her to dodge what had happened. "Is that how you really see it?" he asked, not exactly angry, but certainly a little offended. "Just a momentary slip in decorum? Weren't you the one who questioned our ability to pretend it was just that?"

She ducked her chin. "Morgan . . ."

"I like that you're a straight shooter, Kit. It's one of the things I find really attractive about you. So . . . don't insult us both by ducking now."

She looked at him. "I was just trying to make it easier."

"On?"

"Lilly. Me. I don't know."

He wanted—badly—to step over and fold her right back in his arms again. That was honesty, and there would be no ducking it. But she'd clearly made up her mind about him—them—and he'd have to find a way to respect her decision. "If keeping our hands off one another is something you'd like to be a permanent thing, then that's what we'll do. As you said, we are adults. We live on a small island and have mutual acquaintances, friends, so we might as well figure it out sooner than later. For everyone's sake."

"You're upset—"

"I'm disappointed. I'd be lying if I said otherwise. I know it's complicated. I know we're both at crazy big changing points in our lives, and yet . . . here you are. And here I am. I like us together. I gave it a lot of thought . . . yesterday, last night, all day today. Hell, I can't stop thinking about it. I know I come as part of a package deal, and I would never willingly put Lilly in a situation with someone who didn't—"

"I love Lilly," Kit said. "It's not that. Not from my standpoint, but what about her standpoint? She's been through a lot. So have you. My life is upside down. It just seems like a big risk, trying to make all those things work in tandem. What if they don't? I mean, are any of us ready to deal with that right now if—"

"When are we ever ready to deal with hard things?" he asked.

"I don't want to be irresponsible, just because my hormones have decided to go into a frenzy."

He smiled then, despite his heart feeling like it was teetering on the edge of a huge precipice. "I rather liked your frenzied hormones. My hormones certainly did."

She smiled too, despite the emotions still charging the air between them. "That's just it. We can't let our hormones do all the talking. We have to be smart, make wise choices. It's not just me, or you, it's—"

He crossed the space between them and stopped in front of her, gently taking one of her hands in his, drawing it up between them. "Is that all that's holding you back? Fear of the fallout if we don't continue to want this?"

"Fallout for everyone. It's such a small place, and everyone is so intimate here. It's not like Atlanta, where if I stop seeing someone we go on about our business, likely never to cross paths again. My friends move on and his friends move on. Here . . . my God, everyone would have their nose in, and no one would forget, and"—she looked at him—"it would be hard. Really, really hard. I know it's never a good time for hard stuff, but some times are worse than others. We've both had a whole lot of hard recently. And Lilly has had the hardest of all. I could never forgive myself if I did anything to add to that. She doesn't deserve more tough stuff."

"And you're so certain that's what it would be?" He squeezed her hand when she ducked her chin. "Kit," he said, and she looked back at him. "Have you thought at all about what it could be? I know thinking about the worst-case scenario is a good starting point when figuring out what move to make . . . or not to make. But have you thought what the best-case scenario would be? Yes, there's risk here, but . . . don't you have to at least consider if the possible outcome might warrant taking that risk?"

She smiled then, surprising him.

"What?"

"You sound like a lawyer."

He smiled then, too, even as he sighed. "I'm not trying to sound clinical—"

"I know, Morgan. Maybe I haven't thought enough about how good it might be. I've spent the past year putting all my hopes and dreams into one big basket, only to lose them all. I don't know if I have the strength to do that again and risk failing. I've already stepped out on a ledge somewhat, professionally, by tackling Babycakes. Honestly? I don't know if I can handle more, now. Good or not so good."

Morgan ducked his chin, wishing the clutch in his chest wasn't telling him what he already knew. "Okay," he said at length and looked at her again. "Okay. Thank you for being honest and not just brushing it off. Because it wasn't casual, not for me." He lifted their joined hands and kissed her paint-splattered knuckles before letting her hand go. "If it was just frenzied hormones, this wouldn't feel so . . . well, feel like it does. But I respect your choice and promise I'll step back."

She closed her eyes briefly, and he couldn't shake the feeling he was making a mistake. Maybe the biggest one he'd ever made. But he could decide things only for himself; he didn't get to decide things for her.

"About the dinner," he began. "Maybe it would be better if Lilly and I begged off. Give this more than a day or two to settle out. We'll have plenty of time with Birdie, with everyone—"

"No," she said instantly, with feeling. "That's not fair. I know you wish my answer to this—to you—was different. But, despite what I said yesterday, I think we can certainly handle ourselves. I know it's just a few days from now, but given what we've said here, can't we . . . I mean, surely we can just—"

"Handle it?" he asked. "Yes. We can. Be friends? I'd like to think we'd have that, if nothing else. Lilly cares for you, and we'll spend time together at the center, so . . . yes. I'd be glad we have that much."

"Yeah," she said quietly. "I would be, too. Thank you. For understanding."

"Always." He stepped back. "I, uh, I'm just going to talk to Lilly, then, and make sure she's up for it. Then I'll let Birdie know."

"Good. If Lilly wants to come, then just be there. We'll be fine. Right?" She smiled, a hopeful curve of the lips, but the doubt and uncertainty were still clear in her eyes.

"Sure. Of course."

"Good. Okay."

He held her gaze for another timeless moment, telling himself that walking away from her shouldn't feel so monumental. Except it did, right to the core. He turned and made his way back to the door leading to the front of the shop, and had just scooted around the ladder when she called out to him.

"Morgan?"

He looked back at her, raising a brow in question.

"I'm sorry," She stood among the tarp, paint, and construction mess, looking a bit lost, a little uncertain . . . and a whole lot like the woman he was already falling in love with. "Really sorry."

"I'm really sorry, too." He headed outside while he still could.

Chapter 16

"This sweet potato casserole needs a little time in the oven." Alva handed the glass-covered dish to Kit as she entered the house.

And wow, what a house. Kit had spent the first thirty minutes after she'd arrived wandering around Quinn and Riley's beachfront cottage. It wasn't so much the size—it wasn't much bigger than many of the beach road cottages—but it had been beautifully decorated and styled, which she discovered was how Riley had originally staged it when she'd first met Quinn.

Kit wound her way into the kitchen and popped Alva's casserole dish next to her own pie pans, which held Mamie Sue's famous peanut pie, homemade by Kit in Lani's shop kitchen the night before. She'd worried making the pies might make her feel too melancholy, but it had been healing, redemptive. It had made her feel closer to her mother, grandmother, and great-grandmother than she had in a very long year.

She'd done a lot of thinking the past few days, mostly because of Morgan, but regardless of the reason, it had been time well spent. She was still climbing out from under the oppressive burden of failure, but while rolling out piecrust she'd forced her thoughts on the now. What was done couldn't be undone, and she tried to imagine what her mother and grandmother would say about how she was moving forward and the choices she was making. Would they be proud? Would they think she'd done the right thing about Morgan and Lilly?

"Here, dear, let me help you with that." Birdie moved some of the pans and trays on the cluttered counter to make more room. "My, those look quite yummy. She pointed to the pies. "Yours?"

Kit nodded, smiling. " "And this is Alva's casserole. She's . . . wandered off somewhere."

"I'll go track her down shortly, before she gets into any trouble."

Kit laughed. "Good luck with that. I understand she has a betting pool as to which of the men will carve the turkey."

"So, I've heard." Birdie's eyes twinkled. "I have ten on that delicious drink of water, Quinn." She leaned in closer. "But then, I've always been partial to the tall ones."

Kit would have said all the men were quite tall, but from Birdie's statuesque standpoint, she could see why the spunky older woman had chosen him. Kit hadn't met Birdie until that morning, but she'd liked her immediately. A little younger than Alva, their friendship went back quite a ways. Birdie had already regaled them with stories of some of their escapades that had Kit's sides still aching from laughter an hour later. She imagined more laughter would ensue, now that the dangerous duo were together in the same room. The odd couple appearance of Birdie's gangly height paired with Alva's tiny stature, and Birdie's more bohemian style of dress, with her loose slacks and vividly printed caftans contrasting Alva's tidy suits and pearls, brought a smile to her face.

"Who did you put your money on?" Birdie asked.

Before Kit could respond, there was another knock at the front door and she tensed, but it was, unmistakably,

Franco. She smiled and relaxed again, thinking an already entertaining day was about to get even more so, but she couldn't ignore the fact that she'd been waiting to hear another voice. Morgan had left a message with Dre and Lani that he and Lilly were planning to attend. Kit was sincerely happy about that. She wanted Lilly to have a good holiday, and though the lively group might be a bit overwhelming, they could always steer her to a quieter part of the house to draw pictures.

"*Bon soir, mes amies!*" Franco announced from the doorway, holding aloft several insulated packs containing more food. "My, my, are we an attractive group, or what?" He bent down to kiss Alva on the cheek, then bussed Lani and Riley as well. "And who is this tall drink of loveliness?" he said, walking over to Birdie.

Birdie's blush didn't surprise Kit one bit, as she'd long since figured out no one was immune to Franco's charms.

Birdie introduced herself as Franco bent low over her hand, then kissed the back of it. "Good friend of Alva—"

"And grandmama to the delightful Miss Lilly." He straightened and smiled, even though Birdie's smile faltered a bit. It was obvious she was more than a little nervous about the impending reunion. "A special pleasure to make your acquaintance." He gave her a little wink. "So glad that you could join us."

"I am, too," she said, seeming to relax once again. She glanced at Kit and wiggled her eyebrows. "I may have to change my bet," she whispered, making Kit laugh.

"Another of Alva's pools?" Franco questioned. "No, no, don't tell me. I don't want to know. I lost twenty dollars last time around. So, has *ma ravissante fille* arrived?"

"Not yet," Birdie told him. "Here, why don't we make room for your packages." She turned to the counter, but it was jammed full.

"Now, now," Franco said, "you go have yourself a

drink, sit down, and enjoy. I'll take over here. Don't you worry about a thing."

"Oh, I don't mind. I'm just not sure where we still have room."

"Birdie, don't even try," Kit informed her, with a fast smile at Franco. "He's incorrigible and unstoppable."

"So, I hear," Birdie said, with another little wiggle of the eyebrows, which made Kit and Franco laugh.

"Come on," Kit said, grinning as she slid her arm through Birdie's. "Let's go out on the back deck. I hear Quinn set up an outdoor bar. I'll pour."

"It's not even ten in the morning, dear."

"Mulled cider is on the menu, and mint iced tea since it's going to be quite balmy out today."

"Sounds lovely. I can't believe the weather we're having," Birdie said as they stepped out onto the wide deck. "I saw that it might get up to eighty."

Baxter and Quinn were behind the bar, prompting Kit to think that had to be some kind of crime against nature, to have so much male beauty in one place. Add Franco's swarthy good looks to Baxter's hot blondness and Quinn's smooth Southern charm, and it really was an embarrassment of eye candy. All of it unavailable, of course, but considering she'd just turned down the most eligible bachelor on Sugarberry, she could hardly complain. Besides, looking but not touching was pretty much all she could handle at the moment.

And yet, as she and Birdie settled in comfy chairs by the pool, she was glancing back at the house every other minute . . . and it wasn't to catch a glimpse of Franco or the hot already-spoken-fors.

"I thought Miss Riley had a dog, a rather large one, I'm told," Birdie said as they sipped.

"She does," Kit replied. "He's a mastiff, but I understand he's just a big sweetie. Riley has him down on her houseboat for the day. She didn't want him getting in the way and was afraid he might scare Lilly." Privately, though Kit hadn't met Brutus, she'd bet Lilly would have loved him just because he was kind of an oddball. But, better safe, and all that.

Birdie's expression took on a pensive look and her gaze drifted out past the pool, toward the pergola and the dunes that backed the property.

Sensing Birdie's nerves were getting the best of her again, Kit said, "Don't worry about Lilly. She'll come around. I think today will be a big step in that direction."

"If the dear thing isn't completely overwhelmed. I still feel like a complete boob for all but scaring the poor child off at our picnic. I—"

"You were understandably excited, and she was understandably nervous. She's a great kid, though, and she'll come around. Just give it time. Even if it's not today—"

"Oh, I don't plan on pushing things at all today. I thought it would just be good for us to be in the same crowd together. No pressure that way."

"I'm glad it's working out for you both to be here." Kit had a very good feeling about it. She just wasn't sure how things would go between her and Morgan. She'd worried the intensity of the chemistry between them, now that they'd given in to it, would be all but impossible to hide. After their last conversation, she prayed being together wouldn't be awkward.

She knew she'd disappointed him, but having thought it all over . . . she'd make the same choice again. Yes, they shared something unlike anything she'd experienced before. But that didn't make it automatically worth taking such a big risk. There was a lot at stake. She was just getting to level ground with herself. He was embarking on a whole new life as a parent. And there was Lilly. Kit couldn't begin to know the impact it would have on the child if Morgan started sharing his time, love, and attention with someone new, especially as they were just beginning to establish a new life in a new place.

She sighed and stared into her mulled cider.

"My, my. Whatever is going on?" Birdie wanted to know, shifting around in her chair. "There seems to be some excitement—"

Kit pulled herself from her thoughts and looked toward the house. Everyone was clustered just inside the open French doors off the kitchen and Birdie was right—they were quite animated. Kit wondered if Riley had burned something again, but didn't see any smoke. An exuberant, happy person, Riley was tall and blond and gorgeous and very outgoing, but, as Franco had mentioned, something of a klutz.

A moment later, it was Lilly worming through the throng of adults who raced straight toward her.

Kit was out of her chair in a heartbeat. She knelt down to catch the out-of-breath child in her arms. "What's wrong? Has something happened? Is Morgan okay?" Her mind was racing to a million possible scenarios, so it took a moment for her to realize Lilly was smiling. Bursting with it, actually.

"The turtles," she said, almost completely breathless. "The baby turtles."

Kit rubbed Lilly's arms and smiled at her, her own heart still racing, but everything else in her calming down. "What about the baby turtles?"

She thought Lilly was talking about the small Hawksbills they'd brought back from Jekyll. Compared to the loggerheads in residence, they looked like babies. "Did Morgan take you to see them this morning?"

Lilly shook her head, still vibrating with excitement, so

much that she could hardly speak. "The babies . . . are coming . . . through the sand!"

And then Morgan was there, smiling and handsome and far too sexy for his own good. "Hello, Birdie," he said, bending down to buss her on the cheek. "Happy Thanksgiving."

"And a Happy Thanksgiving to you. What's all this about baby turtles?"

Kit was still crouched down in front of Lilly, who had grabbed her hand and was tugging. "Come on, we have to go help them!"

Kit looked up just as Morgan crouched down beside Lilly and made direct eye contact with her. She'd worried—a lot—about that moment, and whether he'd still be upset with her or put off because she'd chosen not to pursue a relationship with him. But he was grinning and it was as if nothing had happened and everything was as it always was with him. Easy and natural. And right.

"The nest is hatching," he said, almost as excited as Lilly.

Kit's eyes widened. "I thought they hatched at night?"

"They started coming out last night, but they're still coming. Gabe got hold of me early this morning. They're kind of popping up one here and one there. All of his volunteers and students are with their families today, so it's just he and Anne acting as shepherds, so to speak."

"We have to go," Lilly was saying, still tugging. "Dr. Langley needs us to help."

Kit glanced from Morgan to Lilly, then back again, a questioning look on her face that she hoped he'd understand, as she didn't want to have to spell it out. Would Lilly be okay if anything happened to any of the babies as they made their dangerous first trek?

"Gabe said they're doing okay," Morgan put in, understanding her question without her having to speak. "Not much interference. But they're a little disoriented because it's daytime, and they could use some help." He glanced down at the top of Lilly's head, then back to Kit and said, "We'll make it work."

Morgan stood and hoisted Lilly into his arms, and Kit stood, too. "So, you're going out there now?"

He nodded. "We don't want to mess up anyone's dinner or hold things up, so we swung in here first." He grinned. "Canned cranberry sauce is on the counter."

She couldn't help it, she laughed. "And here I was hoping for fried rice stuffing."

"I'll keep that in mind for next year," he said, holding her gaze.

Before Kit could figure out what he meant by that, Birdie had gotten up from her chair. "Would more people be helpful? Or just get in the way?"

They all turned to look at her.

She shrugged. "Sounds exciting."

Lilly held on a little more tightly to Morgan, but her gaze was riveted on Birdie. "Do you like turtles?" she asked tentatively.

Kit and Morgan went still, aware of the significance of Lilly speaking directly to her grandmother.

Birdie's face split into a wide smile. "I've never met one, but I would very much like to. Would you introduce me?"

Lilly turned to Morgan. "Can I, Moggy? The babies need help getting borned."

A bit of a shimmer shone in Morgan's eyes. "Of course. I think that would be great."

"Can Miss Dre come, too?" Lilly asked, looking from Morgan to Kit and back to Morgan.

No sooner had she spoken than Dre, Lani, and Franco joined their little poolside cluster. "What's this I hear about *le petite tortues* making their grand debut?" Franco asked.

"We have to go," Lilly whispered, scrunching down a

little in Morgan's arms now that a crowd had gathered around them.

"Alva and Baxter said they'd stay and keep watch over the turkeys and all," Lani said. "Want some help?"

Kit's eyebrows lifted. "You're all coming?"

"Dre just called Gabe on his cell and he said they could use volunteers. I thought it sounded like the perfect thing to do on Thanksgiving."

"We could be out there for some time," Morgan cautioned. "Of course, you all could come back whenever you wanted." He smiled at the small group, clearly surprised, and just as clearly touched. "The more help the better."

"Did you get the chance to meet everyone?" Kit asked him.

"I did. Thank you all for such a generous welcome. It means more to us than you could know." He turned to Birdie. "So much more."

Her eyes took on a suspicious glimmer then, too.

Franco clapped Morgan on the back and did his best British Baxter imitation. "Off to the turtle races, then, my good man?"

"I believe so." Morgan chuckled and turned to Kit. "Will you ferry some of the group over? I can take three in addition to Lilly."

"Quinn has an SUV, too," Lani said. "We'll figure it out."

And just like that, the caravan of turtle shepherds trekked through the house and out to the rows of cars and trucks. They ended up taking whichever ones were easiest to maneuver onto the loop road, which landed Kit in Morgan's vehicle with Lilly and Dre.

"Thanks for doing this," Morgan said to Kit as he climbed in the driver's seat after getting Lilly settled into hers.

"Of course! I wouldn't miss it." She fumbled with her

seat belt, excited by the adventure ahead and feeling silly for being nervous with Morgan. It wasn't like they were alone. "I can't believe we're getting to see them come out."

Morgan took the buckle out of her hand and clicked it into the slot, smiling and catching her gaze as their hands brushed. But he immediately settled back in his seat and maneuvered the car out onto the loop road, leaving her feeling more discombobulated.

"We don't know how many we'll get to see or how many more will hatch," he said. "Gabe told me they started emerging around three this morning, and there had already been several dozen out by the time we spoke, possibly more by now. He said, even with the sun up, they're still coming out, which is why he called me. Things have slowed down now, but, overall, he's hopeful for a really decent hatch from the nest."

Kit glanced back at Lilly, who was talking to Dre, then said in a quieter voice only Morgan could hear, "What happens to the ones that don't hatch? Can we be sure the ones that do will make it to the water?"

"Gabe and Anne will take care of the unhatched eggs later. They'll want to examine them, see how far they developed, and find out if there were any issues that prevented them from reaching maturity. Today we'll just help the ones who dig out find their way to the water and keep the birds and crabs away. With as many people as we'll have now, I doubt the birds will be a problem. It will just be shooing away whatever crabs scuttle in, then watching until the turtles get past the waves."

He led the caravan the short distance to the research center. Once there, they piled out of their cars, and he corralled everyone together at the trailhead that led to the beach. "The nest is up the beach a bit and situated back by the dunes. It takes the babies a good while to navigate all the way to the water, and they'll probably be more disoriented than usual because it's daylight. Gabe will tell you what to do; just be careful when you approach and don't get too close. Apparently they feel the vibration through the sand and if it's too strong, it might discourage them from coming out, as they'd sense predators. We're just here to keep the crabs and birds away and to make sure the turtles head in the right direction. Once they find the water, we'll watch until they make it out past the waves. They might get tossed back a few times, but that's normal. It can be quite a process."

He scooped Lilly up and led the group down the short path to the beach. Kit fell in behind him with Dre and Birdie. Franco, Lani, Riley, and Quinn brought up the tail end.

"Man, wait until I tell Charlotte what she missed," Lani said, rubbing her hands together. "This is so exciting!"

"I know." Riley took Lani's and Quinn's hands and swung them. "I'm so glad we made it back. This is so cool!"

"And I'm so glad we dressed for the occasion," Quinn said with a chuckle.

Kit heard that and shot him a smile over her shoulder. Everybody had dressed up for the holiday meal, but once on the beach, shoes and heels came off, pant legs got rolled up, and scarves were tied around heads to keep those with longer hair from having it tossed about in the ocean breeze.

It was a very warm day, well into the upper seventies, but the sand was cool underfoot. "We have mud boots in the research center for anyone who needs them, if your feet get too cold," Morgan called out, but everyone was laughing and gabbing and seemed perfectly fine without them, so down the beach they went.

As they rounded the shoreline and came into view of

the nest, Gabe and Anne spied them and their faces lit up. They began to wave, encouraging them closer.

Gabe made his way up the beach and met them a distance from the nest, his face more animated than Kit could ever remember seeing it. "What a great surprise. Welcome to all of you."

Hellos and introductions were made, then Gabe settled in to give them instructions. "We have one hatchling on the beach right now . . ."

Every one of of the volunteers drew in a breath of excitement.

". . . And I think now that enough tunnels have been made out of the nest, we should expect a few more quite soon."

Lilly squealed at that, which made everyone laugh.

"I think we can all identify with her," Gabe said with a chuckle. "Predators haven't been too big an issue today, but orientation is. The babies are wandering a bit, but they're getting to the water eventually. When they get a good distance from the nest, we'll have a pair of you chaperone each one, keeping it protected until it finds it way to the water. Once there, keep a vigil until the little one makes it past the waves. This usually takes several efforts."

As Kit looked around, the group's anticipation was palpable.

"Lived here all my life and never once have done this," Birdie said as they neared the nest. She looked over at Gabe and smiled. "But, if you can use a volunteer who might be a bit more . . . seasoned I believe I will from now on."

"We never turn away any volunteers," Gabe happily replied. "It's a pleasure to have you."

Introductions were made with Anne, who was, more or less, a female version of her husband, not only in occupation, but in appearance. Other than the beard, of course.

"Thank you all for coming," she said, clearly grateful for the impromptu support. "You're about to experience a very special day."

"Look!" Lilly squealed, pointing to a small spot on the sand. A small spot that was moving. "There he is!" She squirmed to get down out of Morgan's arms.

"Hold on there, tiger." Morgan set her down, but took her hand firmly in his.

Lilly surprised Kit by turning to her and reaching for her hand. "Come on!" she urged. "We have to go help him!"

Everyone laughed, following the threesome as they caught up with the newly hatched turtle.

"Oh," Kit gasped. "Look at him. He's so tiny!" She crouched down next to Lilly, still holding her hand, as the turtle, a half-dozen yards away, continued his determined trek. "I've seen pictures, but . . . he'd fit on the palm of my hand."

Privately, looking at the wee fellow, she thought it was a miracle any of them made it to the water. He was so tiny, and had to navigate so much beach with clumsy flippers. But he sure was gung ho about it. "You can't help but cheer him on. Go, turtle, go!" She realized she was grinning like . . . well, like five-year-old Lilly.

"Go, turtle, go!" Lilly called out, crouching down, too, which was equally adorable.

"Moggy," Lilly whispered, when he stood next to her. "He's going the wrong way. Maybe he's 'fraid of the water." She squinted up at her uncle, the sun in her eyes. "Can't he see the ocean?"

"He's got pretty low ground clearance there. But he'll figure it out."

Anne had posted herself on the far side of the baby, keeping watch on his progress. Gabe had herded the rest of the crew up the beach toward the nest, prepping them for the next hatchling.

Lilly held on to Kit's hand fiercely as if the tighter she gripped, the better chance the little turtle would have. Kit understood the emotion entirely and wished she had Morgan's hand so she could squeeze her anxiety out, too. She felt a need to be connected to him as they shared this experience.

"Can't we pick him up and put him in the water?" Lilly asked as the baby continued to meander along the shoreline instead of toward the water.

"He needs to figure it out. It's part of getting his navigation system set up," Morgan said. "We won't let anything happen to him."

"What's a nagavation system?" Lilly asked.

"You know how a car has a steering wheel we use to make the car go where we want it to go?" Kit said.

Lilly nodded, never once looking away from the baby.

"Well, the baby turtle has to figure out how to steer himself to the water. That's called *navigation*."

"He has to make sure his steering wheel works right?" Lilly asked.

Morgan chuckled, Kit smiled, and their gazes tangled up again over Lilly's head. "Exactly," Kit answered, her smile including Morgan.

Lilly looked up at Kit then. "What if it doesn't?"

Kit pulled her gaze from Morgan's and reached over with her free hand to brush Lilly's hair from her face. It had come loose from the pigtails someone had braided that morning. *Morgan?* she wondered She tried to imagine those big hands of his weaving Lilly's silky hair and . . . and she really needed to stop thinking about all the things his big hands could do.

"It will work," Kit told Lilly. "Some just take a little longer to set up than others."

Lilly held her gaze a moment longer as she appeared to

gauge the believability of such a statement, but then there were squeals from up the beach and they stood up again and looked toward the nest.

Riley turned around, blond curls bouncing, and waved to them. "Another one!" She threw her arms around Quinn, jumping into his arms, which sent them laughing and staggering back a few steps, and almost straight down to the sand before he managed to get them righted again. As soon as he set her down, she disengaged from him long enough to perform an elaborate curtsy for the crowd, which made everyone laugh. "Enjoy the show, I'll be here all week."

Laughing, she tucked herself back under Quinn's sheltering arm.

Kit watched the two of them, warmed by how natural and good they were with each other, and without thinking, her gaze shifted toward Morgan. Realizing what she was doing almost the same instant she did it, she would have jerked her gaze right back away again, only . . . he was looking at her, too.

Had he seen the direction of her gaze? Read her thoughts? Mirrored them? She couldn't read his expression at that moment, but neither of them looked away.

Then Lilly grabbed both their hands, dragging them up the beach to see the new hatchling, leaving Anne to monitor the progress of the one by the water.

"We'll get there," Morgan said on a laugh, his gaze catching Kit's again. He didn't say anything, or intimate anything with his gaze; he just looked . . . happy. Content.

In that moment, trudging up the beach with a very anxious five-year-old between them, tugging them along with her toward the miracle of another little birth . . . Kit had to admit, she was pretty happy and content, too.

She shifted her gaze toward their destination before he

saw something in her expression that would send mixed signals, which was highly possible. She was feeling very mixed up right at that moment.

A hush of anticipation had fallen over the group as Kit, Morgan, and Lilly edged in closer. Lilly let go of their hands and wiggled her way through the sea of legs until she had a ringside seat, as close to the nest as Gabe would allow them.

Kit hung back on the outskirts of the group, warmed by Lilly's assertiveness, happy that her desire to help the baby turtles was eclipsing her more reserved nature when around strangers. Especially a whole group of them. Kit glanced up and caught Birdie also watching Lilly, her own expression filled with so much joy and delight, it made Kit's already full heart swell even more.

Quinn and Riley shifted and urged Birdie to move a space or two around the ring, closer to her granddaughter. Initially she balked, not wanting to disrupt the moment, but she ended up not having much say in the matter.

Lilly caught the little commotion, and looked up just as a shuffled Birdie wound up right next to her. "Look, Gramma," she said, her eyes big as saucers. "The sand is moving!"

Everyone in the group had been focused on Birdie and Lilly. Only Lilly had been watching the nest. As one, their attention zeroed back to the sand.

"Oh my," Kit gasped. "Look!"

The sand, which had already been disrupted from the exit of the other babies, started to shift, crumble, and move. And then . . . a flipper popped out!

"Look, look!" Lilly urged. "It's a baby Paddlefoot!" She looked up at Birdie again. "You want to meet him, right?"

Kit could hardly take her gaze off the emerging baby,

but she looked at Birdie, who was excited and clearly flustered. And worried she might somehow screw up the moment.

Franco moved up and took Birdie's arm. "Here, let me help." He assisted Birdie so she could kneel down in the sand next to her granddaughter, heedless of what damage it might do to her pristine white slacks.

For Kit, it was almost as rewarding watching grandmother and granddaughter bond over the baby turtle fighting its way through the sand, as it was to see the baby succeed and free himself to start the long journey to the water.

"He did it!" Lilly squealed, clapping.

Everyone else pumped their fists in the air, but kept their vocalizations to a minimum, so as not to distract the baby from its mission.

Kit's attention moved back and forth, from turtle to Lilly and Birdie, and back to the turtle.

"He's a strong little one," Birdie said. "Look at him go!"

She was right. That baby wasted no time before scraping and clawing its way down the sand, leaving what looked like tiny tire tracks behind him, his rear flippers dragging along as he propelled himself forward with the front two.

"He's going the right way!" Lilly said, literally bouncing on her knees in the sand.

Gabe said, "Why don't the two of you be his chaperones, okay?"

Lilly's eyes got bigger, if that was possible. "Can we?"

"I think it's a great idea." Gabe nodded his encouragement.

Lilly clambered to her feet, heedless of the sand going every which way. "Want to be a chapaporn?" she asked Birdie.

"I'd love to"—Birdie's eyes glistened, then she looked helplessly toward Franco and Quinn and laughed—"if these two strapping young men would help an old lady out."

Grinning, the two men did just that, getting Birdie back to her feet with minimal effort and as gracefully as possible. She didn't even brush at the mess of damp sand on her clothes, but stuck her hand out toward Lilly. "Shall we?"

Only then did Lilly look back at the group and find Morgan in the crowd. "Moggy?"

"Go on," he said. "I'll chaperone the next one. This one is for you and Grandma Birdie. You watched him come out, I think he feels safest with you two."

"Okay!" And without so much as batting an eye, Lilly turned right back around and took Birdie's hand, and their attention was immediately riveted on the steady trucking progress of their little flippered charge.

Kit watched the tall, older woman and the tiny little girl and had to wipe at the tears gathering at the corners of her eyes.

"Funny how things work themselves out," Morgan said quietly from right behind her, a smile in his deep voice.

"I know," Kit said tremulously, fighting the very strong urge to lean back against him. "It's just so wonderful."

Laughing and sniffling at the same time, she caught him wiping his own eyes. She laughed and sniffled again.

"Look!" Riley's exclamation had them all turning back to the nest. "Another one! Two!"

Riley and Quinn paired up as chaperones when the first one launched himself from the nest, making everyone chuckle.

The next one had to work a bit harder to free himself completely.

"This one's yours," Gabe said, clearly meaning Kit and Morgan.

Still standing just behind her, Morgan surreptitiously hooked his finger in hers, where their hands were hidden from view of the others, and tugged. "You game?" he said, leaning down by her ear.

He let her finger go as he stepped up beside her.

That little tug, that one tiny gesture caused every bit of resistance Kit had left to crumble, just like the sand on the turtle nest, as her heart surged up.

"Yeah," she managed. "I am." She realized he was only talking about chaperoning the baby turtle, but she knew in her heart her capitulation was about a whole lot more than that.

"Check him out," Morgan said. "He's done it."

She looked back and sure enough, the baby had finally freed himself. "He's going the wrong way, though!" she exclaimed when the turtle headed toward the dunes and not the water.

"Come on this side," Gabe directed, "and make a barrier with this." He handed them a wide screen of soft black fabric stretched around a frame of thin boards. "We use this to help deflect and focus the light at night, but it works just as well as a barrier. Just plant it in the sand in front of him and when he hits it, he'll shift position. Don't worry. It's soft. It won't hurt him any. Try to get him going the right way sooner rather than later. The sand will cool as he nears the water. He'll figure it out pretty quick."

Morgan took the screen from Gabe with one hand, and, as naturally as if they'd been doing it forever, he took Kit's hand in the other. "We're on it." He looked at Kit and grinned. "Turtle volunteer squad to the rescue."

"It's what we do," she said just as reverently, grinning like a loon right along with him as they headed off after their tiny charge.

Over the next few hours, turtles kept popping up out of the nest, and Kit stopped thinking and worrying and analyzing and just rolled with the wonderful, awe-inspiring tide. She ended up paired with Dre, Lilly, and Birdie on successive runs. Morgan and Lilly took two in a row, and Kit and Anne took another. She and Morgan didn't work alone together again, though with everyone on the beach, it was like one big rescue party anyway.

"This is truly incredible," Kit told Anne, as they guided their current baby toward the water. "I'm so glad I got to do this."

"We're truly thankful you all came. I'm so sorry we've intruded on your holiday meal together, though."

Kit laughed and gestured to where everyone was spread out, dotting the beach here and there as they watched over their tiny trekkers. "Does anyone here look like they'd rather be anywhere else?"

Anne smiled. "True, perhaps, but still, we—"

"Ahoy there, turtle guides!"

Everyone looked up to see Alva coming out from the dune trail, a lunch basket over one arm. Right behind her was Baxter, pulling a giant cooler on wheels.

It was only then that Kit glanced at her watch and realized they'd been on the beach for almost four hours. "Oh my, we should have called them."

"I've got this little guy if you want to go up and lend a hand." Anne winked. "It looks like they've brought the feast to you."

Chapter 17

"Everyone hold hands," Alva instructed. "We'll say grace. Then you can go back and play with your turtle darlings."

Everyone chuckled as hands were linked and smiles were shared. The group, including Gabe and Anne, had assembled at three of the picnic tables situated under one of the larger pavilion awnings.

Alva stood and gave the invocation and everyone said their amens.

Then Franco stood up. "I shall wield *ze* knife." He struck a pose. "Stand back and ready yourselves . . . for some turkey!"

He began to carve; then everyone laughed as Kit held her hand out for Alva to pay up on the betting pool. They laughed even harder when Baxter held his hand out next.

And so it went for the next several hours, with everyone enjoying the leisurely meal and different pairs heading back to the beach as turtles continued to emerge, less often now. No one cared that some food was cold or if sand made its way into unfortunate places. Mud boots and jackets had been fetched as the breeze picked up.

Morgan finally had the chance to chat with Gabe, asking him just how unusual a daytime hatch was.

The doctor explained it wasn't entirely unheard of, especially toward the end of a protracted hatch season. "But I doubt you'll see anything like this again anytime soon. This was a very special day."

"Indeed, that it was." *In so many ways,* Morgan thought. He knew the people who had participated in the turtle hatchings had bonded in a way that would never be forgotten. Longtime friends shared a new experience that strengthened their bond, and those meeting for the first time created an indelible memory together that would likely lead to many more.

Seated between Kit and Birdie, Lilly was finally winding down as they enjoyed some of Kit's peanut pie. He smiled, feeling his heart swell, and thought how right it was, watching the three of them together, seeing Kit and Birdie exchange knowing looks over a drooping Lilly's head and assist her with cutting her pie. Right, wrong, or foolish, he didn't want this day—or that particular union—to end.

"This might be the best Thanksgiving I've ever had," he told Gabe, his gaze still on the three of them. He'd almost thought of them as "his girls" . . . and knew it was something he very much wanted to be true.

Anne joined them, having come up from the nesting area. "Light's fading fast and the nest is getting a bit more active again. I think we're in for a last burst."

It wasn't five o'clock yet, but the sun set early that time of year. It was on the tip of Morgan's tongue to say he'd stay, but Lilly was all but asleep in her empty pie plate. He'd have to take her home soon.

Birdie got up and came over to where the three of them stood. "If you'd like to stay on, I'd be happy to stay at your place for a bit and babysit," she offered. "I imagine Lilly will be out like a light as soon as her head hits the pillow." She glanced back at her granddaughter and smiled. "If she makes it that long."

Right there was proof of how incredible a day it had been. Something Morgan couldn't have imagined that morning seemed like the most natural thing in the world. "If you're sure it's not an imposition,"

"Morgan, dear," she said, putting her hand on his arm. "I'd be delighted."

"I don't have the guest room fully set up, but there is a bed with clean sheets and a blanket in there. If you're sure it's okay, I imagine I'll be here for a time. If you'd be comfortable staying over, we can have breakfast and get you back home in the morning."

"That sounds wonderful. I'm a night bird, and always have a book in my bag, so don't worry yourself. I'll be fine. As long as darling Lilly knows where I am if she needs anything, we'll manage for the night." Her gaze drifted to Kit, who was chatting with Riley, then back to Morgan. "No need to hurry back on my account," she added with an extra twinkle in her gaze.

"We'd really appreciate the help," Anne said to Morgan, saving him from figuring out how to respond to that. Of course, none of the crowd had been shy about trying to get the two of them together that day.

"Kit said she'd stay, too," Anne went on. "Riley and Quinn are going to head back to the house with Alva, pack up leftovers and see everyone on their way, then come back for a spell. I think Lani and Baxter plan to as well. Franco and Dre have to head back across the causeway."

"That's more help than I thought we'd have and I'm grateful for it," Gabe added. "A very thankful and blessed Thanksgiving," he said, speaking louder so everyone would hear.

"Amen," everyone still sitting and standing around the table intoned, lifting a jumble of drinks, cupcakes, and pie forks in unison.

Morgan went over to the table, and with Kit's help,

scooped Lilly directly from her seat into his arms. She hugged him and pressed her cheek to his chest. "More turtles?" she asked groggily.

"Not tonight, sweet pea. Time for home and some sleep. We'll come back tomorrow."

"Okay." She wasn't putting up a fight and yawned deeply, confirming his diagnosis of exhaustion and making him smile. "I like peanut pie," she said, already fading. "It's amazing."

"Ah-mazing," Morgan repeated, then kissed the top of her head.

He looked around at the crowd. "Thanks, everyone," he said, quietly so as not to rouse her. "I can't tell you how much this day has meant to us. We're blessed to know you all and look forward to spending more time with you in the future."

"I think I speak for everyone when I say it was our pleasure," Alva said, bustling around the table with enough energy for three people, despite the long day.

Everyone nodded, waved, smiled, and Franco gave a two-knife salute as he continued carving what was left of the three turkeys while Lani packed the leftovers into portable take-home containers for anyone who was interested.

"Now, you stop by Quinn and Riley's tomorrow," Alva was saying. "I'll leave a care package for you and Miss Lilly in their fridge."

"We will. Thank you."

He hadn't spent much time with the tiny senior, but knew she was quite a pistol. He could see why Kit enjoyed her so much. He'd heard Lani say she was Sugarberry's answer to Betty White, and he had to agree that was a pretty apt description.

"I'll go with you," Birdie said. "My car is still at Quinn's, if we can stop by."

"Unless it's in the way, I can take you back tomorrow to get it when we pick up our leftovers," Morgan told her. "Just come on home with us and we'll get both of you settled."

"Birdie, you come by and get a care package, tomorrow, too," Alva told her, squeezing her hand.

Birdie leaned down and hugged the smaller woman, then they bussed cheeks.

"It was a good day," Alva said, eyes shining.

"Indeed," Birdie agreed, beaming right back.

Morgan didn't see Kit again before they left as she was taking a turn on the beach, but he already planned to catch up with her when he got back. He hoped his tired little one didn't balk at the idea of Birdie staying over, but at this point, he sincerely doubted it.

They managed to accomplish their mission in a little less than an hour. He'd had to wake Lilly up enough to explain about Birdie being there while he finished helping Dr. Gabe, and he was pretty sure she understood it all before she drifted off again. Birdie had his cell phone number and he was only five minutes away if Lilly woke up and panicked in any way. He doubted, however, she'd wake up again until the sun was well up in the sky the following morning. She'd had no chance for a nap or some quiet time that entire day and had literally raced around the beach the whole time they'd been there.

He smiled as he pulled back into the lot at the research center, thinking what an incredible experience it had turned out to be for her. And for him. "A miracle of a day," he murmured. Lilly and Birdie connecting the way they had, sharing such a magical day, was so much more than he had hoped for. And everyone had been great. With him, with Lilly. He truly, truly was thankful.

He emerged from the dune path and headed down the beach as a full moon began its ascent into the early evening sky, and thought about the one other thing he still wanted to accomplish before the day was over.

When he made it to the nest area, only Anne and Lani were there. "Gabe and Baxter are back in the center," Anne told him. "He had evening rounds to do with our current residents."

"Baxter is fascinated by all this," Lani added, with an affectionate grin. "He'd never even seen a live turtle before. I think Gabe has himself a new benefactor. They're talking about ways Baxter might be able to use his show or his celebrity status to help draw attention to the sea turtles' plight, find some way to tie it in."

"That's fantastic," Morgan said, grinning in surprise. "Gabe must be ecstatic."

"He's had quite a wonderful day, yes," Anne added, tired but beaming.

Morgan glanced out at the beach, but the dim light made it hard to see anything.

"If you're looking for Kit, she's by the water, about twenty or so yards down the beach," Lani said, moving to stand beside him. "We had a straggler who just couldn't find the water. She's probably done by now." Lani smiled up at him, not even bothering to hide the knowing twinkle in her eyes. "But she might appreciate the company on the stroll back."

All day people had been trying to nudge the two of them together. But, other than their first team chaperone effort, he hadn't spent any time alone with Kit.

He'd noted that as they worked, Lilly had gone just as often to Kit as she had him. Kit had been relaxed, having fun, and really at ease. She was great with Lilly, so open and loving. They came together so easily, so naturally, and, not once did Kit pull back or even hesitate. He couldn't know if it was just the situation and the heightened emotions that went with it . . . or if she was rethinking her stance on taking a risk on him. On them.

"So . . . that full moon sure is pretty," Lani said quite pointedly, pulling him from his thoughts, making even Anne laugh.

"I'm going, I'm going." With a wave, he took off down the beach at a slow jog, heading in the direction they'd pointed him.

Morgan chuckled. He'd thought it would be uncomfortable, having everyone rooting for him and Kit to get together. But it hadn't been awkward or uncomfortable; it was funny and sweet. Because he completely agreed with them. Kit had been good-natured about it, too. He supposed it was time to find out exactly where her thoughts were on . . . well, everything.

He found her a good thirty yards or more down the shoreline, still standing by the water's edge, looking out at the waves.

"Silly turtle," she said, looking up when she saw him approach. "Four tries, and he keeps getting tossed back. After all his crawling to get there by the very long detour route he took, I'm afraid he's exhausted."

Morgan stopped by her side, looking out at the waves, too, but not knowing where to search in the vastness of the moonlit water. "One thing I learned today is they're the most determined little guys I've ever seen. He'll make it."

Kit sighed, clearly worried. "I hope so."

"All the other ones did," he assured her.

"I still can't get over how tiny they are. I mean, they grow to be so huge. The odds seem insurmountable, starting out that small. It's really a miracle any of them make it."

Morgan had to work hard to resist the urge to pull her into his arms. She was tired and concerned, and it seemed like the most natural thing in the world to hold her. "The journey they make is an incredible one with all kinds of dangers, but they've been doing it for thousands of years. We'll just hope all of our turtles find the flotsam and jetsam out there and ride the tides all the way to the Caribbean without any worries."

Kit sent him a sideways glance, a wry twist to her lips. "You really are the most optimistic lawyer I've ever met."

He grinned back. "Saving the planet, one baby turtle at a time."

She let out a short laugh and looked back out to the water. "Well, he didn't wash up again, so I guess he made it."

Morgan said to hell with playing it safe and shifted to stand behind her, putting his hands on her shoulders and massaging them lightly as he watched the waves with her. "This was a good day, Kit. We did good."

"We did," she said softly. "And that feels wonderful, by the way." But she wasn't relaxing under his touch. "I'm just . . ."

He turned her slowly to face him, keeping her close. "You're a protector. It's your nature to look out, to take care, which means you're also a worrier," he teased lightly, smiling. "That isn't entirely a bad thing. Someone needs to look out for others."

"I used to look out for a whole lot of others. It's been . . . well, it's been a relief, in some ways, not to have to do that anymore . . . but it's been weird, too. It wasn't just my job, it was . . . well, you're right, it was me."

"Being a new parental role model, I think I can safely say it takes one to know one."

Her lips lifted a little again.

"So . . . now you can worry about our baby turtles." He slid one hand to her chin, tipped her face up to his. "But not too much. Okay?"

She didn't try to move away, nor had she stiffened at his

touch. She still had that half smile on her face. "Will you believe me if I say okay back?"

"Not really."

She laughed. "How about I'll try?"

"Good start. I'll take it."

They fell silent for a moment, but their gazes stayed locked on each other. He wanted to slide his hand around to the nape of her neck, urge her mouth to his, and end the night the way he truly ached to.

"It *was* a good start," she said, her voice a little uneven. "Today, I mean."

Morgan's heart kicked into gear along with his hopes. "It was. In a lot of very good ways."

"I'm so happy about Lilly and Birdie. And everyone, all of it. I'm glad you two decided to join us, and that we all came out here. It was really just . . . incredible."

"Agreed. A lot of new friendships started today, and others grew closer. I was thinking about that as I drove back here. Birdie and Lilly . . . I don't even know where to start about how special that was."

"Everyone saw it, too," Kit said. "It touched every heart here."

You touch mine every time I look at you, he thought, barely managing not to say the words out loud. "I—"

"Morgan—"

They started at the same time, then broke off.

"Go on," he said. "What were you going to say?"

She searched his face, his eyes, as if debating to say what was on her mind, and he felt like some part of him was slowly dying inside, as all he could do was wait . . . and hope. He braced himself for the worst, sensing that their closeness was coming to an end. Again. He didn't think he'd handle it gracefully this time. This time he'd fight for what he wanted. For what he knew was already there between them.

Carefully choosing her words, she began. "Today was so good, so . . . unexpected. I had such a good time. With everyone, but especially with Lilly." She held his gaze. "And with you."

Just like that, everything jumbled up inside him. His pulse was suddenly pounding like thunder, echoing in his ears, inside his head. Had she changed her mind . . . did she mean . . . ?

"I'm worried," she went on, and his heart ricocheted back the other way.

"About?" he managed.

"We were a big group today, but I spent a lot of time with Lilly and . . . I loved it." She looked at him. "I love her, Morgan, I really do. I mean, how can I not? Everyone does. But I feel that we have this special connection. I . . . can't explain it, exactly. Maybe it's because we both lost our parents, albeit at very different times in our lives, or—I don't know. But it's there."

"I watched her with you today, too." *And it made me fall even harder for you,* he wanted to add. "She reached for you, looked for you, instinctively."

"I know," Kit said, but she wasn't smiling. "And . . . a part of me feels so good, so touched. I want to be there for her—"

"You are." Morgan was beyond knowing what to think, what to feel. "But . . . the other part of you . . . feels what?"

She didn't respond and looked away.

He urged her gaze back to his again. "Kit, there's nothing wrong with you and Lilly bonding. Or Lilly and Birdie bonding, or Lilly and Dre. I want her to have people she can trust, rely on, and turn to. It doesn't have to be bigger than that." But the longer the conversation went on, the more he realized he wanted it to be a whole lot bigger than that.

"There was no secret today . . . folks pushing us together, making not-so-veiled innuendos. "It was funny and sweet and everyone meant well. And I know it went right over Lilly's head, but—"

"But what if Lilly starts wanting that, too? Is that what you're worried about?"

"I've thought about it. Yes."

"So have I. Would it be so bad, Kit?" he asked quietly. "For her to want that? For us to want that?"

To his complete surprise, her face crumpled, and tears filled those luminous eyes of hers.

He didn't push, didn't prod. He just pulled her into his arms, tucking her face against his shoulder and held on. He cupped his hand to the back of her head, soothing her and wrapping her close. "It's okay," he said, stroking her hair, though he honestly wasn't sure whether it was or not.

"What if . . ." Her voice was muffled against his chest.

He urged her to lift her head and leaned down to catch her gaze. "What if . . . ?"

"What if I let her down, too?" Her eyes, so big, awash with tears, broke his heart. "I don't—I can't risk that. I've let so many people down, my employees, my family—" She shook her head, unable to continue. Tears tracked down her cheeks. She looked utterly and completely defeated.

Morgan began to finally understand the enormity of what she was facing and what he was asking of her.

He framed her face when she would have looked away, brushing away her tears with his thumbs. "You've really been put through it, haven't you?"

"So has Lilly," she managed, her voice rough. "She deserves someone who has their act together, who—"

"She deserves someone who cares about her and who has her best interests at heart." He lifted Kit's face to his. "She has that with you. I know you feel you've lost your footing and you don't trust your instincts. I feel like that every day, being a new parent. I freak out pretty much hourly. And that's on a good day."

"You don't show it. You look . . . you two look perfect together. Like it's the most natural thing. You're great with her."

"Thank you. That means a great deal to me. But, you don't show it, either. You're handling the rebuild of the shop like you could do it in your sleep, volunteering with Gabe, spending time with Lilly, making new, really good friends with the cupcake group."

"Those things don't scare me." Kit looked right at him, the stark helplessness she felt right there for him to see. "At least not like you do."

His felt his heart clutch, and sighed. "Kit—"

"Wanting you scares me. Wanting Lilly scares me. I came here looking for a new start." She smiled, even though her eyes were glassy and tears still pooled. "I was going to take baby steps, slowly get myself back to where I felt steadier, rebuild my confidence . . . work on the guilt that still wracks me. I failed everyone. I lost something generations of people had devoted their whole lives to. Something I'd devoted my whole life to. And, instead, I feel like I just took a huge dive, head first, straight into the deep end of the pool. I'm handling Babycakes okay. It's a slow process and Lani and Baxter are easy and great to work with. But it's still intimidating. I want to do right by them." Her lips curved as she drew in uneven breaths. "I freak out on an hourly basis there, too."

He tipped her chin up, then cupped her cheek in his hand, needing to feel her, touch her. "So, take baby steps with me. With us."

"That's just it. With the shop, I had to dive in. And with you . . . you know we won't take baby steps. We already aren't. It's . . . overwhelming, how you make me feel. I don't know that I ever have felt like that—like this—with anyone, so fast, so . . . fully. I'm in uncharted territory . . . at a time when I'm already floundering. What happens if I just go for it, then completely fall apart when I realize I can't handle it?

"I can barely rely on myself right now. I can't do that to you, won't do that to Lilly." She looked into his eyes with a kind of desperation in hers. "What if you and Lilly start to depend on me, to count on me, and I fail you, too? I don't think I could live with that."

"Aw, Kit." He stroked her cheek, her hair, wishing there was a magic wand he could wave and take the pain away. He could feel the trembling, see the fear.

"It's not all on you, you know. Not the loss of the company and not this relationship. It's a group effort.

"The group named Teddy and Trixie should have had your back where the company was concerned. They let you down when you needed them, counted on them. They let everyone down, putting what they wanted first, above and beyond everything and everyone. You never do that. That's not you. Your employees know that, and I know the Bellamy women who came before you had to know that, too."

He sighed, knowing words weren't enough. She'd experienced the pain, seen the faces, had to deliver the news, and watch as the doors were closed, then watch again when her generations-old family home was sold out from under her.

"All I can tell you is that this group effort—meaning me, you, Lilly—has got your back. When you need something, whatever it is, I got you. And when I need something, I hope you got me. When Lilly needs something, we tag team it. Like we already do when we're all together. Have you noticed that? We just . . . do it. You understand her. You've been in her shoes. What more could she ever hope for than you? Then we just keep doing that, keep being there for each other." He smiled, even as his heart ached for her. "One hourly freak-out at a time."

Her bottom lip trembled with a smile, even as her eyes searched his. The yearning, the want, the desire were there, vibrant and tremulous . . . and so was the fear.

Morgan knew being vulnerable, baring herself to him, was costing her. "I know it would be easier if things happened to us when we were most prepared to deal with them. But we both know that's not how it works. Things happen to us when they happen. The part that is up to us is what we do about it. I know what I want to do about this. About you. About us. Crazy or not, there already is an us. You know that, right? You do feel that?"

She nodded, but he could feel her tremble again in his arms. He wanted to hunt Teddy Carruthers down and wring the bastard's conniving, soulless neck with his bare hands for causing her so much pain.

He wouldn't get a better chance to pour his own heart out. And she needed to hear him before she made up her mind for good.

"So, should we walk away from the good things because the harsh things happened? Or . . . do we cling to the good things, and revel in them, because we so dearly know their value. I mean, otherwise, why the hell are we here?" He worked to soften his tone, gentle his own indignation on her behalf. "I want to revel, Kit. I want to revel in this." His voice shook a little. "I want to revel in you."

His gaze shifted from her big, vulnerable eyes to the quiver of her bottom lip . . . and he lowered his head, soothing her—and himself—in the only other way he knew how. He took her mouth in a kiss saying all the rest of the things he had no words for. He didn't know how else to explain to her what they had and why it was worth fighting for.

She gasped against his mouth, stilled for a moment, surprised . . . then sank right into it with him on a long, keening sigh. He didn't think, he didn't pause, he didn't second-guess.

He claimed.

Even the depth of the carnal kiss they'd shared before didn't touch the connection they were making at that moment. It wasn't slow, and it wasn't tender. It was hot and hungry, no games, no holding back. It was a single kiss, but it laid them both bare. He took, he tasted, he plundered . . . and urged her to do the same. It was only the need to draw in air that broke the kiss apart.

"You know," she said, fighting to breathe and speak at the same time, clinging to his shoulders to keep steady on her feet. "I think you missed your calling . . . as a trial attorney." She managed to shoot him that crooked half smile of hers, standing there with her hair going every which way, her cheeks still streaked with tears, and her mouth looking like someone had just kissed it quite thoroughly.

His heart teetered right over that edge, and there was no hope of pulling it back. "And why is that?" he asked, his own voice sounding like gravel scraping on sand.

"Because, when you defend something you're passionate about there's not a jury in the world who'd deny you your desired outcome."

He grinned, too, resigning himself to the fact that his heart was never going to straighten itself out and get back to a regular rhythm anytime soon. But if she kept smiling at him like that, frankly, he didn't give a damn. "There's just a jury of one I'm interested in swaying to my point of view."

Kit reached up and brushed the hair from his forehead . . . and smiled. "Well"—she took a shuddering, shaky breath, but her smile didn't waver—"I think you can consider me swayed."

Morgan's face split into a wider grin. He wanted to bust out a war whoop, swing her joyously around, dance under the moon . . . and take her right there on the sand.

"I've always thought your grin was mischievous bordering on wicked," she said, not seeming at all put off by that fact. Quite the opposite, if he could be any rational sort of judge. "But right now, it looks downright fierce."

"Is that a bad thing?" he asked, taking in her whole face, her eyes, those streaked cheeks, that soft mouth. "Because you make me feel some pretty fierce things."

She shook her head, and when her gaze drifted from his eyes, down to his mouth, his lips curved in a slow, lazy smile. He bent his head slowly, his gaze staying on hers until their lips met, and then he took her, opened her, reveled in her. The hunger was a slow, consuming roll, but just as ravenous. He slid his hands down her spine, closed his palms around her waist, then moved them down over the curve of her incredibly delicious backside, urging her closer until he molded her body to his.

She moaned softly against his mouth, aware of what she was doing to his body, to him.

"Yes, I want you," he said against her lips as he moved from her mouth, laying a trail of hot, sweet kisses along her jaw, to the side of her neck, and up to the tender softness of her earlobe. "I want to peel these clothes off you and feel every bare inch of you on me."

She shuddered hard against him as he nudged the neckline of her blouse open and continued his seductive trek.

"I want to hear you moan, make you gasp. I want you to arch under me. And over me. And I want to sink every last aching inch of myself into you."

She was trembling for very different reasons as he kissed his way back along her jaw, then framed her face with his palms until she opened her eyes. Eyes that were huge and dark and drenched with the same exact need and want swamping him.

"I want all of you. Do you understand?"

She nodded, her body shaking against his. Or maybe it was him.

"I want your fear, your laughter, your doubts, your triumphs. I want your tears, your joy, your frustration, your excitement." He traced his thumbs over her cheeks and felt his heart tumble the rest of the way down that steep, slick slide . . . and reveled in the ride. "I want your heart, Kit. I want it all."

Chapter 18

"Morgan . . . " Kit was breathless . . . in more ways than one.

"Don't—you don't have to say anything to that. Just . . . taking this one step, that's enough. One step. Then we take another and another. One at a time, okay? Where it leads is where it leads. I'm being honest about where I hope it will go. I wouldn't ask you to try this, knowing how you feel, knowing how hard this is, if I didn't think the payoff would be worth it."

"You're so confident about this."

"You said this was different from anything you'd experienced. Well, it is for me, too. It's easy and natural and very, very good. You make me laugh, you make me think. And I want you so badly my teeth ache. I don't know how long it's supposed to take to figure it out, but I've been told, on more than one occasion, that I'd know it when I was knocked over the head with it." He grinned. "Turns out they were right."

She grinned back because it was impossible not to. He looked so . . . taut, so intense, excited, and . . . worried. It was adorable, charming, and hot as hell, all at the same time. "I'll take that first step with you."

Fierce didn't begin to describe the joy in his smile. "I know I'm pressuring you—hard—but—"

"But you've made me think, too, Morgan. And you're right. We've had a lot taken from us without our consent or any preparation—leaving huge, gaping holes in our lives. I need to think about filling those holes, instead of tiptoeing around them, afraid I'll fall in."

He stroked her cheek, pulled her closer, and it was that very instinct to comfort, to take care that dowsed any lingering doubts she had. There was no telling where it would lead, but he wouldn't be careless, and he wouldn't be thoughtless, and she honestly couldn't ask for more than that.

"It's a natural instinct to duck and cover," he told her. "I think . . . if it hadn't been for Lilly, maybe I would have ducked, too. Losing my brother . . ." He shook his head, and then she was the one reaching up to soothe, to stroke, to comfort. She saw the surprise when he met her gaze again . . . and how that ferocity in his had deepened.

She didn't know it was possible to feel so content and so utterly and inexorably turned on at the same time. Now that she'd finally let her guard completely down and opened herself up to the possibilities, everything inside her ached for him. It was terrifying but it was also exhilarating. She'd just have to cling to that last part, instead of being cowed by the first.

"After all that's happened, I feel I've lost my sister, too. It's not at all the same, of course, but it does make me think about regrets and what will be in the future between us." Kit held his cheek in her palm, held his gaze just as surely. "Asher named you as guardian to his only child. So you know he loved you, you know he respected you. And I'm sure he knew he could count on you, too. When push came to shove, you were family. Keep that in your heart. It's what I'm trying to do."

"Wise words. I just . . . haven't really let myself go there," he said somewhat haltingly. "I've dealt with the shock of it and my tangled feelings about my family and the choices I've made. Then I just poured all the rest of my energy into focusing on Lilly. But I miss him. We were nothing alike, shared very little in our adult lives, but at the core of it all, we were brothers. We grew up together, got in trouble together. When I was little, I wanted to do everything he did. That changed as we got older, but—"

"But it doesn't change—never changes—who you were to each other. Siblings. I know a little something about that." She soothed his cheek with her hand, then slid both hands to the nape of his neck and tugged his mouth down to hers.

"Kit, you don't have to—"

"Sh," she said, kissing the corners of his mouth. "Protectors need protecting, too." Then she quieted any other response he might have made by taking his mouth with her own. It was a marvel to her that every kiss they shared seemed so different, revealed so much more . . . pulled her in that much deeper. They'd shared so much of themselves already, intimate things, things she never shared and doubted he did, either. In the short time they'd been wrapped up in each other, standing on the beach under a full moon, the desire to share the most intimate moment with him, to have him in exactly the very graphic way he described wanting her, had grown from hunger to downright craving.

He sank into the kiss, pulling her deeply into it with him. Her hands roamed, sliding over his shoulders, drawing her palms down over his well-muscled chest, reveling in the thundering vibration of his heartbeat, over his flat belly, finally hooking her fingers into the loops of his trousers and tugging him closer. He growled against her mouth and surprised her by scooping her up against him and wrapping her around him.

"Kit—" he managed as he left her mouth and dropped heated, hungry kisses along her jaw and her neck.

"I know." She felt the same sense of urgency. "Me, too."

He swung her around. "Hold on."

She instinctively wrapped her legs around his waist as he started up the sand toward the dunes. "Morgan . . . the turtles . . . Gabe . . . everyone—"

"Will not come looking for us if we don't go back to the nest. I'm sure they think we're taking a stroll down the beach and will be very happy to chat about that." The moonlight caught his knowing grin as he looked down into her eyes. "We are taking a stroll . . . just up the beach instead of along the shoreline."

"But . . . where?"

The answer became clear as he wound down a short path through the dunes to a clearing where a small grouping of three bungalows, two small and one a bit larger, sat catty-corner to the others. They were weathered and worn, but appeared sturdy and . . . apparently uninhabited.

"What are these?" she asked, looking around as he slid her to her feet. The moonlight made it easier to see, but there were still more shadows than light. She could hear the crash of the waves, but the ocean was hidden from view over the dunes circling the tiny cottages, nestling them and protecting them. It was charming and rustic . . . and pretty much perfect.

"Gabe and Anne had these built about ten years ago to house visiting professors and occasionally student interns who come from other parts of the country—the world, actually—to study and work here. They're mostly used during the spring and summer and sit empty through the winter. Gabe and I have been trying to figure out a way to use them year-round so they are more beneficial to the center."

He took her hand and walked up the short path to the largest of the three, then reached up and felt along the top of the doorframe. He smiled as he lowered his hand again . . . with the key in his possession.

Kit laughed, excited and nervous. "I can't believe we're doing this."

"We don't have to *do* anything, you know," he said, pausing before he unlocked the door. "I just want some privacy, to spend a little time with you away from everyone. So we can be just us . . . for a little while." He leaned down and kissed her, short, sweet, and quite tender. "Okay?"

She nodded, feeling silly for the sudden burning sensation in her eyes . . . happy tears . . . surprised again at how many ways he touched her.

As they entered the bungalow together, she realized she had come to trust him, felt comfortable and safe with him . . . but equally enjoyed that she never knew what he'd do next, that he was confident, bold, aggressive, and not afraid to take what he wanted. The dichotomy of protector and possessor, and her desire to experience both in the most intimate way a woman could, had her taking his hand and turning him to face her before he could light the hurricane lamp on the tiny dining room table.

"Morgan." Without saying another word, she pulled his head down and kissed him.

He groaned, low and deep in his throat as he filled his hands with her. He wasn't shy, and it wasn't awkward. In fact, it was exactly what she wanted. He bumped the two of them backward several steps, clattering into one of the two chairs positioned around the table. "Hold on," he mumbled against her lips.

Hiking her up in his arms, he carried her through a narrow door into a small bedroom, lowered her to the comforter stretched across the double bed, and followed her down.

She'd already come to love the feel of his hands, the way he framed her cheeks, the way he slid his fingers through her hair. He made it personal, like she was the absolute center of his attention. As he did when he lifted his head, just long enough to connect his gaze to hers. "Are you sure?"

She didn't take offense at his presumption of where this was going, because it was going exactly where it had been going since the moment they'd laid eyes on one another. "I thought I made that pretty clear out there in the kitchen-slash-dining room-slash-living room."

His lips curved. "It is pretty cozy."

She wriggled under him and reveled in the way his body jerked and twitched at the feel of her. "I like cozy."

"I'm liking it better by the second," he agreed. Bracing his weight on his elbows, he brushed the hair off her forehead with his fingertips. "I know we haven't talked about things like other relationships and—"

"I'm not in any other relationships." She smiled. "I can barely handle the idea of one at a time. I want only one at a time."

"For a very long time . . . this time."

"I hope so."

"The same," he agreed, "on all counts. The reason I mentioned it is I want you to know you're safe with me. Okay?"

"Oh. Right. I . . . thank you. I'm glad you made sure I knew that. It's . . . been a long time and I didn't catch on to what . . . You're safe with me, too," she blurted, feeling silly for suddenly stumbling over such a simple declaration. "In fact, you're really . . . really safe with me." She smiled up into his eyes . . . and slid her hands down his back, and pulled his wallet from his back pocket. "Meaning, you don't need . . . things. Unless you want to."

He covered her hand, slipped his wallet from her fingers . . . and tossed it across the room.

"Good," she said.

"Oh, yeah," he agreed, and the look in his eyes brought her back to that place of confidence and ease.

She slid her hands back up his body and stroked her fingertips along his jaw, then over his lower lip, following her actions closely with her gaze, wondering how his mouth was going to feel on all those places he'd yet to use it.

"Do you have any idea what it does to me when you look at my mouth like that?" His voice was not much more than a low grumble, and it did delicious things to her insides. Her outsides, too, for that matter.

She grinned, and for the first time, felt a little mischievous and fierce. "Like what? Like a woman who has finally decided to give in to her most carnal desire?"

His grin was slow, wide, and very, very wicked. "I've never been someone's most carnal desire."

"Well," she said, pulling his head down to hers, "you can't say that anymore."

Framing her face again, a slight tension in his fingers now as he shifted her head so his mouth would fit hers more perfectly. "No, I definitely can't." He kissed her deeply, pushed her up the bed, and began unbuttoning her blouse. With the sun down, the air had cooled considerably, but it felt like a caress on her overheated skin as he bared more and more of it to his touch . . . and his taste. Her shirt followed his wallet; her pants met the same fate.

She felt alive and free, desirable and incredibly wanton. Splayed, naked beneath him, as he, still fully dressed, took every advantage of her. His lips were warm, his tongue wet, and his fingers just a little rough.

She responded to all of it, writhing, twisting, arching. He made her moan. He made her beg.

She burrowed her fingers in his hair, urging him to where she wanted him most. She could feel him smile against the soft skin of her inner thigh.

"Demanding," he murmured.

"It's tough being the most carnal desire," she managed, which made him chuckle.

She smiled, thinking she couldn't remember a time in her life when she'd felt so completely and utterly herself. Maybe she'd never known who she really was, she'd been so busy being who she was supposed to be, who she needed to be. With Morgan, nothing was censored, nothing hidden. She could trust him with all of who she was, even—and maybe precisely—when she wasn't sure quite who that might be. Yet.

But she was figuring it out. And loving every second of it.

"You know," he said, teasing her with light kisses along her thigh, up to her hipbone . . . then slowly across to the other one, before trailing equally light and lazy kisses down to the inside of her other thigh. "I think . . . you should get . . . a taste . . . of what it's like . . . to be the most carnal desire."

Her short laugh turned into a gasp, and her hips arched straight off the bed when he slid his tongue deep inside her.

Her fingers dug into the mattress, and everything in her arched and keened as he drove her quite decidedly straight to the edge, and raced her right over. It was almost wrenching, the pleasure he was giving her, and she continued to buck underneath him, shocked at the strength of wave upon wave. She would have pushed him away, thinking any more would paralyze her, but he gentled his tongue, gentled his fingers, and he stayed right where he was.

And the next time, it was slow, and languorous, almost torturous . . . and, at the end, downright volcanic.

"Very . . . very . . . carnal," he murmured against her thigh.

She was shaking, still gasping, even as he made her laugh. And then she was reaching for him, wanting more, but most important wanting him.

He shifted onto his knees and pulled his shirt off and over his head. Onto the pile with the wallet and her clothes it went. Smiling at each other, he playfully shifted his hands to his waistband, teasing her by unbuckling his belt excruciatingly slowly.

It was hard to believe she could go from mind-numbing climax to playful laughter, that she was sprawled open to him, vulnerable to him, and was thinking only of what would happen next.

He slid his belt free, made her eyes go wide when he snapped it once or twice, then tossed it away. "Not that I don't think you'd look incredible in leather," he said, making her laugh all over again. "But not under it."

"Good to know. I like my pleasure to be . . . you know, pleasurable."

"Me, too." His hands went to his waistband. "How'm I doing so far?"

He was just the right amount of cocky without being arrogant, just the right amount of playful, while still taking it seriously.

She knew he was vulnerable, too, knew he understood what it was to be hurt, so it made the moments they were sharing all the more meaningful. No pretense, no posturing. But . . . she decided he shouldn't get to call all the shots. Smiling and giving him a very pointed once-over, she sat up and put her hands over his as he undid the button of his trousers. "You got to unwrap your presents. Don't I get to unwrap mine?"

He barked out a laugh, but lifted his hands straight up and away.

She laughed at the antics. "You're so easy like that."

He grinned, unrepentant. "I know." Then he tackled her, making her squeal, before rolling to his back, carrying her with him. "Go ahead," he flung his arms wide once she'd straddled his waist. "Have your wanton, wicked way with me."

"Well, I'm not very wicked," she said, running her hands down his chest. "But I am feeling particularly wanton." She slid back and flipped open the button and hook of his trousers, then slowly tugged them down until he could kick them off. She didn't even care where they landed.

"Black," she said, running her fingers under the edge of his boxer briefs.

"It's slimming," he teased.

His grin was all the motivation she needed to stroke her hand over the very impressive bulge stretching the front panel. "Not really."

He jerked under the touch of her hand, half groaning, half laughing. She carefully freed him, but had barely drawn the briefs over his thighs when she found herself abruptly rolled to her back as he jerked them the rest of the way off and slid on top of her.

"So unfair." She was having a hard time not giggling. "You got to unwrap."

"But—"

He pressed a finger across her lips. "But if you'd gone any further, we wouldn't have gotten to this." He shifted between her legs and pushed slowly inside of her.

"Oh . . . ohhhh," she said, ending on a very long, very satisfied moan as he filled her. "You may have a point." She pressed a finger across his lips. "Yes, it's one I am liking"—she arched—"very, very, much."

He kissed her fingertip, then nipped the end of it before pinning her hands to the bed and moving inside of her. "Move with me," he coaxed, rolling his hips, and hers lifted again of their own volition.

"Morgan—"

"I know."

For the first time, she heard in his voice the strain of the restraint he was showing. which prompted her to slip her hands free and pull his head to hers. She lifted her hips higher, wrapped her legs around him, and dug her heels into his back. "Now you move with me," she said, and began pumping her hips.

"Kit—"

"I'm not made of glass, you know." She nipped his ear, then his chin, then his bottom lip.

"Sweet Lord, have mercy," he whispered, the deep south of his roots coming through in every reverently spoken word as he gave in . . . and let go.

Kit didn't know which was more exhilarating, more fulfilling; the way he naturally matched her thrust for thrust, going harder and faster, taking her to greater heights than she'd known she could reach . . . or that he'd trusted her enough to cut himself loose of his natural desire to protect, even while possessing.

She wasn't sure who cried out first, who shattered first. All she knew was that she was wrapped around him, and he around her . . . and both held on until all there was left to do was reclaim their breath and let their shuddering, spent bodies revel in what had just happened.

He finally rolled to his side, taking her with him, her leg

wrapped over his, his arm around her as if it was a particular comfort they'd sought a hundred times before.

"I think my eyes are permanently crossed," she murmured, her cheek pressed against his chest, feeling every beat of his rapidly thumping heart. She managed to lift her head just enough to prop up her chin and look at him. "You give great most carnal desire, do you know that?"

"I'm sorry," he managed, "I'm still having an out of body experience. I'll be back with you in a minute."

She snorted and felt him chuckle as he tucked her against him, wrapping her up snugly in his arms.

"It's funny," she said, moments later when their breathing finally slowed.

"What's funny?" he asked, sounding drowsy and sexy and very content as he traced lazy circles on her lower back with his fingertips.

"This was so . . . crazy. Crazy good, but definitely in some other realm. And . . . we're new to each other in so many ways yet."

"But?" There was not a tense muscle in his body at the moment, and she smiled against his chest, glad he still trusted her, believing in the good and not worrying about wherever she was leading him.

"I feel like there is so much I want to know, have yet to find out . . . but, at the same time, I feel like we're already closer than . . ." She trailed off, unable to find the right words.

He shifted her effortlessly on top of him and opened his eyes so he could look into hers. "Even before this . . . crazy good part, I felt that." He searched her eyes, as serious as she'd ever seen him. "I couldn't say that, of course. I was already pushing so hard, and—I know you won't believe me—but that's not something I've ever been compelled to do." He brushed at the hair still clinging damply to her forehead and looked at her the way a man might when he couldn't quite believe his good fortune. "But that was the reason I pushed. It was like I've known you for so very long, and I've been looking for you and looking for you and then, one day, there you finally are. Even in that first moment, it was like, ah, there you are."

He lifted his head, kissed her lightly on the mouth, making her smile against his lips, even as tears—the very best kind—formed in her eyes. "And, every time we spoke, every moment we've spent together, has felt like I was reacquainting myself with someone I already knew so well. We already get it, already know, and are finally just teaming up and getting on with where we're supposed to be."

Her smile grew, and, glassy-eyed, she leaned down and kissed him, tenderly. "If you'd told me that at any other time, I would have convinced myself you truly were a crazy man. A part of me would have had to call myself crazy, too . . . because you're right. It's like the connection has been there all along. It was just a matter of figuring out how in the hell I was going to be okay with accepting it. I knew it was big, or would be, and I wasn't ready. It was the wrong time. Why now? Couldn't you have found me when I had my life together?"

His smile had spread slowly to a grin, and he rolled her slowly to her back, leaning over her, looking down into her eyes. "And then you realize that when you finally meet, when you finally find each other, it doesn't matter. All the rest of it doesn't matter. Life scattered, life together . . . it's just where things begin. It's where the story is when you jump into it. It doesn't stay there. You start writing the next chapter from that moment on."

"Seriously"—she sighed softly, charmed and grinning at the same time, her heart so full she thought it might burst—"you really should be in front of juries, like, every day. Your clients would get off scot-free. Every single time."

"I'm just glad the jury is still not out where we're concerned. It feels like it took an awfully long time to find each other. And I don't want to waste any more of it." He leaned down and kissed her, lingering, and then continuing on a little longer. Then they were laughing and saying meaningless things and kissing, then laughing again.

She was considering if her body was up to another round of most carnal desire, but his phone chirped—from somewhere in the room—with a text message.

To his credit, he didn't go diving off the bed looking for it, even though her first thought was Lilly, so she knew it had to have been his as well.

He rolled off her and they sat up, searching the room in the moonlight, waiting for the phone to chirp again. When it did, Morgan got up and went over to the pile of clothes and retrieved his phone from his pants pocket. "Birdie," he said, confirming her suspicions. He looked up, and even in the dim light she saw his shoulders sag in relief. "She's just letting me know Lilly woke up, had to use the bathroom, asked for some water." He grinned as he scrolled down, the light from the screen illuminating his face. "And didn't seem at all surprised to find Birdie there to help her sort things out before she climbed back into bed."

Kit slipped off the bed and crossed the short distance to him. "That's so good."

"Well, she's probably half sleepwalking, but yes, it's . . ." He sighed, and she could hear the relief and happiness in it.

"Yes," Kit said, slipping her arms around his waist. "It sure is."

She watched as he texted Birdie back, saying he'd be home soon and thanking her for being there and helping out.

Kit leaned her head against his shoulder as he closed the phone and dropped it back down in the pile of clothes, before turning and pulling her more directly into his arms. He kissed her once, then again.

"I know you need to get home, and I want you to go be with Birdie, be there for Lilly," she said between kisses, "but I will selfishly say that, at the same time, I wish this night could go on forever."

"Me, too." Morgan mercifully left the light off as they dressed, fumbling a little to find everything. Their vision had adapted to the moonlit darkness and anything brighter would have felt too harsh.

"My God, how did I not realize how sandy we were," Kit said, finding everything she picked up gritty.

"Because it wasn't sandy where it was important."

She laughed at that and brushed at her pants, though they really needed a good shaking outdoors. And a dry cleaner. A bonfire and a match, perhaps. "Can we come back here and clean up when it's light outside? I mean, the floor is covered in sand and the bed—"

Morgan twirled her around and up against his chest, making her laugh, then silencing her with a kiss. "I'm sure these bungalows have never had a grain of sand in them nor been mussed up a little. But yes. . . I'll get back here and remove any evidence that Goldilocks and her most carnal bear were here."

She giggled. "It might be easier if I did it, since you'll probably have baby bear with you."

"You do have a point."

She sighed deeply and appreciatively. "No, no . . . you're the one with the point."

He chuckled. "I suppose we need to return from our

walk down the beach, report in, see how the turtles are progressing."

"We should." She glanced down. "But you realize I have not a hope in hell of not looking like . . . well, exactly like what I look like."

"They're going to know eventually."

She pushed up to her tiptoes and kissed him, meaning it to be a hard, fast kiss, but somehow getting a little caught up in it. He helped it along by wrapping her up in his arms and urging her to continue.

When she finally broke the kiss, he was the one who spoke. "But, not tonight. This one is all ours."

She smiled. "Exactly. And thank you."

"I'll call Gabe, let him know we're heading out. He'll understand, and he'll . . . come up with something. There's a path from here that winds back to the center and the parking lot."

"I rode here with you, so—"

"We'll go by Riley's and get your car; then I'll drop you off. Where are you staying, anyway? I've never asked."

"Well, nowhere permanent yet. I've kind of squirreled myself away in the half apartment-half storage space over Lani's shop. I keep meaning to go look for a place, but haven't gotten to it yet. Riley told me today that she'd get listings for me to look at, not that there's much to choose from if I want to stay on the island. Which I do." She leaned her cheek to his chest. "It's funny, but it already feels like my place, this island. Like if I'm not going to be in Atlanta anymore, in the house I grew up in, then I want to be here. Not even over the bridge, but . . ."

"I know. Sugarberry is like that. I was going to have my office in Savannah, thinking Lilly would be in school and I could do the short commute, but once I got here, I realized I don't want to be that far from her. Honestly, even that was an excuse, because Savannah's only twenty minutes away. The island, the people remind me a lot of how I felt in Colorado. Savannah doesn't."

"When does Lilly start school? I hadn't even thought of that, but she is kindergarten age, right?"

"Well, she's only been taught privately—"

"Didn't she just turn five? How much could she have been taught?"

Morgan's lips twisted in a wry grin. "Oh, you don't even want to know."

"Oh, right. Oil paintings versus watercolor impressionists, or something like that. But . . . four or five years old?"

"That's why I want her art experience to be more about Gabe's turtle coloring book and finger painting—for now. I haven't talked to the school here yet, but I did look into it before we moved. It's just one school from kindergarten through eighth grade; then they go over the causeway for high school. It's small, with only one class per grade and sometimes even those are joined together when there aren't enough students to warrant teaching the grades separately."

"Wow, that is small. But it is a small island. I never thought about that. But, I think it's kind of cool. She'll make the dearest friends in her whole life and still get almost a private school level of attention. No overly crowded classrooms."

"I thought the same thing. I know there are pitfalls in having the same small group to deal with for so many years, especially if there are any problems."

"Nowhere to hide."

"Exactly. But, I think . . . all in all . . . that Lilly would do really well with the more relaxed, low key environment and a smaller group rather than a larger one. She's very assertive and chatty on the one hand, but she's still painfully shy, too. Especially in big crowds."

"I think she'll fit in well. Would she start now, or next fall?"

"That's what I need to figure out by Christmas. I wanted her to get to know more people on the island first, maybe find a way to meet some of the kids, if possible, but take it slow. I had been thinking I'd wait and let her have the summer to adjust, make new friends, so she'd feel more comfortable about belonging here before starting next fall. But . . . seeing her today . . . now I'm not sure."

"Well, maybe take her to the school, meet the teacher she'd have, watch how she is there. You'll know what's right."

Morgan chuckled. "Well, that would be a first. I'll do whatever feels right at the time anyway."

Kit hugged him and they slid their arms around each other's waists as they left the bungalow and started down the path to the parking lot. "That seems to be working out pretty well so far."

He paused beside the passenger door to his SUV and she looked up into his face. How was it that he'd become so dear to her, so quickly?

"Happy Thanksgiving, Kit. I am so thankful for this amazing, unexpected day. Actually, it warrants an ah-mazing, as Lilly would say."

Kit grinned. "Me, too. Thank you for being so sure. About us. For not letting it go. For not letting me go." She tipped up on her toes, kissed him. "My most carnal desire."

He laughed against her lips. "You know, if you're not careful, my ego will swell, and the next thing you know I'll be having Dre make me MCD T-shirts with my own logo or something."

"I'm happy with the things you already have that swell," she said, tugging him close so they bumped hips. "And quite nicely, too, thank you." She laughed outright when he spluttered a surprised laugh at that. Then winked at him as she climbed in and started to pull the passenger door closed. "But, at least now I know what to get you for Christmas."

Chapter 19

Morgan knocked on the door to Babycakes, then stuck his head inside. "Kit?"

There were no saws buzzing, no hammers pounding, no music pumping, but it was the Saturday after Thanksgiving, so he wasn't surprised. Actually, it was because no workers would be in the place that he and Lilly were there.

He opened the door and shuffled the two of them inside, closing the door behind them against the rain that had begun the night before and wasn't showing any signs of lightening up. "Be careful," he told Lilly. "There's buckets and tarps, ladders. Just walk around them, okay?" He held on to her hand. She had her turtle journal clutched to her chest in the other.

"Where's Miss Kit?" she asked, looking ridiculously adorable in her little green boots and matching raincoat with the turtle-head hood. Where Birdie had found them yesterday when she and Lilly had taken a little jaunt together while he caught up on some work, he had no idea.

"I'm right here!" Kit came out from the back, smiling as she wound her way through the clutter. "Ooh," she winced when she caught her elbow on a ladder.

Morgan stepped across the tarp and balanced her by taking her other elbow. "You okay?"

"Yes," she said on a laugh. "It's just . . . well—" She gestured to the front room.

Morgan did a quick scan of the torn-out walls, scraped paint, half-removed wallpaper and the various construction detritus. "Love what you've done with the place."

"I know," she laughed. "It's a good thing I've seen the drawings on how it will eventually look or I'd begin to wonder if the transformation was even possible." She turned to Lilly and crouched down. "Do you want to see the drawings of how it will look when it's done?"

Lilly nodded, but her attention was focused, quite raptly, on Kit's apron. Kit noticed the direction of her gaze and straightened, so Lilly could see the full effect of the apron Dre had designed.

She'd described it to Morgan, but, as she'd said, it truly defied description. As a work of art, it was stunning—rich in detail, colorful, and whimsical. Of course, Morgan was thinking how nice it would be to slip Kit right back out of it, but he suspected he'd be thinking that no matter what she was wearing.

"Isn't it cool?" she asked Lilly, untying the apron at her waist so she could open it up fully.

"Ah-mazing," Lilly whispered, making Morgan and Kit smile at each other.

Kit pointed out each fairy, and Lilly could guess who most of them were. "Miss Dre drew these, did you know that?"

Lilly's eyes went wide. "Really? You can draw on your clothes?"

Morgan made a half-choking noise, and Kit just laughed. "Well, Miss Dre is an artist, and you know how artists can make a painting on canvas?"

Lilly nodded, but Morgan wasn't sure how much she understood of that.

"Well, Miss Dre used an apron as her canvas, so I'd have

something beautiful and special to wear when we open the shop."

"Oh," Lilly said, then seemed to consider. "Can Miss Dre color on my clothes?"

Both adults chuckled at that. "Well, we'd have to talk to her about that. Maybe we can get you your own apron," Kit said. "Would you like that?" Before Lilly could answer, Kit went on. "Because, I was thinking, since it's raining so hard and no one is shopping for cupcakes much today, maybe Miss Lani and Miss Alva would let us use their kitchen next door."

Lilly wasn't immediately sold. "And I get to wear an apron? With pictures on it?"

Kit looked over Lilly's head at Morgan. "I'm pretty sure you have a budding artist here. She's all about the drawing."

Morgan smiled. "You may be right."

Kit looked back to Lilly. "You liked the peanut pie I made, right?"

That got an enthusiastic nod.

"Well, when I was your age, my great-grandma taught me how to make piecrust. My first official job was to help sprinkle the flour on the countertop so my great-grandma could roll the piecrust out really smooth."

"I have a great grandma, too. Gramma Birdie."

Kit smiled. "Aw. I think she's great, too."

Neither Morgan nor Kit attempted to explain what great-grandma meant, too charmed by Lilly's sweet sentiment to risk ruining the moment.

"She got me this raincoat." Lilly tipped her head forward, muffling her voice. "It's a turtle."

Kit laughed. "It's fantastic."

Lilly lifted her head and smiled. "Ah-mazing," they said at the same time and laughed all over again.

"I love it," Kit said. "I wish it came in my size."

"I could ask Gramma Birdie to find you one," Lilly said seriously.

"Aw, that's the nicest thing. Well, maybe we can. I heard you and your grandma went shopping."

Morgan and Kit had talked on the phone several times the day before. His intention to see her during the serendipitous shopping excursion had fallen through, as Kit had ended up helping Lani in the cupcake shop when the Black Friday hoards had descended. Sugarberry wasn't exactly a shopping mecca, but there'd been quite a hustle and bustle all through the shops surrounding the square. Without being obvious, there was no way she could duck out.

"We went to get stuff to paint with," Lilly told Kit.

"You did?" She nodded to the journal Lilly had in her arms. "Did you draw things together?"

"Gramma likes to color, too. She makes up her own pictures. And she uses brushes. She showed me—" Lilly looked up at Moggy questioningly.

"Watercolors," Morgan said.

"Watercolor," Lilly repeated to Kit. "We made cottages."

Kit's brows furrowed. "You painted pictures of cottages?"

"No," Lilly said in that five-year-old way of silently rolling her eyes. Silly adults. "We made . . . cottages."

"Collages," Morgan supplied.

Kit nodded, silently forming *oh* with her mouth. "That sounds pretty cool. Did you bring some to show me?"

Lilly nodded, then looked expectantly at Morgan again. He lifted the little tackle box he had in his hand. "We brought supplies. In case you wanted to try them out."

Kit's face lit up in delight. "You want to make collages?"

Lilly nodded, looking truly excited.

Kit pursed her lips and her expression turned to a considering one. "How about we make a trade?"

Lilly's expression immediately turned wary, and she held her journal a little more tightly against her chest. "A trade?"

"I teach you how to make peanut pie, and you teach me how to make cottages."

Lilly snickered. "It's not cottages. It's . . . co—" But she broke off, apparently knowing she couldn't put it together right, and looked at Morgan again.

"Collages," he supplied.

"Right!" Lilly beamed proudly back at Kit, who was clearly swallowing laughter. "Cottages."

Kit stood. "Sounds like a great plan. So . . . your Uncle Morgan said you wanted to see the shop. I'm afraid it doesn't look much like a shop yet, but when we get over to Lani's kitchen, she has all the drawings in her office. This front room is where we'll meet with our customers, take their orders, and talk about the parties they want us to take cupcakes to."

Kit motioned them toward the back room. "Back here, will be a kitchen like Miss Lani's, where we bake the cupcakes we'll be mailing to people and the ones for the parties, too."

She helped them weave through the construction mess. "Right now, it's hard to see what it will look like, but the drawings will show you."

She stepped to the rear service door and opened it. "We don't have a door between the shops yet, so I'm afraid we have to duck out in the rain, but the construction guys put up a covered walkway, so it's not too bad."

Morgan noticed that Lilly had looked all around the front room and the back, too, as Kit had talked, but hadn't asked a single question. Just as they were to step out the back door, she tugged on his hand. He bent down when she motioned him to come closer. "What is it?"

"I like the other bakery," she whispered. "Can we get our cupcakes from Miss Dre?"

Morgan grinned. "Well, they're not finished here yet, so there aren't any cupcakes in this bakery. In the meantime, we can get cupcakes from the other bakery, yes."

"Will Miss Kit be mad?" Lilly glanced to where Kit was waiting by the door.

"No, she won't be mad. We can try the cupcakes here, too, once this bakery is all fixed up. Let's go next door and have some fun, okay?"

Morgan caught Kit's questioning gaze as he straightened. He paused by the door so the girls could head out first. "I'll explain later," he said and winked. Kit took Lilly's hand then, and they made their way through the covered walkway to the back door of Lani's kitchen, giggling and squealing as the wind buffeted them with rain, anyway.

Morgan headed up the rear, watching the two of them and enjoying the contentment he felt, happy with how things were flowing forward. It was happening sooner than he'd imagined. With Birdie and with Kit.

"My, my, who do we have here!" Alva remarked, as they ducked in the back door of Cakes by the Cup. "You're like three wet little puppies."

She glanced up at Morgan. "Well, maybe not so little," she added with a wink at him.

She bustled around, helping them off with coats and showing Lilly where to wipe her boots. "Do you have shoes to put on? Or would you like to wear your rain boots? Very nice rain boots they are, too, by the way." Alva glanced at Kit and Morgan, making him think she was quite aware of how Lilly had come by her turtle-themed outfit.

Lilly reached for Kit's hand as Alva spoke to her, but she didn't shrink back. Apparently the time spent on the beach with everyone helping the turtles had gotten her past a good part of her shyness, at least with that particular group. Alva hadn't been there until the end, but Lilly seemed to be mostly relaxed with her, too.

"Uncle Moggy has my shoes," she told Alva, only shifting slightly closer to Kit's side. "But I can't get the boots off by myself."

"Well, I think we can figure that out. Come on in. Miss Lani had to go to Savannah to meet with Mr. Baxter, so I'm holding down the fort."

Lilly's eyes went wide. "You have a fort?"

Everyone chuckled. "Some days I think running a real fort would be easier, dear, but I meant I'll be out front taking care of the customers who come in to buy cupcakes." She looked at Kit. "Lani said you know where everything is now, so just help yourself to what you need. Between the crazy sales of yesterday and this weather, we don't expect to have much business." She glanced back at Lilly. "We might have a cupcake or two leftover, though, and I was hoping maybe you and your Uncle Morgan would take them with you."

Lilly nodded enthusiastically, though she remembered to glance up at Morgan to make sure it was okay. He nodded back.

"Aprons are on the wall. Miss Lani has more in those drawers just below. Some she's collected from all the way back when she was your age. She said feel free to borrow one." Alva looked at Lilly. "You can pick one out, and we'll give you a hook on the apron wall to hang it up when you're done. Then, every time you visit the kitchen, you'll have your own apron to wear. Just like Miss Kit does, and like I do." She modeled her apron, which featured a pink-maned My Little Pony.

Lilly nodded again, seeming somewhat more contemplative. "Can I see them?"

Just then the sound of a jingle echoed in the kitchen. Alva clapped. "Customers! You all make yourselves at home." With that, she bustled out of the kitchen to the front of the shop.

"Let's check out what's in the drawers," Kit said, motioning Lilly over after Morgan helped her off with her boots and on with her sneakers.

Lilly looked at Morgan. "You need an apron, too."

"Well—"

"Mr. Franco had one on," she said, which was true. Franco had put on an apron to carve the turkey, beachside. "It had a big, pink cat on it. Do you like pink cats?" She looked more than a little dubious about his possible response.

"Why don't we see what's available," Morgan said, catching Kit's gaze and seeing her fight to keep from laughing.

"Yes, why don't we go see what's available." Kit headed over to the apron wall. "How do you feel about pirates?"

Lilly clapped and looked instantly more interested. "Uncle Moggy, pirates!"

Kit was all but bursting as she handed Morgan an apron with Johnny Depp's smiling face covering the front. "Here you go, Cap'n Jack."

Lilly tugged on Kit's apron and whispered, "His name isn't Jack."

"That's the name of the pirate on his apron," Kit said, still dangling the apron from her fingers.

Morgan took it and slipped the loop over his head. "You know," he said conversationally, "pirates like to plunder. And they like hot wenches."

Kit's eyes went wide as she spluttered a laugh, even as Lilly was saying, "What's a hot wenches?"

Kit pointed a finger at him in warning, and immediately crouched down in front of the small antique set of drawers, distracting Lilly by opening the first one. "These were Miss Lani's when she was a little girl. See if you can find one you like."

She straightened as Lilly began going through the stack and turned to Morgan. "You are being a very bad influence," she whispered so only he could hear.

"Well, if you really like pirates, just wait until later. I plan to be a very, very bad influence." He glanced down to make sure Lilly was engrossed in her task, then leaned in and gave Kit a fast kiss. "Good morning." He liked seeing the sparkle his kiss put in those green eyes.

"Good morning, yourself," she said, making him wish they had an hour or two—or a week—somewhere private.

He'd settle for a few hours of pie making and collage painting, but was already plotting how they could spend more alone time together . . . the sooner the better.

He slipped his hand toward hers and hooked their little fingers together, tugging her a little bit closer, even as she turned back to watch Lilly.

"You can look through the other drawers, too," Kit told her. Then, to Morgan, she said, "So, the shopping trip yesterday . . . it went really well it seems."

"Ah-mazingly well," Morgan said, making her laugh. "Lilly and Birdie are thick as thieves. I'm learning that Lilly might be shy with new people, and in some cases, she stays that way, but once she decides she likes someone, she's all in."

Kit glanced up. "Kind of like her uncle, then."

Morgan's lips curved. "Kind of like, yes." God, he wanted to sweep her up in his arms, kiss her hello the way he really wanted to. Instead, he squeezed his finger around hers. "She's going to go see Birdie's house tomorrow. Apparently Birdie's set up a little art studio in what used to be her potting shed. She does really beautiful watercolors.

And now that the two of them have made *cottages* together, Lilly is all about learning art."

"That's fantastic. It's wonderful they have something like that to share with each other."

"I was thinking, maybe over the Christmas holiday Dre will let us see where she works, and she can show Lilly that kind of art, how it can be a business, too."

"Starting her on a career path so soon?" Kit teased. "You really are a Westlake, after all."

It was a testament to how comfortable they were with one another, and how much he trusted her, that her comment made him laugh rather than wince. "No, but you know how she is when she gets on to something, like with the turtles. I just thought—"

Kit leaned into him, bumping elbows. "I know what you thought, and it's a great idea. I love that Lilly's making so many new friends here, people who are becoming important to her. I know nothing will fill the void of her losing her parents, but I think it's great for her to make new connections before she has a chance to close herself off. She won't even think about that now."

Morgan knew Kit was truly thinking about Lilly as she spoke, but he also knew it was her own experiences that were coloring her concerns. He hadn't thought as much about how losing her parents had affected her, as he had losing the family business. Even though she'd been an adult when they'd died, and it had happened over a half dozen years ago, he wondered just how much that event had caused her to pour herself into her job, her work, the company, and thereby remove any risks of a more personal nature.

And he understood, more and more, why she'd been so tentative with him. He thanked the stars and fate and whatever else had had a hand in it, that their coming together had been easy and natural. She'd have never considered a first step with him if it hadn't been.

"This one!" Lilly said, scrambling back to her feet. The open drawers were littered with a toss of aprons. Before Morgan could say anything, Kit leaned down to take the apron from her, so they could see it.

"Land of the Lost," Kit read out loud, holding up the apron, which had a scene from an old television show on the front.

"Dinosaurs!" Lilly exclaimed, her face all lit up.

"I know," Kit replied. "Awesome. Here, turn around and we'll get it tied on." Once they had the deed done, she said, "Can you do me a favor and put all of Miss Lani's very special aprons back in the drawers while we get out the stuff to make pies?"

Lilly was still admiring her apron, smoothing her hands over the front of it, squinting as she looked at the dinosaurs, which were upside down from her viewpoint. "Okay," she said, and after another long moment admiring herself, she knelt back down and got to work.

Kit tousled the top of her head, then took Morgan's hand and crossed the kitchen to the storage cupboards where Lani kept the bins of flour, sugar, and the like. "Good thing they're extinct," she teased Morgan, "or, given that rapt look on her face, you might be making a trip to the dinosaur zoo and research center."

Morgan chuckled. "The turtle fixation is looking better and better all the time." He held on to Kit's hand when she went to reach for the cupboard door, and gently tugged her back a step. He leaned down and kissed the side of her neck, his back blocking the view from Lilly.

"What was that for?" she asked, smiling up at him over her shoulder.

"For being just what Lilly needs. For being what I need."

The moment he'd said it, he wondered if he shouldn't keep those thoughts to himself, at least for a while longer. But when his comment didn't give her pause, he was glad he'd said what was on his mind.

Her smile was sweet, as was the color blooming in her cheeks. "I'm just being me. And you both make that very, very easy." She tipped up on her toes, gave him a quick kiss. "So, thank you for being what I need, too."

Then it was all about the pie business as Lilly came scampering over, practically tripping over her apron, which was still a bit on the large size for her tinier-than-average frame. Kit solved that problem by flipping the bottom of the apron front up and clipping it on each side with bag clips. Lilly wiggled, making the bag clips rattle, and they laughed.

"You know, Miss Lani likes to have music on while she bakes. What do you say we play some music while I show you how to make piecrust?"

"What's a crust?" Lilly asked.

At that question, Kit positioned Lilly on a step stool, so she could see over the worktable, and Morgan took on the job of errand boy, fetching whatever the two of them needed as Kit asked for it, directing him where to look. She showed Lilly how to sprinkle the flour and powder the work surface with it.

As soon as she realized she got to put her hands in things, Lilly's entire attitude about the project changed. Then it was laughter and a few squeals—when his little color-inside-the-lines, neat and tidy fanatic got flour on herself for the first time—mixing, rolling, along with dancing, and even a little singing.

When Alva popped into the back an hour later, she smiled at the messy trio. "My, my, it sure smells like heaven back here. You all look like you've been pretty busy."

"We made peanut pie," Lilly said, beaming proudly, with flour on her face, her apron, her hands, and a good bit of the area surrounding her.

Alva beamed right back, clearly charmed. "Well, if you're willing to share a bite, I'd love to try some."

Lilly looked at Kit, who nodded. "We'll have plenty to share."

"I was thinking since it's slowed down up front, maybe you want to clean up a little and come out and see about choosing which of those cupcakes you want to take home for later." Alva winked at Morgan and Kit. "I think these will be even better, though, if you wait until tomorrow to try them."

Between the pies and cupcakes, Morgan prayed the rain let up soon, so he could run the sugar energy out of his little five-year-old, up and down the beach if necessary. Lilly had asked a ton of questions about the turtle babies, and wanted to go back and see the nest, make sure they were all out and okay. Morgan wanted to wait until Gabe and Anne had had time to excavate the mound and remove anything Lilly didn't need to see, and also to check the beach, make sure none of the babies had washed back up for good.

With the rain, all of that would be delayed a little longer, making him doubly grateful Birdie had gotten Lilly interested in painting and drawing. Something to keep her distracted until they could get back to the beach.

Alva had Lilly over at the sink, getting her washed up, so he went over to help Kit clean up the work surface. "I don't want to rummage through Lani's office with her gone. My copy of the plans for the shop is upstairs," Kit told him.

Morgan wiggled his eyebrows. "Are you asking me upstairs to see your etchings?"

She laughed. "I meant that I needed to go up and get

them. It's a mess up there, so I wasn't planning on having Lilly up. I'm thinking maybe we can do our painting on one of the worktables, just put down some paper—"

"We're going to get cupcakes!" Lilly announced, freshly washed up and hand in hand with Alva by the door to the front of the shop.

"You two finish cleaning up," Alva said, not even bothering to hide her knowing look. "I'm sure it will take us a little time to choose. Plus, I want to show Miss Lilly the antique cash register, maybe show her how it works."

"What's a regsist—" She broke off. "What is it called?"

"A cash register. When a customer buys a cupcake, it's where we ring up the sale and tell them how much money it will cost. Then we put the money in the register drawer," Alva told her, already opening the swinging door. "Come on. I'll show you." She shot another wink at Kit and Morgan as she hustled Lilly back up front.

"I think I'm going to be conspicuously absent from the next Cupcake Club Bitch 'n' Bake," Kit said, laughing. "If I thought they took an overactive interest in my sex life before—"

Morgan spun her neatly around and kissed her flour-covered lips. "I have an overactive interest in your sex life," he said as she slid her arms around his neck. "Although I'm not much for talking about it. I'm more of a show and tell guy."

"Are you?" She grinned against his mouth as he kissed her again. "So, wanna come see my shop plans?"

"I thought you'd never ask."

Laughing, Kit directed him to a different door off the kitchen, which led up a very narrow staircase to the second floor, and provided him with a very delightful view as she climbed up ahead of him.

"Fair warning," she said as she opened the door, "it's a

disaster. And not just the storage side. I haven't had any time—"

Morgan cut her off by taking her hips in his hands and turning her around and into his arms. His mouth was on hers a moment later, and he backed them into the room, gently kicking the door shut behind him. "Funny," he said, still kissing her, "I don't notice the mess at all."

She smiled, then sighed and tipped her head back as he trailed kisses along her jaw to just below her ear.

"I've been dying to do this since we walked into the shop," he said, continuing his delicious journey as he slid his hands down her back, over the curve of her backside, and pulled her to him. "Dying."

"I know," she managed. "I've been dying for you to do this since you dropped me off the other night."

He grinned, loving her honesty and that she felt comfortable telling him what she was thinking. "I really wanted to see you yesterday."

"I know, and I wish we could have made that work." She nudged his face back to hers and looked into his eyes. "But, you're here now."

His eyes widened. She couldn't possibly mean—but then she was tugging at his apron ties and, well, no one had to tell him twice. They all but ripped the clothes from each other. No teasing, no toying.

"You know," he said, scooping her up so she wrapped her legs around his hips. "We don't always have to—"

"We don't," she agreed, breathless. "Except, right now we do," she countered, then took his mouth in a kiss that went straight through him and sent any thought of stopping flying right out of his head. If he'd thought about carnal desires before, she was shedding a whole new light on her most carnal desire right at that moment.

He didn't even ask where the bed was, instead turning

and backing them up against the nearest wall. He hiked her up, still kissing her, as she wrapped herself more tightly around him.

"Hold on," he said, and slid her slowly down, pushing inside her. They growled, already moving with each other even before he was fully sheathed.

"Have I told you," he ground out, as he took her . . . and she took him right back . . . "how much I love . . . that you're really . . . really . . . safe?"

She gasped as he pinned her against the wall and drove deeply into her, but she was moving right along with him. Then there was no more talk. She dug her fingers into his shoulders, her heels into his back as she found his mouth again and slid her tongue inside, matching the rhythm of him sliding into her.

It was fast, furious, and over far, far too soon. He had to forcibly swallow a shout when he came, shaking with the intensity of it. His knees threatened to buckle, but he braced against the wall, waiting as she continued to shudder, both of them breathing as if they'd run a marathon. He kissed the side of her neck, then nipped her ear lobe. "You're . . . that was . . ."

"I know," she breathed. "Right?"

They let out a breathless chuckle at that, and he was half stunned they'd done what they'd done. Not that he was complaining. Finally, he shifted her off him, and let her feet slide to the floor, then rolled so his back was to the wall, and held her tucked against him, both of them still a bit wobbly-kneed.

"You know . . . I do have a bed."

"Yes," he said, still working on even breathing. "But it was way, way over there somewhere." He tucked her head to his chest and rested his cheek on her hair. "And the wall was right here."

"Walls. So handy like that," she managed. "I will never look at them the same way."

"Me, either," he said with a surprised chuckle. When he'd followed her up the stairs, it had been with the notion of torturing them with the chance to kiss each other hello in the way he'd truly wanted to. He'd never imagined this. Much less that she'd be the one to instigate it. "We should probably get dressed."

"Probably."

"Go downstairs. Be responsible adults."

"Alva is a responsible adult."

"True."

"We're always the responsible adults." Kit leaned her head back then, and he looked down into deep green eyes that were sated and content, but still had a bit of the devil in them. "It's nice to know we don't always have to be." She reached up and pulled his head down, kissing him again, taking her time and letting the emotion they hadn't expressed during their wild animal coupling shine through.

He let her lead, let her show him, let her express herself . . . as his heart pounded for entirely different reasons. She smiled up into his eyes as she finally broke the kiss, then settled her cheek against his chest, nestling in his arms as if it were her natural, rightful place.

And it was. If there had been any doubt he was in love with her, that moment ended the debate.

Chapter 20

"Baxter has meetings all this week, so we're going to get our Christmas tree on the weekend," Lani said as she cored a row of cupcakes. "He found a place about an hour and half from here where we can chop down our own, go on a hayride, the whole thing." She paused between coring out the centers of the rack of vanilla bean cupcakes in front of her. "You know, I definitely don't miss the snow and the cold, but it's not the same, buying your tree from some parking lot. Riley said she and Quinn are going to tag along, even bring Brutus. Can you imagine him on the hayride?"

"He could be the hayride." Charlotte was filling pastry bags with almond buttercream frosting to top her cardamom chocolate cupcakes.

Everyone chuckled.

"Isn't that waiting a bit long?" Alva asked. "I've had mine up since the day after Thanksgiving. A Liles tradition."

"We were going to ask if you wanted to go with us," Lani asked.

Alva scoffed. "My dear, not to put a damper on your own enthusiasm for those real trees with all their falling needles and watering requirements, but until you've seen the magnificence that is my seven-foot white tree, tipped with silver, you simply haven't lived."

"Well, no, that is true. Clearly, I have lived a life of neglect and deprivation," Lani teased.

"Yes, well, dear, we can't all be on the forefront of modern décor."

"True," Charlotte said. "Although, one year, when Lani and I still lived in New York, we did wrap a single string of lights around our very tiny and very pathetic fake ficus tabletop tree. We made sandwich baggie florets, which we spray painted and then used metal bread bag ties to affix them to the branches."

"Yes, it was truly a . . . statement of some kind," Lani added, "right up until the heat from the lights created a noxious fume from the spray paint that almost got the restaurant below us shut down by the health department."

"Ho ho not," Charlotte deadpanned.

"Well, dears, not everyone appreciates creativity. I'm sure it was . . . quite lovely."

Kit hid her own smile, but she caught Lani and Charlotte exchanging grins and had to swallow a snicker. "I'd love to see your tree, Alva."

That had Lani's and Charlotte's expressions instantly changing to ones of warning and chagrin. Charlotte tried the throat slash maneuver, but . . . it was too late.

Alva had already lit up like the proverbial Christmas tree. "Why, Kit dear, I'd love to show it to you."

"Every ornament has a story," Lani said brightly while shaking her head behind Alva's back and crossing her eyes, as Charlotte pantomimed slowly choking to death.

"Every one of them," Charlotte added with equal, overly enthusiastic cheer.

Kit determinedly did not look at either one of them and focused on Alva. "Sounds sentimental and lovely."

"Every year I have a new theme."

"Oh." Kit struggled to maintain her smile. "Really.

Themes. How . . . interesting. And every year has its own stories?"

"Why, yes. I wouldn't put just anything on my tree. I have to be inspired. Usually, I decide right after taking down the old one, but it depends. Then I spend the whole year finding just the right things. Every ornament I choose has a reason for its inclusion."

"Sounds really . . . amazing."

"Seven foot tree," Charlotte reminded her, working hard to keep the edge of snark from her tone. "So many ornaments."

Kit sent Charlotte a quick glare as Alva came around the table to her side. "I have pictures of last year's tree here on my phone. I got this last year, too. They call it a smart phone, but my goodness, it's far more incredible than merely smart. Look."

"What was last year's theme?" Kit asked as Alva handed her the phone after she opened the photo file. "Oh. Look. Cats. Lots and lots of . . . cats." She clicked through the first handful of photos. "Who knew cat ornaments came in so many . . . styles."

Lani and Charlotte had to turn back to their worktables, but Kit could see their shoulders shaking with barely restrained mirth. Well . . . they'd tried to warn her.

"The year before that, it was pineapples." Alva took the phone back and opened a new folder.

"Pineapples. Wow. Seems like it would be hard to find enough ornaments to really do the tree justice."

"Oh, it was, dear. One of my biggest challenges. I had to make more than a few myself, just to keep it from looking sparse." She handed the phone back to Kit. "See?"

"Oh . . . my. Yes." Kit kept her attention on the phone and didn't dare to so much as glance in Lani's or Charlotte's general direction. "How . . . unique." She handed the phone back to Alva and asked the obvious question, but mostly so she could get those pictures out of her head. "So, what is this year's theme?"

Alva clasped her phone in hands and propped them beneath her chin. "Angels." She reached out and took Kit's arm, and squeezed. "We've had a few more angels in heaven this year . . . and well, a few more have come to live with us right here on Sugarberry." She looked up at Kit, her eyes a bit shimmery.

Kit's were, too. "Oh, that's . . . thank you," she said, sincerely touched. She hugged the smaller woman, and saw Lani and Charlotte had turned around and were looking all sentimental.

For shame, Kit mouthed over Alva's head, wagging a finger at them. *For shame.*

"I don't think I'll have any trouble decorating this season," Alva said as she straightened and smoothed her apron. "If you've any you want to include, I think that would be wonderful."

"I—I don't have any of my family's ornaments . . . or mine. My sister . . ." Kit trailed off, not wanting to go there, or she would start crying in earnest. "But I'll start to look when I'm out and about. I'd like to contribute one if I can."

"That would be lovely, dear," Alva said. "Birdie is going to have one for the tree, too."

Lani sniffled loudly. "Oh . . . group hug! Group hug!" She and Charlotte bustled around the tables and they all hugged in the center of the room.

"I can't believe how much my life has changed in such a short time," Kit said, sniffling, too. "I couldn't have imagined this or any of you. You've all become so important to me so quickly. I don't know what to say, except, thank you for taking me in like this, making me so welcome."

"You were due," Alva said, patting her on the back. "And we're happy to have you."

After another squeeze and a few self-deprecating laughs over their huddling in the middle of the kitchen, being all sniffly together, they each went back to their respective tables and back to work on their cupcakes.

Since only cupcakes made from Lani's personal, original recipes were sold in her shop, Kit had asked the night of her first after-hours bake what they did with the cupcakes made in Cupcake Club. Mostly, they were donated to various groups and causes, spreading cheer and goodwill, and so it was a win-win thing all around.

Lani looked across the kitchen at Kit. "So . . . do you and Morgan have tree-buying plans? Want to join us?"

Kit girded herself for the latest round of "let's out Kit and Morgan as a couple." She should have kept Alva talking about her trees. "I have no idea what he and Lilly plan to do about a tree this year."

As one, all three women paused, turned, and leveled her a look. *Really?*

It was Alva who spoke up. "Dear, I don't know why you insist on pretending you're not seeing each other. It's been a week since you all came that day and made pie together, right here in this kitchen."

"Lilly wanted to see Babycakes," Kit explained. "She was confused about how that business will work—still is. She really liked the peanut pie on Thanksgiving, so I thought it would be fun to teach her how to make it."

"Like you were taught when you were a little girl," Alva said pointedly.

"Yes, like I was taught." Kit whisked flour and spices together, pretending to be oblivious to Alva's meaning. "Lilly showed me some collages she made with Birdie—and isn't that just the most wonderful thing?" Hoping to distract Alva from the conversation, she continued. "I think that's all the Christmas present I need this year, seeing Lilly and her grandmother enjoying each other, especially after that rocky start."

"Oh my yes," Alva agreed. "Birdie is simply rhapsodic over it. I have never seen her so happy. She said to me the other day how it's helped her begin healing after the tragedy of losing her poor Delilah."

"It's worked out to be a good thing for Morgan, too," Kit added, relieved at the topic change. "With Lilly not in school yet, having Birdie spend time with her has really allowed him to get a leg up on starting his practice here."

"Well, now, sounds like the two of you keep pretty well in touch, seeing as you know all about his day-to-day doings. " Alva's razor sharp gaze landed back on Kit, even as she kept an innocent smile on her face. "I think it's wonderful you've overcome that silly misunderstanding."

Kit sighed. She should have known better. Alva was like a pit bull. "You mean . . . about him being a Westlake? He is a Westlake."

"Well, dear, I'm just glad it hasn't stopped you from taking that first step together, that's all. A man's family, who he's from, is important and all, but seeing what he's done for himself and for his darling niece, I believe he's become successful despite, rather than because of his roots, and he should be commended for that." Alva pointed a spatula in Kit's direction, flinging small bits of salted caramel in her general direction as she punctuated her comment.

"You could do far, far worse than that man, believe you me. Besides, the three of you look just darling together." She sighed, clasping the sticky handle in both hands. "And the way he looks at you?" She fanned herself. "I've seen it with my own eyes."

"They're both googly," Lani said. "I've said so since day one."

Kit dropped her chin. She knew when to accept defeat.

Since their day on the beach, she'd crossed paths with everyone, in and around the shop, and they'd each taken turns trying to wheedle it out of her. Collectively, she never stood a chance.

"We're just . . ." Kit set her bowl and whisk down on the worktable and looked at their hopeful faces, thinking she was lucky Franco and Dre hadn't made it over the causeway that evening. God only knew what they'd have gotten out of her. "We're getting to know each other better."

Immediately, their expressions brightened and they opened their mouths to say something all at the same time.

"But we're trying to keep it low key," she cautioned. "Lilly doesn't need to get her hopes up about anything. She has made many friends here and, for now, I'm just one of them."

All three women sighed quite happily.

"I'm so happy for you," Lani said. "And yes, I know, I know . . . we'll be careful with Miss Lilly, but that doesn't mean we can't tell you how much we like Morgan and you, and the two of you together is just really wonderful."

Charlotte and Alva were nodding along with her.

"And isn't life so much better when you're having regular sex?" Alva asked.

Lani, Charlotte, and Kit choked a little at that. But Lani and Charlotte were snickering as they looked at Kit speculatively, and Kit knew her beet red cheeks defeated any possible chance she had of denying it.

Alva smiled sweetly. "I mean, it's just us girls here. Surely we can be honest with each other."

Lani turned her speculative gleam on Alva, tapping her corer against her other hand. "So . . . does this mean that you and Hank . . . ?"

Charlotte and Kit turned to Alva and gave her the same

speculative look. Kit's expression might have been extra twinkly. After all . . . fair was fair.

"Now, now, dears, a lady doesn't kiss and tell," Alva replied, but surprised them by adding, "And Hank . . . well, he's not my Harold. No one could replace that dear man." She sighed, then looked up at them. "But, I must admit, having the attentions of a nice looking gentleman does put a little lift in a girl's step."

She looked so cute and twinkly, all Kit and the other two women could do was beam right back at her.

"Well, I'm happy for both of you," Lani said, then looked at Kit. "We had our doubts, too, you know. About his family. They certainly didn't do right by Birdie, quite the opposite."

"What do you mean?" Kit asked.

"Blocked her from seeing her own flesh and blood, like her kind wasn't good enough to be seen around the fancy place they live in," Alva explained. "When Delilah married into the family, Olivia about had a stroke, then immediately set about trying to train the girl to not be an embarrassment. Hounded her—shamed her, if you ask me—into leaving her poor mother behind.

"But now that we've met and gotten to know Morgan," Lani continued, "and of course, seen how wonderful he is with Lilly, plus all he did to make sure Lilly and Birdie got together . . . I mean, he's a good guy, Kit. A really, really good guy. He's nothing like his family."

"Ask me, I think it's kismet," Charlotte offered, her accent more crisp as they'd gotten their sniffling under control. "I mean, look at what happened with your family and Morgan's. It's an odd connection you share. And you both end up here at the same time? Starting your lives over? It's the universe showing you your new path."

Kit smiled. "I don't know what it is," she cautioned

them, knowing it would do no good. "But I can say that in my wildest dreams, I couldn't have imagined I'd be looking forward to this particular holiday season. And, so far, it's been . . . well, it's been very special."

They held each other's gazes, getting all sentimental and shimmery-eyed again, and Kit sensed another group hug in the offing. The oven timer went off right at that moment, making them all jump, then laugh at themselves.

Charlotte bustled over and slid out the supersize rack of cupcakes.

Kit had turned back to her bowl and whisk and her batter in the making, when Alva said, "So, dear, now that you've let us know about your burgeoning romance—"

"You mean confessed under interrogation?" Kit teased.

"Call it what you will, dear, but come now, surely you'd rather be with your new beau on a Friday night than with the bunch of us."

"Morgan is at home with Lilly, and . . . well, I haven't been over to his place yet."

"I understand you want to keep things low key, dear," Alva said. "But the three of you do spend time together. Surely there would be nothing amiss in the three of you having a movie night. Some popcorn, a family friendly movie."

"That's just it, Alva. We're not trying to be a family. We're just . . . getting to know one another. Morgan and I want to do that a little more on our own before doing family-type things."

Alva tsked and went back to her task. "Well, if you all can't see what we plainly see, then fine. Just seems a bit silly to waste time posturing about when you could be enjoying each other the way you were meant to."

"If it's meant to be," Kit replied, "it will be. I've jumped into a lot here, and—"

"And all of it has been quite wonderful, has it not?" Alva pointed her caramel-covered spatula at Kit again. "You need to trust your instincts."

"I'm working on it," Kit said dryly, but inside, the comment dinged her a little. All she'd wanted to do was take baby steps toward a new future, but felt that she was making gigantic strides after the catastrophic year leading up to her move to Sugarberry. She worried it was all going to backfire on her at some point. Given her history, probably when she least expected it. But there was no way she could explain that to this group.

"Don't push her, Alva," Lani chided. "If she and Morgan are happy, then that's all that matters. He seems to be doing pretty well by Lilly, so it's not our business to tell what they should or shouldn't do."

"Fine, fine," Alva sniffed. "For heaven's sake, when did watching a movie and having some popcorn together become a federal offense?"

Lani and Charlotte rolled their eyes behind her, while still smiling at Kit.

"I haven't had a chance to ask, but what was the final count on the turtle hatch?" Lani asked brightly, clearly changing the subject.

Kit could have kissed her. "Gabe said it ended up about seventy-five percent. Given the time of year and all, he thought it was really successful."

"The weather has been so horrible all week, it's really lucky they hatched when they did," Lani said.

"It really is. Gabe and Anne mentioned that this much rain could have flooded the nest at a critical time, when the babies were working to emerge, so they were very, very lucky."

"I've wanted to get back out there to explore the center," Lani said. "I hate to say it, but since moving here, I've never gone out there and checked it out. Still haven't been inside yet. Baxter hasn't stopped talking about it, so I'm sure we'll make it happen."

Charlotte sighed. "I can't believe I was in New York, trying to pretend I couldn't hear Carlo's grandmother putting the black curse on me and my family under her breath every time we were in the same room, when I could have here helping with the Great Turtle Hatch."

Lani made a sad face. "I'm sorry his family is still being so brutal."

Charlotte lifted a shoulder. "His sisters have thawed. Slightly. But . . . it will be a challenging road."

"So, still no date yet?" Alva asked.

Charlotte shook her head. "Carlo wants to just go ahead with it. He wants us to be married. I-I want to be married, too. And maybe it will never get easier, so we shouldn't wait. But every time I try to imagine that day, with half his family cursing me as I walk down the aisle and my own parents disapproving of my choice"—she shuddered—"it's a nightmare. There is nothing about that day that appeals to me. We're happy as we are. I don't see the reason to make so many people unhappy and upset."

"What about your happiness?" Kit asked her. "Carlo won't consider eloping? Or a smaller ceremony?"

Charlotte shook her head. "His mother and grandmother would never forgive him and his sisters would lynch him. They had to go through it, so it's only fair he face the same gauntlet."

"I don't know, Charlotte. I know you love him and I know he loves you. But if he's always going to bow to his family's happiness over yours . . ." Kit let the statement trail off.

Charlotte nodded. "I know, I know. Trust me. I've thought about that. A lot. I think about us starting a family, all of that, and it's so daunting. I can't see where it's ever going to be okay with his family or mine. I've already chosen my own life over the one my parents would choose for me, and I have come to terms with their disapproval. We live on different continents and maintain separate lives. But Carlo . . . while he has chosen his path here, in Georgia with me . . . he does care about his family, loves them deeply, is still so close to them. I see how it tears him up. He really wants to make everybody happy." She smiled, bleakly. "But there is no feasible way to accomplish that."

Lani rounded the table to her and pulled her into another hug. "I'm sorry."

Charlotte hugged her back. "Thank you. That's why we're just kind of going on as we've been going. We're happy, we're together, and we only have to deal with our respective families long distance."

"Not everyone has to be married," Lani said. "You've committed to each other."

Charlotte nodded, but didn't say anything more.

Kit watched, listened, and couldn't help thinking of the situation between her and Morgan. Since Thanksgiving, she'd kept her focus on her life as it was now. On what was happening with Morgan and Lilly, and how things were unfolding for them on Sugarberry. She'd very purposefully put his extended family, and hers too, for that matter, from her thoughts. They'd each chosen to distance themselves from their immediate families, but that didn't mean the families had simply ceased to exist. At some point, she'd have to deal with that part of things. She just wanted . . . a stronger foundation with Morgan first, for them to have developed a relationship together, time to get to a place where it wasn't Morgan and Lilly, and Morgan and Kit, and Kit and Lilly. But Morgan, Kit, and Lilly.

Listening to Charlotte, though, she found it hard not to consider the reality of what would happen if and when they wanted to take a step like Charlotte and Carlo wanted to take. What then? With her family, it didn't matter as much. She doubted Trixie or Teddy would notice, much less care, what she did with her life or whom she married. Though if she married a Westlake, she could well imagine Teddy trying to make that work to his advantage. Dear Lord, the very idea made her cringe. Maybe she just wouldn't tell them.

But with Morgan, it would be different. There was Lilly to consider. And her two grandmothers, one of whom was a Westlake. At some point and for many points in the future, Olivia Westlake would factor in to Morgan's life. If Kit became a permanent part of that scenario, she would have to deal with Olivia as well.

"Dear, I do believe you've whisked that pour bowl of flour about half to death."

Alva's words broke into her thoughts, and Kit looked down, only to realize that during her ruminations, she'd picked up her bowl and started whisking again. If only her concerns could be whisked away so easily.

Chapter 21

"Lilly has never decorated a Christmas tree? How is that possible?"

Morgan glanced over at Kit as he drove along the loop road toward his cottage. "Because Westlake trees are professionally designed and decorated to match the theme and décor of whatever events may be taking place that particular season."

"Trees? Plural?" Kit laughed. "What, like one in the family room and another one in the living room?"

"More like two in the grand foyer—one on the first landing of the central staircase, one in the upper balcony vestibule—and, well, that's just within eyeshot of the front door."

Kit shook her head, still laughing. "We definitely had very different childhoods." She settled back into her seat. "Well, I think it's doubly wonderful that Lilly and Birdie are going to make ornaments together. It's already great they've bonded over making art together. And, if Lilly's never decorated a tree, then today's craft endeavor is a more fantastic thing for them to share."

Morgan glanced over, then reached out, took her hand, and squeezed. "Actually, it was the art that started it. I've been talking to Lilly about getting our tree, and we've been trying to figure out what to decorate it with. I want her to have one, but I wanted it to mean something, and not just have a bunch of store bought ornaments on it. So, they decided to make them. Originally, Birdie thought she'd have Lilly over to help with her tree, but we decided to wait until Lilly's a bit older before they share that particular task."

"Why?" Then Kit's expression softened. "Oh, right. She'd have ornaments from Delilah's childhood, I imagine."

"Boxes of them. We felt it's too soon to have Lilly looking through things her mom made. Maybe next year, when she's a little older and a bit more time has passed. Instead, they're making ornaments to go on our tree."

"Oh, speaking of that, we—you, me, Lilly, and I'm guessing Birdie would be welcome, too—have been invited to go with Lani and Baxter, Quinn and Riley, to chop down a Christmas tree next weekend. I don't know how traditional you are about putting a tree up at a certain time, but—"

He laughed. "Confession. I don't have any Christmas tree traditions."

Kit opened her mouth, then shut it again and smiled. "Right. The tree on every stair landing thing probably didn't start just since Lilly was born."

"I'm pretty sure it started whenever the first Christmas tree in history was ever decorated, where, I'm sure there was a Westlake in attendance who took one look and thought, hey, this would make a good centerpiece for our royal feast, impress the neighboring kings and such."

Kit laughed. "You're so bad."

"I'm not exaggerating. Probably."

"Didn't you have a tree in all the time you lived out west? You said that was where you experienced more traditional holidays and learned what you wanted for yourself, your kids, and now . . . for Lilly."

"I did see the kind of holidays I'd like to have, but that was from being around friends and their families. I didn't put up a tree in my place. I mean, it was just me. I guess I got enough holiday spirit from osmosis. Western mountain towns are crazy for decorations and traditions this time of year."

"Well, with all that snow, it would be pretty festive. Was that fun? Having white Christmases? I've spent all mine here in Georgia."

"It was pretty cool, I'll admit. Especially the first few. This is my first one back east in what feels like a lifetime, but . . . I'm enjoying seeing it through Lilly's eyes."

"Does she say anything . . . I mean, the whole Santa thing and wishing for Christmas presents? Does she mention her mama and daddy?"

Morgan slowed and turned into his driveway. He turned off the engine, but didn't get out. "She's only mentioned them to me once since we've been here. But I've heard her saying her prayers at night. And she includes mama and daddy up in heaven in her list." His eyes sheened over. "I don't know if I should bring them up or just let her do it when she's ready. She's so young, and I don't want her to forget them. Since she fell for the turtles, and then Thanksgiving happened, and now with Birdie . . . her life is very full and she's happy. Happier, for sure, than when we got here. She's rarely solemn anymore. Still shy around new people, but so much more relaxed and herself now that she has all of you. I'll be honest . . . I don't know what to do, so I just . . . play it day-to-day."

Kit reached across the console and took his hand. "That's all you can do. She's making good memories here, memories she'll associate with the holidays when they come next year. She'll look forward to them, and you can't ask for more than that. Later, or whenever curiosity or emotion prompts her to talk about her mama and daddy, she'll ask. I think she knows she can say anything to you, ask you anything."

Morgan squeezed her hand. "I hope so. Sometimes I feel incredibly ill prepared for this. I'm so worried I'll screw up something important and scar her for life." He chuckled, but the worry was real.

Kit tugged on his hand until he looked at her. "A wise man once told me that all Lilly needs is someone who cares about her and has her best interests at heart. I don't think any person feels prepared to be a parent, no matter when it happens, or how many times it happens. She seems like she's doing really well. And that's what you have to have faith in."

Morgan smiled.

She noted the dry edge and cocked her head. "What?"

"Nothing. For someone who has been so nervous about moving forward—with good reason—you are amazingly wise in the ways of relationships and life."

She tugged him closer and leaned over the center console until their lips brushed. "Well, I keep saying I'm afraid to do things, and yet I keep doing them, so, I don't know how wise I am. But just because I'm doing them, doesn't mean I'm not still afraid. Maybe that's the key, to just jump in. When my parents died, and suddenly Mamie Sue's Peanut Pie company was mine and Trixie's, it was ridiculously overwhelming. I either stepped up and figured it out, or let it fall apart. If I'd thought about what I was facing, I'd have completely freaked out."

Morgan smiled and kissed her lightly. "Is that what you did with me? Just tried hard not to think about it so you wouldn't completely freak out?"

She nodded, rubbing noses with him. "Kind of." When he widened his eyes in surprise, she laughed lightly. "Well, with the company, eventually, I figured it out. I had to make myself hang in there. Since there was no real alternative—at least for me, there wasn't—that's all I could do."

"And me? You have an alternative. I mean, you could have stuck with the things you'd already jumped into and walked away from us."

"*Could have.* But I'd already had something in my life I was utterly and completely passionate about so I understood bigger than life, once in a lifetime things you have to do because not doing them is surely something you'd always regret. I knew when I met you— okay, when you continued to push me—it was like Mamie Sue's."

He slipped his hand through her hair, cupped her head, and drew her closer. "I'm glad I'm someone you thought you would regret not knowing." He searched her eyes. "Someone you're passionate about. Bigger than life."

"Once in a lifetime," she whispered and was smiling when he kissed her.

The kiss deepened, and the words were in his mind, in his heart, on the tip of his tongue, but he held on to them. Far too soon for declarations of any kind, but he couldn't keep the hope from blooming fully to life any longer. When he lifted his head, he kept his palm cupping the side of her face, tracing her bottom lip with his thumb. "I'm glad you agreed to come here today. Even though you've never been here, it's like you're missing when you're not around. Lilly will say something, or I'll be on a call, or . . . any of a number of things, and I want to turn to you, tell you, talk to you. It just seems like you should be there."

She didn't respond, but her gaze on his didn't waver.

"Since the rain has finally let up and it's gotten warm again, humid even, I thought we'd take a walk on the beach. There's a path through the dunes behind the house, straight to the beach. Maybe a picnic. I didn't want you to think I wanted you here just so—"

"I could see your etchings?"

He grinned. "Well, I won't lie. I imagine you being in every room of the house, but I dream about having you in my bed . . ." He trailed off, his body already painfully hard.

"Well, since we're being so open . . . I'll admit I've thought about how it would be, to wake up together. It's the lust of something new, I know. But . . . it's not to say I don't think about . . . everything you mentioned. Eventually."

"Well, for now"—he leaned in and kissed her again—"I'm just happy you're here. Today. But let's not spend our time sitting out here in the driveway. Want to make some sandwiches, go for a walk on the beach?"

He got out and went around, helping her out and into his arms. She laughed, going quite willingly, sliding her arms around his neck. "Do you honestly think once we get inside behind closed doors we'll make it to the beach?"

"Why, Miss Bellamy," he said, tilting her face to his, kissing the corners of her mouth. "Whatever are you suggesting?"

She tipped up on her toes and kissed him quite solidly on the lips. "I'm suggesting that perhaps the stroll might be put off just a wee bit." Her eyes twinkled. "When we've worked up more of an appetite for the picnic." She laughed then. "Besides, we had to deal with sand once before and I thought maybe we'd rather take advantage of a nice, soft, sand-free bed this time around, so by the time we get to walking on the beach, we're more likely not to have to deal with that particular issue."

He grinned. "We'll bring a blanket anyway."

She laughed and was smiling against his mouth as he kissed her again. She leaned into his arms, and he scooped her up against him and turned toward the house . . . and froze.

"What—oh no, I'm daring on a good day," Kit said on a laugh, "but we're making it past the hood of the car."

Morgan slowly slid her to her feet, but kept her facing him. He framed her face, held her gaze.

Her smile faltered. "Morgan, what's—"

"Remember how you said you were keeping your eyes on the here and now, and not letting yourself imagine the bigger picture? Well, the picture's about to get a little bigger. Maybe a lot bigger. Please trust me and let me do the talking, okay?"

"For heaven's sake, Morgan," came an imperious Southern voice from a short distance behind him.

It was Kit's turn to go completely and utterly still.

"Are you going to stand in your own driveway—if you can call it that—and leave me waiting on your doorstep, or would you care to introduce the young woman to your dear mother?"

Chapter 22

As Kit stood there, half wrapped around Morgan, trying to process what was happening, she knew she'd been right about one thing: The bigger picture had definitely happened when she'd least suspected it.

She supposed it could have been worse. Olivia could have shown up thirty minutes later . . . and caught them naked and in bed. Of course, if she'd knocked first, Kit could have at least hidden in the closet. Or something.

Looking at Olivia Westlake, Kit doubted she was the knock-first type. Clearly, she wasn't the call-first type, as Morgan was obviously as surprised as Kit to see her on his doorstep.

Deep end of the pool, she thought, *I'm back!*

Morgan carefully shifted Kit to his side and slid his arm around her waist. Whether to bolster her or himself, she wasn't sure.

"Hello, Mother. I'm sorry to have missed your call letting me know you were planning to visit."

"Let's not play coy, dear, shall we?" Olivia smoothed a hand over her sleek hairdo, the color as shiny and dark as her son's.

And what a marvelous feat of perfectly teased, styled, and executed engineering it was, too. In fact, Kit couldn't have said if Olivia Westlake was forty or sixty. She either had the most amazing genetics ever or had been assisted in her youthful appearance at the hands of exceedingly skilled surgeons. Her makeup was expertly applied and, from her calf-length, black cashmere coat to her hand-tooled leather purse and boots, her couture shouted expensive, tailor made, and sporting only the most exclusive labels. She was imposing on the scale of Cruella DeVille—only less friendly.

"We both know you wouldn't have taken my calls," Olivia went on to say, "so I didn't bother."

"Why have you come?" Morgan asked. "And where is your car . . . and driver?"

"I've sent Thomas back to Savannah. There was an issue with our rooms and he's gone to straighten that out."

"Rooms?"

Her smile could only be called such because the corners of her mouth inched slightly northward. "You certainly didn't think I'd be staying here." She gave his cottage a dismissive glance, indicating she'd likely need a thorough cleansing just for standing so close to it.

"No," Morgan agreed. "I certainly didn't think that. Why have you come? I told you Lilly and I would visit—"

"I've come because my patience with this little . . . escapade of yours has finally worn thin."

"Mother, I believe you know me well enough by now to realize that when I decide to relocate, I generally don't return. You know full well that I intend to stay here, raise Lilly so she'll have the benefit of being close to both sides of her family."

"Yes, yes, point taken. We've exhausted this topic many times over," she said, waving a weary, heavily-ringed hand. "However, the holidays are upon us, and surely you don't mean to exclude Lilly from her rightful place with her family during the upcoming festivities. Coraline told me you wouldn't be returning for Thanksgiving, but we've not received a single word of your plans for Christmas. There is much planning being done, and so I've come to make certain we're all in concert with one another, and that you'll be present. We've got your rooms ready and expect to see you no later than the twenty-first, preferably by the nineteenth."

Kit noted Olivia hadn't once asked about Lilly or even wondered where she might be, since she clearly wasn't with the two of them. Morgan had explained how his family was more about business than sentiment, and to her it had seemed as if they followed the *better seen and not heard* edict when it came to child rearing, but until that moment, Kit had never comprehended what he had really been trying to describe.

"Now, am I to be kept out here on the stoop like some poor relative, or shall we go inside and finish getting our calendars in order?"

"I can save you the trouble," Morgan said. "We aren't planning to travel back to Atlanta for the time being. Perhaps after the new year, or during spring break."

"Spring . . . break? Whatever in the world is that?"

"It's the seasonal vacation for kids in school."

"Not in any reputable school I know of. And you wonder why we choose private education. Surely you don't mean to enroll a Westlake in public . . . oh my—" She broke off, then pulled a small hankie from her bag and pressed it to her cheek, then her other cheek. "I'm becoming quite taxed, Morgan. I really should sit a spell."

"You could have rebuilt Rome in three days with one hand tied behind your back," Morgan said. "I think you'll manage."

At any other time, Kit would have been shocked that Morgan would speak like that to his own mother. But, after less than ten minutes of exposure, Kit had to keep from doing a little fist pump in solidarity.

"Unless Thomas is close to returning, I'll call you a cab to take you back to Savannah. Or all the way to Atlanta."

Apparently realizing she wasn't going to have the upper hand, even with witnesses, Olivia changed tactics. "Surely you don't mean to deprive me of some time spent with my darling granddaughter. I've come all this way."

"And, until this moment, you haven't so much as asked how she's doing. I must have missed all those calls from you as well, these past few months. I know Lilly has."

If Morgan's pointed reply so much as dinged Olivia's armor, she didn't let it show.

"You know what it's like this time of year, the chaos, the madness of organization, not to mention all the end-of-year business to be taken care of. And this year, in particular, what with dealing with the horrible tragedy we've suffered. It's been beyond brutal. But I've shouldered it, with no help from you, of course. The very last thing I'd do is visit any of that on the poor child. I've kept my distance and handled what needed handling. I'm sure she understands."

"She's five years old. I'm not sure she grasps the tricky nuances of managing a business and a household during trying times. She only understands actions and how people treat her."

"Well, she will certainly understand one day, as it is her birthright I'm working so hard to safeguard."

Kit thought she might have felt Morgan actually shudder at that. Or maybe it had been her.

Just then a sleek town car slowly tooled past the front of the house and quietly eased to the curb, the purring engine barely making a rumble.

"Ah, good. Your ride is here," Morgan said.

"And my visit with my granddaughter?"

"Her name is Lilly. And she has other plans today."

"Surely nothing as important as the chance to spend time with her grandmother."

Morgan smiled. "Surely not, as that is exactly what she's doing."

It took a moment, but his meaning registered. Even someone as cold and seemingly unfeeling as Olivia had a visceral response to the knowledge that her flesh and blood was enjoying time with the Other Grandmother, the shunned one, the one who didn't measure up to Westlake standards.

Yes, how that must rankle, Kit thought.

Olivia's expression went from rigid to downright glacial. "I see." She stepped down from the porch and walked toward the two of them still standing in the driveway, in front of Morgan's SUV.

Kit had to work not to shrink back behind Morgan as the woman neared.

She stopped just in front of them. "I'll assume, since you couldn't bother to make introductions, that this isn't someone of any importance to you or that you've forgotten her name altogether." Olivia didn't so much as flicker a glance at Kit. "Please be advised, however, if this is how you're going to conduct yourself, perhaps I'll have our lawyers revisit that agreement Asher regrettably made with you regarding my granddaughter's care. I'll hardly allow her to be subject to a string of questionable women parading in and out."

Morgan slipped his hand in Kit's and held on firmly. "Mother, this is Kit Bellamy. I didn't introduce you, because, frankly, given this exchange, I'm embarrassed."

"Well, I should think so." Then Olivia seemed to gather his meaning and looked downright horrified. "Embarrassed? By *me*?" She all but spit that last word out.

She paused and looked directly at Kit. "Wait. Surely, you're not related to the Bellamy family who—"

"Who your exceedingly wealthy law firm helped my

equally wealthy brother-in-law dismantle and destroy a generations-old family business and decimate countless lives? Entirely aided by a whole lot of billable hours put in by the smug, arrogant lawyers you employ? Yes, that would be me," Kit said, the words spilling out before she'd realized she was going to say them.

Olivia swung her astonished gaze back to Morgan, instantly dismissing Kit as apparently unworthy of a response. "Did you know this? Know of her connection to Atlanta? Surely not, or you would never have taken up with her." She turned back to Kit then. "If you've followed him out here to seek revenge for what was purely the fault of your own gross negligence and seduce your way into this family and his trust fund, the way your sister did with the Carruthers family, then—"

Morgan stepped between the two women, his face mere inches from his mother's. When he spoke, his voice was quiet, but with a steel edge that made even Kit shiver. "You're going to want to be very, very careful about the words you choose to use right now."

"Are you—are you actually threatening me?" Olivia asked. "Has she gotten you wound that tightly around her—"

"She is not after my fortune. Hell, *I'm* not after my fortune. You know better than anyone, I've never touched a dime of it. As for Kit, I had to persuade her to give me the time of day. Trust me, being a Westlake was no selling tool."

Olivia's expression made it clear she couldn't comprehend such a thing. "Then she's an even bigger fool than I thought. As are you, if you think—"

"I don't think anything," Morgan said quite calmly. "What I know, however, is that I love her. Very much. And if I'm fortunate enough to convince her to marry me, she'll make me—and Lilly—the happiest people on earth. I can only hope you haven't destroyed any chance I might have had."

"If you think I'm going to allow this . . . woman," she spit out, "to raise my grand—"

Morgan dropped Kit's hand and slid his other arm neatly through his mother's, then march-stepped her straight down the driveway toward her waiting town car.

"What on earth—why I never! Unhand me this moment! How dare you—"

"No," Morgan said quite heatedly as Thomas leaped from the car and scrambled to open the rear passenger door, looking uncertain as to what to do about this unexpected scene.

Kit was still standing, frozen, on the driveway, trying to process what Morgan had just said. He loved her? Wanted to marry her? Had that been grandstanding, for shock value?

Morgan's words—or more the steel tone of them—drew her attention back curbside. "I want you to be part of Lilly's life and she yours. But if you ever decide to drop by unannounced, again, issuing orders and expecting command performances, I will find it very hard to think it's a good idea to expose her to you. If you ever speak to Kit again in that manner, I will assume you don't want a relationship of any sort, with any of us."

"Are you . . . blackmailing me? Thomas, are you hearing this? He's my witness," she told Morgan. "How dare you—"

"No," Morgan repeated, leaning in closer.

Kit and Thomas had to strain to hear.

"How dare *you*. How . . . dare . . . you. You may rule your world, but you don't rule mine. You don't rule Lilly's. And you most assuredly will never have a hand again in Kit's. I will say this one more time. I want you and

Lilly to have a relationship. Hell, I'll be happy if you learn to call her by her first name. For the time being, however, we're going to focus on our lives here, without any interference or assistance from you. So . . . please consider this my RSVP to your invitation. I'm afraid we won't be able to attend."

Then Morgan seemed to find some semblance of calm and stepped back, handing the care of Olivia to Thomas, who took her arm.

"But I sincerely hope we can find a way to share some time together, just us. Just family. No social events, no obligations, no guests, no company circus. Just a meal, some conversation, and quality family time. That's all I've ever wanted. If you decide this is something you also want, then please call me. Call us. We'd very much enjoy that."

Olivia opened her mouth, then shut it again, apparently unable to decide if it was some other form of attack . . . or if he could possibly be as sincere and honest as he sounded.

"I'm sorry," Morgan said. "About today. I wish it wasn't like this. I wish we weren't like this. I just don't know how else to handle it. If it were only me, I'd simply walk away. But now I have family of my own, and as long as you force me to take a stand, that's what I'll do. I hate that it's come to this. Especially when it seems so easy, so simple, for it to be so much better."

Kit watched raptly as Olivia took in Morgan's heartfelt words. For a split second, Kit thought Olivia wavered, thought she saw true understanding, even a desire to reach out to her son as he'd asked her to. Family member to family member. Mother . . . to son.

But in the time it took Kit to wonder, Olivia's expression smoothed to an almost inhuman degree, until she looked like a cold, lifeless wax figurine. Her voice was a shard of ice. "I will be in contact with your lawyer to set up visitation. Fight me on this, and you'll be very, very sorry. You may not take pride in your name, but my granddaughter will. I will see to it." With that, she turned her back to him, and Thomas quickly helped her into the car.

Kit's gaze flew to Morgan, devastated for him. But he was clearly not surprised by his mother's response, and not even particularly upset by it.

Kit flew down the driveway, straight to him as he lifted a hand in a short wave. "And a very merry Christmas to you, too, Mother dear."

Chapter 23

As soon as the car was out of sight, Morgan immediately turned to Kit. "I'm very, very sorry you had to witness that."

"You don't need to apologize," Kit said. "I'm very, very sorry that your mother is . . . well, the way she is. You've explained it, but if I hadn't seen it, I would never have understood it. I think it's the same kind of thing, albeit on a very different level, as I've observed with my own sister. Like Trixie, your mother is hardwired differently from most people. I thought, for a moment there, she might capitulate and allow some real feelings to come through. I don't know, but maybe she just can't be vulnerable, or she doesn't feel like the rest of us do. I'm just . . . sorry. For you. For Lilly." She took his hands, put them on her waist, and urged him to pull her close.

Morgan hadn't been worried about his mother or her threats . . . but he'd been terrified her surprise visit might have robbed him of the best thing that would ever happen to him. "Kit . . ."

He couldn't put into words how her acceptance made him feel.

He pulled her close and wrapped her against him, realizing only then how worked up the confrontation with Olivia had made him. The feel of Kit in his arms went a long way toward soothing distress he hadn't realized he felt. Or maybe it was because of his strong feelings about Kit that Olivia had been able to rile him. He finally had a vulnerable spot.

He tipped her face up to his. "How in the world did I get so lucky?"

Kit smiled up at him, and his heart found its rhythm again, just like that. "Well"—she wiggled her eyebrows—"define getting lucky."

He barked out a laugh, then went with his heart and scooped her up and spun around, making her squeal long and loud. He spun her again, then carried her to the front door of the cottage, piggyback style. "Well, you know I'm a—"

"Show and tell guy," she finished, then leaned down and nipped the side of his ear. "I'm counting on that."

He carried her into the cottage and straight to the bedroom. "That's the house, tour later," he said, as it went by in a blur. He kicked the door shut and turned so she could drop back on the bed. Then he sprawled out next to her, pulling her close when even a few inches was just too far away.

"So, where's all the showing," she said, reaching for the buttons of his shirt. "I believe we have a hearty picnic to get suitably hungry for."

"Oh, I'm hungry all right," he said, but covered her hands and lowered them. He and Kit had to deal with his mother's appearance or he'd forever worry it would come back later to haunt them. "I am really sorry."

"You had no more control over it than I did. It was a shock, sure. But . . . you handled it."

"I'm not proud of the way I did that, but—"

Kit pressed her finger over his lips. "I was there, too, remember? You did what you had to do, spoke the only language she'd understand. And any harshness you meted out in the beginning, you more than made up for with your heartfelt plea at the end."

"I did mean that. I truly wish we could be a family first, business second . . . or never."

She stroked his cheek. "I do know. And I'm sorry she doesn't seem able to function that way, because she's missing out on two of the very best people I have ever had the privilege to know."

He turned his head, kissed her palm, then tucked it on top of his heart. "This is where I feel you. This is where I know you," he said, keeping her hand pressed over the steady thump. "I want you to know me the same way."

"Maybe I already do." She searched his eyes. "Did you mean everything you said outside?"

He tried to think back over what he'd said. His mother had pushed his buttons as always and he'd shot back whatever had come to mind. "Oh." He realized what Kit might be talking about. "You mean . . ."

Kit spoke softly. "Normally, I like to stand up for myself. That way I always know I can. Being self-reliant has been very important to me, especially since my parents passed. But this past year . . . it shook me so hard. Not only did I not take care of me, I didn't—couldn't—take care of everyone else who depended on me." She pressed a finger to his lips when he tried to comfort her.

She continued to search his gaze, but there was no fear in hers, no worry. No doubt. "It wasn't until I met you . . . and you got me to reach out even though I was at my shakiest, urged me to hold on when I needed it, and not be so damned determined to shoulder everything alone . . . that I realized it's not a sign of strength to be wholly self-sufficient. It's merely a sign of vulnerability, because you don't have faith—or haven't cultivated enough faith—in those around you to work together as a team. Maybe if I'd done more of that with Mamie Sue's, I'd have seen what was coming."

Her lips curved in a slow smile. "I won't lie. Your mother scares the ever living crap out of me." She cupped his cheek. "But I don't have to take her on alone. And now . . . neither do you. I don't want to do life all by myself. I don't want to prove that I can. I don't want to prove anything. I want to do life with you. And with Lilly. And figure it out together, like you said, taking care of each other, letting me care for you and letting you take care of me right back."

Her smile deepened, and a decided spark entered those green eyes of hers. "So . . . I'm asking . . . did you mean what you said out there? Or were you just trying to shock your mama by proclaiming to love one of those Bellamy tramps."

Morgan choked out a laugh at that, but his heart was pounding so loud he had to focus to make sure he was hearing what he thought he was hearing, and not just what he so desperately wanted to hear. "If you're asking do I love you," he said, cupping her cheek, "then, yes. I love you, Katherine Mary Margaret Bellamy. And most definitely yes, I plan to marry you, if you'll have me. Well, me and the most adorable five-year-old ever."

Kit grinned, beaming up at him. "How did you know my full name?"

"I have read one or two articles about you, remember? Besides, I wanted you to know, without a doubt, that I know exactly whom I am proposing to."

"So . . . you've thought about this proposal."

"Well, I can't say that in any incarnation, my mother was part of it, so . . . not exactly how I'd hoped it would go. But if you plan on saying yes at any future point . . . when you feel absolutely like it's the right thing to do, I would happily give you a do-over, in the most romantic—"

She jerked his head down and kissed him. Rolling him to his back, she straddled his waist, still kissing him . . . until they had to come up for air.

Morgan blinked once, then again. "So . . . should I take that as a yes?" "

"Depends."

His eyes widened even as he laughed. "On?"

"Do you think Lilly should have siblings—well, cousins, whatever the heck they'd be—at some point? Not tomorrow, but—"

He pulled her down, kissed her fast, hard, and deep.

She let out a long, shaky sigh, when he let her up for air. "So, okay . . . check that one off. How do you feel about big sloppy dogs? I've always, always wanted one, but I could say it's for Lilly, because all kids should have a pet, if that earns me more leverage."

"Are you trying to see if you can scare me off?"

"Well, I just lived through your mother—which, I'm pretty sure, is the scariest thing you've got. I'm just trying to feel out your reaction to every possible thing on my side that I can. Fair is fair, right?"

Morgan rolled her to her back and grinned down into the bright green eyes and wide smile he hoped to be looking into for a long time to come. "Oh, so very, very right."

He started to lower his head, but she blocked him. "Dog?" she said. "No ducking."

"Dog," he agreed. "Cat, gerbil, fish, sea turtle. I might draw the line at snakes. Never really liked them."

"Deal. Not a fan, either." She pretended to think about it. "Yep, that's pretty much all I got."

His grin was slow, wide, and—he hoped—very wicked.

"Oh . . . you got much more than that." He slowly worked his way down the front of her body, taking a very detailed inventory of every inch of her . . . assets.

"Yes," she said on a long, appreciative sigh as her hips arched beneath him. "Yes, I do." She slid her fingers into his hair and urged him to where she wanted him most. "And to think I imagined a life all about pie would be enough." She arched sharply, cried out, as he found her very best asset.

She dragged him up, refusing to let him linger, and he gladly complied. She wrapped her legs around his waist and he found her in one, slow thrust, lifting her up to reach deeply inside of her. "Right," he growled, as they began moving together in a rhythm that was all theirs. "Because this . . . this is . . ."

"Ah-mazing," they said together, laughing, even as they went roaring straight past the edge, on a long, shuddering sigh.

Epilogue

"This one is from Miss Dre." Morgan handed the brightly wrapped present to Lilly, who was sitting beside the Christmas tree—her very favorite, bestest tree ever as she'd called it—buried in a mound of torn wrapping paper, ribbons, bows, empty boxes, and enough art supplies and sea turtle paraphernalia to last until at least the new year.

She tore it opened, then gasped as her very own, miniature apron fell out. She spread it out, looking at it in awe. "Miss Dre painted a whole ocean. Look! There's Paddlefoot! And Donatello!"

Kit shifted from her spot between Morgan's outstretched legs and leaned over Lilly's shoulder. "She's got other ocean critters on there, too. Whales, fish. Look." She pointed at each figure. It was another tremendous work of art. Kit shook her head, unable to comprehend how anyone had that kind of crazy talent.

Lilly looked up at Kit over her shoulder. "Do I have to wear it just for baking? Can I wear it with my paints Gramma got me?"

"I think it would make a fine art apron."

"Would Miss Dre get mad if I painted in it?"

"Well"—Morgan scooted over and surrounded them

with his legs and arms—"since she loves art as much as she loves to bake, I think she'd totally be happy with that."

Lilly scrambled up so she could try it on, half trampling Kit and Morgan in the process. Morgan took the opportunity to lean in and kiss Kit, then another on the side of her neck.

"Eww," Lilly said, grinning wildly. "Kissing." It was a game with them now. Lilly knew when she said that, what happened next.

Morgan didn't disappoint. "Eww? Kissing?" He crawled across the living room floor, sending Lilly squealing down the hall as the kissing monster followed her.

Kit could hear the peals of laughter and squeals as the kissing monster, once again, founds its prey and silenced it with all the love the poor "victim" could take.

They came crawling back with Lilly riding on Morgan's back. He dumped her into Kit's waiting lap, then both leaned down and kissed her again, making her squeal in another peal of laughter.

"So . . ." Morgan said, when they'd caught their breath and pulled ribbons and wrapping paper out of their hair. "There is one more present."

Lilly's eyes went wide. "There is?"

"This one is for Kit."

Kit's eyes went wide. "It is?"

Morgan grinned. "I was going to wait until your birthday, but then it sort of fell into my lap a bit sooner than I'd anticipated, and I couldn't say no."

Kit's expression was confused.

"But, first, we need to pick up all this stuff. To make room."

Kit and Lilly both looked confused.

"Come on," he said. "I'll get the trash bag."

Kit and Lilly exchanged looks, then smiled and Kit shrugged. "Come on, you heard him." They crawled around the floor, grabbing up all the paper, balling it up, shoving it in the bag Morgan held open for them. Kit stacked up empty boxes, trying to make orderly sense of Lilly's haul. Between the two of them and the rest of the turtle rescue gang, they'd gone a teensy bit overboard for her, but it was Christmas, after all.

She turned around after getting the last bit squared away, to find Morgan and Lilly deep in a powwow by the kitchen table. Whatever Morgan was telling her, Lilly was solemnly listening to, and then was nodding her head, and all but jumping up and down excitedly.

"Sh," Morgan said, pressing his fingers to his lips. "It's a surprise."

Lilly turned to Kit with both hands over her mouth, but her eyes were like saucers.

"What on earth did you get?" Kit asked, totally flummoxed.

"Wait here," Morgan said, then stood and scooped up Lilly. "Come on, you need to help me finish wrapping it, okay?"

"Okay, okay, okay!" She was literally jumping in his arms.

Kit was tempted to follow them as they exited to the garage, but thought better of it. They were excited, and she didn't want to ruin the surprise.

She took the moment to pull her knees up, wrap her arms around them, and take in everything around her. It had been an incredible month. *Ah-mazing,* she thought with a smile. *Beyond so.*

She'd been so worried about how Lilly would handle Kit being a part of hers and Morgan's lives, but it had gone much like Morgan had predicted it would. It was more love for Lilly, and happy people were happy. It hadn't been awkward or difficult. It had been as easy and natural as all the rest.

Suddenly, Kit heard thumping and bumping coming from the garage and scrambled to her feet. "Are you guys okay?"

Lilly came bursting into the room and flung herself at Kit, who caught the energized little bundle in her lap. "What is it?"

"Close your eyes." Lilly had already closed hers, though she knew what was making the noise. "Moggy said," she whispered. It was almost a squeal, as she was still being a Mexican jumping bean in Kit's lap.

Kit laughed and closed her eyes. "Okay, they're closed."

"They're closed!" Lilly shouted, making Kit cover her ears.

She swore the ground might have trembled a little, or there was thunder happening in the floorboards.

"Okay," Morgan said. "You can open your eyes. Merry Christmas, Kit."

She opened her eyes . . . and about fell over in shock. "Oh. My. God. What is that? A small horse?"

Lilly leaped out of her lap and ran over to the mutant-sized puppy squirming in Morgan's arms. Morgan looked at Kit and gave her a sheepish shrug. "Riley and Brutus joined a doggy playgroup over on Tybee, because she heard a mastiff came by to play and she thought it would be fun for him to have a friend his own size. Turns out the friend was pregnant. By what kind of dog, we're not sure, but I'm guessing nothing small."

Kit's eyes bugged. "That's . . . going to be a Brutus?"

"Well, I don't know if she'd like that name."

Kit's heart melted. "It's a girl puppy?"

Morgan nodded and Lilly was already pulling Kit's hand. "Come on. Pet her. She loves it. I put the bow on her collar."

Kit let Lilly pull her over to the squirming mass of happy puppy. She was velvety gray and ridiculously soft.

"My God, Morgan, her paws are already the size of baseballs!"

"What is her name?" Lilly wanted to know, already hugging all over the dog. Apparently her fussy sensibilities didn't extend to getting dog slobber all over her.

"I had planned to get a pound puppy," Morgan explained. "But then the puppies were born and Riley had pictures and they just wanted to find homes for them, and . . . well . . ."

The puppy broke loose and leaped into Kit's lap, snapping her from her stunned moment of disbelief, making her laugh as she was knocked to her back and proceeded to get a very thorough licking all over her face.

"We'll have to come up with a name for you," Kit said, finally getting the dog's face in her hands. "Look at you. Look at you."

Then she looked up at Morgan. "I love her. And I love you." The puppy lurched up and licked Lilly. "And she loves you, too!" Kit added on a laugh. Morgan joined them in a tumble of puppy and five-year-old on the floor.

Kit finally managed to get close enough to give Morgan a big, wet kiss on his cheek. "Did you happen to get a life preserver?"

"Afraid we'll drown in the dog slobber?"

"Well, that . . . but I meant for me."

"Why?" He tugged her to his side as Lilly and the puppy went bounding over them and down the hall in a squeal of laughter and puppy barks.

Kit pushed the hair out of her face and pulled him next to her. "Because I'm pretty sure I'm never getting out of the deep end of the pool. Just keep helping me tread water, okay?"

"Promise."

She was still laughing as she kissed him.

Author Note

The research facilities mentioned in this story are fictional, but research centers just like them do exist on Georgia's barrier islands and in coastal areas stretching from Virginia all the way down to the Florida Keys. The plight of the endangered sea turtle is very real and an ongoing concern all over the world.

If you are interested in learning more about these amazing (ah-mazing!) creatures, would like to contribute in some way, or perhaps even "adopt" a sea turtle of your very own, a good place to start is The Georgia Sea Turtle Center, a research and rescue facility on Jekyll Island, Georgia. Please take a peek at their wonderful website and learn more about their organization at:

www.georgiaseaturtlecenter.org.

Alva's Sweet Potato 'Tater Cupcakes

2½ cups all-purpose flour
1½ teaspoons baking powder
½ teaspoon salt
¼ teaspoon baking soda
½ teaspoon ground cinnamon
¼ teaspoon ground ginger
⅛ teaspoon ground nutmeg
⅛ teaspoon ground clove
⅔ cup buttermilk
½ cup sweet potato puree
1 teaspoon vanilla extract
1 stick unsalted butter
¾ cup brown sugar
2 eggs

Preheat oven to 350 degrees F. Line 18 muffin cups with paper liners. (Yes, I know 18 is a pain, but that gives you an excuse to try that cute 6 cup silicone cupcake pan you got for Christmas! They work, too . . . but the cupcakes come out denser.)

1. In a medium bowl, combine the flour, baking powder, salt, baking soda, and spices with a whisk. Set aside.
2. In a 2-cup sized measuring cup, stir together buttermilk, vanilla, and sweet potato puree. Set aside.
3. In a large mixing bowl, cream the butter and brown sugar until fluffy. Scrape down the sides of the bowl.
4. Add the eggs one at a time, beating well after each addition. Scrape bowl as needed.
5. In three additions, alternately add the flour mixture and the milk/puree mixture. Blend only until they are incorporated (or, as I call it . . . assimilated. Like

the Borg.) Do not overmix or this will activate the gluten in the flour. (And the only gluten I need activated are the ones I sit on all day while I write.)

6. Use an ice cream scoop to fill each muffin cup approx ⅔ full. (Does this ever work out for you? No? Me, either. There's too much math in baking. I prefer to wing it. I figure, the Cupcake Size Monitoring Team isn't coming to my house, so who cares if they are different sizes when done?)
7. Bake for 20–25 minutes or until a toothpick inserted into the center of the cupcake comes out clean. Enjoy how great your kitchen smells right now!

Browned Butter Cream Cheese Frosting

1 stick butter, cut in half (¼ cup each)
1 8-ounce package cream cheese, room temperature
1 teaspoon vanilla
3 cups powdered sugar
1–3 tablespoons milk, optional

1. In a small saucepan over medium heat, heat ¼-cup butter until browned. (If you've read my cupcake blog, you know that whenever I activate a burner and melt anything, I keep my EMT on speed dial. He's a very cute EMT though, which motivates me to try braver recipes. Don't judge. Expanding one's horizons is a good thing.)
2. In a small bowl, cut up the other half stick of butter into small cubes. Pour the browned butter over them and stir until all are melted.
3. In a mixing bowl beat the butter, cream cheese, vanilla and sugar until smooth and creamy.
4. Add 1–3 tablespoons cold whole milk only if needed to thin to a spreading consistency. (Did you know that skim or low fat milk can make your powdered

sugar taste dusty or flat? Use whole milk. I mean, come on, there's a stick of butter in there and you're going to skimp on milk?)

Makes about 4 cups.

Mamie Sue's Peanut Pie

For this recipe, you need 1½ cups shelled, roasted, and partially crushed peanuts. You can use already roasted peanuts, but you know Mamie Sue would have roasted her own. If you'd like to try, the steps are below.

Roasting the Peanuts

Preheat oven to 350 degrees F.

1. Place 1½ cups raw peanuts in a single layer in shallow sheet pan.
2. For unshelled peanuts, bake 20 to 25 minutes.
3. For shelled peanuts, bake 15 to 20 minutes.
4. Stir once or twice during cooking time.
5. Cook until slightly underdone. Please note! Peanuts continue to cook when removed from oven.
6. Let cool completely before shelling and using in the pie recipe below.
7. Crush the peanuts in large and chunky pieces, with some halves still almost intact. Put approximately ½ cup in a sealed bag (freezer bags are good) and roll over the bag with a rolling pin. Repeat with the remaining peanuts until all are done.

Making the Pie Shell

Make your own 9-inch pie shell. Sure, you can buy one premade, but do you think Mamie Sue did that? Give this a try:

1¼ cups all-purpose flour
¼ teaspoon salt
⅓ cup shortening
4–5 tablespoons cold water

1. Whisk together flour and salt.
2. Using a pastry blender, cut in shortening until pieces are pea-size.
3. Sprinkle 1 tablespoon of the water over part of the mixture; gently toss with a fork until moist. Move that moistened dough to the side and repeat, one tablespoon at a time, until all the dough has been moistened.
4. Work the moistened dough into one ball with your hands.
5. Place ball on a lightly floured surface and use your hands to flatten, then use a rolling pin to roll the dough from center to edges into a circle approximately 12 inches in diameter.
6. Wrap the pastry around the rolling pin, then unroll it over a 9-inch pie plate. Gently press the pastry into the pie plate without stretching it.
7. Trim around the pastry to leave approximately a ½-inch ring beyond the edge of the pie plate. Fold the extra pastry under and crimp with your fingers.

Making the Pie Filling

3 eggs
½ cup granulated sugar
1½ cups dark corn syrup
¼ cup butter, melted
¼ teaspoon salt (if you are using already shelled, salted peanuts, eliminate the salt from the recipe or reduce to taste)
½ teaspoon vanilla
1½ cups shelled and roasted peanuts
9-inch unbaked deep-dish pastry shell—use one you made (or a premade shell)

Preheat oven to 375 degrees F.

1. Beat eggs well, until you see foam. (Yes, foamy eggs are good.)
2. Add in the following one item at a time, mixing each until incorporated, but do not overmix: sugar, corn syrup, butter, salt, and vanilla.
3. Stir in the peanuts.
4. Pour the peanut mixture into the unbaked pastry shell.
5. Bake at 375 degrees for 50–55 minutes. Allow to cool before cutting.

Makes one pie.

Lilly's Ah-mazing Turtle Cupcakes

2 cups all-purpose flour
1 teaspoon baking soda
6 ounces unsweetened chocolate, melted
1 cup (2 sticks) unsalted butter, softened
1 cup granulated sugar
1 cup firmly packed light brown sugar
4 large eggs, at room temperature
1 cup buttermilk
1 teaspoon vanilla extract

Preheat oven to 350 degrees F. Line two 12-cup muffin tins with cupcake papers. Set aside.

1. In a small bowl, sift together the flour and baking soda. Set aside.
2. Melt the chocolate in a double boiler over simmering water on low heat for approximately 5–10 minutes. Stir occasionally until completely smooth and no pieces of chocolate remain. Remove from the heat and let cool to lukewarm, 5–10 minutes.
3. In a large bowl, on the medium speed of an electric mixer, cream the butter until smooth. Add the sugars and beat until fluffy, about 3 minutes.
4. Add the eggs, one at a time, beating well after each addition.
5. Add the chocolate, mixing until well incorporated.
6. Add the dry ingredients in three parts, alternating with the buttermilk and vanilla. With each addition, beat until the ingredients are incorporated, but do not overbeat.
7. Pour mixture evenly into cupcake papers and bake for 20–25 minutes. Remove from the tins and cool completely.

8. Note: While oven is still warm, toast the pecans used in the frosting on a cookie sheet. See recipe below.

Cutest Sea Turtle Frosting Ever

Pecans:
7 dozen (approx 3 Cups) pecan halves, toasted

Ganache:
4 ounces dark chocolate
½ cup heavy cream
2 tablespoons light corn syrup
1 teaspoon pure vanilla extract

Caramel Sauce:
2 cups sugar
½ cup water
½ cup heavy cream, heated to lukewarm in microwave (30 seconds)
2 tablespoons butter, cubed or cut up in small pieces
¼ cup heavy cream, heated to lukewarm in microwave (30 seconds)

Making the Ganache:

1. Chop chocolate into small pieces. Set aside.
2. In a small, heavy saucepan over low to medium heat, warm the cream until it begins to steam. Remove from heat and pour over the chopped chocolate, stirring until the chocolate is completely melted.
3. Add corn syrup and vanilla, stirring until completely mixed. Let sit and cool to room temperature, stirring as needed.
4. Frost cupcakes, keeping a cup of frosting in reserve.
5. Arrange 5 pecans on the top of each cupcake, to form a turtle head, and four flippers, pressing gently into the frosting. (The flippers will touch in the middle. The head butts up against the top two flippers.)

Making the Caramel Sauce:

1. In a medium saucepan, add sugar and water. Stir. Cook the ingredients on medium-high heat. Carefully watch the sugar syrup change colors to an amber-brownish color around the outer edge, or if using a candy thermometer, heat to 350 degrees F.
2. Remove from heat immediately and, using a wooden spoon or whisk, quickly stir everything to keep the sugar water from burning. It should be a gold-amber color.
3. Continue stirring, while adding ½ cup of warm heavy cream and butter bits. (NOTE: When the cream comes into contact with the syrup it will start bubbling violently.) Continue to stir until the sugar crystallization dissolves.
4. Add the remaining warm heavy cream (¼ cup) until caramel sauce is nice and smooth.
5. Pour into heat-proof measuring cup and let cool slightly.

Finishing the Cupcakes:

1. Spoon 2 teaspoons soft caramel on top of the center of the pecans. Let the caramel set for a few minutes to firm up.
2. Heat remaining Ganache if necessary to soften. Drop a teaspoon of Ganache on top of the caramel to finish off the turtle shell.

As Miss Lilly would say . . . these are ah-mazing! Enjoy!

Makes 24 cupcakes.